Loved By You

"When past wounds meet seconds chances, every heartbeat counts."

Alexandrea LeChelle

Content Warning

Just a heads-up before you dive into this story—this book is a slow-burn, emotional rollercoaster. Some parts touch on sensitive topics, like miscarriage, grief, and family struggles. Plus, some moments explore anxiety and panic attacks, mixed in with several moments of laughter and lightness. You'll also find a fair share of adult language and some steamy, explicit scenes. Take care of yourself, and feel free to step away if it gets too heavy.

DEDICATION

For those who have loved deeply, through every storm and every heartache. For the love we give to others, the love we receive from family, and the love we discover within ourselves. May you find strength in vulnerability, healing in connection, and light in the love that endures—even in the darkest of times. This story is for you—may it remind you that love, in all its forms, has the power to rebuild, restore, and renew.

Contents

Prologue

Xavier University - September 2014

RIGHT HERE. THIS MOMENT.

This was where life spread out before me, soft and thick like a summer quilt. I wanted to lay in it forever. The music of the Isley Brothers drifted from the speaker, wrapping my dorm room in a melody that stirred memories deep in my soul. It was the kind of music that made you feel like time slowed just for you. I always favored the old songs, the ones that echoed the past and whispered of love in every note. It wasn't that I couldn't move to the beat of today's music, but when it was just me, Nessa, and the quiet of the night, nothing else compared.

Tonight, the room was heavy with the scent of coconut and berries, the fragrance of her hair, twisted just so. Nessa's body pressed against me; warm, brown skin melting into mine as we lay together, fitting like two puzzle pieces. Her voice, soft and sweet, filled the room as she spoke of summer days and nights, of parties and resorts, her words dancing in the air like fireflies. I closed my eyes and let the sound of her voice sink deep into my heart. Every word was a promise of the forever I wanted with her, a forever where I'd listen to her voice long past the day when the sun set for the last time.

"Zay, do you hear me?" Vanessa asked, turning her face towards mine, her eyes searching for the answer before I could give it. "My parents want to visit in a few weeks to get to know you, officially," she said, a hint of worry in her tone.

"I'm down with that," I told her, my lips finding the tip of her nose in a kiss as light as a whisper. "You know I've been wanting to meet them. Especially since Ma damn near adopted you since I brought you around."

"That's because I'm her favorite," she laughed, a sound like sunshine breaking through the clouds. "Even if I almost burned down her kitchen." We laughed together, the memory as sweet as the bread pudding we'd shared earlier. "You think you can handle them, though? My mom... you know she has her ways."

"I'm not worried about them," I said, my thumb tracing the softness of her bottom lip. "Besides, me and your daddy got some things to talk about."

"Like what?" she asked, her eyebrows raising in curiosity.

"That's for us to know and you to find out later," I teased, her pout bringing a smile to my face. "Aww, what? Your little nosy ass mad?"

"No," she said, a playful pinch to my chest. "Just so you know, my Daddy and I are thick as thieves. He'll just tell me when I ask him."

"Uh-huh," I replied, my fingers brushing her cheek, her skin smooth and warm like a summer evening. "What you think about forever with me?"

"Forever," she asked, her lips curving into a smile that could stop the world from spinning. "You sure you can handle me forever?" Her fingers traced the lines of the tattoos on my chest; her touch, like her original artwork, was forever imprinted on my skin, marking me as hers. I don't know if she knew this, but she possessed me. All of me. Her hands worked their way down my stomach, to the hardness growing at my hips.

"Without a doubt. You are mine forever, love," I said, my voice thick with the truth of it. My heart swelled in my chest, the weight of it pressing against my ribs. Shifting her beneath me, with my soldier's attention resting between her warm center. The heat sent the smell of her sweet arousal to my nose. A unique fragrance all her own. I'd bottle that shit and wear it as cologne; if I knew I wouldn't have to beat a nigga's ass if they thought they could get what was mine.

"And what does this forever entail?"

"I see us with a house by the Lakefront, babies running around, me coming home to you every night." I left trails of kisses from her chin to her exposed breasts, only stopping to take her erect nipples into my mouth and suck gently. I could feast on the dark chocolate kisses for the rest of my life.

"You want me to have your babies?" She chuckled, her eyes bright and sparkling, illuminating the dim light of my room.

"Yep, all ten of them." My lips moved to the crevice of her neck, right behind her ear. The spot never failed to make her sweet river flow between her lower lips.

"Ten!?! Boy, you crazy!" She played at trying to push me off of her for a bit before settling her arms around my neck. "You can have two." She brought my head up to meet her deep kiss. "Three at the most." Her mouth covered mine again as she moved her hips against my hardness. Our tongues twirled in a dance all their own, traces of cinnamon and sugar lingering from my mom's bread pudding we'd eaten earlier. She was hot and slick as she rocked her warm, wet folds up and down my shaft, letting the tip of my dick graze against her opening, but not enter. *Always with the teasing.* I pulled back to calm my excitement, as she had a nigga ready to tear her ass up.

"I'll take it. Two boys and a girl that looks just like you. I'm going to renovate a fixer-upper for us. After working all day at designing building plans, I'm going to come home to you and the babies, just in time for dinner."

"Now, you know I can't cook." Vanessa's delicate fingers stroked the hairs on my head as I licked the valley between her breasts. Two perfectly round chocolate mountains. A soft moan sounded from deep within her throat as I took her right nipple, the sensitive one, into my mouth again before letting it go with a juicy plop. My thumb and index finger massaged the rosebud at the center of her warmth, teasing it into a hardened pearl, before slipping my middle finger inside her, circling it just around the rim of Vanessa's opening, preparing her to take all of me. If she was going to have me on the brink of ecstasy, I would have her right there with me. It was a long summer without her, me working two jobs and her traveling. We needed to make up for lost time.

"That's okay; Ma will teach you by then. We got all the time in the world."

"And what am I going to do while you're at work? I hope you don't expect me to stay at home all day." Vanessa's usually soft voice came out deep and raspy between her heated breaths. Her hips moved to inch my finger deeper inside, making it hit that ridged spot over and over again. Soft moans escaped soft, tender lips as I moved my middle finger and thumb in sync with each other. The way her muscles tensed let me know she was getting close. I removed my finger from that sweet spot and sucked her essence from it while gazing deeply into her eyes, lust seeping from those chocolate orbs.

"Naw, you gon' start teaching art at one of them schools around here and sell your stuff on the side in one of them fancy galleries in the Quarter."

"You sound so sure," she murmured, her voice like the soft rustle of leaves in the wind. My uncle Luther was singing in the background now, complimenting the feelings I had. I knew, at this moment, that this was what I was made for—to love her, to build a life with her, to hold her close as the world spun around us. I entered her, gushes of her wetness making me harder than I already was. A gasp escaped from deep in her throat as I moved in and out slowly, ensuring she felt each stroke.

"It's going to happen," I said, my words a vow, as steady and sure as the Earth beneath us. "Straight like that."

Part I

"Footsteps in the Dark, Pts. 1 & 2" - The Isley Brothers

Chapter 1

XAVIER

REALITY WAS A MOTHERFUCKER.

That thought was my constant companion for the past six years. No matter how many hours I buried in the company, no matter how far I ran toward the next milestone, that feeling of something missing followed me like a shadow. We'd made it. Khalil and I turned our dream of an affordable, sustainable housing company into reality. We were doing good—more than good—but the space inside me, that void, refused to be filled. I'd wrestled with it, tried to smooth it over with success and accolades, but still, it lingered.

Khalil was talking, his words buzzing around the room like bees seeking flowers. I tried to focus, to latch onto his enthusiasm. He was telling me about a company—Wright Horizons—that could push our company, EcoVision Urban Solutions, to the next level. We'd dreamed of this since we were in college, sketching our ideas on tattered napkins in my mom's kitchen, whispering about the future late into the night in our college dorm. Now, we had an office in New Orleans, a team of people we'd mentored and employed, and a vision that stretched further than the horizon. But even as Khalil spoke, I could feel it—something in me still unsettled.

"Say bruh, tell me about this company again." I turned, giving him my full attention, hoping it would push away the gnawing ache inside.

"Man, I done already told you. Wright Horizons," Khalil said, smacking his teeth like he couldn't believe I needed to hear it again. His eyes sparkled with the kind of excitement only he could muster.

I glanced at the presentation he'd put together. "I don't know, man. They don't look like they trying to do what we do. Know what I'm saying?"

Khalil moved, sitting in the chair across from my desk, leaning forward with his elbows on his knees. "I know what you're saying, but look at the numbers."

I flipped through the slides until the financials stared back at me. Billion-dollar revenues, investors we could only dream of having. Khalil was right. Partnering with Wright Horizons would be a leap beyond anything we'd imagined. But still, a familiar hesitation settled in my gut.

"And you think they'll rock with us," I asked, the uncertainty coating my words.

Khalil pointed at the screen, his voice alive with energy. "You see that dude next to the bald guy? I met him at that conference I went to in New York. He's pushing for sustainable infrastructure, saying it's gonna be their priority in the next few years."

"Years," I echoed, skepticism lining my voice. "You went to that conference six months ago. What's changed since then?"

He looked at me, his hazel-green eyes shining the same way they did when I'd first talked about starting this company back in college. Khalil and I went back like four flats on a Cadillac. Grew up together, faced life together, survived Hurricane Katrina and the chaos that followed. Khalil had been there through it all, the brother I never had. My mother and his auntie were best friends, damn near raising each one of us as their own, after Khalil's mother ran off when he was a toddler. They'd eventually left New Orleans too, but Khalil came back for college, back to help build something out of the ashes. Now, here we were; but that same fire that burned in him seemed to sputter in me.

"We need to act fast before somebody else gets to him," he pressed, his eyes cracking with the kind of enthusiasm that was all Khalil. We were both being powerhouses of men at 6'6". His thick, black hair was cut in his signature short, curly bush with a low fade on the sides, complementing his clean-cut, sandy-brown skin. He was always the dreamer, the one who leaped first. His laugh was infectious, presence magnetic. He could charm the socks off a snake if he had to. It's what made him the perfect partner in this venture. Khalil was the face, the voice, while I worked quietly behind the scenes, laying the bricks one by one.

"I don't know, man," I said, leaning back in my chair. "How we gonna get a meeting with them? They bring in hundreds of millions, Khalil."

He grinned a slow, confident smile that lit up the room. "Ain't that the tip we trying to be on? Why not us?"

"Yeah, but what are we supposed to do? Just walk into the office? Ain't no way we getting a meeting with them."

"Why not?" Khalil questioned. All through college we mapped out the business plan. By the time we graduated, all we needed was capital. A year and some change of working two, sometimes three, jobs finally got us in a position to do our first project, *for the sake of other things being neglected.* I shook my head to rid myself of the nasty taste of regret, a bitter cough syrup absent of medicine or relief for my heartache.

"You doubt we can do this?" Khalil asked, his voice softer now, probing. He knew me well enough to read the lines on my face, the worry that sometimes crept into the corners of my eyes.

"Khalil, man, you see the type of stuff they on. We ain't ever done anything on this scale before." I palmed the back of my head, the words of my therapist echoing in my mind: *You are worthy of everything, no matter your setbacks.* But those words felt hollow, a fragile shield against the doubts swirling in my chest.

"Yeah, but who says we can't?" Khalil walked over to my side of the desk, smacking one hand into my chest. "Besides, we don't have a choice now."

"Why not?"

"Because...We got a meeting with them a few weeks from now." My eyes shot up at him as he stared back, crossing his arms over his chest.

"How the fuck you got a meeting with them? When you had time to do all that?"

"Cause I'm Khalil *Muthafuckin* Grant. I does this," Khalil bragged, laughing, all thirty-two teeth showing.

"Man, how you did all that?"

"You already know. I know somebody, that know somebody, that know somebody. Boom, boom, bam! We got a meeting," he replied, wiping his shirt in feigned modesty.

Walking over to the window of our office, I glanced outside at a few of the abandoned homes we'd renovated, now filled with families, kids playing in the front yards, laughter spilling into the street. We'd built this community, brick by brick. It was a sanctuary, but standing here, looking at the work we'd accomplished, I still felt like I was chasing something I couldn't quite grasp.

Turning towards Khalil, I took a deep breath. If we were able to get a company like Wright Horizons to work with us, we could create more havens like the one on our street and throughout the city. "How likely is it they'd agree to work with us? Give me the numbers."

Khalil laid it out, detailing the projections, and the potential. "I'm just saying, Zay. They ain't got a choice but to rock with us." Khalil added, shrugging his shoulders.

Crossing my arms, I thought about it. Khalil stood to my right, waiting in silence. I could feel the adrenaline picking up in my veins, the excitement of knowing this may be something real, even if the nagging feeling in my stomach persisted.

"This isn't going to work," I said, my gaze lingering on the figures Khalil had explained.

"Zay, it's all right there. It can work."

"Nah, this presentation isn't going to work." I walked over to the whiteboard hanging at the back of the office, wiping away everything written on it.

"We need to show them what they'd miss out on if they don't pick us," I said, an idea sparking in the back of my mind.

Khalil's eyes lit up. "Now you talking some sense. What you thinking about, bruh?"

I touched a finger to my lips. "Check this. You say Wright Horizons is already doing numbers in the billions, right?"

"Yeah." Khalil stalked over to where I was standing, crossing his arms again.

"So that means they can have a whole section of the company doing this."

"Yeah, and?" he replied, raising a thick eyebrow, his eyes flickering with curiosity.

"Well, with us, as small as we are," I sneered, waving my hand around our office littered with several awards and framed pictures from the work we'd done in the city.

"Zay, we done brought in a few million. I wouldn't say we're small."

"I know that, man. But compared to Wright Horizons, it's a drop in the bucket. Which is why, if they gonna pick us to work with, we need to focus on one thing." Another slow, big smile crept across my face.

"And what's that?"

I turned to the whiteboard on the wall, wiping it clean. "Image," I said, writing the word in big, bold letters. "They're doing this for image. We need to make them see us as the key to that image."

"Image?" Khalil asked.

"Yep. Any company trying to hop on the eco-friendly bandwagon today is only doing it for the image."

"I'm tracking." Khalil got re-focused, his face taking on a more serious look, his hazel eyes concentrating on formulating a plan.

I leaned back on his desk, folding my arms across my chest. "And what better image than to do it with an up-and-coming company? One that's spent their whole life savings on trying to do just that." Khalil walked over, dapping me up, his smile just as big as mine.

"That's what I'm talking about, man. I don't know what you doing in that head of yours, but it's doing something. So, what you thinking?"

I brought Khalil over to my desk and started explaining all the ways Wright Horizons would look better by working with us. We brainstormed dozens of speaking points to make our company stand out among the others we'd have to outsmart.

"So tell me, do you think this is something we could rock with?" The buzz of excitement under my skin sent my knees rocking.

"I think so. I still want to look into the company more, see what they've been doing in New York, know where to hit hardest.

Buy, this might work." Khalil looked at some of the notes we put together. "Shit, if you with it, I'm with it."

My lips pursed as I took a deep breath. "Like you said, we ain't got a choice now."

Khalil nodded, his gaze sharpening as the plan started to form between us. This was how we worked, feeding off each other's energy, building ideas until they became something tangible. We spent the next few hours brainstorming, talking through strategies, each word pushing back the darkness in my mind, if only for a while.

We were on the brink of something big, maybe the biggest thing we'd ever done. But as I watched Khalil, his face animated as he talked about our next steps, I felt that familiar emptiness stirring inside me. We were building a legacy, leaving our mark on the world. But even with all this, I couldn't shake the feeling that I was still missing a piece of myself.

Her.

Chapter 2

Xavier

THREE MONTHS LATER...

It's going to be okay. Inhale. Exhale. It's going to be okay. Inhale. Exhale.

"Damn, man. Slow down." Khalil's voice pulled me out of my head, and I glanced back to see him lagging behind, chest heaving as he struggled to catch his breath. Yes, we were the same height, but where I was lean muscle and sinew, Khalil had the bulk of the linebacker he used to be in high school. Hands on his hips, mouth gaped open, he looked at me like I'd lost my damn mind. "Fuck wrong with you, man?"

"What you mean?" I kept up my pace, the muscles in my legs screaming to go faster, to outrun whatever was chasing me inside my head.

"Fuck you mean, what I mean? You got me out here running like I stole something. You good?" Khalil's words came out between breaths, but I could hear the concern laced in his tone.

"Yeah." I turned to face him, jogging backward, forcing a smile that didn't reach my eyes. "Why wouldn't I be?"

Khalil squinted at me, suspicion written all over his face. "Maybe 'cause we'll practically be living in Houston for the rest of the year?" His words hung in the air, heavy and unavoidable.

I smirked, my eyes darting away from his gaze. He wasn't about to get the satisfaction of knowing how much that weighed on me. We'd scored the deal with Wright Horizons, a collaboration that could put us on the map in ways we'd only dreamed. I should've been elated, but the thought of being in Houston? It sat like a stone in my gut.

"Yeah, and?"

"Stop bullshitting. You know you anxious about running into Nessa. It's gonna happen eventually." Khalil's eyes bore into mine, searching for the truth I was trying to hide, even from myself.

I kept my face blank, the smirk still playing on my lips, though inside, my stomach twisted. "Why would I be anxious?"

Khalil shook his head, not letting up. "Man, you and I both know you and Nessa never really ended." His words struck a chord, one I'd been avoiding for years.

"We did, Khalil. You forgot?" I wished I could forget. Every night since I let her walk away, I've regretted it. By the time I realized what I'd lost, it was too late.

He laughed, a sound that held no humor. "You gonna spin the block if you see her? Try and see if something still there on her end? I know your ass still loves her."

He is not going to let this conversation go. "What do you want me to say?" I stopped abruptly, turning to face him. "Do I miss her? Yes. If I had the chance, would I go back and change how things went down? Of course, but I've been blocked for six years, man. On everything. Phone, social media, hell, even email. I fucked up. Anything happening between us would be a gift from God himself." My heart pounded in my chest, the weight of my words sinking into the ground beneath us. "Look, you trying to finish this run or what?" I needed to move, needed to escape the whirlpool of thoughts that threatened to drag me under.

Khalil stared at me, the worry in his eyes clear as day. "Finish? Fuck you mean, finish? We done already ran around the neighborhood three times. That's double what we usually do." He looked at me like he was trying to piece together a puzzle. "Nah, you got it. I'm heading home. You sure you good?"

No.

"Yeah, just trying to get some energy out. Nervous about being away from home." It was half the truth, but it was the only one I could give him.

"Yeah, alright. I'll see what's up with you later." We dapped each other up, and I watched as he turned to jog back toward the house. I took off, letting my feet and legs carry me away from everything I didn't want to feel.

The streets were empty, the neighborhood still asleep. This was my sanctuary—the early morning runs where the world was silent except for the sound of my breath and the rhythm of my feet hitting the pavement. The oak trees lining the streets stood tall like silent sentinels, watching over the homes they guarded. I pushed on, making my way toward the lakefront, the steady beat of my footsteps a temporary balm to the chaos in my mind.

But no matter how far I ran, she was always there.

Vanessa.

She appeared like a ghost, her image shimmering in my mind as clear as the first day I saw her. The memory of that day washed over me—the way she moved, the way she laughed, how she lit up every corner of the restaurant with her presence. She was magnetic, a force of nature I hadn't been prepared for. I felt my legs pump faster, my body trying to outrun the memories, to leave them behind in the dust.

Inhale, exhale.

I weaved between other joggers and cyclists, pushing through the burn in my calves as it crept into my thighs. I slowed to a walk, hands on my head, trying to catch my breath. In truth, it wasn't just Vanessa. It was everything—the project with Wright Horizons, the move to Houston, the weight of my past pressing down on me. New Orleans had been my anchor and my chain. It held all my traumas but it also held all my love.

It's going to be okay. Inhale. Exhale. It's going to be okay. Inhale. Exhale.

Half an hour later, I was home, the scenarios still swirling in my mind. What would I do if I saw her? Would she be angry? Dismissive? Had she moved on completely, leaving me nothing but a faded memory? I pulled out my phone and typed in her best friend's name on Instagram, searching for traces of her life.

Jackpot.

There she was, in a picture with Kelly, holding matching smoothies. My eyes zoomed in on her hand, recognizing the small paintbrush tattoo on her wrist. Did she still have her "X" tattoo, or had she covered it up? I scrolled down to another picture of her by a pool, her skin glowing under the sun, that warmth I remembered so well. I marveled over her toned body, the one I took great pleasure in holding and loving when we were together. The sun made her cocoa-kissed skin emit this warmth and radiance against the white bikini she wore. She looked different, more grown, more sure of herself. But underneath, I could still see the girl I fell in love with.

How I missed leaving trails of kisses up and her body, little spots of electricity passing between us. I slid the picture around to focus on her face. My chest tightened. I missed her. I missed us. I zoomed in on her face in one of the pictures, her smile not as bright as I remembered. There was something there, a shadow of what used to be.

I kept scrolling until I reached a birthday picture Kelly had posted of Vanessa, blowing out candles. *God, she was beautiful in this picture.* It easily became my new favorite. Her hair was pulled back into a tight bun. It showed off her face. Soft round cheeks, perfectly sized button nose, round, brown eyes that made me want to give her anything she wanted. Smooth, walnut-brown skin met soft black, wispy baby hairs that framed her hairline. *I wonder if her hair still smells like mangoes, coconuts, and shea butter.* I felt my finger move on its own, tapping the heart icon before quickly undoing it.

Shit.

I dropped my phone on the counter, rubbing my face with both hands. What was I doing? What was I hoping to find in those photos? We were set to move to Houston before the summer, and I didn't know what I'd do if I ran into her. The thought scared me as much as it thrilled me. I'd built a life here, one brick at a time, trying to fill the voids left by my father's abandonment, the wreckage of Hurricane Katrina, and the nights spent worrying over my mother's health.

I loved this city, and I hated it in equal measure. It was the only place that knew me, all the broken pieces and patched-up parts. But maybe, just maybe, it was time to leave it behind.

Chapter 3

Vanessa

A FEW MONTHS LATER...

Painting calmed the chaos that shook my soul.

I'd read that in an art history book my mother bought me in high school. I didn't know then how true those words would become; how they would echo throughout the hardest moments of my life. Acrylics and plaster became my language, the way I shaped the world I longed for. When I told my therapist about my love for the medium, she encouraged me to express it more. What she didn't know was that I'd already been selling pieces under a pseudonym at a local Black-owned gallery called Roots + Rhythm Collective. The owners wanted more from me, but between the demands of working at my parents' foundation and the endless events, my time was stretched thin.

I wanted to create something that bore my name, that stood on its own, without the weight of my parents' influence. That's what brought me to Heritage Community Center, brush in hand, adding the final strokes to the mural on the cinderblock wall at the back of the entrance hallway. The hum of colors on the wall grounded me, each swirl of paint bringing me a step closer to the calm I craved.

Soft snickers pulled me from my thoughts. I turned to find a group of teen faces peering at me from around the corner. Smiling,

I dropped my brush on the paint-splattered drop cloth and moved toward their hiding spot.

"You know," I said, rounding the corner, "it's easier to see what I'm working on if you're not trying so hard to hide."

Their eyes widened in surprise, a mix of curiosity and nerves dashing across their faces.

"Miss, what're you doing," one of the girls asked, stepping forward with a bravery that made my heart swell.

"Mrs. Collins asked me to paint a mural for the center. Want to see?" I invited the girls over to take a look. They exchanged glances, hesitating for only a moment before following me like a line of ducklings back to my workspace. As they gazed at the mural, I seized the opportunity to close a few paint tubes and wipe the smudges of color from my hands.

"Wow. How did you do all of this?" Another girl breathed, awe evident in her voice.

"Well, I just let it flow from my mind. Do y'all like it?" Their heads bobbed in unison, eyes wide with wonder as they took in the details. Warmth spread through me, softening the edges of my self-doubt.

I met Mrs. Collins, the community center director, at one of my parents' foundation events a few months back. She mentioned wanting to bring to life the center, and when I hesitated, she simply smiled and said, "Think about it." Those words stayed with me, and eventually, I made it here, pouring pieces of my soul onto this wall. It was a welcome respite from the watchful eyes in my mother's office; a place where I could breathe.

"Yeah. I've never seen something like it before," said the girl who had spoken first. "Just graffiti and stuff like that."

"Well, graffiti can be beautiful too," I replied, turning to pack away my supplies. "But it takes practice, just like any form of art."

"Can you show us how to paint like this?" Another girl asked, her eyes shining with hope.

"Ummm, sure." I picked up a fine brush and dipped it into the remaining white paint on my palette. "These letters could use a bit of highlighting. Want to help?"

"Like to make them pop more?" the girl asked, excitement creeping into her voice.

"Exactly," I giggled. "Just follow the curves of the letter with the brush." The quietest of the bunch stepped forward, carefully taking the brush. I watched her hold her breath, steadying her hand as she painted a fine line along one of the letters in "Heritage."

"That was good. What's your name?"

"Jourdan."

"And I'm Payton," the leader said with a confident smile. "This is Tyri."

"It's nice to meet y'all. I'm Vanessa." The sound of footsteps made us turn to see Mrs. Collins approaching, her caramel skin glowing under the fluorescent lights. She wore her graying sister locs styled in twists that cascaded over her broad shoulders.

"Oh, Vanessa. This is absolutely stunning," she said, her eyes lighting up as she took in the mural. "The way you've captured the neighborhood beautifully, I'd think you'd lived in Third Ward your whole life."

A shy smile crept across my face, and I felt a surge of pride mixed with vulnerability. "Thank you, Mrs. Collins. Walking around the neighborhood really inspired me." I looked over to the girls, my secret audience for the past week, as they gossiped amongst themselves. "I know I grew up in River Oaks, but there's so much history and culture here. I wanted to make sure I honored it well."

"Mrs. Collins," Payton chimed in eagerly. "Can Vanessa teach an art class here? I want to learn how to paint a mural, too!"

Mrs. Collins chuckled. "Well, that sounds like a wonderful idea. How about you girls head back to your class, and Ms. Taylor and I will talk it over?"

The girls scampered off, their laughter echoing down the hallway. Mrs. Collins turned to me, her eyes gentle but direct. "We'd love to offer the kids more than just academics and sports. We're on a tight budget this year, with the property tax increase, so it would be volunteer work only. What do you say?"

My face scanned the mural, then towards the corner the girls just turned, and then back at Mrs. Collins. The thought of teaching made my heart race with both excitement and fear. Could I do this? Could I step out and share this part of myself openly? "Maybe I can do a class or two, see how it goes?"

Mrs. Collins gave me a knowing smile and patted my arm. "Definitely. I'll put you on the schedule for next week, and see how sign-ups go. Thank you, Vanessa."

"Thank you for letting me be a part of this," I said, feeling a flutter of joy in my chest.

Mrs. Collins nodded, her heels clicking as she walked away. I turned back to the mural, my heart swelling as I took in the scene before me. It was more than just paint on a wall—it was a piece of me, brought into the light. I reached for my phone, snapped a picture, and posted it on social media with a smile. I was late for drinks with Kelly, but for the first time in a long time, I felt like I was exactly where I needed to be.

I rushed to gather my things, the butterflies in my stomach turning into something warm and hopeful. I was finding my way, one brushstroke at a time.

"I'M SO SORRY!" I pleaded, rushing to the table where Kelly was waiting, her face already breaking into a grin. "I got to talking with some of the kids and Mrs. Collins. Completely lost track of time."

"Girl, you're good. I know you run on CP time." Kelly waved off my apology with a laugh, her dark, lustrous hair gleaming in the soft lighting of the restaurant. It fell just past her shoulders, framing her round face and highlighting her almond-shaped eyes, which were always lit with a mix of warmth and determination. Her caramel skin, kissed by the Texas sun, seemed to glow with an inner light. Even in hospital scrubs, Kelly exuded beauty and confidence.

A young waiter approached our table, and Kelly's melodic voice filled the small café as she ordered our usuals. Her presence was magnetic, drawing everyone in without trying. We'd stumbled upon this hole-in-the-wall Chinese spot when one of our regular places became too crowded, and now we were practically family here. They knew our orders by heart and had a table reserved just for us, the best seat in the house where we could people-watch without the sun blinding us through the front windows.

Kelly flashed a smile at the waiter. "Please hurry with those drinks." She turned to me with a wink as I slid into the chair across from her. "I got our usuals. Is that ok?"

"Perfect." I sank into my seat, finally relaxing. Kelly always had that effect on me.

The waiter hurried off, but not before sneaking a glance back at Kelly, clearly smitten.

"Do you just attract men wherever we go?" I asked, raising an eyebrow.

"Like my Grandma always said..." Kelly started, eyes gleaming.

"Stay marketable?" I finished, and we both burst into laughter. Her grandmother's words of wisdom always made us giggle.

Kelly rolled her eyes, setting my purse beside hers on the chair between us. "No. Well, yes, but no. I'm talking about the other one—'You catch more flies with honey than vinegar.'"

"You know, I never understood that," I mused, smoothing my hand over my tight bun to ensure every hair was still in place. "Why would anybody want to catch flies?"

"Girl, I don't know. You know the old folks talk crazy," Kelly smirked. "How's the mural coming along?"

"I finished it today," I said, pulling up the picture on my phone and handing it to her.

"Nessa, this is amazing!" Kelly exclaimed, her face lighting up as she took in the details. Even she didn't know about the pieces I'd been selling under a pseudonym. This mural was the first glimpse into the world I kept hidden.

"And you see the highlights in the letters?" I pointed to the subtle lines. "I showed some girls how to add them. They were so excited. They remind me of us at that age—sassy and inquisitive."

Kelly looked up at me, her eyes softening. "You just look so happy. I haven't seen you like this in a long time." She reached across the table, squeezing my hand. "It makes me happy, considering...everything."

"Yeah." The weight of the past few years pressed on my chest for a moment. The darkness, the depression that had threatened to swallow me whole after college. I moved my hand to my stomach, feeling the phantom ache of that pit I had to crawl out. Quickly, I stuffed those memories into the mental cabinet I labeled "Dark Ages" and locked it shut.

Just then, the waiter returned with our drinks. "One classic Long Island for the lady way too young to be drinking it," he said with a smile, handing Kelly her glass, "and a Sake Sangria for her equally gorgeous friend."

Kelly grinned, batting her lashes playfully. "Oh, you're too kind. It's a favorite I picked up from the men I date. You know, the more established men I date."

The waiter cleared his throat, suddenly understanding her not-so-subtle message, and hurried away.

"You did not have to say all that," I laughed. "What happened to honey and vinegar?"

"Girl, you know dudes be bugging. If he's not about to pay my bills, I don't want him."

"Kelly, you're about to be a board-certified pediatrician. How many men can afford to pay your bills?" I teased, taking a sip of my drink.

"Exactly. I'm exclusive," she replied, shimmying her shoulders with a proud grin. Kelly took a sip of her drink, her eyes never leaving mine. "Question."

"What?" I asked, flipping aimlessly through the menu.

"I know we don't talk about the past much, but I've been curious," she said, her voice suddenly serious.

I looked up, meeting her gaze. "Curious about what?"

"You don't have to answer me. If it's too much, I'll understand." She hesitated, then pressed on. "Do you ever think about what might've happened if Zay knew everything that was going on back then?"

My stomach clenched at the mention of his name, my eyes darting to a spot on the wall just past Kelly's shoulders. A knot of emotion twisted inside me, memories threatening to spill over.

He could've known, but he was too ignorant to listen.

I forced myself to look back at Kelly, blinking away the sting of tears. "Look, don't worry about it. It's not a big deal." Kelly cast a concerned look at me, trying to reassure me. "It's in the past."

"No, it's fine." I insisted, taking another sip. "I've talked about it in therapy. I'm...past it now."

At least I hoped I was.

"Are you still mad at him?" Kelly asked, studying me carefully. "I mean, it's been six years."

"Not anymore," I said quietly. "He was dealing with a lot—work, Ma Josie's cancer. Would it have helped if he'd just let me in instead of pushing me away? Yes. But what's done is done."

"One more question." Kelly arched an eyebrow. "Do you still love him?"

I side-eyed Kelly, tilting my head to the side. "Kelly, it's been six years," I said, trying to sound casual. "I've moved on."

"I'm still not hearing a 'no'," she pressed, her eyes twinkling with curiosity.

I shot her a look. "No, okay? Satisfied?" I waved to the waiter, signaling we were ready to order. "That's all in the past. If I ever see him again, it's cool. He's doing him, and I'm doing me."

"So, if you ever saw him again, there'd be no spark? No longing?" Kelly probed, her eyes narrowing slightly.

"I don't have to think about that because I will never see Zay again." I took a long sip of my Sangria, my throat suddenly dry. "I'm in a good place now. This is where I want to stay, not the past."

The waiter arrived, saving me from further interrogation. "So, ladies. What can I get for you?" He asked, keeping his eyes on the tablet he used to take orders.

"Pan-fried shrimp dumplings for me. Extra dipping sauce. Kelly, Kung Pao chicken and jasmine rice, right?"

"Yes, extra spicy, please." Kelly handed the menu to the waiter with a smile.

"Alright. I'll be right out with those. Can I bring another round of drinks?"

"No, thank you. Just some water with lemon, light ice." Kelly replied. The waiter nodded and hurried off, leaving us in a silence that Kelly quickly filled. "Speaking of the past, guess who hit me up today." Kelly's eyes lit up mischievously, the gossip bubbling at her lips.

"Who?" I asked, more out of habit than curiosity.

"Khalil." Kelly's smile was wide, all teeth and sparkle.

"You say that like I should be shocked. I know you two have kept in touch since you graduated," I replied, my heart quickening at the mention of his name. I took a stealthy breath, trying to steady my nerves.

"Unlike you and Zay, we didn't block each other on everything," she quipped. "Khalil would've reached out to you too if y'all hadn't made us choose sides after the breakup." Kelly eyed me suspiciously, swirling the straw of her drink around the glass, her bottom lip tucked gently under her top teeth. "Guess what he told me."

Nope, nope, nope.

"Whatever you're about to tell me," I warned, "I don't want to hear it. Got it?"

"You sure? It's really good," she teased, her eyes dancing with the secret she was dying to spill.

"No, Kelly. I'm serious. I'm focused on the present."

She pouted. "Come on, girl. I'll die if I don't tell you." Kelly's round eyes pleaded in my direction.

She really thinks those puppy dog eyes are going to work on me.

"How long do you want your eulogy to be?" I taunted, raising my right eyebrow to the heaven Kelly would reside if she didn't drop this subject.

"Fine," Kelly resigned, throwing her hands in the air. "As you wish."

The waiter made his way to our table with our orders and placed the plates before us. "Enjoy. Let me know if you need anything." He scurried away, barely making eye contact.

"Kelly, you scared the man. He'll barely look us in the eye." I used my chopsticks to plop a dumpling in my mouth. My tongue watered as the strong flavors of soy sauce and ginger mingled together in my mouth, a subtle heat hitting the back of my throat as I swallowed. "Mmm. These are delicious."

"If he's that easily scared, he needs nothing to do with me," Kelly shrugged. "How are the dumplings? Switching it up on me, huh?"

"So good! Let me get some of that chicken."

Kelly spooned some of her dish onto my plate. "Honestly, after the last two shifts I had this week, anything tastes good."

"What'd you do today?" I halfway waited for Kelly's response. Yes, I shot down whatever information she had pertaining to Xavier, but my mind raced with a million scenarios of what it could be.

"Rounds all morning, then the pediatric emergency after lunch. I had a long call shift in the Pediatric Ward the night before. I'm exhausted."

"That sounds like a lot, but it'll pay off. Just two more years until you take the exam?"

"Yes." Kelly took another bite before continuing. "Now, if my dad could get with the program about the fellowship I want to do, that'd be great."

"He's still mad you don't want to go to his practice?"

Kelly rolled her eyes. "You know how he is. It's either his way or the highway." She smirked. "All he wants is his perfect doctor of a daughter as a trophy on the shelf in his family medical practice. It's fucking exhausting being 'on' all the time."

"I know what you mean. Sometimes I definitely feel like I'm playing a part." I sipped some water to wash down the remainder of the dumplings in my mouth.

Kelly laughed breathtakingly. "Bitch, you are playing a part."

Did she just? My chopsticks paused halfway to my mouth. "Excuse me?"

"You heard me." Kelly set her fork down. "Since you graduated, you've been following Aunt Viv's script, not your own."

"Kelly," I started, but she cut me off.

"I'm not just your best friend. I'm your sister. Blood couldn't make us any closer." She waved over to the waiter. "And as your sister, I'm telling you it's time to cut the umbilical cord."

"Well, if you must know," I replied, leaning in. "I'm thinking about teaching an art class at Heritage Community Center, and I don't plan on asking my mother."

"Oh really? I'll believe it when I see it. You know Aunt Viv controls your schedule. I'm surprised she hasn't called you while we've been here."

I was silent before responding. "We talked on the way here," I admitted with a sheepish grin.

"See what I mean. Nessa, you're a grown-ass woman. Cut the umbilical cord already."

"Hey, I'm working on it. What do you think I've been unpacking in therapy?"

"Well, tell your therapist to hurry it up. I'm ready to have my friend back and be in these streets before summer's over." Kelly downed the rest of her drink, shimmying in her seat.

I felt a flutter in my chest, the excitement of stepping into something new. It scared me, but also thrilled me. I was finally breaking free, piece by piece, from the cocoon that held me captive for so long.

"We need a night out. I took off the weekend of you and Aunt Viv's birthday. We're going to the club. Drink as much as we want. I'll have time to bounce back before my next set of rounds."

"That sounds good. You know the dinner is going to be lame anyway." I took my wallet, swiping Kelly's hand away. "I got this. You're paying for everything when we go out for my birthday." I handed the waiter my card when he returned.

"What are you going to wear?"

"I don't know, girl," I replied, looking at my watch. "I gotta get going. My show starts in 45 minutes. And you know I-69 is full of traffic."

As we stood to leave, Kelly pulled me in close for a tight, reassuring hug. "You know I'm always here for you, right?"

I stepped back and took her face in my hands. We were each other's ride-or-die, down to do whatever to support the other. "Yes, Kelly girl. And I'm forever here for you, too." I gave my friend a peck on the cheek. "Get some rest, Dr. Reid. I'll talk to you later."

"And you sure you don't want to know what Khalil said?" Kelly implored, again.

"No, Kelly! Please don't ask me again."

"Fine." We walked out of the restaurant arm in arm, before parting ways to head to our cars. I really loved my best friend. Even if she did push me beyond my comfort zone.

As I walked to my car, I couldn't help biting the inside of my lip. As many times as I'd told Kelly I didn't want to hear what Khalil told her, it now consumed my mind. My gut told me it had to be about Xavier. *Clearly, Vanessa, or else Kelly wouldn't have been so enthused about telling you.* As I drove home, so many thoughts popped into my head. How was he doing? Did he miss me? Did he want to see me? Did he regret pushing me away? Does he still love me? Or was he lying to himself the same way I had when Kelly asked if I still loved him?

Chapter 4

Vanessa

"Emily, do you know what the plan is for social media engagement this year?"

My mother's assistant sat across from me, her fingers flying over the tablet on her lap. "Mrs. Taylor never mentioned social media. Just a few local press," she replied, not looking up.

"That's not going to work." I sighed, rubbing my temples. "Between you and me, we need to get The Taylor Foundation, the gala, and all other events in front of people across the country. What's the point of hosting all these fundraising events if barely anyone knows about them?"

I pulled up a list of local social media managers on my screen and sent their contact information to Emily. "Look, reach out to these candidates. See if you can get another staff member to help with the interviews. Let me know who you think might be a good fit." I looked at the assistant, who continued to look down at her tablet before looking back up.

Emily glanced up, her eyes wide. "Yes, Ms. Taylor. I'll get on that right away."

"Look, Emily. Call me Vanessa," I insisted, a slight smile tugging at my lips. "Mrs. Taylor is my mother."

"But you're so much like her!" Emily exclaimed, her voice bright with admiration. "Your attention to detail, your innovative ideas. It must've been amazing to have Mrs. Taylor as your mother."

If only you knew.

I forced a smile, shaking my head. "No, no, no. There's only one Vivian Taylor." Knocks sounded on the door to my office, a warning before it swung on it's hinges, revealing the visitor.

"Vanessa, sweetheart! Look who came to pay me a visit." My mother swept into the room, her presence as commanding as ever. Behind her, Wesley trailed with a sheepish grin, sidestepping around her to approach me.

"Van, long time no see." He pulled me into a friendly hug, and I stiffened at the contact, praying my mother wouldn't get the wrong idea. Wesley was all chiseled good looks—dark honey-green eyes, a neatly groomed beard framing his full lips, his complexion sun-kissed and freckled. But as attractive as he was, our history taught me he wasn't what I needed. We were better off as friends.

"It's good to see you too." I forced a smile as I pulled back. "What are you doing here? I thought you were working in your dad's New York office?"

"I've got a few meetings upstairs today," he explained, glancing between me and my mother. "I ran into Mrs. Viv on the elevator. She insisted I stop by."

Because of course, she did.

"Wesley was filling me in all that he's done since you two left graduate school," my mother said, her smile too wide, her eyes dancing with a calculated gleam. "I thought it would be a nice surprise. Besides, he has something he wants to ask you. Don't you, Wesley?"

"Uh, right," he stammered, clearing his throat. My mother moved to sit in my chair, settling in as if she owned the space. "Van, this new project I'm working on is a luxury apartment complex. Your mother mentioned you just finished a mural at Heritage Community Center in Third Ward. We'd love to have you do one for the complex."

"Doesn't that sound fun, sweetheart?" My mother beamed, her voice dripping with enthusiasm. "You know how much you love painting."

I shot her a sideways glance, my irritation simmering just beneath the surface. "I don't know. My schedule's pretty busy with work around here and volunteering at the community center." I sat in the chair opposite her, hoping she caught the pointed stare I aimed in her direction. This was her, always inserting her plans into my life.

"It wouldn't be for a few months," Wesley interjected. "Not until major renovations are completed."

"See?" My mother clasped her hands, her eyes sparkling with determination. "Plenty of time for you to move some things around," my mother added, biting her lip. *This lady doesn't quit.*

"I can even set up a meeting with our partners," Wesley offered. "You can get a feel for the project, then decide."

Before I could open my mouth to respond, my mother cut in again. "She'll be there. Send me the details, I'll make sure of it." I seethed silently in my chair, glaring at her. This was Vivian Taylor at her finest—always steering the ship, never mind the destination I wanted.

"Okay, then," Wesley said, looking between us with a knowing smile. "I'll see you around, Mrs. Viv. Van." He gave me a wink as he left, the door closing softly behind him. He knew all too well what it was like to have your life mapped out by someone else.

"Bye, Wesley," my mother sang. "Tell your mother I can't wait to see her at my birthday dinner. It's been too long."

"Emily," my mother called without turning to face her, "give my daughter and me a moment, will you?" Emily gathered her things and rushed out without a word, closing the door quietly behind her.

"Vanessa, sweetheart. What's wrong?" My mother asked, rearranging items on my desk with her usual precision. "You look like a sourpuss."

I rolled my eyes toward the ceiling. "Mom, we talked about this. Why do you insist on butting in on my life?"

"Vanessa," she said, her voice taking on that familiar tone of exasperation, "I am not butting in. I'm giving you a gentle push in the right direction. The sooner you realize that, the better. My mother did the exact same thing, and look how I turned out."

I stood, crossing my arms as I looked down at her. "Mom, I don't need help making decisions. The sooner you realize *that*, the better." I moved to replace the items on my desk how I wanted them. "I know you gave up your career to raise me and took care of me after college, but I can figure things out on my own now."

"Vanessa. I'm your mother. I know what's best for you," she replied, her voice softening, though urgency remained. She moved from behind my desk, her face softening, juxtaposing with her urgent voice. "You need something to occupy your mind. It's been almost two years since you started acting like yourself again. When are you going to settle down? Give Wesley a chance. He's a good man."

"Wesley and I operate better as friends," I said, frustration edging into my tone. "I wish you and Mrs. Lisa would understand that."

"Good God, Vanessa," she sighed, her patience thinning. "You're practically thirty and still haven't settled on something. Don't you want a career? A family of your own? Kids? The world isn't over because it didn't work out before."

I felt like the wind had been knocked out of me. "Wow, Mom. Really? And, for the record, I'm about to be twenty-seven. I have time to figure things out. When, and *if*, I fall in love again, it'll be on my own terms."

She waved a dismissive hand. "That's not what I meant, and you know it."

"Then what did you mean?" I demanded, my voice rising.

"All I'm saying is that if you want love, Wesley is a catch. Any girl would be lucky to have him."

"Then they can have him." I leaned back on the desk, crossing my arms over my chest.

She sighed, standing to face me, her eyes searching mine. "I just don't understand you, Vanessa. Why do you have to make things so difficult? Let me help you."

"Help me?" I almost laughed. "Or control me?" I watched her face shift, a flicker of hurt crossing her eyes. "I want to love my career and the person I choose to be with. You loved your career before you gave it up, and you and Daddy are so in love it's nauseating. Is it so hard to believe I want the same thing?"

My mother laughed softly, a wistful sound. "Your father and I...that was...different." Her voice softened, a hint of vulnerability creeping in. "I just want you to be taken care of."

I exhaled, letting my arms drop to my sides. "Mom, I know, but it's not going to be by Wesley. His definition of love is whatever wins his parent's approval. I know his mom is your soror and friend, but is that what you want for me? To be someone's trophy?"

"But sweetheart, you are the prize." She walked over to me, taking my hands in hers. "I just want you to be happy."

"And I will be," I said, my voice gentler now. "But it has to be my way, not yours."

She took a deep breath, squeezing my hands in hers. "Just take the meeting with Wesley. It can't do any harm."

I sighed deeply, nodding. "Fine. But it's just for the mural. Nothing else."

A relieved smile broke across her face as she gathered her purse and walked to the door. "I'll take it. Besides, I already told Emily to schedule the meeting for next week, in the private lounge."

"Mom!" I protested, but she was already heading for the door.

"See you Saturday for my birthday dinner, darling," she sang, pausing at the doorway. "And you're getting your hair done, yes?" Without waiting for a reply, she blew me air kisses and disappeared down the hallway.

A silent scream welled up inside me, and I grabbed my belongings, following her out of the office. Some things never changed, and yet, somehow, I was determined to carve out my own path—even if it meant pushing back against the force that was Vivian Taylor.

THE SOUND OF TEENS chattering in the hallway was a welcome relief from the tension that simmered between my mother and me earlier. It was as if the walls of the community center absorbed the stress, letting me breathe again. I walked around the large room, laying out brushes, paints, and canvas sheets. The students trickled in, laughter and smack talk echoing through the space as they found their usual spots at the tables. The room came alive with their energy, the late evening sunlight streaming through the large windows, bathing everything in warm hues of yellow and orange.

I raised my hand, signaling our agreed-upon gesture for quiet. The students gradually settled, their eyes turning toward me.

"Hey, everybody. I know y'all are excited since we're painting today," I began, my voice calm and steady. "A reminder that today's about exploring. We're just practicing adding colors to the canvas and getting a feel for the materials. Focus on how the paint moves, and how it blends. Don't worry about making it perfect."

Low murmurs and the rustle of supplies filled the room. Teen angst mixed with genuine excitement, a familiar rhythm in this space we had carved out together. I pointed to the easel at the front of the room, a larger version of the mini ones I'd set up on each table—an investment from my own pocket.

"First things first," I continued, "let's meet our new best friend—the canvas. It's your own magic portal to create whatever you imagine."

Cary, one of my more spirited students, shot his hand up, his eyes gleaming with mischief. "Ms. Nessa, you said we could paint whatever, right?"

"Yes, Cary," I replied, bracing myself for what was about to come, "anything you can imagine in your mind."

"So I could paint Johnny and fix his jacked-up fade?" Laughter rippled around the room.

Don't laugh, Nessa. I fought to keep a straight face. *And don't even think about looking at Johnny.* We all knew his haircut was looking a little rough.

"Absolutely, Cary," I said, letting a smile slip. "As long as you're okay with him fixing that hairline." I joked back, pointing to the edge of his hairline. More laughter erupted, and the atmosphere lightened even further.

As the students dipped their brushes into the paint, the room buzzed with chatter and ideas. I moved around, offering guidance, showing them how to mix colors, and letting their creativity flow.

I stopped at Jourdan's table. She stared at her blank canvas, eyes clouded with uncertainty.

"What's wrong, Jourdan? You haven't gotten started," I said, placing a gentle hand on her back.

"I don't know, Ms. Nessa." She hesitated. "I can't think of anything to do that makes sense."

I bent down beside her. Using my hand to guide hers into a random color on her palette, I moved her hand along the dry canvas. "Well, Jourdan, it doesn't have to make sense. Art is your own secret language," I whispered. "Use it to tell stories, express feelings, and create a world that's uniquely yours."

Her eyes lit up, the fear giving way to a flicker of confidence. She started painting abstract yellow lines, her movements becoming more fluid, more certain. Around us, laughter and excitement filled the room as I moved from table to table, turning the class into a joyful exploration of creativity.

"Okay, anybody want to share what they've put on their canvas?" I asked, removing my own canvas from the easel at the front of the class. Hands shot up and I grinned at their eagerness. I pointed to a boy in the class who was on the more reserved artsy side. "Keon, come on up. Tell us about your painting."

He walked to the front, holding his canvas with care. "Well, I thought about what you said, about it not needing to be perfect," he began. "I thought about all the things people think are perfect, but still have flaws." He explained how the dilapidated houses on his canvas represented happy moments for the people living in them, even if they seemed broken on the outside.

I knew this boy had something special about him. Once Keon finished his explanation, the class clapped and a few of the boys dapped him up on the way to his seat.

I joined in with the clapping. "Well done, Keon! Basquiat would be proud."

"Who's that?" Tyri piped up from the back of the class.

"He was a famous Black artist who created some really wonderful pieces. Famous pieces."

"So like, he was getting that bread, huh?" Cary added.

I laughed. With these kids, everything always came back to money. "Yes, Cary. Jay Z paid around $4.5 million for one of his pieces."

"Nah, tell me how to paint like him," Cary declared, and the class erupted in laughter again.

"Well," I said smiling, "maybe, if you focus, you might learn to do that. Let's master the basics first, okay?" The room turned into a whirlwind of colors and laughter. I shared stories of other Black artists, their work, their struggles, and their triumphs. Slowly, these kids were finding their place in my heart, each one carving out a space where there was once emptiness.

I moved over to Payton's table, noticing her deep concentration. "How's it going, Payton?"

"Alright." She said, not taking her eyes off her canvas. "These brushes are kind of weird. My lines come out funky depending on which direction I paint them."

"That happens to me too," I reassured her. "Just keep practicing and you'll find your rhythm."

"Thank you, Ms. Nessa," she said, glancing up at me with a smile that warmed me from the inside out. "You know, I really like your class."

"I'm glad."

"You should do this all the time," she continued, her voice earnest. "Like everyday instead of once a week."

"You think so?" I asked, surprised by the sincerity in her eyes.

"Yeah. I have friends at school who wanted to sign up, but they can't make it on these days."

"Well, I'll have to see what I can do about that," I said, patting her back before moving to the front of the room again. The chatter died down as I raised my hand once more.

"Everyone, look at what you've created today. Each of you has a painting, a story waiting to be told. I'm so proud of each and every one of you. Just remember, art has the power to unlock whatever your heart desires. I'll see you all next week. Make sure you put your materials back where they belong. Let your canvases dry on the counters next to the windows. You should be able to pick them up next time you're at the center."

As they cleaned up, I felt a deep sense of fulfillment wash over me, a feeling I hadn't experienced in a long time. In this room, I was free to be myself. No expectations, no rules, no one else's plan for my life. Just me and the kids, and the beautiful chaos of creativity.

I watched them file out, their smiles and laughter lingering in the air like a warm embrace. I glanced at my watch, realizing I was late for my hair appointment. My mind buzzed with the thought of more classes, more time in this space that felt so right. The guarded walls I had built around myself softened here, with these kids. And maybe, just maybe, they were helping me paint a new picture of what my life could be. For now, I'd have to put that thought away, but it was a seed, planted and waiting to grow.

Chapter 5

Xavier

"Man, when we get some time, I want to research the plans for this building," I said, staring out the floor-to-ceiling windows of the downtown Houston office Khalil and I shared. The space was a perk from partnering with Wright Horizons, a temporary command center for the duration of the project. Below, the streets shimmered with luxury cars, gleaming under the late afternoon sun. Tree-lined sidewalks offered sparse shade to the pedestrians, a faint attempt at softening the city's hard edges.

I started to turn away when a familiar figure caught my eye. I squinted, my pulse quickening. But before I could be sure, they slipped into a car and drove off, swallowed by the flow of traffic. *Man, you tripping.* I shook my head. *Ain't no way that was her.*

The phone buzzed in my pocket, jolting me back to the present.

"Zay, I don't think I'm gonna make it to the meeting today. Can you hold it down?" Khalil's voice came through, tense and rushed.

"What you mean, man?" I asked, already feeling the anxiety rise in my chest.

"I thought I'd be on the plane by now, but my flight keeps getting delayed."

"See. I told your ass to ride with me. That's why I don't mess with them death traps." I unbuttoned the top of my shirt, trying to calm my racing heart.

"I know, man. I know." Khalil continued to explain, but I could barely focus. My eyes drifted back to the street below, hoping for a glimpse of that familiar face again. "But don't worry about it. You got it, bruh."

Yeah, but you're the one that keeps me in check when they keep adding all this unnecessary luxury shit. I rubbed the back of my neck, staring at the presentation on my desk. This whole project was supposed to be about sustainable construction, about revitalizing communities, not installing marble floors and gold-plated faucets. The partnership that began with the promise of redeveloping abandoned projects back home had turned into something unrecognizable. Now, we were converting old apartments in Houston into high-end condos, the exact opposite of what we'd set out to do.

"Yeah, I know," I sighed. "It just looks better if we're both there. More professional."

"I know. If I have to change on the airplane, I will." Announcements blared in the background of the call. "Look, they're saying something about my flight. Hopefully, I get there just in time. Do that meditation shit you do, just in case."

"Yeah," I muttered. "Let me know how you make out."

The line went dead, leaving me with nothing but the silence of the room and the uneasy feeling in my gut. I glanced back out the window, my thoughts drifting. Was it really her? My heart thudded at the thought, my pulse quickening as I imagined Vanessa walking these very streets. It had been so long, but some things stayed with you, like the imprint of a dream you could never quite shake off.

My phone buzzed again. *Ma.* I exhaled, grateful for the distraction.

"Hey, Ma," I answered, forcing a smile into my voice.

"Hey, son. How you doing?" Her voice was cheerful and light, the sound of home.

"Aww, you know. Working." I replied, sinking into the chair by the window, and staring out at the city without really seeing it.

"You're not working too hard, I hope?" she teased.

"That's the only work I know how to do." I chuckled, though it felt hollow.

"Well, you know I'm proud of you."

"I know, Ma." I could almost see her smile on the other end, the way it would light up her face.

"It's good to see you getting back to yourself."

"Myself?" I asked, a frown creasing my forehead. "What you mean, Ma?"

"Yourself," she repeated gently. "Peaceful. Happy-ish. After my diagnosis, you lost your joy for a while."

My chest tightened at her words. "Well, Ma, I thought I was losing you."

The memory of that time came flooding back—the day she sat me down, her voice steady but eyes betraying the fear she tried to hide. Stage 2 cancer. She swore me to secrecy, determined to fight it without drawing attention. I'd spent months driving her to chemo, watching the illness strip away her strength, her hair, her vibrancy. I spiraled, drowning in stress and grief, losing myself in the process.

"Well, I'm still here, standing," she said softly, her voice pulling me back. "And you are, too. Ain't God good?"

"All the time," I murmured, blinking back the sting in my eyes.

"How are you really doing, son?" Her tone shifted, becoming more probing. "You've accomplished so much, so fast, but you never take any time to enjoy it."

I stared at the floor, swallowing the lump in my throat. What was I supposed to say? Business was booming. Ma's been cancer-free for almost five years now. On paper, I had everything I'd ever wanted.

"I'm okay, Ma," I lied.

"You ran into Vanessa yet?" she asked, cutting straight to the heart of it. "I know she been on your mind nonstop since y'all started working out there."

You ain't gotta say it out loud, Ma.

I closed my eyes, the familiar ache flaring up. "No, Ma. Look, let me call you later. I have a virtual session with Dr. Rivers in a few, and this meeting with Wright Horizons a couple hours after that. I need to get my mind right." I stood to walk over to my desk.

"Alright, son." She paused, and I could hear the love and concern wrapped up in her words. "Remember what I said. Everyone deserves second chances."

"I will, Ma. Love you."

"Love you, too." She hung up, leaving me in the quiet of the office. I walked back to the window, staring at the spot where I thought I saw her. *You're imagining things, Zay.* I turned away, shaking off the what-ifs.

Sitting at my desk, I tried to focus on the presentation, my eyes glazing over the words. This partnership with Wright Horizons was supposed to be our next big step. But now, it felt like a betrayal of everything we'd built EcoVision to be. I clicked through the slides, repeating Khalil's talking points in my head until they blurred together.

The chime of my laptop broke the silence. *Dr. Rivers.* I took a deep breath and clicked into the virtual session. His calm face appeared on the screen, his office backdrop a soothing mix of earth tones and soft lighting.

"Good to see you, Xavier," Dr. Rivers greeted, his voice a steady anchor. "How have you been since our last session?"

Exhaling, I ran a hand over the waves of my haircut. "I've been better."

Dr. Rivers leaned forward slightly, his attention unwavering. "Speak more on that. Tell me what's been on your mind lately."

I leaned back in my chair, the familiar tightness in my chest returning. "I guess it's the old stuff coming back. The fear of not being enough. All the things I've been through... They all left these scars. Even though I've done the work, it's hard to shake the feeling that I'll either be abandoned or exposed as a fraud."

Dr. Rivers' expression was sympathetic but firm. "Xavier, you've done incredible work addressing those wounds. Let's remind ourselves of how far you've come. When you first started therapy, you were buried under the weight of these issues. Now, you've built a successful company, you're managing your emotions better, and you're more self-aware than ever before."

"Yeah, I know I've made progress," I admitted, though doubt still clung to me like a shadow. "But every time something good happens, I'm just waiting for the other shoe to drop."

Dr. Rivers' eyes were steady, grounding. "That's the imposter syndrome talking, Xavier. You've worked hard for everything you have, and it's okay to accept that you deserve your success. Remember, your father's abandonment doesn't define your worth. You do."

I took a deep breath, trying to internalize his words. "It's just hard. Sometimes I still feel like that scared kid who's going to be left behind."

"That's natural." Dr. Rivers leaned back, his voice gentle. "Those early experiences shaped you, but they don't have to dictate your future. You've built a life and a career on your terms. Keep acknowledging your fears, but don't let them control you. You've proven time and again that you're capable and resilient."

A flicker of hope sparked inside me. "I guess I need to keep reminding myself of that. It's just tough, especially with the stakes being so high now."

"Absolutely," Dr. Rivers agreed. "High stakes can trigger old anxieties. But think about how you've navigated challenges before. You've faced some of the toughest moments life can throw at you and come out stronger. Use that strength as your foundation."

I looked out at the cityscape, feeling a sense of calm wash over me. "Thanks, Doc. I needed to hear that."

"You're doing great, Xavier," Dr. Rivers said warmly. "Let's keep this momentum going. We'll continue to address these feelings, but don't forget to celebrate your successes along the way. How about we check in again next month?"

"That sounds good," I replied, feeling a bit lighter. "I'll keep working on it."

Dr. Rivers gave me a reassuring nod. "Excellent. Take care, Xavier. I'll talk to you soon."

"Thanks, Dr. Rivers. Talk to you soon."

After the call ended, I sat back in my chair, letting his words wash over me. I wasn't the same person who had started this journey. I was more than my past, more than the fears that clung to me. But knowing that didn't make the struggle any less real. I busied myself with the presentation, committing Khalil's talking points to memory. I practiced dropping my New Orleans accent, aiming for a more neutral tone that wouldn't immediately peg me as the boy who grew up on crawfish and bounce music. A notification flashed on my phone, reminding me of the meeting in fifteen minutes. I stood, grabbing my suit jacket and the printed project updates the CEO of Wright Horizons had requested.

I caught my reflection in the mirror on Khalil's desk. Thank God I got a haircut yesterday. I straightened my tie, taking a deep breath.

You got this.

With one last glance at the window, I turned and headed out of the office, determined to face whatever came next.

MAN, FUCK PLANES, FUCK the sky, and anything else that wasn't on the ground! Khalil's flight was finally arriving in Houston, but he'd missed the entire meeting with Wright Horizons. My heart raced as I wrapped up the project updates in front of the executive board of the real estate development firm. With every meeting, it became painfully clear that they had partnered with Khalil and me for the optics, not for any shared vision. The power to make real decisions was concentrated solely in the hands of the CEO. Every time I sat in those meetings, I kicked myself for not following my gut. This deal went against everything our company stood for, yet we were stuck unless we found an easy way to back out.

Our startup was supposed to revolutionize the architecture and construction industry—integrating sustainable design, virtual reality technology, and urban planning to provide affordable housing solutions. But now, here I was, giving updates on marble tile and hardwood floors for luxury condos. I fought to keep my cool, a task that was usually Khalil's forte. That's why he was supposed to be here, not delayed by weather and flight schedules.

"Once all the structural repairs are made, we'll be ready to add the eco-friendly appliances and technology to the building which will put us a few weeks ahead of schedule."

I clicked to the last slide, clenching my jaw to stifle the frustration boiling within me. The tall executive sitting front and center—whom I immediately pegged as the CEO's son the first time we met—stood up and extended his hand. *Some people got it so easy, silver-spoon ass nigga.*

"Xavier Morris, thank you for giving the updates. We'll review the numbers with finance, and make sure everything is staying within budget."

"That's a bet." I forced one of Khalil's charismatic smiles as I packed my belongings.

The older man beside him, undoubtedly the CEO, nodded toward me. "Mr. Morris, help yourself to a drink down in the building's private lounge. Tell Arthur I sent you down; he'll take care of you. We'll be in touch."

I forced myself to smile, gave them both a firm handshake, and walked out of the conference room, my footsteps echoing in the marble-floored hallway. As I passed by the glass windows, I kept my face composed, but inside, a storm raged.

Inhale. Exhale.

Man, fuck this shit.

The lounge was dimly lit, a stark contrast to the sterile brightness of the office floors. Groups of people sat at tables, their low murmurs blending into an ambient hum. I made my way to the bar and sank into a stool. The bartender approached, a man with gray-flecked hair and a warm, knowing gaze.

Resting my elbows on the bar, I let my head drop into my fingertips. The weight of our situation pressed down on me. Khalil and I had been ecstatic when Wright Horizons agreed to partner with us. Adding them to our portfolio meant a step up in notoriety, bigger clients, and more projects. More money. *But not all money is good money.*

"Big meeting upstairs," the bartender asked, not needing an answer.

"Aw man, 'big' don't even cover it. Can I get a Hennessy and Coke?"

He laughed, a deep, hearty sound. "You ain't at no cookout, young blood. How about a scotch on the rocks?" He gave me a quick once-over, then smirked. "I'll make it a double. You look like you need it."

"You must be Arthur?" I took a sip of the drink he set in front of me. *Got damn. This shit was smoother than a motherfucker.*

"That's what the people call me." He smiled, the corners of his eyes crinkling in a way that reminded me of my grandfather. Pops had been the only father figure in my life after my dad left. I hadn't seen or heard from him much after Katrina.

"What's this? I ain't ever had no scotch like this before?" I took another sip, letting the warmth settle in my chest.

"That is a 30 year Macallan Scotch. Only the best of the best for the people that come in here." Arthur wiped the bar, his movements slow and deliberate. "What business brings you here?"

I sighed and took another sip, the tension in my body starting to ease. "Trying to keep a real estate project going with Wright Horizons. They agreed to partner, but it feels like we're fighting a losing battle just to stay true to our mission."

Arthur chuckled, a sound rich with life's wisdom. "Well. Easy part's over now. Enjoy your drink."

"Thanks, my man." I nursed the rest of my drink, feeling the frustration slowly dull. I shot Khalil a text with the rundown of the meeting. "Say, Arthur, how much do you know about Wright Horizons?"

The bartender relaxed against the back of the bar, crossing his arms over his chest. "Well, I've been working for people like the Wrights' for decades. They have a different kind of drive. Not survival, something else. Not all of them, but some. Just depends on who it is."

"You think Wright Horizons is a good company?"

He shrugged. "I don't know too much about all of that. They own this building and I've had a steady paycheck for 30 years. That's all the good I need." His eyes studied mine. "You think it's a good company to work with?"

I stared into my glass. *Hell no.* "I don't know."

"Well, you might want to think about that then." Arthur moved away to help someone else, leaving me with my thoughts.

"Mr. Morris, you're still here."

I turned to the grating voice behind me. *Not this goofy-ass nigga again.*

"I'm glad I caught you. Jeffery is scheduled to call you in the morning with this but, since you're here now, I'll let you know." The younger Wright wore a pensive expression, his plastic grin barely concealing his diffidence. "Unofficially, Wright Horizon Realty has agreed to move forward with the renovations."

Of course. They got everything they wanted.

"I know this isn't what we initially discussed," he continued, "but this is how things work at this level. You have to give a little to get a little. EcoVision is going to be a major name in the industry by the time we're done."

"That's good to hear, Mr. Wright," I said through clenched teeth. "I'll let Mr. Grant know."

He extended his hand. "Hey, we're business partners now. Call me Wesley. Xavier, right?"

The fuck kind of name is Wesley. "Yes. We'll be in touch, Wesley."

He nodded, turning to leave. "Oh, and I have an artist I'm trying to convince to paint a mural in the community space. Old friend of mine. We'll meet with them in the coming weeks. I'll send the details once they confirm." Wesley headed to the exits of the private lounge.

I turned back to the bar, releasing the breath I'd been holding. "Say, man, can I get another?" Arthur nodded and refilled my glass. I took a sip, the rich taste washing over me, soothing the fire in my gut.

"Everything went according to plans?" Arthur asked.

"Seems like it." I took another sip of the brown liquid, warmth spreading through me. "I got a question for you, Arthur."

"What's that young brother?"

"You ever felt like everything you ever wanted was falling into place, but something was still missing?"

"Yeah." Arthur crossed the bar and leaned toward me, resting his elbows on the lacquered surface. "Usually a woman's involved. Let me guess, the one that got away."

Man, you don't know the half of it.

"Nah, man. Nothing like that," I snorted off, though my tone lacked conviction.

"Well, whatever it is, whoever's missing, you'll find them soon enough."

I shot back the remainder of my drink, the burn catching the back of my throat. " Thanks, Arthur. I'll see you around." I placed the glass on the bar and stood. Walking out of the lounge, the reality of what we were accomplishing finally hit me. While I wasn't fully satisfied with the direction, we were in the room. Maybe that meant something.

I dialed Khalil. "How'd the meeting go? You ain't curse nobody out, huh?"

"Nah, man. Everything is moving full steam ahead. Wright Horizons is getting everything they want."

"Man, I don't even care. We still in there." Khalil's excitement buzzed through the line. "We going out this weekend. We need to celebrate."

"Yeah, yo' ass just need to get out that airport." We were both silent. "Damn, man."

"What?"

"We really made it, huh?" The realization sent chills through me, a mixture of thrill and unease.

"Man, I told you we would. I don't know why you doubted me." Khalil replied.

I looked to the ground, a rare smile playing across my lips. "Yeah, man. Look, I'll hit you up tomorrow. It's going down this weekend. You know I don't do club shit, but I'll make an exception this one time."

"Say less. I already got something in mind."

"Yeah, man."

Chapter 6

VANESSA

THE PRIVATE DINING ROOM of Mastro's Steakhouse was draped in elegance—glistening chandeliers, mirrored walls without a smudge in sight, glass-encased shelves lined with vintage wines, and the soft murmur of a water feature on the outdoor terrace. Warm, ambient light glowed from the crevices of the coffered ceilings and flickers of candles at each table. Nearly fifty guests mingled or took their seats, wrapped in designer cocktail dresses and tailored suits, all here to celebrate my mother's 25/30 Birthday Dinner.

Just say you're fifty-five, Mama.

The restaurant, nestled in the heart of Uptown Houston, was upscale, the epitome of my mother's taste. Each table was topped with peony and eucalyptus arrangements in shades of mauve, cream, and earthy greens, their subtle fragrance wafting through the air. From a distance, soothing vocals and gentle instruments added to the atmosphere. I was sure my father called up Mom's favorite event planner to ensure every detail was perfect, from reserving the largest dining room to footing the bill for every guest. His adoration for her was endless, each gesture a symbol of his love.

Why can't I have that?

My mother glided through the room, soaking in the attention, her closest friends—Wesley and Kelly's mothers—flanking her sides. At the moment, they were deep in conversation with Kelly, Wesley, and his father. Not in the mood for that group, I made my way over to my father at the bar. Though I was the spitting image of my mother, it was from him I got my softer demeanor. A titan in his field before retiring, he was a force to reckon with in private equity. Yet, when it came to us—my mother and me—he was soft as cotton, forever willing to give us the world.

"Daddy, you really outdid yourself this year," I said walking up and taking a seat at the bar next to him.

"Hey, sweet pea. You finally made it, huh?" He wrapped me in a bear hug, kissing the top of my head. At 6'4", he was a giant among men but the warmest soul to me.

"Hey, this time it's not on me," I laughed. "I had to wait for Kelly to pick me up. I'm staying with her this weekend."

"Ah, so you're playing hooky from your mama?" He chuckled, his deep voice rumbling like a soft drum. "Have you said hi to her yet?"

"No, she looked busy," I replied, glancing over to where my mother still held court. "I think her and Mrs. Lisa are trying to get Wesley and me together again. Ever the persistent ones." I let out a small sigh. "Daddy, sometimes I wish she'd just relax. Let me live my own life like you do."

He regarded me with his warm eyes, a hint of sorrow in them. "I know, but she means well. We just want you to be happy." His gaze lingered on me. "So, tell me. How are you doing? How's therapy going?"

"Cool," I said, toying with the napkin in front of me. "Camille suggests I have a conversation with Mom about her overstepping. I keep asking Mom to come to a session with me, but she finds a way to dodge it. I'll circle back at the end of the month."

"Yeah, that's the lawyer in her still at work." He chuckled softly. "Other than that, how are things?" My father always knew when something was off with me, but never pushed or prodded like my mother. "Are you sure you're okay? Happy?"

I sighed, feeling the weight of his question settle on my shoulders. "Yes, daddy. Why do you keep asking me that?"

He tilted his head, studying me with that watchful eye only he had. "Sometimes I get the feeling you aren't. Call it Daddy's intuition." He chuckled.

I smiled at my father. "It's not your intuition," I replied, trying to deflect. "I think you're just scared of letting Daddy's little girl go."

"Hey now, my intuition set us up something good. Me, your mother, you, your children, your children's children." He laughed heartily, taking another sip of the cognac in his hand. "All those investments I made early on paid off quite nicely thanks to my intuition."

"Alright Daddy," I chuckled. "I get it."

"Don't play about me and my intuition," he said, giving me a knowing look. "I worry about you a lot, you know. I know you're in a better place now compared to after college, but I still worry."

"Daddy, you don't need to worry."

"No, I do," he said gently. "I'm your father, that's my job. You used to have a twinkle in your eye. I haven't seen it since you left college and moved back here to Houston." My stomach tightened at the mention of that dark time, and I found myself looking away. *Well, a lot happened back then.* "You know you can talk to me about anything, right?"

"I know." I gave him a reassuring look. "Unfortunately there's nothing to tell. Besides, as people grow up, twinkles leave their eyes. That's life."

"Look at me, look at my eyes," he said, pointing to his eyes. "Still twinkling, aren't they?"

"Daddy, I think that's just the alcohol," I teased, grateful for the change in tone. I glanced toward the other side of the room where my mother was waving us over. "I think we'd better head to the tables."

"Yeah, I agree. Let's go celebrate my lady." My father and I locked arms as we walked across the room taking our seats at a table near the center of the room. "And remember it's your birthday weekend, too. Don't think you have to dedicate all your time to your mother. That's my job."

"I know, Daddy. That's why I'm leaving early, remember? Kelly has a whole weekend planned."

"You want to use the driver?"

"No, sir. There you go worrying again. We'll be fine. I promise." He patted my back before taking his seat beside my mother. I settled in at our table, Kelly and her parents across from me, Wesley next to me.

How convenient.

As the guests found their seats, my father rose to welcome everyone. He spoke warmly of my mother, celebrating her dedication to Taylor Philanthropy and our family. He ended his speech with a toast, wishing everyone a lifetime of the love and happiness he shared with my mother. I caught the wink he shot me before taking a sip of his champagne. Shortly after, waiters brought out appetizers of jumbo lump crab cakes, foie gras, lobster bisque, and house salads. The main course followed—succulent cuts of meat and sides like lobster mashed potatoes and roasted Brussels sprouts. As conversations flowed around me, I found myself returning to my father's words.

Am I really happy? I sat, stuck in my thoughts, moving the barely touched pieces of Chilean Sea Bass and Brussels sprouts around my plate. My phone buzzed, pulling me back to the present.

Kelly Girl: You ready to go?

Vanessa: Yes! Let me tell my parents bye.

"Hey, Mom, Kelly and I are about to head out," I said, standing up.

My mother's eyes flicked from me to Kelly. She squinted slightly, sensing mischief. So did Charisse, Kelly's mom.

"Vanessa, you're leaving my dinner early?" Her voice carried that familiar note of disappointment. The rest of the table continued with their previous conversations.

"I'm not leaving early. It's almost over," I replied.

"Well, can't you do something tomorrow?" My mother turned her attention to Kelly, who had walked over. "Kelly, your mother and I are having brunch tomorrow with Lisa. Why don't the two of you join us?"

Kelly tilted her head and flashed her wide, innocent eyes. "Come on, Aunt Viv. I really want to spend some quality time with my best friend. Between my residency and Nessa's work at The Foundation, we barely have time for each other. Enjoy the rest of the dinner. It's absolutely gorgeous, just like you."

Kelly's smile was her secret weapon. It had gotten us out of trouble since childhood, charmed our way into clubs in college, and now, melted the hearts of patients and their parents alike.

Charisse leaned over, adding to the plea. "Come on, Viv. Let the girls have fun. Don't you remember what we used to get into before we settled down and got married?"

My mother looked suspiciously at both of us. "Well, if you insist. Why don't you take Wesley with you? I'm sure he'd love to celebrate as well."

"No, I think he'd be into it," I said quickly. "Besides, it's a girls' night." I kissed her cheek. "Happy birthday, mom. I love you. I'll call you tomorrow."

"I'll be waiting," my mother replied, her tone resigned as Charisse patted her hand, laughing.

Kelly and I were nearly out of the restaurant when we bumped into Wesley entering through the front doors.

"Hey, where are you two going?"

"We're heading out," Kelly chimed in. "I got us a section at Plush Playground. You want to come? I might have an extra VIP ticket."

"No, thank you. That's not really my scene." He gave a polite smile. Wesley had always preferred the quiet sophistication of country clubs and private lounges over nightclubs. Honestly, I couldn't see the appeal.

"Oh come on, Wesley. You can't be boring forever. Live a little," Kelly teased.

He chuckled. "I live just fine. Van, did you think about the mural? I know your mom said you would, but I wanted to check with you. I'd love to get the meeting on the books next week."

"Uh, sure. Why not? Just send me the details."

"Great. You two enjoy your night. And happy early birthday, Van."

As Wesley walked away, Kelly turned to me with a sly grin. "So, guess what?"

"What now?"

"I invited Khalil to come out tonight," she said, watching my reaction closely.

I tried to play it cool. "Oh, yeah? That's nice..."

Kelly raised an eyebrow. "Relax. He said Xavier wouldn't come. You know he doesn't do the club thing."

"Right." I felt a strange mix of relief and disappointment wash over me. "I mean, that's fine. It's not like it matters."

"Sure, it doesn't," Kelly said with a knowing smile. "Let's just go have some fun, okay?"

"Okay," I agreed, trying to ignore the way my heart skipped a beat at the thought of possibly seeing Xavier.

An hour and a half later, Kelly and I were swaying to the DJ's set at Pulse Playground. We'd swung by my place on the way, trading our reserved cocktail attire for barely-there mini-dresses and sky-high stilettos. Kelly donned a fuchsia body-hugging dress with mesh cutouts along the torso and chest, effortlessly turning heads. I opted for a backless, low-cut, silver number with slits along the sides of my hips. The dress hung on by two thin chains of Swarovski crystals, crossing at the back of my neck and dipping low beneath my arms. Under the club's lowlights, the shimmer of my dress set off a glow against my smooth, chocolate skin. My curls relaxed into soft waves that cascaded down my back. Tonight, there was no doubt in my mind—I looked good.

"Pulse is lit tonight, huh?" Kelly shouted as we maneuvered our way to the VIP section on the second floor, overlooking the dance floor. The DJ blasted Houston Rap classics, the bass thumping through our veins.

"Yeah, it's crazy in here," I yelled back over the music. Kelly tapped away on her phone again, a sly smile on her face. "Who are you texting?"

"Nobody. Look, there's Nyah, Antonio, and Lynn," she said, changing the subject quickly. We flashed our wristbands to the bouncer and slid into the plush VIP section Kelly reserved for the night. Nyah and Lynn, our high school partners in crime, joined us, along with Nyah's drag of a husband. Though we'd split up for college—Kelly and I at Xavier, Nyah and Lynn at Texas Southern—we'd rejoined when Kelly and I moved back to Houston.

"Ahhh, the birthday girl is here," Lynn exclaimed, sweeping me into a tight hug. "Bitch, ass out, titties out. You look *the fuck* good."

"You know it's bad when Lynn calls you out," Kelly joked. "You know this girl hates coming to the club."

"Hey, clearly, I needed to make my presence known." I glanced at Nyah and Antonio cuddled up on our section's couch. "Hey, Nyah," I shouted. "Now, why is he here," I teased.

"Girl, what are you talking about? Kelly said Antonio could come."

I shot Kelly a quizzical look. "Kelly, what is she talking about? You said you only invited Khalil."

Kelly pressed her lips together, then flashed the same disarming smile she'd used on my mother earlier. "Nothing, she's tripping off the tequila already."

"Kelly, I know when you're up to something. I just want to have fun," I whined.

"Will you just chill and enjoy your night? You know I always got you."

"Yeah, if you say so."

Two shots of tequila later, we lost ourselves to the music, moving as if we were all stitched together by the rhythm. The DJ seamlessly transitioned between the hottest tracks, each beat pulling the crowd tighter into a frenzy. Neon lights roamed the dance floor, catching the glint of our jewelry and the shimmer of my dress. We were magnetic, drawing eyes from every corner of the club. Below us, bodies heated and pressed together as the room pulsed with energy.

Out of the corner of my eye, I spotted a Damson Idris look-alike a few sections away, his eyes tracing my figure. I flashed him a quick wink before turning back to Kelly and Lynn.

"Hey, I thought we were looking for hoes, not texting them," I teased, trying to swipe Kelly's phone. She dodged my hand, glancing at her screen again.

"I'll be right back," she said, slipping away toward the VIP section's exit.

"I'm going to the dance floor. You got somebody checking for you," Lynn nudged, her eyes motioning behind me. I turned to see the guy from earlier a few steps away, his gaze fixed on me.

"What's up, shorty? I'm Chris. What's your name?"

"Amber." *A little white lie won't hurt.*

"Okay, Amber. You from Houston?"

"Maybe. Are you from Houston?" Another lie slid easily off my tongue.

"Nah, I'm from Atlanta. Just out here with my homeboys, trying to see what's poppin with Houston." Chris went on, droning about how Houston was just like Atlanta, his voice a dull hum against the vibrant energy of the club. My interest faded quickly.

I cut him off, flashing a polite smile. "You enjoy the rest of your night."

"Damn, it's like that, shorty?" He clutched his chest in feigned rejection before getting the hint and retreating to his section.

Thank God. He was corny as fuck.

As I surveyed the room, I noticed a stir behind me, muffled voices filtering through the club's noise. I couldn't make out the words over the music and the crowd singing along to ClubGod. But then, a scent wafted over—cologne, rich and familiar. The kind that made the hairs on the back of my neck stand on end. My body buzzed, a sudden jolt of electricity coursing through me. My mind drifted back to those warm hands, the strong arms that used to hold me close. My eyes fluttered closed for a moment, my teeth sinking into my lower lip.

Stay focused on the future, Vanessa.

"This is section 128, right?" The voice, deep and unmistakable, sliced through the noise and hit me like a lightning bolt. My heart stopped, then roared to life, thundering in my chest. I turned slowly, the club around us dissolving into nothing. There he was—Xavier, standing not even ten feet away. Time seemed to slow, the air around us thickening, charged with every unsaid word, every lingering feeling.

"Zay?!"

Chapter 7

XAVIER

I TURNED, NOT NEEDING to see her face to know it was her. *It couldn't be.* My heart hammered against the walls of my chest. The small dimple in her right cheek, the mole just beneath her left eye, the golden flecks that brightened her gaze—all of it hit me at once, like a punch to the gut. *Vanessa.* She moved toward me with the fluid grace of water, her dress clinging to every curve like liquid moonlight. Silky raven hair cascaded down her back, brushing against skin that glowed under the dim lights of the club. I took her in, every detail searing into my memory. I wanted to pull her into my arms and feel her warmth against me, but I was frozen, entranced by the sight of her.

This can't be real. I'm daydreaming. What kind of weed did Khalil have me smoking?

I pictured this moment in a thousand different ways, rehearsed it in my mind countless times. Yet now, standing before her, I was speechless. Vanessa stopped a few steps away, her familiar scent—peony and cashmere mixed with a subtle hint of vanilla and amber—filled the space between us, stirring up feelings I'd buried long ago. It was a jolt to my system, her presence igniting every nerve.

"Nessa." My voice barely found its way out, choked by the storm raging inside me.

"What the hell are you doing here?" Her eyes blazed with a fire I hadn't seen in years. She glanced around, clearly looking for her best friend. Her shoulders tensed, struggling to keep her composure.

"Khalil told me to meet him here. I can stay out of your way if you want," I offered, every inch of me hoping she'd say no.

Please don't agree with that.

She shook her head, her voice wavering as she spoke. "I'm sorry. I just never thought I'd see you again." Her words tumbled out in a rush, her gaze darting to the side. She bent down to pour herself a shot, throwing it back without hesitation, wincing as the liquid went down her throat.

"Yeah. I know what you mean." I crossed my arms over my chest, resisting the urge to reach out and touch her. My hands itched to grab her, hold her, and never let go. "Happy Birthday."

"It's not my birthday…yet." Her eyes shifted away, avoiding mine. Unable to resist, I reached out and tilted her chin with my thumb and forefinger, bringing her gaze back to me. Her lips parted, a small gasp escaping as her shoulders softened for the briefest moment.

"Close enough." Her eyes flickered with a mix of emotions—anger, confusion, something else I couldn't place. When Khalil mentioned celebrating tonight, I expected a quiet bar, not this nightclub. The moment I laid eyes on her, I knew Khalil had planned more than just a night out. "Man, it's been a long time, huh?" I said, my voice thick with all the years and distance between us.

"What five, six years," Vanessa replied quickly, her eyes scanning the room like she needed an escape.

Six years, eight months, and ten days.

Vanessa folded her arms near her waist, the motion pushing the fabric of her dress taut. Her gaze stayed locked on mine as if daring me to look down.

Apologize.

"Hey, Nessa. Can we talk?" My voice was almost lost in the thumping music around us.

"This really isn't the place to talk!" she shouted over the music. "Besides, we don't have anything to talk about."

"Yes, we do," I insisted. "It doesn't have to be right now. I'll be here for a few more months until I move back home."

"Move back home?" Her eyes widened. "What do you mean back?"

"Uh, yeah. Me and Khalil have been working with a company out here for the last few months. We moved to Houston for the time being."

She poured herself another shot, the tension in her shoulders making me ache to soothe her. "You live out here?"

"Yeah. Temporarily, at least."

"Oh God." She threw back the shot, wincing as it went down.

This is not going to be easy.

The woman standing before me, the one who meant everything to me, was a bundle of nerves. Her fingers fidgeted with her phone, and it killed me knowing the comfort she once found in me was replaced with unease.

"You good, Nessa?" I took her hand in mine. The touch sent a shockwave through me, every nerve ending sparking to life. Her hand tensed, and without thinking, I started massaging the inside of her palm—a trick I used to calm her down back in the day. She pulled away abruptly.

Damn.

"Yes, I am." She took a deep breath, eyes darting to the dance floor. "This is all just...a lot," she added, biting her lip and looking down at the dance floor.

Since when was she ever rattled?

"I know what you mean." I'd always known that one day I'd run into her again, but it did nothing to prepare me for the reality. The fire that smoldered in my chest for years now threatened to blaze uncontrollably.

Electricity hummed between us, a current that was always there. From the first moment I laid eyes on her, I knew. Vanessa had this way of living life that was both wild and soft, a duality that pulled me in deeper than I'd ever thought possible. The ease with which she lived life and the way she supported those she loved, even to a fault, made me fall in love with her, quicker than the speed of light and harder than granite.

"Kelly's ass thinks she's slick," she muttered, glancing around. *Her best friend Kelly—not somebody I wanted to see tonight.* The last time I saw her she cussed me out like she was my mama or something.

"How is she doing?" I asked, trying to steady the trembling inside.

Vanessa smiled, a ghost of the warmth I remembered. "Good, as usual. Working on her residency. I'm texting to see where her ass is right now. She picked a fine time to disappear," she finished with a roll of her eyes.

"Yeah, Khalil should be coming over too. Said he got a section since I finally decided to come out. Now I know why."

She laughed, a genuine sound that cut through the tension. It was like music, filling a void that had been silent for far too long. "This feels like the last time they set us up. Minus the arguing, of course."

"How could I forget?" We both paused and she stared deep into my eyes. Memories of the past played in my head with an endless loop of silent stories, stolen kisses on warm summer nights, late night embraces on twin beds. Then, a somberness fell around us, darkness filling her eyes, the rims beginning to water as they twinkled in the dimly lit club. When I went to reach for her again, she turned toward the throngs of people on the dance floor.

I took her elbow gently, pulling her closer to shout above the noise. "Listen, I'm sorry...about everything."

Her eyes met mine again, a storm brewing within them. "It's okay. That was a long time ago." She shouted back in my ear, her hand holding onto my waist to steady herself. Her touch sent chills up my side. When she moved away, she was half smiling again. I almost believed it.

"Yeah," I murmured, unable to tear my eyes away from her. The love of my life stood before me, just out of reach. *I bet I have the goofiest smile on my face right now. I don't even care.* "Look, we should get together sometime and—"

A loud, shrill voice shattered the fragile bubble around us. Vanessa turned toward Kelly, who burst into the scene with energy only she could possess. "Zay? I don't believe it." Vanessa moved toward her friend as I followed. Kelly pulled me into a hug, patting my back. "When Khalil said he'd have to beg you to come out, I didn't think you'd show up."

"He can be persuasive," I smiled. "How's it been?"

"Good. How about you?" Kelly said, patting my arm as we released.

"Can't complain." I turned my attention back to Vanessa, who scowled at her friend.

"Apparently, he and Khalil live out here now. But I bet you knew that, didn't you?" Vanessa and Kelly exchanged a few looks at each other, their secret language I could never figure out, even after years of knowing them in college.

Kelly threw her hands up. "That's what I tried to tell you before. You didn't want to hear it, remember?" Kelly looked at me again. "Where is Khalil, anyway? I swear he was right behind me."

Just then, Khalil made his way through the VIP section and bear-hugged Kelly from behind. "I'm right here. I had to scope out the scene."

Our best friends hugged, clearly happier to see each other than Vanessa was to see me. *Understandable.* "Nessa! You look good, girl. Damn, it's been a long time, huh?"

"Yes." Vanessa laughed nervously as she and Khalil embraced quickly.

"Kelly, you ain't say it was crazy like this in here. Not like the other spot," Khalil shouted over the fast beats. Kelly introduced Khalil and me to the rest of their friend group, including Nyah and her husband, and Lynn, who'd made her way back to the section.

"I just want everybody to have a good ass time. It's my bestie's birthday so you know we're about to show out." The group cheered as Kelly and Khalil poured everybody a shot. The energy of the music enveloped the space around us. The DJ mixed hip-hop and R&B hits that hypnotized the crowd. Vanessa and I exchanged some playful banter as the tension from earlier subsided with the vibes set in the nightclub. Our bodies gravitated toward each other. When Vanessa realized she was dancing on me, she laughed and pulled herself away.

After a while, she made her way to the back of our section, where I sat on the top of the couches to smoke from the hookah. She smiled at me again, butterflies sending my stomach into somersaults. She stood before me, her sweet perfume wrapping the air around us. The muscles in my body relaxed and my mind felt at ease for the first time in years. I thought back to what the bartender said the other day.

"Whatever's missing, it'll find you soon enough."

And it had. I missed my love. *My Nessa baby.* Not having her in my life made me feel incomplete.

She leaned close and yelled into my ear. "Are you having a good time?" She took a puff of the hookah as she swayed to the music.

"Yeah. What about you?"

"I had an answer, but you made me change it," she said before smiling. She handed me her mouthpiece to take a hit.

Her response sent me blushing. "I hope it was for the better."

She inhaled deeply, running her fingers through her hair before exhaling. She nodded, letting the smoke curl around her lips before speaking. "I don't know, we'll see how the rest of the night goes."

We stared into each other's eyes for what felt like an eternity. Running into the woman who held your whole heart in the palm of her hands only to realize there was no chance in hell she'd ever return it to you. Agony laced with longing threaded its way through every muscle fiber of my being. It didn't matter that I hadn't had Vanessa in my space in years. Her presence now did something to me. I'd put in so much work to slash the doubt that'd filled my mind during college. Now I could truly appreciate how calm her spirit made me.

Peaceful. Fulfilled.

"What's on your mind, Zay?" she asked, her voice softer now.

"Nothing and everything," I confessed, my heart racing.

Fuck, I am still in love with her.

I turned my head and laughed, taking a sip of the drink in my hand before licking my lips. "Are you thinking about something?"

"I am." She searched my face, her expression unreadable. "Treat me nice and I might share it with you."

"Okay, I'll hold you to that." I chuckled. "How are you? Really?" I questioned as we gazed into each other's eyes. *Please be okay.*

"Good. So, what brings you to Houston?" Her eyes narrowed, suspicion lacing her tone. This was her world now, one she'd worked hard to keep me out of.

"A project, actually..." I said, my gaze trailing over her again. I couldn't help it; my eyes had a mind of their own.

"Why do you keep looking at me like that?" She tilted her head, challenging me.

"Like what?"

"Like you can't believe I'm standing here," she said, pinching my cheek playfully.

Fuck. I licked my lips, feeling my resolve crumble. "It's just good to see you again." She flashed that beautiful smile of hers, the dimple in her right cheek deepening. "Look, about before..."

"Zay," she sang in my ear, playing with the collar of my shirt. "Let's not ruin the night with the past. I don't want to get into anything heavy. Not tonight. It is my birthday, remember?"

Just then, Kelly called her over to the other side of the table. Vanessa left me to dance with her friends, and I leaned back, watching her move. Her laughter, her light—it was all still there, shining brightly even if it wasn't shining for me.

Khalil poured him a drink and sat next to me, looking between Vanessa and me, then smirked. "Bet your ass happy you came out now."

"I don't know what you talkin' about, bruh." I bit my lower lip as I stared at Vanessa, dancing with her friends.

"Uh-huh. I know you thanking me. You ain't even gotta say it," Khalil teased, sipping from his cup. "So, what's it looking like? You think she still feeling you?"

"I don't know, man." I watched her, my mind racing. Her hips swaying to the music had me in a trance. It was cute seeing her get a little ratchet as she sang along to the songs, especially knowing she grew up in a world of private schools and trust funds. Her words said one thing, but the look in her eyes said something else. There was a pull between us, something undeniable.

"Look, if you're trying to see if there's still something there, go ahead and apply that pressure. Show her there's nobody else in the world she needs but you."

"What if she's not with all that?" I asked, my chest tightening.

"Shit, at least you tried," Khalil said with a shrug.

I glanced across the section to where Vanessa danced with her friends. When she turned around, her eyes found mine. I tapped two fingers over my heart—a silent question, a signal only she would know. She hesitated, her body still moving to the beat. Then, just before she turned away, she tapped two fingers against her chest, the gesture so subtle anyone else might have missed it.

She remembered.

Maybe, just maybe, all hope wasn't lost.

Chapter 8

Vanessa

Xavier Morris. What are the fucking odds? There were no odds. As soon as Kelly said she knew he was in Houston, I knew coming out tonight was part of her master plan. Khalil had to be in on it too. Part of me wanted to slap Xavier across his beautiful face. The other part wanted to throw myself into his arms, bridging the gap of time and hurt that kept us apart.

No, that's the alcohol talking.

When he grabbed my hand, warm tingles rushed up my arm, sending radiating pulses to my core. I fought with sheer willpower to look past him and stare at everything but him. Unfortunately, I couldn't resist. The heels I wore allowed me to stand just a few inches shorter than his 6'6" frame. The black button-down short-sleeve he wore, unbuttoned at the top, gave me a peek at the muscular chest underneath. How badly I wanted to bury my face there again.

How many shots have I had so far?

My eyes were drawn to his neatly trimmed mustache and goatee outlining his soft, full lips. Thick dark hair gave way to smooth milk chocolate skin that beamed purple under the club lights.

Good God, this man is fine.

"You like my surprise?" Kelly's voice cut through my swirling thoughts.

"You could've told me what you were trying to do," I snapped, still unable to tear my eyes away from Xavier.

"Why? So you could talk yourself out of coming? Besides, I didn't know for sure he would come. He likes to go out as much as you do." Kelly added, rolling her eyes. "And I did try to tell you. You wouldn't let me remember?"

"Girl, I don't know why you're tripping," Lynn chimed in, giving me a sideways glance. "He's still fine as fuck. I see why your ass didn't wanna leave New Orleans," she added. "Khalil not too bad either. What's happening with him?" Lynn asked, elbowing me in my side.

"Khalil don't fuck with bitches unless he fucking bitches," Kelly said.

"Damn, Kelly. That's mean," Nyah added. Kelly rolled her eyes as she bounced to the music.

"Lynn, he's cool, but he does play around a lot. I don't think I've ever seen him in a relationship."

Nyah shrugged while sipping her drink. "He sounds like you, Kelly." I choked on the drink in my hand.

"Khalil wishes he had game like me. Anyways," Kelly turned her gaze back to me, raising a brow. "What were you and Zay talking about? Ms. 'There's No Sparks.'"

"Nothing." I turned, catching Chris still staring at me from across the club. I turned back to my friends, hoping he'd take the hint.

"Nah, girl. That didn't look like anything. Y'all were eyeing each other and practically saying 'I love you'," Lynn cooed, drunkenly.

"Girl, shut up. That did not happen." *No, we were definitely giving each other googly eyes.*

"Right." Kelly squinted her eyes as she looked at me. "Especially since you don't love him anymore." Her words were a statement and a question rolled into one.

Ignoring my best friend, I swayed my hips to the DJ's mix of some song rapping about peaches and eggplants. The hum in my body told me Xavier's eyes were on me. *Look, just to be sure.* I turned my head, letting my hair swing over my shoulder, and sure enough, there he was, eyes moving up from my lower half to lock with mine. He tried to play it off with a laugh, but I saw it.

I leaned against the balcony to get a better view of him. His waves were deep, inky ripples that stopped at the crisp line around his face. That bright white smile, framed by kissable lips and a jawline sharp enough to cut glass. When he licked his lips, my breath hitched. If I didn't know better, I'd think those shots were starting to hit.

Would it be so bad if I hooked up with my ex tonight?

My mind screamed "Absolutely not!" but my body whispered something else entirely. This was the man who had wrecked me and smashed my heart into pieces with his selfishness. He apologized tonight and tried to explain himself. There was so much we needed to unpack, so much left unsaid. But all I could focus on was this man standing before me, the man who knew every button to push, every part of me that needed touching.

"Do you want a real answer or a 'Vanessa' answer?" Kelly piped up, interrupting my thoughts.

Shit, did I say that out loud?

"If it were me, I'd do it. Worry about the repercussions later," Lynn added. "That is a fine ass man right there."

I smirked in Lynn's direction. "Bitch, not too much."

"Girl, it's your birthday. You want to leave here and be the only one not getting any? Nyah and Antonio are probably about to bounce any second. Lynn, we all know who you're calling. Y'all know I can pull any dude in this club."

Xavier licked his lips again, his eyes trapping me in their intensity. "Y'all, I can't hook up with him. What if we wake up and one of us regrets it?"

"Nessa, I'll tell a joke, but I'll never tell a lie. The only person that's gonna wake up and have regrets will be you with your overthinking ass." Kelly nodded in Xavier's direction. "That man wants you, and not just for tonight. Trust me."

My heart quickened in my chest. *Fuck, Vanessa. What do you want?*

I didn't have time to think. Bottle service girls flooded our section with sparklers, top-shelf tequila, and a birthday cake. One of them held a neon sign that read "Issa Hot Girl B-Day." The DJ boomed over the speakers. The DJ played 2 Chainz' "Birthday Song" throughout the entire club as he spoke into the microphone.

"Alright, Pulse! Make some noise for pretty girl Nessa over there in VIP! Raise your cups, raise your bottles, and show some love on her special day! Happy Birthday, Nessa!"

When the bottle service girls made their way out of VIP, Kelly pulled me to the center of our section as sparklers lit up around us. She opened a bottle of tequila, pouring it straight into my mouth as the crowd cheered. When the music faded to the background and everyone in our section sang *Happy Birthday* to me, I blew out the candles on my cake. Out of the corner of my eye, I saw Chris trying to slide into the scene.

Ugh, some men can't take a hint. I turned my back to him, hoping he'd leave.

"Damn, shorty. You ain't say it was your birthday. I should've been kicking it over here with you. You need some extra company?"

"No. I'm good. You should go back to your section."

"You sure? Birthday girls can't turn up alone."

"Nah, she good." Xavier's voice was deep, sending vibrations down my spine as he circled his arms around my waist from behind. Chris looked Xavier up and down, getting the message and slinking back to his group.

"Thank you," I breathed out, turning to face Xavier.

"Don't mention it, love." People struggled to pass by us, and Xavier pulled me closer. His body pressed against mine, his hand sending jolts of electricity through me as he held the bare skin of my back.

"Can I tell you something?" He looked at me, his eyes filled with an emotion that made my heart squeeze.

"What?" His hesitation made my heart race. He took a hit off the hookah behind us, blowing the smoke away.

"I've missed you. Everyday."

"Couldn't have missed me that much. You pushed me away, remember?" I laughed, trying to hide the hurt that still festered.

Xavier's grip on my waist tightened, his thumb brushing along my spine.

"I shouldn't have done that," he admitted, his voice low. "I'm sorry. I didn't know how to deal with all the shit I was going through at the time." He took another drag of the hookah, blowing it out slowly. Nearly six years, and it felt like we were right back in that space. Just me in his arms, the world outside drifting away.

How many drinks have I had tonight?

"You do look beautiful tonight. As always." His words melted something inside me. I hated him, I never wanted to see him again, and yet here I was, like putty in his hands.

"You don't look so bad yourself. Not as rough around the edges." I let myself lean into his embrace, his thumb drawing circles on my spine.

Nope, nope, nope. This ship has sailed, sunk deep in icy waters.

"Don't do that."

"Why not?" His New Orleans drawl dripped like warm molasses into my soul, seeping into all the cracks and crevices, left behind from the bomb that detonated our relationship.

"You know why," I whispered, my lips brushing his ear. His hand slid lower, stopping just above the thin fabric covering my hips. The DJ slowed the tempo down and mixed a Keith Sweat beat with songs by Quavo and Future, Beyonce, and Megan Thee Stallion. The mashed-up songs couldn't have been more on point with the way I was feeling in Xavier's arms. I was positive the combination of cognac and tequila had my mind on another level. Not to mention the contact high I was getting from all the illegal smoke filling the club. I'd let my guard drop low enough for the feelings, the love I'd thought I'd buried long ago, to resurrect from the dead.

I nuzzled into his neck, inhaling his scent—a mix of cardamom and sandalwood, like cozy nights and crackling fires. My body warmed from the inside out.

Why do you smell so good?

"Let me make things up to you." He crooned into my ear, the deep bass of his voice sending a ripple through me.

He is making it fucking impossible for me to resist him.

"I don't know, Zay." His forehead pressed against mine, his breath mixing with mine. My eyelashes fluttered as I tried to regain control of my body's reaction to him. His sweet breath tinted with cognac and tobacco made my head woozy.

Maybe a little taste won't hurt.

"You might be right," he replied, licking his lips. "But how am I supposed to walk away, now that I've got you in my arms. A place I never thought you'd be again."

God, I wish you would stop doing that.

I pulled back to look up at him again. This time, I didn't mistake the lust in his eyes. I'm sure they were mirror images of my own. The DJ mixed Megan Thee Stallion's *Red Wine* with Keith Sweat's *How Deep Is Your Love*. Xavier moved his hand to cup my face, sweeping his thumb across my bottom lip, and tugging it gently.

"Why do you do this to me?" I breathed out, just barely loud enough for Xavier to hear me over the bass thumping through the room around us.

"I could ask you the same thing." He brushed his soft lips against mine, a shadow of a kiss.

Yeah, I think I can sleep with him tonight. Repercussions be damned.

"Kiss me, Zay."

"I don't know if I'll be able to stop."

"Don't."

Xavier's eyes darkened as he swallowed. "You wanna get out of here?"

I couldn't speak. All I could do was nod. He grabbed my hand, leading us through the exit of the VIP section. I stumbled in my heels trying to keep up with his long strides. We were almost out when Kelly and Khalil blocked our path.

"Where y'all going?" Kelly asked. A quick movement of my eyes to Xavier was all she needed to understand.

"Yeah, we"re about to roll out. Y'all good?" Xavier dapped up Khalil, then entered into a conversation of their own, off to the side.

"Are you happy with your birthday surprise?" Kelly shouted into my ear, grinning.

"I should've known you were up to something when you insisted you drive and I wear this." I looked over to Xavier and Khalil still in conversation. "Why didn't you just tell me he was living out here?"

"For the last time, I tried. Look, Khalil, Lynn, and I are staying for a little while longer, then hitting up Onyx. If you want to roll with us, you can. But if it were me, and the love of my life were right in front of me, I'd be going home with him."

"I do not—" I began.

"Girl cut the bullshit. You love him, and he loves you. Stop whining and see what happens."

Oh, I hate it when Kelly's right.

I'm a grown-ass woman with grown-ass needs. If I want to get some birthday dick, at least I'm going to do it with someone I know can satisfy me, not some random dude in the club.

"Happy Birthday, Nessa. I hope you make this year everything you want it to be," said Kelly as she hugged me tight.

"Thank you, Kelly. I love you and your crazy ass." I looked over to Xavier and Khalil. Xavier dapped him up then walked over and grabbed my hand again, circling his thumb over my palm.

"You ready?"

"Yeah, I'm ready."

Khalil gave me a side hug. "If y'all end up getting back together, don't forget about us...again." Kelly laughed, clinging to Khalil's side...for balance, I suppose.

"Leave them alone Khalil. Hey, Zay! Take care of my girl, alright? Or this time I'll be the one to fuck you up."

We laughed, making our way out of the club, looking like teenagers, grinning at each other. The conversation was sparse during the drive to my apartment. Each time we caught each other's eye, we giggled like fools. His hand rested on my thigh, sending a warmth spreading through me. I sank into the seat, closing my eyes, letting the emotions of the night wash over me. I didn't know what would happen after tonight. I didn't want to think about it. All I wanted was this moment. This feeling.

Home.

Chapter 9

Xavier

Xavier University - September 2012

"Aight man, I'm bout to roll out." I grabbed my keys and gave my best friend Khalil a quick dap.

"What you 'bout to get into?" His eyes were glued to that TV screen, hands gripping the controller like it was his lifeline.

"Bout to hit up Shadow and get a cut. My shit gettin wild." I glanced in the mirror, seeing how my usual low-cut fade was trying to grow up into a full bush of tight coils.

"Aww, shit. Not Lil Shadow," Khalil said, his eyes finally leaving the screen. "Nah, man. I'm comin, too. Gotta check on my boy." He hopped up quickly, sliding on his Nike slides, grabbing his wallet and keys. "Let's hit up Essence Cafe when you done. I been thinking bout them Crawfish Beignets for days, bruh."

"Fo sho'! And while we at it, you need to get ya shit lined up too, nigga." I flicked his forehead before dashing to the door.

"Shut the fuck up. At least I don't look like I been sleepin' under the bridge." We laughed at each other as we walked out of Khalil's dorm room, joking and clowning, just like old times.

We walked up Magazine Street, the heart of Uptown New Orleans. The ancient oak trees stretched over the sidewalks, giving shade to the tourists passing by the shops and cafes snuggled up in the old shotgun houses that lined the streets, windows open, music pouring out like a river of sound—zydeco, blues, bounce. It all flowed into the air.

We turned the corner near Essence Cafe, and there it was, gleaming black in the sunlight—a shiny Mercedes parked all clean and pretty on the curb. I caught my reflection in the tinted windows, and couldn't help but smooth a hand over my fresh cut.

"Say, Shadow got me right, huh?" I asked, admiring my crisp fade.

"Yeah, he got you lookin' straight. Now I can be seen with you in public," laughed Khalil. We made our way inside the cafe, barely getting two steps in before the owner rushed toward us.

"I know that's not who I think it is." A short, sturdy woman stopped in front of us, peering over her glasses. "Aww, Xavier Morris and Khalil Grant. Look at y'all!" She grabbed us in hugs that damn near took the wind out of me.

"Hey, Mrs. Johnson. How you doing?" I said, feeling the warmth of her welcome wrap around me like a blanket.

"Oh, I can't complain, Xavier." She turned to Khalil. "Lord, Khalil! Last time I saw you, you wasn't nothing but teeth and bones." We all laughed, the sound of it filling the small space.

"Mrs. Johnson, we were just here a few weeks ago," Khalil said, his eyes softened by the memories.

"I know, but I can't get over seeing you back in town," she said, a touch of wistfulness in her voice. "How's your daddy doing?"

"He aight. Working as usual."

Mrs. Johnson cupped Khalil's cheek, her touch as tender as a mother's. "Glad to hear it. Now, I know y'all hungry. What y'all want? I'll fix it myself."

"Aww, Mrs. Johnson you already know," I said, grinning.

The old woman swatted at Khalil and me. "Of course, crawfish beignets! Allison, bring them to the table in the back and get them some of that Blue Booty Punch."

Mrs. Johnson and her husband opened the restaurant when Khalil and I were still in elementary school. I remembered walking here from the bus stop after school to meet my mom before going home. She worked as a waitress in the cafe to make ends meet until she got her nursing degree from Xavier University. Even though she made decent money from nursing, Ma didn't earn enough to pay for me to go to college. That's part of the reason I'd decided to attend the same school instead of going somewhere out of state. Not having to pay for housing, in addition to the scholarships I received, made it possible for me to further my education without putting too much of a dent in her pockets.

Sliding into the plastic booths was like coming home for me. It felt like an extension of my own mother's kitchen. Khalil and I spent countless times here eating everything Mrs. Johnson and her husband offered on the menu. I swept my eyes across the homey space. Mardi Gras Indian memorabilia lined the walls. Framed pictures of Mardi Gras parades from years before filled in the spaces surrounding elaborately decorated headdresses and costumes. The local radio station sent bounce mixes of top hip-hop and R&B songs into the air. Everything that made New Orleans a gift to the world was found right here in Essence Cafe.

"Aw man, I'm 'bout to fuck them beignets up. You think she'll give us extra," Khalil asked, his eyes twinkling, "since she love us so much?"

"Yeah, Mrs. Johnson knows what she doing in the kitchen. The lady don't miss." Soon enough, she was walking back from the kitchen, carrying hot platters full of Crawfish Beignets and Red Beans and Rice. Khalil's eyes lit up.

"Aww, Mrs. Johnson, you ain't have to go all out like this," he said, his eyes as big as the saucers placed before us on the table.

"Don't wanna hear none of that. You know y'all parents would want me to take care of y'all. Now eat."

We dug in, talking about our summer break and classes. The bell above the door jingled, and I glanced up. Two girls walked in, looking like they stepped off a magazine cover. One had on low-rise jeans and a soft pink shirt slung off her shoulders. When she moved the big sunglasses off her face, I recognized her but couldn't quite place her name.

Then I saw her friend. *Goddamn*. Forgive me, Lord. She moved like a dream. Sunlight spilled in through the windows, settling on her hair, loose waves and curls bouncing softly around her face. Her eyes were downcast, fixed on her phone, but I caught a glimpse of her long lashes, her full lips painted a bold red. Her top barely reached her navel, glinting with a belly ring and a fine gold chain. Her legs, smooth and long, went on forever under the distressed jean shorts she wore. My heart started pounding, each beat echoing in my ears. I couldn't look away. In all my life, I'd never had a girl make me react this way—transfixed, hooked, stuck on stupid.

"Zay, you heard me?" Khalil snapped his fingers in front of my face. "Man, the fuck you lookin at?" He followed my gaze to the entrance of the cafe. "Damn, man!" Khalil exclaimed, now understanding the reasoning for my distraction. "Hold up, ain't that Kelly?"

"Kelly who?" I responded, my gaze still on that girl. Damn, she was beautiful as fuck.

"Man, Kelly, Kelly. She used to come stay with her grandma down the street from me. You know, the one I told you that I...Hold up, let me go see." Khalil slid out of the booth, swaggering over to the girls. He hugged one of them, and they turned to walk toward our table.

"Kelly, you remember my boy Zay? He used to be at my house all the time."

"Yeah, I think so," Kelly said. "And all the block parties my grandma used to throw."

"Move over, Zay. Y'all sit down." Khalil motioned them to sit. I shuffled closer to the wall as the second girl slipped into the booth beside Kelly.

"I was just telling Nessa it's a small world." She pointed to her friend, who was looking between Khalil and me.

"What you doing out here, Kelly?" I asked, finally able to tear my gaze away from Nessa.

"I'm going to Xavier. Well, we both are," Kelly said, gesturing to her friend.

Lord, you stay looking out for ya boy.

"Oh, that's what's up. Me and Zay in our second year there," Khalil added. "Damn, that's crazy. I ain't think you'd ever go there."

"Me either. I had to beg my parents and promise I'd go to whatever med school my dad wanted. That was slight work compared to her."

Nessa turned to me, her voice soft and smooth. "Yeah, Kelly's mom had to convince my mom to let me come here. Otherwise, I'd be at Rice University back home." Nessa turned to her friend. "Can I tell you again how glad I am that she said yes?"

Hearing her voice for the first time was a soothing balm to my soul. I was smitten with it. It sang to me and made my ears ring. "What's your name again?"

"Nessa, well Vanessa. Vanessa Ann Taylor." *Of course, she got a cute ass name.*

"Oh, okay. So what y'all been up to since school started?" Khalil waved to Allison to get Mrs. Johnson.

"Class mostly. Other than that, Kelly's been showing me around." We made eye contact for the first time since she and Kelly walked in. My breath caught in my throat. I saw the slight exhale she gave before a soft smile spread across her lips.

I cleared my throat, making an easier path for my words to come out again. "What classes you taking this semester?" I struggled to calm the curiosity I had for this girl.

"Bio 101, Art History Survey, Public Speaking, Calculus, and Intro to Economics."

"Damn, where the English and History at?" Khalil asked.

"Our parents forced us into AP classes all throughout high school so we tested out of a few courses," Kelly replied.

Smart girl. I like that.

"Man, Pops tried to make me take one of them my senior year. That was the hardest class I ever took. Damn sho' ain't pass the exam." He laughed.

Mrs. Johnson strode over to the table as Khalil finished his sentence. "Well, look what we got here." She raised one brow, her years of wisdom recognizing something was brewing. "How can I help you?"

"Mrs. Johnson, you remember Kelly Reid? Her grandma stayed down the street from us."

The old woman scratched her head. "Are you talking about Ms. Hall? Wasn't her daughter name Charisse?"

"Yes, that's my mama. I'm Charisse's daughter, Kelly," she piped up.

"Aww, well look at that. Today must be the day for reunions." She laughed. "And who is this?"

"Hi, I'm Vanessa Taylor, Kelly's friend. Our moms are best friends."

"It's nice to meet you. Y'all see something from the menu you want? I'll put in the order."

I watched as both girls turned the laminated menus over in their manicured hands.

"I don't know, it all looks so good." Vanessa looked at him. "Xavier, right? What do you suggest?"

My heart melted in my chest. I could listen to her say my name all night long. "You can't go wrong with the Crawfish Beignets. They're Mrs. Johnson's specialty."

Vanessa looked at the older woman. "Then how can I refuse," she smiled.

"Those red beans smell so good. My mouth is watering. I'll take that," Kelly added.

"Good choices. I'll have Allison bring them out shortly." As Mrs. Johnson took the menus and headed to the kitchen, we fell into conversation, Kelly and Khalil doing most of the talking, catching up. Vanessa and I offered a few laughs and one-off remarks. Any chance I got, I admired Vanessa's beauty. The way her laugh was airy and bright and how her head tilted to the side, her hair swaying whichever way she moved. Every so often, I'd catch her staring back at me.

"That was so good," Vanessa said, wiping her mouth.

"See, I told you. Best crawfish beignets anywhere." I responded, sending a warm smile her way.

"What y'all got going on the rest of today?" Khalil asked.

"Show her more of the city. We were going to go down to the French Quarter."

"Aww, hell nah. That ain't the city. Not the real city anyway." I replied.

"Oh really," Kelly retorted. Vanessa was silent, her eyes still focused on me.

"You wanna see the city, you need somebody from the city to do it," Khalil added.

"So, show us the real city," she said, raising an eyebrow.

Khalil and I looked at each other with knowing glances. "How much time y'all got?"

"It's the middle of Saturday. We have all the time in the world." Kelly looked at Vanessa. "You down?"

"Where you go, I go."

"It's up then," Khalil exclaimed. "Let's get out of here. Y'all ready to walk?"

"My car's parked outside," Kelly said.

The car outside. Of course, it belongs to her.

"We'll meet y'all outside. Let us take care of this." All four of us scooted out of the booth and made our way to the front of the cafe. Kelly and Vanessa exited first, leaving Khalil and me waiting to pay for their meals. Mrs. Johnson took care of us, but we didn't want to be too greedy with her hospitality.

"They enjoyed the food?" Mrs. Johnson asked, walking over to us.

"Of course they did. They even ate some of ours."

She looked at the girls standing outside. "They seem nice." She looked squarely into our eyes. "Y'all be careful. Them girls ain't like the ones y'all used to."

I laughed. "I don't know what you talkin' bout, Mrs. Johnson."

"You know what I'm talking about. Y'all mess over them, I promise y'all will be the ones with broken hearts. Now, go on ahead. Don't worry about the bill...this time. And don't be a stranger."

"Good lookin' out, Mrs. Johnson," Khalil joked. We each hugged the woman, before making our way outside.

"Bye. And I meant what I said. Be careful."

A FEW MONTHS LATER...

The night air was thick with music and laughter spilling from the house party Khalil dragged me to. We were halfway through our second year, and Khalil acted like he was trying to double as a party promoter. I made my way to the front steps and sank down, feeling the bass thumping through the floorboards. Reaching behind my ear, I pulled out the blunt I'd tucked there, and sparked up. I took a deep pull, letting the smoke sit heavy in my lungs, breathing out slowly.

Cars cruised by, headlights catching the edges of shadows as Oldies played, floating through the night air. I took another drag, the quiet outside giving me the peace I needed. The door creaked open behind me, and I shifted on the steps, making space for whoever was leaving the party chaos behind.

"Hey, do you mind if I sit here? It's crazy in there."

Finally looking up, my heart gave a quick, hard thud in my chest when I realized it was Vanessa. "Yeah, you good," I managed, trying to play it cool.

"Why are you sitting out here alone, Zay," she asked, her voice soft, almost drowning out the hum of the city around us. She lowered herself beside me, her perfume mixing with the scent of smoke. It wrapped around me like a spell, pulling me deeper into her orbit.

I shrugged, taking another hit. "Crowds not really my thing. Just needed a breather." When she smiled, it was like the streetlight at the end of the yard shone just a bit brighter, the fluorescent rays casting their glow on her smooth, brown skin. "You enjoying yourself?"

"Yeah, I'm enjoying myself...now," she said, leaning back, her eyes locking with mine. My heart warmed at that, and I felt a smile pulling at my lips.

"So, how you like Xavier University? And the city?" I asked, watching the way her eyes sparkled when she looked at me.

"It's great. I mean, I did have the best personal tour guide," she teased, nudging my shoulder. Her laugh—it sent me flying. I glanced down at my feet, trying to hide the grin stretching across my face.

Boy, you crushing hard.

"You know I had to show you the real," I said, giving her a sly look. "Can't have you going to all them fake ass tourist spots, acting like a stranger." Her gaze dropped to my lips as I licked them, feeling the tension thrumming between us. I held out the blunt to her. "You wanna pass?"

She shook her head. "No, I hate smoking like that. I can never get a good pull."

I exhaled off to the side again. "You ever took a charge before?" I asked, arching a brow. She shook her head again, and I grinned. "Look, hold the blunt in your mouth. I'll blow from the other side."

She followed my lead, her eyes never leaving mine. She brought the blunt to her lips. As she inhaled, I blew from the lit end. She tried to hold the smoke in, but it rushed out in a fit of coughs. I reached out, placing my hand on the small of her back.

"You good, love?"

"Yeah, yeah. I'm fine," she laughed, a little breathless. "See, this is why I don't smoke blunts."

"Challenge accepted. Next time," I teased, not missing the way she bit her lip.

"Next time?" she echoed, her eyes searching mine.

"Yeah, next time," I said, letting the words hang in the air between us. I watched her lean back on her arms, her eyes drifting up to the stars.

"You ever think about what's up there?" she asked, her voice soft. "Like, if aliens are watching us or something?"

"If they are, they're probably jealous of this view," I said, not meaning the sky one bit.

"Real smooth." She turned her head and smirked, that soft smile playing on her lips again. "Seriously. You think there's life out there beyond Earth?"

"I think the universe is too big for us to be alone," I replied. "Maybe they're out there smoking alien-grade weed, looking down at us, laughing they ass off."

She laughed, her voice a melody that wrapped around me like a warm breeze. "Alien-grade? You might be onto something." The quiet settled in, a peaceful kind of silence that felt right with her beside me. She scooted closer, her knee touching mine.

"You want to try something different?" I held up the blunt again, watching her eyes flicker to mine.

"Yeah," she whispered, her voice like a secret meant just for me.

I took another pull, then leaned in close, tilting her chin up with my fingers, our lips just a breath apart. Slowly, I exhaled the smoke into her mouth, our lips barely touching. She closed her eyes, letting the smoke fill her lungs, then opened them again.

"How was that?" I asked, my voice low, heart pounding against my ribs.

"Mmm," she muttered, her eyes holding my captive. "That was nice."

"You want another one?"

She nodded, leaning in closer this time. Our lips brushed, soft, slow. When I went to pull away, she grabbed my hand, her eyes searching mine.

"What?" I asked, my voice catching in my throat.

"What are you thinking about, Zay?" Her words were a whisper, her breath warm against my skin. "I can see the gears turning every time I look at you."

I laughed, trying to keep it light. "Oh, so you pay attention to me like that?" My thumb found a spot behind her ear, one that made her eyes flutter.

"Yep" she breathed, leaning into my touch. "Kiss me."

"Naw, love, I can't do that," I said, feeling my heart twist. I knew if I crossed that line, I'd be lost to her forever. And that was something I wasn't sure I was ready for. Not yet.

She pulled back, her eyes falling to the ground. "Why not?"

"Don't think I'm not tempted to," I replied, letting the truth slip out. "You just...you something else, you know that?"

She rested her head in her hands on her knees. "Really? Is that a good thing or a bad thing?"

"Definitely a good thing." A comfortable silence grew between us again.

She leaned her head on my shoulder, the weight of it feeling like home. "Tell me the craziest thing you've ever done."

"Uhhh, I don't know. I don't really do crazy," I said, chuckling. "Especially if it involve me getting up there with them aliens."

"Not you being afraid of heights," she teased me, "Can't be tall as you are?"

"Well, believe it. We all have our Achilles heel," I laughed, then asked, "What about you?"

She hesitated, pulling her hand away from my arm. Instinctively, I grabbed it, holding it firm. "You really wanna know?" she asked, her voice low and full of mischief.

"Yeah, tell me. What's the riskiest thing Vanessa Ann Taylor's ever done?"

"Not my government name," she giggled, eyes shining. "I can't tell you...not yet, anyway"

I stared into her eyes, my heart working to construct a place for her in my heart. "You scared to take risks?" The street lights twinkled in her eyes as she leaned in closer.

She leaned in, so close I could feel her breath on my lips. "Only if it's worth it." Her eyes bore into mine, asking a question without saying a word. "You still sharing?" she asked, her voice like honey.

I took another deep inhale, then brought my mouth to hers again. This time, she leaned in all the way, our lips meeting in a soft, slow kiss. When we pulled apart, she looked at me with those eyes that made my heart flip.

"We should hang out sometime," she said, her voice soft but sure. "I think I might need another tour."

"Oh yeah? You know I got you," I replied.

"I know." She stood, me following her lead. "I guess I'll see you around."

"Why don't we get out of here?" I suggested.

"And go where?" she asked, her eyes curious and bright.

"Anywhere you wanna go."

She thought a moment before she looked at me again. "Okay. Let me make sure Kelly's straight." She disappeared into the house as I texted Khalil that I was leaving. Before I knew it, she was standing in front of me again, taking my hand in hers.

"You ready?" I asked.

She looked up at me, a smile playing on her lips. "Yeah. Show me everything."

I grinned, my heart feeling lighter than it had in a long time. "Bet."

Chapter 10

Vanessa

Gentle kisses sprinkled like raindrops on my forehead as soft fingertips trailed down my spine, leaving a wake of goosebumps on my skin. A sleepy smile tugged at my lips, and I stretched, tangled in the covers, reaching out to the warm body next to me. My fingers traced over hardened muscle, finding their way across the planes of his stomach, chest, and arms. It all felt like a dream, hazy and blurred at the edges. Last night was a whirlwind of city lights and quiet moments. The last clear memory I had was when Xavier and I drove back to my apartment, the night around us quiet and still.

Inside, the cool air of my apartment greeted us, chasing away the sultry heat that clung to us from the nightclub. We walked into the kitchen, and Xavier moved about it with a familiar determination, filling two glasses with water, adding a packet of electrolytes to each. His hands were steady, his movements deliberate, muscle memory from the dozens of nights we'd gone out back in college, Kelly and Khalil in tow. He handed me a glass, and we stood there, drinking in silence, the cool liquid sliding down my throat, bringing me back to myself.

"I should go, let you get some rest," he murmured, starting to pull away.

"No," I whispered, the gentle plea slurring at the end as I reached for his hand. "Stay, please. I don't want to be alone tonight. If you leave, I'll never forgive you."

He hesitated, a flicker of something crossing his face. "You sure?"

"Yes," I murmured, my eyes already closing. "Stay with me, Xavier."

Truthfully, I was tired—the kind of tiredness that seeped into your very being and made you feel like you could sleep for a century. Xavier sensed it too, because he guided me toward my bedroom, his arm firm around my waist. His fingers worked the zipper on my dress, easing the fabric from my shoulders, the cool air kissing my skin as the dress pooled at my feet. He found an oversized shirt and boy shorts, handing them to me.

"Here, put these on," he said softly, his voice a soothing command in the quiet room.

I nodded, too drained, too tipsy to speak, slipping into the clothes he handed me. They were soft and smelled faintly of laundry detergent. Xavier's eyes never left mine as he handed me a pair of fuzzy socks and motioned toward the bathroom, and I followed him without a word.

In the bathroom, we stood side by side at the sink. I caught a glimpse of us in the mirror—my eyes half-lidded with fatigue, his face etched with a gentle concentration. Nervous giggles escaped my lips as I took in the sight of how domestic we looked. Sitting me on the counter, he washed my face, the cool water waking me up just enough to feel the quiet care in his touch. Then, he brushed my teeth, each motion tender and unrushed, a quiet rhythm that felt like the most natural thing in the world.

Back in the bedroom, he pulled back the covers, easing me into bed. I sank into the mattress, the exhaustion starting to pull me under. He leaned over, tucking the blanket around me, his hands gentle and warm.

I heard him move around the room, the rustle of his clothes as he undressed, the quiet run of the water as he washed his face. The mattress dipped beside me, the warmth of his body crawling over me as he slipped under the covers, pulling me close. His scent, warm and unmistakably him, cradled me. I nestled into his embrace, letting the steady rhythm of his heartbeat lull me into a deep sleep.

"Good morning," he whispered, his voice a low rumble in my ear, his strong arms pulling me into his warmth.

"Morning, Zay." I sighed as his hand smoothed the hair away from my face, his lips pressing soft and tender against my cheek. "Thank you for staying."

"You said you'd never forgive me if I left you alone on your birthday. I couldn't risk giving you another reason to never talk to me again." His lips found my neck, nuzzling into the space just below my ear. "How you feeling?" he asked, his eyes searching mine.

"Better than expected," I giggled, feeling the roughness of his beard against my skin. "Thank you for taking care of me. I'm sure I was a hot mess."

"Not at all," he murmured, pulling back to look at me. "Had to make sure the birthday girl was taken care of." He kissed my lips this time, shifting over me, his body fitting perfectly between my thighs. "What you got planned for today?" he asked, his voice husky as his lips brushed against mine.

"Sunday Funday with Kelly and Lynn at Chapman and Kirby," I replied, already feeling the fatigue settling in. "I don't know how I'm going to survive after last night. I'm so exhausted."

"Don't go," he said, his kisses trailing to my neck. "Let me take care of you today. We can grab some food...reconnect."

"How about a rain check?" I whispered, melting into his touch, his hands roaming over my body. "I need some time with my girls."

He sighed against my skin. "Okay," he uttered, his lips finding mine again, slow and deep. "How much time do you have before you need to get ready?"

I didn't register his question, lost in the heat of his touch. I wrapped my arms around his neck and grazed my nails along his shoulders. My body arched into his, and I moaned against his mouth, feeling his desire pressing against me. His lips moved down to my neck, his hand squeezing my ass, pressing me into his hard length, and I felt the world blur around us.

"Vanessa!" The voice cut through the haze, yanking me back to reality. "Nessa! Wake your ass up! I've been calling your ass all morning!" The door slammed, and I jolted up, my heart racing.

I reached for my phone, scrolling through my notifications, I saw the many texts and calls I'd missed from Kelly. I ducked under the bed to grab my slippers, so I could stop her before she made it to my room.

"Is that Kelly?" Xavier asked, rolling out of the bed to grab his clothes.

"Yes," I whispered back. "Kelly, wait! I'll be right out!"

"She just walks in your house like that?" he asked, pulling on his shirt.

"Why wouldn't she? We have keys to each other's places," I explained, trying to smooth my hair.

Kelly's footsteps echoed down the hallway leading to my room. "Nessa, you're about to make us late. And I need to talk to you...like real bad!" *Fuck.* I put a finger over my mouth to Xavier. I cracked my bedroom door open just enough to poke my head out.

"Kelly, can you please wait for me in the living room? Please?!" She narrowed her eyes at me, suspicion and frustration oozing from them.

"Fuck, is Zay in there? My bad, girl. I didn't think he'd still be here. It's 10:30."

"Look, give me a few minutes. I'll meet you in the living room."

I closed the door as her footsteps echoed down the hallway. "Good morning, Zay!" she sang behind her.

"She got the worst timing in the world," he muttered, his arms coming around my waist, pulling me close. Instantly, my body relaxed into his as my head rested on his firm chest. He moved his hand to hold my head in place, lifting it slightly to kiss my forehead.

There was no way on Earth I should be feeling this way toward the man who broke my heart and tore it to pieces with venom-drenched words. They took up residence in my innermost self, only to leave me hollow and abused.

Girl, snap out of it.

"I should get going, huh?"

"Yeah," I whispered, our eyes locking in a silent goodbye.

"Is your number the same?" he asked, searching my face.

"It is. Do you still have me blocked?" I smirked, my fingers trailing over the tattoos on his arms. My artwork was imprinted into the smooth walnut of his skin. Intricate webs of illustrations littering his arms, back, and chest. Dark lines and shading representing our tragic love story.

I still can't believe he let me design these.

He chuckled. "For the record, you blocked me first." He showed me his phone. Sure enough, I was unblocked.

I took my phone, showing it to him as I found and unblocked his number. "This still your number, right?"

"Yeah. Let's get together sometime. I really wanna talk. About everything."

"Sure. I'll check my schedule," I said, trying to play it cool.

"Yeah, just let me know." He followed me to the front door, his fingers intertwined with mine.

"Bye, Zay!" Kelly shouted from the living room.

"Bye, Kelly," he shouted back before caressing my face one last time. I opened the door and he leaned down, pressing a thumb to my lips before walking out.

I shut the door behind him, turning to see Kelly's inquisitive eyes on me, ready to get the details of last night.

"What?" We moved to the living room and plopped on the cloud-like couch that was so big it seemed to take over the entire room.

"I just have one question." She paused, her eyes glinting with mischief. "Was it as good as you remembered?"

I rolled my eyes, resting my head on the back of the couch. "I wouldn't know," I said, side-eyeing her. "We got interrupted."

"Y'all didn't do anything when you got home?" She narrowed her eyes.

"No. I passed out right after I begged him to stay."

"Damn, girl. You did go ham on those shots."

"And who was it pouring the tequila down my throat?"

"You right," she giggled. "I'll take the blame. I just wanted you to have a good time." She eyed me for a minute. "I'm assuming you did because you haven't stopped smiling since you and Zay were in each others' faces all night."

"Chill out, Kelly!" I laughed, throwing a pillow at my friend. "Yes, it was nice seeing him again."

"And waking up next to him." Kelly raised her eyes suggestively, biting her lip and bouncing her shoulders. "When are y'all going to talk about getting back together?"

"Nobody's talking about getting back together." I propped an arm on the back of the couch, resting my head there as I looked at Kelly. "Look, there's things Zay and I need to discuss."

"Yeah, like you know what," she interrupted, her voice going soft.

"Look, I'll tell him, okay? Right now, I want to enjoy my birthday with my best friend in the whole wide world," I said, crashing into Kelly and giving her a hug.

"Girl," she started laughing. "Have you even brushed your teeth? Get the fuck off of me." She struggled to push me off, but I held on tighter. "Come on, now. Go wash your ass. Get cute. I have some Hydration IVs waiting for us at Lynn's house before we do round two."

"Alright," I said as I stood up. "I won't be long."

Part II

"A House Is Not A Home" - Luther Vandross

Chapter 11

Vanessa

THE DAYS AFTER MY birthday slipped by, each one blending into the next like brushstrokes on a canvas. Xavier and I were texting here and there, his name popping up on my screen enough to stir a quiet storm in my chest. I wanted to see him again, but the memory of our last conversation in college held me back. It ended with me screaming at him, his face meeting my hand. The fallout was fierce, Khalil stepping in just to pull me away. I rubbed at the phantom sting in my palm, as I erased the memory from my mind.

I wrapped up my afternoon art class at the community center, a yawn escaping my lips. The kids were getting the hang of the painting techniques I'd taught them, and though I loved every minute of it, I needed rest. The hangover of my birthday weekend clung to me like a heavy fog.

I am never drinking that much again.

I scrubbed the paint brushes and palettes in the sink, watching as the colors swirled down the drain. The room around me glowed with the orange and gold hues of the setting Houston sun, turning everything into shades of a dream. I paused, admiring the beauty of it, thinking maybe next time I'd bring the kids outside to paint the world as it was.

After cleaning up, I grabbed my purse and phone, ready to head home for some much-needed sleep. I tapped out replies to my mother, Kelly, and Wesley as I stepped out into the evening air.

"Nessa." His voice came from across the street, smooth and deep. I looked up, my heart giving a little jump when I saw Xavier walking toward me. It happened every time—at the club, in my bed, that first day at Essence Cafe.

He walked with a calm stride, his tall frame catching the light of the setting sun, skin glowing a warm, deep brown. His eyes held a soulful intensity, one that seemed to see right through me. It wasn't just his looks, though they were enough to make any woman stop in her tracks. It was his energy, the way he carried himself, that quiet confidence that pulled me back then and drew me near now.

"Zay. We have to stop meeting like this," I said, laughing to ease the tightness in my chest. Butterflies tried to break free inside me, my smile widening despite my efforts to keep it cool. I couldn't let myself fall again, not like before.

It only leads to disaster.

"Man, what? How's your day been?"

"Good," I squeaked out. "What about you?" As Xavier made his way toward me, the smell of him hit me all at once.

Mmph. So good.

"Eh. It's straight. Better now."

"That's good. So...why are you out here?" I asked, trying to keep my eyes off his, those eyes that could pull me under in a heartbeat.

"I was walking around the neighborhood, getting a feel for it. What you doing here?"

"Uh, I just finished a painting class for kids...well, teenagers."

"Oh, really? You started your non-profit?" He smiled that bright, easy smile that used to melt my heart. Those walls I'd built around it felt like tissue paper now.

"Um, not exactly," I mumbled, glancing at the ground. I could feel my stomach twisting. "I'm just volunteering."

"Oh, okay." He nodded, his eyes not leaving mine. "Hey, you busy? I'd really like to talk. Catch up."

God, I didn't even know what he was saying. My mind was too busy drowning in his voice, the deep drawl of it's bass. The way each word seemed to connect to the one before it.

"Umm, no actually. What did you have in mind?"

"You want to walk around the block? It's a park down the way. If not, we can drive somewhere and catch a happy hour or something."

I shook my head side to side. "Nope," I laughed. "No alcohol. I had enough over the weekend."

"I feel you," he chuckled. "You want to walk? It's not too hot out."

"Sure." We turned toward Emancipation Park, the silence between us buzzing like cicadas. Each brush of his hand against mine sent heat rushing through me, my body betraying the front I was trying to keep up. I pulled my bundles of curls into a bun on top of my head, trying to focus on anything but the man beside me.

"Look, about the past," Xavier started, his voice breaking the quiet like shattering glass. "I just wanted to apologize. I never got the chance."

"Never got the chance or was too stubborn to say it when it needed to be said?" The words flew out of my mouth sharp, laced with all the hurt I'd kept inside. I saw him wince, his jaw clenching, and I felt a pang of regret.

"I deserve that. It's just..." He slowed his steps, struggling to find the right words. "I never thought I'd see you again. And, now, seeing you the other night and—"

"Look," I interrupted, stopping in my tracks. "I appreciate the apology. Better late than never, right?"

"Right...Is there something else you want to say?" he asked, his eyes searching mine.

What does he mean? Is there something else I need to say? Does he know?

I stopped walking, staring at him, confused. "Is there something you want me to say?"

"Aren't you sorry for giving up on us? I know I was messed up, but you left me high and dry at my lowest point. You didn't give me a chance to get my shit together or make it right. I know shit was bad, but I love you with my whole heart."

"Did you forget how you pushed me away any chance you got? I left because I had a good reason." My armpits pricked with heat. A sheen of sweat crossed my nose and cheeks as my face grew hotter—and not from the early fall Texas heat. "None of it would've happened if you'd just let me help you instead of trying to do everything by yourself. Keep things to yourself," I huffed and continued walking, picking up my pace.

"Nessa, your idea of helping was using your parent's money. There's some shit you can't fix by dropping a bag." Xavier took a deep breath, his face settling into deep resolve. "I'm just trying to say, I didn't need that from you. I just needed you to be there, but you couldn't do that," he said, softening his voice.

"There it is," I muttered. "I'm sorry for being too selfish to give you what you needed, even if it broke me." I shook my head, feeling like this was a mistake, like I needed to walk away now before I got too caught up.

He stepped in front of me, taking hold of my elbows. "Nessa, are you happy? Like really happy? Be honest with me."

He let go when I shot daggers at his hands, his arms dropping to his sides, the tension tightening his muscles underneath the short sleeve polo he wore.

I don't know anymore.

I sighed, looking anywhere but at him. "You could say that."

"Happier than when you were with me? Before all the bullshit." His voice was quiet, but I could see the tremor in his hands.

I clenched my jaw, staring at the ground. I didn't want to answer that. I couldn't bear to say it, not out loud.

"Yes," I lied, the word heavy like stone on my tongue. I finally looked up at him, watching as he tried to hide the pain in his eyes, the same pain that punched the back of my own. We stood still, mere inches separating us, a soft hum vibrating between us. It evaporated as I spoke again. "Xavier, we've grown up. We've moved on. Let's not ruin it by going back to the past, okay?" I said, trying to keep my voice steady.

His jaw clenched underneath his low-shaven beard. He swallowed, before giving me a broken smile. "I agree. We good?"

"We were always good, Zay." I squeezed his shoulder, his muscles flexing in my hands.

"Yeah," he replied, grabbing my hand still on his shoulder. The air froze around us. "Make sure you do what's best for you, always."

"Of course. You too." I pulled my hand away, tapped two fingers over my heart, then opened my arms. "Truce?"

"Truce," he echoed, pulling me into a hug. His embrace was too familiar, too safe. My face pressed against his jawline, and I breathed him in one last time.

The scent of his warm, intoxicating breath sent chills up and down my spine. My arms squeezed tighter around his waist, my manicured nails digging into his sides. *I don't want to let go.* He moved his arms from the tops of my shoulders down to my waist, inhaling the scent of my hair. When I pulled my face back, our lips brushed gently, my eyes meeting his. I bit down the urge to stay, to get lost in him again.

"I'd better go," I whispered, feeling the world tilt around me.

"Yeah, me too." His voice was low, rough with all the things left unsaid.

"This is it, Xavier. Friends," I whispered, pressing my forehead against his lips. He squeezed me tight one last time before letting go.

"Friends," he repeated, his voice hollow.

I swiped at my hair with my fingers. "We should link up, sometime...you know, with everyone else. I had fun with you and Khalil in the mix."

"Yeah, me too." His face was stoic, aside from the glassiness of his eyes. "You know when Kelly and Khalil get together, it gets crazy." I didn't miss the deep rasp in his voice, the subtle hitch as he spoke.

I laughed, fighting back the stinging of my own eyes. I turned, walking back to the community center, pausing to glance back one last time. "See you around," I called out, more to the memories than to him.

Back in my car, I scrolled through my phone, searching for the number of the person who could make sense of the mess in my heart.

"Calm Roots Counseling. How can I help you?" The receptionist sang into the phone.

"Hi. It's Vanessa Taylor. Does Dr. Smith have any openings tomorrow?"

"Virtual or in-person?"

"It doesn't matter. Either is fine," I said, my voice cracking a bit. The call connected to my car as I situated myself in the seat and started the engine.

"Nothing tomorrow, but she has a virtual slot open for 4:00 PM on Thursday. Will that work?"

I was supposed to meet Wesley at 4:30 that day. *Oh well, he'll just have to wait.*

"Yes, I'll take it." Xavier's sudden reappearance in my life had knocked me off balance. I needed clarity. I needed to understand why, after all these years, he still had this hold on me.

※

FOR NEARLY TWO DAYS, I moved through the world with the kind of nervous energy you'd see in a bird trapped in a cage, fluttering and frantic, with no clear way out. My mother kept barging into my office like she was on some internal timer, demanding updates on every little thing I was working on. Each intrusion chipped away at my already thin patience. At least she'd agreed to sit in on a session with my therapist in a few weeks. Maybe I could use this emergency appointment to prepare for that instead of diving headfirst into the Pandora's Box that was Xavier.

I settled into my chair, the screen glowing in front of me as Dr. Camille Smith's serene face appeared. She had that calm, unhurried energy, like a deep exhale that made you want to release everything you'd been holding in.

"Good afternoon, Nessa," Dr. Smith greeted me, her voice like silk with a hint of warm, earthy undertone. The kind that soothed and probed all at once, no judgment, just observation. That is, until I started retreating into myself. Then, it was like being held at gunpoint. Today, her locs were gathered in a soft scarf, little whiffs of hair peeking out from under the Ankara-printed fabric.. "How have you been since our last session?"

"It's been a bit of a rollercoaster," I admitted, my gaze darting from her calm face to the collection of African masks that hung on the wall behind her. "I ran into Xavier recently."

She leaned in slightly, her interest piqued, but her energy remained grounded. "Xavier? How did that happen?" Her tone held a kind of openness, like the conversation was a slow river, not rushing but flowing steadily.

I exhaled, wrapping my arm around my chest and chewing at my gel manicure. "He showed up while I was out for my birthday with some friends. Then we bumped into each other the other day. He's been living in Houston for the past few months, and I never saw him. Now, it's like he's everywhere all at once."

Dr. Smith nodded, her gold hoops swaying slightly with the movement. "Interesting. The universe has a funny way of bringing people into our lives, especially when there's unfinished business. How did you feel when you saw him again?"

"Fine, I guess" My voice trailed off as I rubbed my temples. "Conflicted, honestly."

"Conflicted? How so?"

"Because we decided to be friends," I started, trying to make sense of my feelings in my head. "Something that should be so simple, seems unreasonably complicated."

Her gaze softened, the kind of understanding that felt like she could see all the mess I was trying to hide, yet didn't flinch at the sight of it. "It rarely is, Vanessa. You and Xavier played pivotal parts in each other's lives. Why would being friends be complicated?"

"Because I shouldn't still have feelings for him. I should be able to say 'Let's be friends,'" and mean it, but I don't. And now, I'm stuck between wanting to protect myself and wanting...him." I took a sip of water, letting the coolness calm the storm whirling inside me. My fingers fidgeted, tracing invisible lines on the desk.

She tilted her head slightly, as if weighing her response carefully. "It sounds like you're trying to shield yourself from getting hurt again. How did Xavier respond to your suggestion of just being friends?"

"He agreed, but I know him. I could see it in his eyes, the hurt he was trying to hide. He always does that—pretends like everything's fine when it's not." My hands found their way to my lap, hiding my chewed-up nails as I bit the inside of my cheek instead.

Dr. Smith smiled faintly, scribbling something in her journal. "Let's reflect. What are you really afraid of, Vanessa? Is it the past, or something deeper?"

A knock at my door pulled me out of my thoughts. Wesley strolled in like he owned the place—soft smile, calm demeanor.

"Hold on just a second," I muttered, muting the microphone. "Wesley, I thought we were meeting in the private lounge?"

"Change of plans. We're in the small conference room in my dad's office," he replied, his voice casual.

"You could've texted me that," I said, arching an eyebrow.

"I figured we could walk there together. Catch up."

"It's fine. I'll be up in ten, fifteen minutes tops."

"Take your time," Wesley offered, flashing another smile before slipping out. I unmuted the microphone and sighed.

"Sorry about that."

Dr. Smith waved it off. "No worries. Where were we?"

"I just want confirmation," I admitted. "That I made the right choice."

"Reassurance is natural, especially in complex situations like this. But let's focus on what you're feeling right now. Do you believe you made the right decision?"

"I don't know. That's what you're supposed to tell me."

Dr. Smith gave me a penetrating gaze. "Now sis, we both know I'm not doing that. Tell me what you're thinking."

I let out a deep breath. "On one hand, I want to move forward, and leave the past where it is. But on the other hand, there's this part of me that still wants what we had, what we could've had. But I'm scared. Scared of the mess."

Dr. Smith paused, her eyes narrowing just slightly, as if she were carefully weighing her next words. Her voice, usually smooth and warm, carried a new firmness. "I'm not going to tell you which direction to go, but I will say the universe is presenting you with an opportunity for honesty and growth."

A lump formed in my throat. Tears gathered at the corners of my eyes, and I blinked rapidly to keep them from falling. "I'm scared of getting hurt again," I whispered. "The pain from before... It was suffocating. Like being buried alive. I can't go through that again."

Dr. Smith nodded slowly, her bracelets jingling softly as she shifted in her seat. "Vanessa, I think you already know this, but I'm going to say it out loud for you. Whether you choose to stay friends with Xavier or explore something more, you can't keep this secret between you. The miscarriage... it's a part of your shared bond. It's something that you've been carrying alone, and it's weighing you down. Until you share that burden with him, until you let him know the truth, any progress you make, together or apart, will be built on a shaky foundation."

Her words hit like a punch to the gut, and I gripped the edge of my desk to steady myself. "I don't know if I can do that," I whispered, the tears now spilling freely. "What if it destroys him? It nearly destroyed me."

Dr. Smith leaned forward, her gaze steady but compassionate. "Vanessa, I can't promise to tell you exactly how Xavier will react. But he deserves to know. And you deserve to release the hurt you've been carrying alone." She gave me a moment, then said gently, "Let's explore this more in our next session. No matter what decision you make, we need to work on how you communicate these truths—to Xavier, but also to yourself. It's time to let those bags go, baby girl."

I nodded, my throat tight. "Yeah. I think I'll take some space to think."

"Take all the time you need," she said, her voice softening. "We'll continue next week, and I'll see you for the session with your mother as well. Be gentle with yourself in the meantime."

"Thanks, Dr. Smith," I mumbled, wiping my eyes again. My mother knocked once, then entered my office without waiting for a response. "I'll see you next time." I ended the call and grabbed my purse.

"Hey Mom, I'm about to head upstairs to meet with Wesley."

"Oh, is it about the mural?"

"Yeah...Did you need something?" I breezed past my mother, heading down the hallway, toward the receptionist as she trailed me.

"Who were you talking to? Wesley said you were on a call."

I took a deep breath. "I had a therapy appointment."

"I thought we weren't meeting with your therapist for a few weeks?"

"We are. I just needed to fit in an extra session today." As we stood by the doors leading to the lobby of Taylor Philanthropy, my mother's face softened for a moment.

"Vanessa, what's going on between us?" She looked at me with concern. "I feel you're keeping things from me. You can talk to me, you know."

"I'm not keeping anything from you. I'm just trying to figure things out on my own for once."

"Vanessa, I'm your mother. My entire existence is to take care of you." She reached out to me, trying to touch my chin. "Is something going on, sweetheart? Please tell me. I'm worried about you. You don't have the best track record with decisions."

I side-eyed my mother as heat rose to my face. "Wow, thanks for the vote of confidence."

"That's not what I meant, Vanessa, and you know it."

"Look, nothing's wrong. I'm just trying to get to this meeting since I'm already late." I moved toward where Wesley waited by the reception desk. He smiled at me, then embraced my mother in a hug.

"You ready, Nessa? The company's waiting upstairs."

"Yeah, let's go. And just so you know, I'm not making any promises about this mural."

My mother pursed her lips at me. "I swear, Vanessa. Give them a chance. This could be the first step in this journey you're on."

"Yeah, sure," I muttered as the three of us moved to the elevators. The doors dinged open, and folks stepped out. My mother fussed over my hair, dusting imaginary lint off my shoulders.

"When are you getting your hair touched up? Your edges are looking a little sweated out." She fingered her hands through my wavy extensions.

"It's the humidity, mom. My edges will lay down once I wrap my hair tonight." I gathered my hair into a low bun, a few tendrils framing my face, and then stepped into the elevator without another word. Wesley followed me inside, a smirk to his face.

"Parents, huh," he grinned.

After we passed the receptionist at Wright Horizons, I decided I'd give this meeting fifteen, thirty minutes tops, before I let them know I didn't have the time. Wesley rattled off facts about the company, but my mind wandered. When one of my father's old colleagues stopped me, I waved Wesley on.

But when I finally stepped into the conference room, my feet froze. There, sitting at the table, were Khalil and Xavier.

If the Good Lord had a sense of humor, He sure picked the wrong time to show it.

Chapter 12

XAVIER

THE MUSCLES IN MY body seized as the conference room door swung open and Vanessa walked in, her hair pulled into a loose bun, leaving her face open to the world, save for a few strands framing her round, sad eyes. Thick lashes curled around them like whisps. Her lips, full and glossed, drew my attention more than they should have. A white bodysuit clung to her form, accentuating the curves that led from her breasts to her waist. Loose, light-washed jeans slung low on her hips, almost casual in contrast to her top and matching heels. Wesley gestured for her to take a seat beside him. My heart did a double beat.

That's your friend now, remember.

"Van, you made it," Wesley said, rising to his feet to make introductions. His hand settled on the small of Vanessa's back, guiding her into the room. *The fuck?* My blood boiled at the sight. *What the hell did he just call her? What the fuck is Van? And why is his hand so low? And why is she letting his hand touch her like that?* She didn't even flinch, just let his hand linger there as if it were natural, normal. My jaw clenched. I had to take a deep breath to keep from reacting.

She's not yours anymore. She made that plain as day.

"Sorry I'm late. I was on a call," she shared as she stepped closer to the table.

"This is Xavier Morris and Khalil Grant. Gentleman, this is Vanessa Taylor, my highly-recommended muralist."

"Wesley, stop," Vanessa said. "You had one conversation with my mother."

"And she was very convincing," Wesley chuckled. "Besides, you were the genius behind our class mural in high school." Their easy banter grated on my soul. Khalil and I exchanged glances that spoke volumes. Just what was going on between these two? Too familiar, too close. They weren't just acquaintances, that much was certain. Vanessa dared to smile, like everything was normal between us as if we hadn't exchanged heated words days ago.

"Hi," she said, her voice directed more at Khalil than me as she shook his hand then mine. "Small world, huh?"

"What are you talking about?" Wesley asked, brows furrowed.

"We, uh, we know each other," Khalil jumped in, trying to ease the tension.

"Really, how so?" Wesley's eyes darted between Vanessa, Khalil, and me, curiosity written all over his face.

Khalil's eyes urged me on. "We used to—," I started.

"We dated a little bit." Vanessa cut me off with a nervous laugh. I stared at her. A little bit? I was ready to settle down and make a life with her.

"Really? Van, sit here," Wesley said, motioning her to the seat across from me. Vanessa hesitated before sitting down, biting her lip. She plastered on a fake smile.

"You good?" I mouthed. When Wesley and Khalil got caught up looking over papers, she tapped two fingers over her heart. A signal. Now, it felt hollow. She'd moved on. Wesley's repeated touches against her arm, the way she avoided looking at me—it all pointed to that truth.

"For our first project, Wright Horizon Realty and EcoVision Urban Solutions are working on the first sustainably resourced luxury condos here in Third Ward," Wesley announced, drawing her attention.

Vanessa's eyes shot to mine, judgment flickering in them.

"Really, Wesley? More luxury housing? Doesn't Houston have enough?" she asked, challenging him, yet holding all the fire in her gaze for me.

"Van, you know what my father says. There could never be enough," Wesley grinned. "Besides, this is just to get people interested in the concept."

"Nessa," I interjected, trying to soften the blow. "We're hoping the same ideas can be used in future projects for affordable housing. Right, Wesley?"

"Right," Wesley said, his eyes narrowing. "You know, Van and I go back too. Our mothers are college friends. They've been trying to marry us off for years," he added, laughing as he winked at Vanessa. "Van, I'm still surprised your mom let you go all the way to Xavier, instead of Rice with me." He turned to me with a smug look.

Of course Vivian Taylor approved of him.

"Wesley, stop." Vanessa shot me a look of apology, then changed the subject. "Tell me more about the project. What exactly do you want?"

As the conversation moved on to project details, I let Khalil take the reins. My heart pounded in my chest, every beat echoing in my ears. Under the table, I felt a nudge. Vanessa's foot. I glanced at my phone; a new message.

Nessa Baby: I'm so sorry.

Xavier: For what?

Nessa Baby: For downplaying our relationship.

Xavier: Nah, you good. I'm just surprised.

Nessa Baby: Surprised? Why?

Xavier: I didn't think you'd settle for a goofy ass nigga like him.

Nessa Baby: You sure about that? Apparently they're my type.

Xavier: Man, fuck that.

Nessa Baby: Fuck you too

"The building plans look beautiful. I'm worried what it will do to the existing community," Vanessa said, biting her nails.

"It'll be fine," Wesley dismissed. "It'll bring new businesses and customers to the area. Right, gentlemen?"

"I agree with Vanessa," I shared. "I got a chance to walk through the neighborhood the other day. This might not be sustainable for the current businesses and families, long-term."

"Perhaps the revitalization will bring customers to existing businesses, so it'll even out," Khalil added, noticing Wesley's tightened jaw.

Khalil, we've seen this happen back home, after Katrina. You know that's not how this plays out.

"Either way, I can't wait to get this project finished. So, Van, will you do the mural?" Wesley rested his hand on top of hers. She pursed her lips to the side and then gave him a half smile. Wesley returned the gesture.

I swear if they look at each other like this one more time I'm sliding his Scar-looking ass across the table.

"I don't know, Wesley. Let me think about it," she replied, pulling her hand back.

"Alright, but I'll need a decision soon. We can discuss it more later." Wesley gestured to the hallway leading to the rest of Wright Horizons offices. "Oh, Khalil, let me introduce you to the head of the finance department. You missed him at our last meeting." They left the conference room, leaving Vanessa and me alone.

"So, we decided to be friends, but now we barely know each other?" I asked, my tone cooler than I intended. Vanessa rolled her eyes as she continued to thumb through her phone. "Van, I'm talking to you," I snapped.

"What's your problem, Zay," she shot back, finally looking up.

"Nothing. We only dated a little bit. Why should I have a problem?"

"I forgot how much of an asshole you could be." *That one stung.* We glared at each other until I let out a breath, trying to calm the storm inside me.

"I'm sorry. I'm not trying to be mean, but you got me feeling some kind of way." Vanessa tilted her head, her lips parting as if to speak but nothing came out. "Are you happy with him?" I asked.

"Look who finally learned how to communicate," she sneered, rolling her eyes. "I'm not with him."

"You sure about that?"

"Careful, Zay. Some might think you're jealous." She walked closer, her perfume, that familiar scent of peonies and warmth, enveloping me.

"You know you can do better than that," I said, my voice softer now. I know I agreed to be friends, but seeing her with Wesley, all buddy-buddy, it just wasn't sitting right with me. She didn't belong with anyone else. *Especially not Braxton.* She was mine.

"What? You mean like you?" She shook her head. "Been there, done that."

"I know I fucked up before, but I've changed. Tell me to my face there's another man out here for you." She was silent. "Exactly. College me was young. I didn't know half of what I know now about being there for you. But I'm here now, Nessa."

"That's good to hear. I'm glad you're in a better place. But we agreed to be friends." Her voice cracked when she emphasized *friends*, betraying the mask she was trying to wear.

"You sure about that?" I took her hand in mine, pressing a kiss to the back. Her eyes met mine, and for a moment, it was just us and the tension simmering from me to her.

Khalil's entrance shattered the moment. We jumped apart like kids caught doing something they shouldn't.

"Uh," Khalil started, clearing his throat. "Say bruh, Wesley says we're good to go." He walked up to Vanessa, pulling her in a gentle hug. "Why you lying to old dude, Nessa? Downplaying my brother like that."

She laughed, a genuine sound that hit me straight in the chest. "I'm sorry about that. I don't think quickly on my feet." She gave Khalil another hug. "Wesley likes to ask too many questions."

"Yeah, yeah. Tell Kelly I'll be hitting her up," Khalil replied, patting her back.

"For sure," she replied. "We all need to link up again sometime." She turned to look at me once more, something hiding in her eyes. "Bye." She grabbed her belongings and left.

"Damn, Zay. Nessa and Wesley. Didn't see that coming. You think they messed around?"

"She said they didn't, but I don't know about that." I kept my eyes on the hallway where she disappeared.

"So, what you gonna do now?" Khalil's voice was low.

"Only thing I can do." I turned to him, my hands fidgeting in my pockets. "Fix all the old shit. Show her I've changed. Then remind her why she fell in love with me in the first place."

Chapter 13

◆

XAVIER

XAVIER UNIVERSITY - JANUARY 2016

THE APARTMENT WAS CLOAKED in an unsettling quiet, the kind that feels thick, pressing, like the air itself is holding its breath. Shadows stretched long across the walls, their edges blurred by the dimming light of the evening. I stood in the living room, my back pressed against the cool plaster, trying to find something solid in the chaos swirling around me. Exhaustion clung to my body like a second skin. My fists were balled tight, nails digging into my palms, the only anchor I had in the suffocating tension between us. Across the room, Vanessa stood with her arms wrapped around herself, like she was holding her very being together. The silence between us was a chasm—deep, vast, and widening with each passing minute.

"I just don't get it, Nessa," I said, my voice strained and thin with the weight of everything I hadn't said. "Why can't you understand that I need to do this on my own?"

Her eyes met mine, and I saw the unshed tears loitering at the edge of her resolve. Hurt and confusion danced across her face, and it killed me that I was the reason for it. She shook her head, her voice breaking as she tried to hold on. "Xavier, I'm trying to help you. We're supposed to be a team. But every time I try to be there, you push me away. What do you expect me to do?"

I couldn't look at her. The heaviness of everything—the pressure of my mother's illness, the struggle to make EcoVision work, the crushing sense of failure—wrapped around my chest like a vice, making it hard to breathe. I wanted to scream, to break something, to make the unbearable silence stop, but the words tangled in my throat.

"It's not that simple!" I blurted out, my voice cracking under the strain. "What I look like accepting your parents' money. They'll forever think I can't stand on my own and take care of you the way I should."

"You're being ridiculous!" Vanessa stepped closer, her hands reaching out, desperate to close the gap between us. "Xavier, this isn't about the money. It's about us, about supporting each other. Why won't you let me in?"

I laughed bitterly, the sound harsh and empty in the room. "Support me? It feels like charity. Like you'd rather throw money than understand my struggles."

Her face twisted in anguish, and for the first time, the tears that had been threatening finally broke free. "You think I don't understand struggle? Just because I come from a family with money doesn't mean I haven't faced my own battles, Xavier. God, you have no idea how exhausting it is being around you lately. You make me feel like I'm not enough for you, that nothing I do is ever good enough. If I wanted to feel this worthless, I'd go back home."

Her words hit me like a punch to the gut, but the frustration inside me wouldn't let go. "Maybe you don't get it because you've never had to fight for something without a backup plan. I need to prove I can make it on my own. For us."

Her eyes blazed with anger, but beneath that, I saw the hurt—the deep, aching hurt that I put there. She took a step back, pulling her arms tighter around herself as if she were holding in all the pain

I couldn't see. "You think I haven't fought for us? I've been here, trying to stand by you, but all you do is push me away. I'm tired, Xavier! I'm tired of feeling like I'm walking on eggshells, like I'm failing you at every turn."

Her voice cracked, and I felt something inside me crack with it. I wanted to reach out, to tell her I was sorry, that I didn't mean any of it, but the words tangled in my throat, knotted up with all the fear I couldn't unravel.

"I'm trying, Vanessa," I said, my voice breaking under the weight of my own helplessness. "I'm trying so damn hard to be enough, for everybody, but I feel like I'm drowning. I don't know how to do this—how to fix this."

Her shoulders sagged, her face a mask of sorrow and defeat. "And I can't keep drowning with you, Xavier. I need to breathe too."

The tears I'd been holding back slipped down my cheek, unnoticed until I felt the cold sting of them. I reached out as if to touch her, to pull her close and make her stay, but my hand fell back to my side, useless and heavy. "I don't know what to do," I whispered, the words raw and jagged, barely making it past the lump in my throat. "I don't know how to fix us."

Vanessa shook her head slowly, her eyes filled with a sorrow I couldn't bear. "Maybe we can't fix us. Maybe we're just...broken."

Her words hung between us, a devastating blow I wasn't ready for. The last thread holding us together snapped, and I felt it deep in my chest, a pain so sharp it nearly broke me to my knees.

"I'm sorry," I murmured, my voice barely audible, nothing more than a broken whimper.

Vanessa closed her eyes, a single tear slipping down her cheek. "Me too."

"Do what you got to do, Vanessa."

She turned, her footsteps soft but heavy with finality, and walked to the door. Every step she took felt like she was walking away from more than just the room—from us, from everything we planned. The door clicked shut behind her, and the silence that followed was unbearable, crushing in its emptiness. I sank to the floor, my back against the wall, my head in my hands, as the failure of everything we were—everything we could've been—crashed down on me.

The darkness closed in, swallowing me whole.

Chapter 14

Vanessa

Xavier University - Late February 2016

I paced the length of my bedroom, my footsteps sinking into the carpet, the tension coiled tight in my chest. The room felt small, as I downed another bottle of water, hoping it would help, but the anxiety bubbling inside me was impossible to drown. Kelly sat cross-legged on my bed, flipping through the instruction booklets of the three pregnancy test brands we'd bought at the drugstore, her own nervous energy mirroring mine.

"Try jumping jacks" she suggested, her voice laced with the same kind of worry I'd been swallowing for days. "Might help get the water through faster."

I shook my head, feeling a hollow ache in my stomach that had nothing to do with the tests. "It's not going to change, Kelly," I said, my voice flat, lifeless. The truth hung heavy between us. I sank onto the bed, pressing my face into the pillows as my words trembled. "I'm pregnant," I choked out, rolling over to look at her. My vision blurred from the tears welling in my eyes. "We've gone through three boxes. They all say the same thing. Positive." The word felt like a weight in my mouth, heavy and unmovable. I wiped my face, trying to clear the tears that kept streaming, but it was like fighting a flood.

"What are you going to do?" Kelly asked softly, her concern piercing through my despair. "Are you going to tell your parents?"

I closed my eyes, the thought of facing them too much to bear. "I don't know," I choked through heavy sobs. "I don't even know where to start. They think we're still together."

Kelly's hand moved to my shoulder, grounding me. "You need to tell Zay," she said, her tone gentle but firm. "He has a right to know."

"Why should I?" I snapped, my voice brittle, sharp. "He left me, Kelly. Or did you forget?"

Kelly sighed, her patience endless, even when I didn't deserve it. "Technically, you left him, but it doesn't matter. You can't keep this from him."

"I couldn't if I tried. He blocked me. Everywhere." I collapsed into her lap, the tears spilling freely now. She stroked my hair, her hand comforting but unable to stop the ache inside me.

A beat of silence passed before I heard her shift, reaching for her phone. "Let me try," Kelly said, tapping the screen as she dialed Xavier's number. His voice came through the speaker, deep and familiar, making my heart stutter in my chest. I froze, breathless.

"Zay," Kelly started, but before she could get another word out, the line clicked dead. She tried again, but this time it didn't ring. The rejection was like a punch to the gut.

"Just forget about it," I uttered, sinking deeper into the bed. "It's your birthday. We should be celebrating, not dealing with my mess." I felt guilty pulling her into my storm. We hadn't seen each other since winter break—she'd graduated, and moved on to med school, while I was still here, stuck in this endless loop of heartbreak and uncertainty. We were supposed to be out in the city, celebrating her, celebrating Mardi Gras. Instead, we were holed up in my room, drowning in my problems.

Kelly wouldn't hear it. "Nope," she said, standing up and pulling me with her. "It's my birthday, it's Mardi Gras, and we are not sitting in this room all day. We're going out." She tossed me a pair of jeans and a cute top, her determination leaving no room for argument. "Get dressed. You need to get out of this house."

An hour later, we were walking down Canal Street, the noise and color of the parade filling the air. For the first time in days, I felt the weight lift, just a little. The rhythm of the music, the laughter of the crowd—it all helped me forget, if only for a moment. I smiled at Kelly as a band marched by, my heart easing, my mind beginning to clear. But then, like a bad dream come to life, I saw him.

Xavier.

Across the street, his smile was wide and loose, eyes so low they seemed closed, his arm slung around some random girl. My breath hitched, and my entire body went cold. The world tilted on its axis, the noise of the parade fading as my vision tunneled in on them. She was pressed close to him, her hand low on his waist, her body language protective, possessive. As if she really had a right to what was mine. The sight of them together sent my stomach plummeting, and I gripped Kelly's arm, trying to steady myself.

Kelly's eyes followed my gaze, and when she saw him, her face hardened. "I know you fucking lying." She began to move to the group across the street, her rage bubbling to the surface.

"No, Kelly. Please. Let's just try to get out of here," I pleaded, restraining her.

But, Kelly wasn't having it. "That bitch ass muthafucka," she growled. "He can't answer the phone, but he can be out running around with some hoochie. Fuck that, Nessa. I'm about to beat his ass."

"You don't think I want to do that!" I snapped, my voice breaking. "You don't think I want to drag his ass from here to St. Charles? But what's the point?"

I was shaking, my heart pounding so hard it felt like it might burst. We turned away from the parade, weaving through the crowd, my tears blurring everything around me. I could barely see through the flood, but I kept moving, one foot in front of the other, just trying to make it back to Kelly's car before I fell apart.

As we walked away, I couldn't hold it in any longer. "I don't understand, Kelly," I whispered, my voice cracking under the weight of my grief. "How can he just move on? I thought we had something real. I thought he loved me."

Kelly's hand squeezed mine. "Guys are idiots. But don't think for a second this is about you. He's the one messing up, Nessa. You tried."

"Did I?" I whispered, my tears falling freely now. "I was there for him, for his mom, for all of it. And he just... shut me out."

"You two didn't talk about this, did you?"

I shook my head, shame settling into the pit of my stomach. "No. I didn't want to add to his stress."

Kelly sighed, her voice softening. "Nessa, if you don't tell him how you feel, how's he supposed to know? You can't expect him to read your mind."

I closed my eyes, leaning my head against the cool glass of the car window as her words sank in. The truth of it weighed heavily on me. "I just don't know what to do."

Kelly looked at me, her face soft with concern. "Whatever you decide, I'm here for you, okay? Always."

"Thanks, Kelly." I managed a small, broken smile. "Happy birthday."

THE NEXT MONTH FELT like moving through a haze, a constant blur of monotony. Work, class, the cold silence of my apartment—each day passed, filled with exhaustion and sadness. With Kelly back in Houston, I was left to wrestle with my thoughts, alone. I walked into my empty duplex and made my way to the kitchen. When I opened the fridge, all that greeted me was expired milk and a few half-empty condiment bottles. In the sink, a pan sat with burnt remnants of eggs I couldn't even remember cooking. I gagged at the sight. I couldn't remember the last time I'd eaten properly. But what did it matter? Even if I wasn't nauseous, my broken heart stripped me of any appetite.

I didn't know hearts could shatter into a billion pieces. Growing up, I thought love was simple. My parents made it look so easy—my headstrong mother and calm, steady father balancing each other like the two halves of a perfect whole. That's what I thought Xavier and I had. But I was wrong.

So wrong.

I dragged myself to my bedroom, collapsing onto the bed, the growing emptiness inside me too much to bear. The words tumbled out in a whisper, heavy and full of rage.

"Fuck him!"

The memory of that night—of the way everything fell apart—haunted me, playing on repeat in my mind. I had gone to Xavier's, ready to fix things between us, to fight for us. But what did I get? *"Do what you gotta do."* His voice, flat and emotionless, echoed in my mind, each syllable cutting deeper into my chest. I stood there, waiting—hoping—for something, anything from him. A word. A glance. A reason to stay. But he sat there, cold and detached, watching me gather my things without a care in the world.

And when I left—when I stood in his doorway for the last time—he didn't stop me. He didn't even flinch.

I told myself I was done. I told myself I was better off. But when the calls stopped going through, when I realized he blocked me, a knife twisted in my chest. He couldn't have loved me. He couldn't have meant any of it if he let me go that easily.

I swiped at my eyes, forcing myself to sit up, the fury in my veins boiling over. Staying in this apartment wasn't going to fix anything. If my life was going to fall apart, then I wasn't going to suffer alone. He didn't get to cut me out like I was nothing, like I hadn't been there for him, like I didn't matter.

And now I was stuck with his child? Fuck that shit.

I wiped the tears falling down my face and sat up. I pulled a sweatshirt and leggings from my dresser, throwing them on quickly. Xavier didn't get to cut me out so easily and make me feel disposable. If my world was going to turn upside down, he was coming with me. I don't care what shit he had going on.

I grabbed my keys, hands trembling, and headed out the door. The drive was a blur of emotions—anger, hurt, desperation—all swirling together as I tried to make sense of the storm inside me. Hurricane Vanessa was brewing and due for landfall. Thirty minutes later, I parked in front of Xavier's place, staring at the door, trying to muster the courage to walk up.

I stepped out of the car, every part of me trembling as I walked toward the house. As I neared the door, the smell of smoke and alcohol hit me, making my nausea rise again. It wasn't just Xavier's place tonight—it was a full-blown party. Music boomed, and people milled in and out of the door, laughing, drinking, and celebrating. Meanwhile, I was here to confront the father of my child.

"Nessa!"

I turned quickly upon hearing that familiar voice. "Khalil! What is going on? Who are all these people?" I struggled to shout over the loud music. The bass made my anxious jitters and nausea worsen.

"You know we're trying to save some money to start this business." Khalil's hazel eyes were glossed over, his smile wider than usual.

"Why are y'all throwing a party when I could just ask my dad? This is unnecessary and foolish. The cops could come."

"Everything is legal, girl. Besides, Zay said he didn't want the money. I gotta respect that. You wanna drink?"

I rolled my eyes. Whatever Xavier wants, Xavier gets. No matter how it impacts the people around him. "No. Look, where's Zay?"

"You sure?"

"I'm not in the mood. Where's Zay?" A couple of people passed by, bumping into me and sending another wave of vomit to the bottom of my throat. The acid sat bubbling, waiting to erupt at any moment.

"I don't know. He somewhere around here though."

"Ugh. Okay."

"Wait. Say, Zay!" Khalil shouted over the music. Xavier made his way across the room. I stilled as the, now former, love of my life stood before me. His pupils were dilated, eyes dazed, bloodshot, lids barely able to stay open. I regretted not checking my mirror before getting out of the car. I was sure I looked as crazy as I felt with tear-stained mascara smudged around my eyes and cheeks.

"Zay." I so desperately wanted to embrace him and beg him to come home with me. But all I could do was stand there, frozen.

He looked back at me with disgust. "Fuck you doing here?"

"Zay, chill out bruh," Khalil warned.

"We need to talk."

"I'm busy." His words hit me like the acid that threatened to cover the front of his crisp white T-shirt.

"Please," I begged, my voice cracking.

"Fuck nah. We ain't got shit to talk about. You said you was done, remember?"

"Zay, come on man. You better than this."

Xavier looked around the room, massaging his jaw and avoiding eye contact with me. "Come on." I followed him back to his room and he closed the door behind us.

"What you want?"

"The fuck is wrong with you? This isn't you, Zay!" Although we were in his room, I still had to shout over the music booming through the wall.

"Why the fuck you care about what's wrong with me? You said you was done, right? What you doing here?"

"I needed to see you."

"You seen me. Now leave. That's what you good at doing anyways."

Tears pricked my eyes. "Zay, stop being like this with me. It's me." When I grabbed his arm, I felt his muscles recoil under my fingers.

"I ain't being like nothing."

I wiped my eyes, looking up at him. I didn't know who this person was who stood in front of me. Xavier's once warm and kind eyes were now ice. His glare felt like stones being thrown my way. "Why?"

"Why what?" His throat moved up and down as his jaw clenched.

"Why did you leave? Why did you end us?"

He raised an eyebrow in my direction. "You must be confused. You did that shit." Xavier moved to sit on the edge of the bed, lighting his blunt.

"But you let me walk away like it was nothing. Zay, you love me. We love each other!"

He inhaled deeply, before walking over to me. He exhaled the thick smoke in my face, then stalked away. "Loved. Past tense. That shit died when you walked out the door."

"What did you want me to do? You wouldn't talk to me. You wouldn't let me help you. You complained about every suggestion I had. You wouldn't let me take care of you."

"I don't need you to take care of me!" His voice boomed. "I just needed you to be there and stop trying to make everything perfect for Vanessa's little world! I know you don't get it because you got parents that buy your way into whatever you want. But us, regular people, got real shit to deal with on a daily basis."

"Again with the money. I told you I had you for whatever you needed. Why do you keep throwing it in my face? Stop being stubborn and take it!"

Xavier charged over and stood face-to-face with me again. He was so close his flared nostrils brushed against my own.

"It's not about the money! There's some things you can't throw money at and expect it to go away. But you don't understand that. Nah, all you understand is when shit get real, when it get tough, you run. So go ahead and run up out of here and back to ya Momma and Daddy. You good for it."

"Look at me," I said, grabbing his face. "I'm here. I'm right here. You're talking reckless and I'm still here. Don't you see what you're doing to me? To us. We need you."

He flung my hands from his face. "Need me? You don't need me! You got everything you could ever need! All you gotta do is call ya people! It's done the next day."

"No, Zay, you don't understand. We need you." Thick tears lay on my lower lids. I felt the avalanche ready to spill at any minute. I know Xavier was hurting. We both were. If he could just listen for a second, everything could be right again. We could *fix* this together. "I need the real you right now. Not whoever this is."

"News flash, love. This is me."

Vomit inched its way up my esophagus. I bent at the hips to breathe, hoping it would work its way back down. I was already embarrassing myself. I couldn't add puking all over the place to this situation. "No. I need you, Zay. I'm—"

The door flung open. Khalil walked in with a cup in his hand. "Say, y'all good? I can hear y'all out here."

"Yeah. We good. Nessa was just leaving." Khalil looked from Xavier to me. His eyes followed as my hands moved up from my knees to rest on my stomach. He caught the desperation and meaning in my eyes. A message Xavier was too upset to hear.

"Look, Zay, why don't y'all take a drive? This ain't y'all. You need to talk this out the right way," Khalil suggested.

"I don't need to do no more talking!" Xavier tried pushing Khalil out of the door frame. "I'm done with all this fucking bullshit!"

"Zay, you fucking trippin', my boy. You need to calm your ass down and listen."

"I'm tripping? I'm tripping? She's the one tripping! Coming here crashing my shit! Playing fucking mind games, talking about she needs me when she's the one that abandoned me! Who the fuck side you on anyway?"

"Say bruh, I'll fuck you up right now," Khalil said, pushing Xavier back into the room. "I don't give a damn who you is."

"I can't take this shit! I'm done." Xavier grabbed his keys from the floor before walking up to me and staring into my eyes. They were mirror images of each other. Perfect pairs of glossy orbs swirling with pain, anger, hurt, and regret. Yet he was too stubborn to step outside of his own pain to see beyond it. "Don't you see I'm going through a lot right now! And then you come here with bullshit...This why I can't be with your selfish ass, Nessa."

"Zay, stop! You don't mean that!" Hot tears streamed down my face.

"Nah, take your crazy ass home. Grab you a drink on the way out." His eyes moved up and down my body. "You look like you need it."

This nigga. Fury overtook me. I swiped everything on top of his dresser to the floor, the contents crashing to the floor.

"Is this what you want, Zay? You want me to be crazy?" I slapped his face, barely registering the sting in my palm. My vision grew blurry from the mix of smoke and tears that stung my eyes. Rage swelled in my veins, leading to an assault of punches and slaps raining down on Xavier. "I'm not fucking selfish." I felt strong arms pull me off of Xavier. He said something to me, something I couldn't make out over the ringing in my ears. When I was standing again, I looked at Xavier one final time, my chest heaving.

"Fuck you, Zay," I spat, before turning to leave forever.

When I made it to my car, I couldn't stop myself from throwing up on the curb. My throat burned as the never-ending stomach acid and bile continued to pour from my body. When I finally gathered myself, I got into the driver's seat and started the ignition. Out of nowhere, I rammed my fists into the steering wheel, center console, dashboard, anything that seemed strong enough to let out the pain inside my heart. I screamed, hoping Xavier would hear my pain and rush to me to soothe it away. It was a useless attempt with the music from the party seeping into the streets. Two months ago, I'd given Xavier the knife to stab into my heart. Tonight, he'd twisted it further into my soul, leaving it to fester. I didn't know how, or if, I'd be able to heal from this.

Chapter 15

VANESSA

"OH MY GOD. THAT was brutal," Kelly cried.

I wiped the sweat beading around my temples. "Why did we decide to get into Pilates?" I grimaced, my legs threatening to give way as I stood from the torture device called The Reformer.

"Because, only with Pilates do you get bodies like this," Kelly said, admiring her physique in the mirrors of the studio. "Smoothies?"

"Yes, please." I slung my light jacket across my shoulders, pulled my tote bag onto my forearm, and rested my large shades on the bridge of my nose.

"Thanks, Kathy," Kelly called out. "We'll see you next week for another round of torture." As we exited the studio, we waved goodbye to our Pilates instructor and walked across the street to the designer smoothie bar we frequented post-class. After we ordered, we sat in a booth at the back of the shop.

"This dragon fruit bowl is so good," I said, heaping a spoonful of the chilly frozen fruit into my mouth. The roasted pumpkin seeds and fresh-made pieces of granola added a nice crunch.

"I know, right." Kelly took a sip of water. "So, have you talked to Xavier since you told him you wanted to be friends?"

"No, not really. I'm trying to keep my distance until after my next session with Dr. Smith. But his ass just keeps popping up everywhere. For Houston to be so big, it sure feels small."

"Really? How so?"

"You know how Wesley wants me to do this mural for his next project?"

"Yeah. And?"

"It's a fucking partnership with Xavier and Khalil. They're renovating that old apartment complex near the community center."

Kelly choked on her water. "Is that why you called me so many times? I'm sorry, girl. My last shift was crazy. Kids back in school. All kinds of germs going around. Speaking of, make sure you're taking extra vitamin C since you're at the community center all the time."

"Let me add that to my grocery order."

"But continue. Wesley, Xavier, partnership. Crazy," Kelly replied as she shook her head.

"I just don't understand. Two weeks ago, I had everything under control. My life was moving in the right direction. Now, I feel like I'm unraveling at the seams."

I twirled my spoon around my bowl, the plump blueberries sinking into the pink froth.

"Can you believe he tried to imply that we should get back together? After blaming me for part of our break-up."

"Yes. I can definitely believe that." Kelly looked at me blankly. "What? I knew from the way he looked at you at the nightclub he wanted to be back with your indecisive ass. And again, you were the one that ended things first."

I shook my head, eating more of my smoothie bowl, before it turned into liquid mush. "Whose side are you on anyway?"

"Truth. You want another dose?" My friend arched an eyebrow as she awaited my answer. One thing I could say about my best friend is that she kept it real with everyone. She didn't care whether you were close friends or strangers.

"Just say it."

"I don't care what you and Xavier end up being but you need to tell him about the baby. If whatever y'all have going on grows to something more, or doesn't, you don't want to keep a secret like that from him. It'll eat away at you and all this growth you're doing will be pointless."

"It wouldn't be a secret if he hadn't pushed me away," I retorted.

"Nope, I'm not letting you play the blame game. You said you don't want to live in the past, right?"

"Yeah. So?"

"Well, grown up Vanessa needs to put her grown woman panties on." Kelly slurped more of her green smoothie.

"What if he blames me? What if he hates me?"

"Then fuck his ass. There are plenty of others. You think I don't know how you were popping that pussy in grad school. Nyah told me about y'alls escapades."

"Oh, hush." I scooped some bananas into my mouth. The sweetness contrasting with the tartness of the fruit. "How are your patients doing?"

"Good. Well, all except one. There's this little girl that has a brain tumor. Prognosis isn't great. She'll be lucky to make it to Christmas."

"Oh, Kelly. I'm so sorry to hear that." I reached across the table to smooth my hand over hers. "I don't know how you do it? It's one thing for adults to go through horrible things. But kids? They're innocent."

"Don't speak too soon. Pretty soon you'll be in the same position as me with those kids from the center."

"But they aren't sick," I laughed.

"No, but each one of them will have their own special place in your heart just the same." Kelly went on to talk about some of the toddlers she'd met during her rounds in the Pediatric Intensive Care Unit. I laughed at the stories of the young children calling her Dr. Barbie. As she continued, my phone buzzed on the table. I looked down, still listening to Kelly, to see that Xavier sent me a message.

Asshole: I'm sorry. For yesterday. I didn't mean to come at you like that. I was caught off guard.

Vanessa: You're fine. I think it caught us both off guard.

Asshole: We're still good?

Vanessa: Yeah... I guess so...

As we left the smoothie bar, I carried Kelly's words with me. I knew that, in the end, it was my heart that would guide my steps. I trudged into my apartment and struggled to kick off my shoes. The soreness from Pilates this morning settled in quickly. I shrugged off my hoodie and tossed it aimlessly to the entryway table, grabbing my phone and heading to my bedroom. The moment Xavier kissed me replayed in my mind, warmth spreading like fluid brushstrokes through my body. The addictiveness of being desired by him made me crave even more.

I needed to be honest with myself. Yes, I still loved him, even after everything. It was instant attraction when we first met. I tried so hard to not look at him, looking at me from across the table in Essence Cafe. *Things were so simple then.* I went into my closet to grab a lounge set to put on after my shower.

After cleansing my mind and my body, I walked into the room I used as a makeshift studio. It was my private oasis away from everyone else's opinions. I started my soothing Paint Session playlist from my phone. The voices of SZA, Summer Walker, and Jhene Aiko wrapped me in a melodic flow, promising to bring about peak creativity from the inner workings of my mind.

Picking up one of my soft charcoal pencils, I sketched out a few circles and lines on the canvas to map out the form of the face I couldn't seem to get out of my mind. Light gray markings made out the sharpness of his jaw, the angles of his cheekbones. Broad strokes outlined his neck and led to the strong roundness of his shoulders, angled in a ¾ profile. As I moved to add an assortment of deep brown and white to my pallets, my phone buzzed, stopping the music. *Xavier*.

Zay: WYD?

Vanessa: Painting. You?

Zay: Just left Buffalo Bayou Park. Had to get my run in. Let me see what you working on

Vanessa: Ummm no...It's not ready yet.

Zay: Come one, now. I bet it's perfect already

Vanessa: No it's not. Besides, this one is not coming out of the vault.

Zay: Yeah, yeah

Zay: I don't like how we ended things the other day. Let me take you to dinner. Make things right. As friends?

I hesitated. On one hand, I could definitely stand to see Xavier more. On the other hand, I wanted to put some space between the moment we shared the night of my birthday and the reality of our demise. We couldn't just hop back in like nothing ever happened.

Vanessa: Actually, can we met up week after next? Tuesday, at the community center.

Zay: Yea. What time?

Vanessa: I should wrap up my art class around 6:00.

Zay: I'll be there. I'm gonna let you get back to work, Picasso

Vanessa: I prefer Waring

Zay: Who is that?

Vanessa: Bye, Zay

I focused on the canvas in front of me, trying to ease the jitters going through my veins. I rolled a base of white paint over the canvas fabric and faced a fan toward it to quicken the drying process. Then, I mixed the colors that would serve as the skin color on the portrait I wanted to capture perfectly. When I was sure the base was dry, I used the sketching from earlier to fill in the outline. With each deliberate stroke, the canvas captured the essence of my tangled feelings.

This was a language I spoke fluently, a dialogue between the canvas and my restless heart. Each dab of paint whispered understanding, bridging the gap between confusion and clarity. As the figure unfolded before my eyes, so did the tension within me, the swirls of browns dancing around, emphasizing the shadows and highlights of the portrait, mimicking the complexities of love and choice in my own heart.

But it wasn't just a painting. It was all my fears and anxieties coming to the forefront of my life. And just like a painting, one wrong stroke of color had the potential to destroy days, months, even years of work. This portrait needed to be perfect in every stroke, every shade, every highlight. I needed it to be perfect.

So lost in the process, I jumped when my doorbell rang. Hours passed since I started. I took deep breaths as I bounded down the hallway leading into my entryway. Looking into the peephole of my door, I saw nothing. I slowly cracked the door open and looked down to find a plastic takeout bag with a note attached.

Nessa,

I don't have your address, but I remembered how I got here the night of your birthday. I don't know if you've learned to stop and eat when

*you're in a creative groove, so I got you something, just to be sure. Eat
up and enjoy,*

Zay.

An elevator ding went off further down the hallway. *He was here?*
Grabbing the bag, I locked my door then rushed to get my phone in
my studio room.

Vanessa: Zay, you didn't need to bring me food.

Zay: I know. I wanted to. Now please take a break and eat, then
finish your secret masterpiece. I hope I get to see it one day.

My cheeks blushed right there on the spot. I opened the bag and
my mouth watered from the savory aroma of fried fish, jalapeno
peppers, and dirty rice hitting my nose. Can't even describe the
feeling when I saw the container of peach cobbler

Frenchy's? My man knows me too well.

Vanessa: Thank you

Zay: Anytime, love

Vanessa: What do you know about Frenchy's?

Zay: I just know my baby. See you soon.

Chapter 16

Xavier

THE AIR IN THIRD Ward had a familiar weight as back home—history, struggle, and hope all woven into the atmosphere. As I strolled past the new luxury condos, I couldn't help but feel the unease settling deeper into my gut. This wasn't what Khalil and I had envisioned. What was supposed to be an eco-friendly, community-driven project for the people who'd lived here for generations was quickly morphing into yet another exclusive enclave for Houston's wealthy elite. I felt like a sellout, plain and simple. Every other project we'd taken on always circled back to giving something meaningful to the people, but this one...this one felt we'd let them down.

Wright Horizon's vision for this build was clear, and it wasn't about community. It was about wealth. The same wealth that pushed residents further and further from the heart of the city, replacing homes with condos, culture with commerce. It gnawed at me, the realization that in order to do "bigger" things, we had to compromise our values. But how far could we bend before we broke?

I checked my watch, making sure I was on time for Vanessa's invitation to meet her at the community center this afternoon. Wesley mentioned something about her mural here weeks ago, and though I didn't need an excuse to see her, the mural was a good one to get here early. She always poured her soul into her art, leaving behind pieces of herself in each stroke, each color.

Walking up to the community center, I took a deep breath. I wasn't sure what to expect, but if anything, I knew being around her, seeing her in her element, would feel like coming home—even if we weren't fully there yet.

Inside, the hallway felt alive—vibrant, humming with the sound of young voices and clattering feet, like the building itself breathed along with its visitors. The mural Wesley talked about dominated the far end of the corridor, drawing me in like a magnet. Massive graffiti-style letters spelling "Third Ward" loomed large, the Houston skyline painted in sharp contrast. But that wasn't all—spaceships, oil rigs, slabs, cassette tapes, and astronauts swirled in a kaleidoscope of color and culture. It had Vanessa's signature all over it. A work of art so undeniably hers you wouldn't mistake it for anyone else's. My fingers itched to trace the lines, to get lost in the world she had created.

"Hi, welcome to Heritage Community Center. My name is Mrs. Collins. How can I help you?" I turned to find Mrs. Collins approaching me, the apples of her cheeks rounding into a warm smile.

"Hi, I'm Xavier Morris," I replied, offering a handshake.

"Oh, that's right. Vanessa told me you'd be stopping by today. You're a bit early, huh?"

"Yeah, I was hoping to check out her mural I've heard so much about."

"Oh, yes. It's beautiful, isn't it? Really captures the neighborhood and city." We admired the mural together. "If you follow me, I can take you to her classroom."

I followed Mrs. Collins down the corridor as the sound of laughter and teenage banter grew louder.

When we reached the art room, I spotted Vanessa immediately. Her back was to me, but the golden-brown warmth of her skin caught the light streaming through the large windows, making her glow like something ethereal. Her hair—wavy tresses, slightly unkempt—framed her face as she moved between the tables, guiding the young artists. I stood still for a moment, watching her as if I were observing something sacred. She wasn't tense like she was the last time I saw her. No, this was different. She was in her element, surrounded by the magic of her own making.

My eyes traced over the rest of her body. A vintage Prince graphic tee skirted over the black biker shorts she wore. When she leaned in to assist a student, it was only right that I admired the plump roundness of her ass, the lean lines of her legs. They taunted me, knowing I wanted to run my hands up and down and squeeze until my fingers broke. I bit my bottom lip to quell the stirring in my chest. Mrs. Collins cleared her throat.

"I'm sorry," I chuckled. "I guess I was distracted."

"Uh-huh," Mrs. Collins hummed, raising an eyebrow. "Like I was saying, Vanessa is something special. I was ecstatic to meet her at one of her parent's foundation events. I know she works for them but, between you and me, I think she's wasting her talents."

"I know what you mean." My eyes stayed on Vanessa as Mrs. Collins and I stood across the hallway.

I love this woman so much.

"It's a shame the center is closing at the end of next summer."

"Closing?"

"Yeah. We just don't have the funds to run it. Especially with the tax rates going up in the area with all those new condos and whatnot."

My chest tightened. "Do the instructors or kids know?"

"The instructors and staff, yes. We haven't told the kids just yet. Don't want them checking out. There are already few spaces they can go to just to be kids, you know?"

"Yeah, I know what you mean." I bit the insides of my cheeks as my hands fidgeted in my pockets. Vanessa looked so happy and in her element here. How would losing this place affect her when it was gone?

"You can wait here. Her class should be over soon. It was nice meeting you Mr. Grant." Mrs. Collins gave me a heartwarming smile.

"That sounds great. Thank you. Nice meeting you too."

"Umm huh." Mrs. Collins looked at me, the apples of her cheeks rounding high as her eyes narrowed. "No problem," she said before walking off.

Leaning against the wall, I couldn't help but smile as I witnessed Vanessa's graceful movements as she guided young fingers across the canvas. Her laughter blended with the background of teenagers chatting. She was oblivious that I was standing here. To any other person walking by, I'm sure I looked like a stalker.

"Wow, Natyri, those brushstrokes are fantastic! You're turning this canvas into a masterpiece," Vanessa exclaimed. The young lady beamed with pride as her fingers carefully maneuvered the paintbrush under Vanessa's encouraging gaze.

As Vanessa approached a group of students huddled around a collaborative painting, she noticed me standing by the doorway. Her eyes lit with a mixture of surprise and...delight? She smiled and waved her hand for me to enter. I didn't hesitate to move toward her as she met me by the doorway.

"Zay! You're here early. Afraid I was going to back out of meeting up?" Her voice was light, teasing.

"I don't know what you're talking about," I shot back, trying to match her ease, though my heart raced at just being near her again. "I just came to see this mural Wesley won't shut up about."

"Uh-huh. Sure," she quipped, raising an eyebrow playfully.

Her eyes held mine for a moment longer than I expected, so I broke the moment, gesturing to the productive chaos happening in the room behind her. "What's going on here? I'm not interrupting anything, am I?"

"No, no interruption at all." She smiled a little softer this time. "We're just creating a little magic here. Come have a look."

The teens, sensing a new audience, greeted me with curious glances and suspecting smiles. Vanessa introduced me to her young protégés. Heat and sweat pricked my forehead and armpits. It's was only a room of teenagers and the love of my life. *Why was I so nervous?*

"Everyone, this is Mr. Morris. He's an old friend from college."

"Ms. Nessa, is that your man?" One girl asked, her eyes narrowing curiously.

"No, Tyri." She laughed nervously. I could tell from the girl's facial expression we were thinking the same thing. *I'm definitely her man.* I don't care what lie she was telling herself. The truth comes from the mouths (or looks) of babes. "Mr. Morris and I went to college together."

"So, if he's not your man, do you have a man?" I saw Vanessa flush at the question. I never would've thought kids could be so nosy. This same thing happened when I visited her classes when she volunteered at the Boys and Girls Club back when we were together. Of course she claimed me back then.

"Tyri, Ms. Nessa a baddie. She probably got a whole roster."

"Okay, we're done with that. Payton, why don't you tell Mr. Morris about your painting, hmm?" She walked away, giving me a bemused smile before hurrying over to two boys getting ready to start a paint war.

"So, what are you creating here? It looks fascinating!"

Payton, a nonchalant expression on her face, met my gaze with unenthusiastic teen angst. *How does Vanessa deal with them at this age?* "We're working on form and portraits."

"Oh, okay. Who's this supposed to be?"

Payton looked across the room. "Jacobi," she answered, shrugging her shoulders toward one of the boys Vanessa was scolding. "I'm trying to capture how annoying he is."

Looking over the painting again, the girl definitely mastered turning the poor boy into a caricature. "I think you did a great job. Especially with the exaggerated teeth and forehead."

Payton laughed, her nonchalant attitude momentarily breaking into a huge grin. "You see it too, huh?"

I laughed. "Yeah. I bet he jokes all the time. Reminds me of my best friend."

The girl peered at me with narrowed eyes again. "Are you and Ms. Nessa really just friends?"

"Yeah, that's what she says."

"Hmph, if you say so." Payton turned her attention back to her canvas.

"What are we talking about over here?" Vanessa asked, coming over just in time.

"Paintings and friends," I replied.

She mimicked me, licking her lips and lowering her eyes, to mock me. I hadn't realized I'd done that at all. "We're supposed to be friends and you're making it hard for me to remember that."

"My bad." I let out a nervous laughter, instinctively licking my lips again.

Vanessa smacked my chest, soft chuckles spilling from her smile. "Stop that."

"Hey, keep your hands to yourself, Mike Tyson." She rolled her eyes and then turned to the shuffling of feet complementing the occasional clatter of paintbrushes being placed back in their drawers. Vanessa rolled up her sleeves and joined the children in the cleanup effort. As I observed her, a warmth blossomed within me—an appreciation for the woman who effortlessly nurtured creativity in others, realizing she always did the same for me.

The room, now in pristine order, seemed to echo with the hum of shared satisfaction at a day well spent. Vanessa glanced around, a sense of fulfillment radiating from her. As the last paintbrush was put away, she and I lingered in the quiet aftermath of creativity. The teens, now free to explore their own adventures, scampered out of the room leaving Vanessa and me alone.

"Mrs. Collins told me the center might close," I said gently, not wanting to break the fragile peace between us but knowing it had to be said. "If there's anything I can do...I mean, anything to help, you know I will."

"Even if it means ending your partnership with Wright Horizons?" She played with a few stray pieces of her hair while she bit the inside of her mouth. Her eyes narrowed, the tension in her face mirroring the conflict I felt inside. "Not going to lie. I never thought you'd work with a company like them. Wesley's father is all about lining his pockets."

"And what about Wesley?"

"Him, not so much. He just wants his father's approval. Taking over Wright Horizons has always been the plan for him." Vanessa's voice softened, her gaze falling to the table as she continued to twirl the pieces of hair that framed her face.

I reached out, grabbing her hands to stop the fidgeting. Her fingers laced through mine, and that familiar spark, our electricity, coursed through me again. The connection between us never fully disappeared; it lay dormant, waiting for moments like this to remind me of what we had—and what we could've had.

"Stop doing that," she said, pulling her hand away gently, through her eyes further softened with an amused glint. "Go ahead and take a seat. No one else is using this room for the rest of the day."

"Sorry," I muttered, turning and sitting in the chair across from her. "It's just...I don't know. This whole project, it doesn't sit right with me anymore. Don't get me wrong, the building is beautiful. We're working with materials we only dreamed of having access to. But..."

"It's not like saving the world, huh?" Vanessa gave a small nod, her eyes searching mine as if trying to figure out how deep that unease ran. "It's still great what you and Khalil built," she said, her voice gentle but firm. "But don't get sidetracked by the money."

"Yeah, I've been trying to tell Khalil the same thing."

Vanessa's expression shifted, her smile returning as she leaned forward, a playful twinkle back in her eyes. "Speaking of money," she said, her voice light but with that edge. "Where's my cut?"

I raised an eyebrow. "Your cut? What you mean?"

"Yeah, EcoVision Urban Solutions?" she teased. "That's my name y'all are using. I came up with it, run me my coins."

Her laughter was infectious. I remembered the exact day she came up with that name for the company, back when things between us were light and easy. "I don't know about that, love," I said, matching her grin.

"Oh, please. I could sue you, you know. Intellectual property and all that," she quipped. "I know someone. And she's damn good."

I laughed, the tension melting away as I shook my head. "You wouldn't do that. Besides, it felt right."

"Of course it did," she replied, smirking. "I came up with it!"

"That's why I used it." Our laughter echoed in the room. "So, what's up? I know you didn't ask me here for a payout."

Where earlier the air was light, laughter, and creative energy, it pressed down, heavy clouds charged with unspoken truths lingering between us. The smell of paint clung to the air. The soft afternoon light filtered through the large windows, casting muted shadows across the space, making everything feel like it existed in a place between past and present.

Vanessa stood across from me, her arms wrapped around her chest. Her eyes were distant, staring at the floor as though the weight of the words she was about to speak might break her. I swallowed hard, the muscles in my chest tightening with each passing second.

"You remember the night came over? When you and Khalil threw the party?" Her voice was a whisper, but it cut through the room like a cold wind.

I nodded slowly, my heart sinking. "Yeah... I'll forever apologize for the way I treated you that night. I should've known better." My thumb brushed away the tear that slipped down her cheek.

"Well," she sniffled, still not looking at me. "I came to talk to you. I really needed to talk to you."

"I mean, you did more than just talk. You beat my ass." I tried to lighten the mood, though my laughter came out weak, almost desperate.

But she didn't laugh. Her silence stretched between us, heavy and impenetrable. She shook her head. "Not about us, Zay. I didn't care about that. Well...a part of me did. But that's not what I came to talk about." Her voice trembled, the walls of the room closing in on us.

"What was it then?" My voice barely rose above a whisper, the uncertainty gnawing at my insides.

She finally lifted her gaze, locking onto mine with a look that shattered every ounce of composure I had left. "Zay..." she started, her voice cracking under the weight of what she was about to say. "I was pregnant."

The words hit me like a punch to the gut, leaving me breathless. I blinked, my mind racing to catch up with what she'd just said. "What?" My voice cracked, the disbelief thick in my throat.

"I was pregnant, Zay. With our baby."

I stared at her, my body frozen as her words sank in, my heart spiraling. *Pregnant? A baby? Our baby?* My mind swirled in chaotic confusion as questions clawed their way to the surface. My pulse quickened, and I could feel my jaw set, the clench of my teeth trying to hold back the flood of emotions spewing in my mind.

"I...I didn't know," I stammered, shaking my head as if that might somehow make it easier to process, make it unreal.

Vanessa stood there, a picture of fragile strength, her arms still hugging herself as though she could shield herself from the pain of her own words. Her eyes, usually filled with light, were hollow now, filled with a grief that cut me deeper than any physical blow could.

"What happened to the baby?" My voice was barely above a rasp, thick with the ache swelling in my chest. My palms were slick with sweat, my stomach twisted in knots. I was terrified to hear her answer, yet I knew I had to ask.

Her eyes flickered with something—pain, regret, maybe both—before she looked down again, her voice a frail whisper. "I tried to hold on and wait for you to be in a better space. I wanted to let you know sooner. But...I lost it, before I got the chance."

The room tilted, my entire world going along with it. Everything felt wrong. Her quiet confession shattered the remainder of the resolve I had inside of me, and before I could think, I stepped forward, pulling her into my arms. She collapsed against my frame, her body shaking with silent sobs as I held her tighter, more for me than her, trying desperately to piece together the fragments of her heart, her soul—both of us shattered by a truth too heavy to bear.

I buried my face into her hair, inhaling the faint floral and warm sweet scent of her, trying to anchor myself to her in some way, to keep from drowning in the guilt, the sorrow, the regret. "I'm so sorry," I whispered into her hair, my own tears slipping down my face. "I wasn't there when you needed me. I should've been there."

She buried her face into the crook of my neck. The tremors of her pain vibrated through me. All I could do was hold her, helpless to fix what was already broken. Helpless to undo the past that carved these scars between us.

"Tell me you're not mad at me," she asked softly, her voice hoarse from crying. "The one thing my body was made to do and I couldn't get it right."

My chest tightened at her words, self-blame etched into each one. "No, Nessa baby. It wasn't your fault," I said softly, my hands running up and down her back in soothing circles. But deep down, I knew it wasn't enough. Nothing I could say would take away the pain of what she'd gone through alone. The guilt gnawed at me, knowing she carried this loss by herself. "Hey," I murmured, pulling back to look into her eyes. "You can't blame yourself for this. If it was meant to be, we'd have a baby here right now. That's just how life works sometimes."

Vanessa let out a sad, half-hearted laugh. "You sound like my mother."

I stiffened. "She knows?"

Her gaze softened, though pain remained. "Who do you think took me to the hospital?"

Her words pressed down on me again. I could only imagine what her mother thought of me, knowing I hadn't been there, knowing I'd failed Vanessa in the most profound way, a manifestation of her last words to me. "What did she say about what happened?"

"I don't remember much outside the fact that she never told a soul. Not even my dad," she replied quietly. "We swept it under the rug. I graduated, moved back home, started grad school. We never talked about it again."

I hesitated, my mind racing to make sense of everything. "I came to your place the day before your graduation. Waited around for a few hours. You never came."

Vanessa sighed heavily. "I stayed at the hotel with my parents. My things had been packed and moved for at least a week." She wiped the few remaining tears from her eyes, staring deeply into my own, shimmering with unshed tears. "I missed you, Zay. I missed what we had. But...I can't bring myself to go back. I don't want to return to that dark place."

"Is this why you want to remain friends?"

"This...being friends, this is all I can give you right now."

Her words pierced me, slicing through my hopes of what we could've been, but I understood. I didn't have a choice. "I get it," I whispered, squeezing her hand gently. "I don't want to pressure you to do anything you're not ready for."

"Then you need to stop looking at me like that."

"Like what?"

"Like you're in love with me."

"I am," I said, my voice steady, holding her gaze. She needed to see it, to feel the gravity of what I was saying because it was more than just words. It was everything. "I never stopped, Nessa. Not for a second."

"Don't make this harder on me, Zay." She leaned forward, pressing her hand into my chest. "Seeing you again is already confusing enough."

I took a deep breath, trying to find the right words, the ones that would break through the walls she built around her heart. "Look, I know I wasn't there for you when you needed me. I shut down, I pushed you away…and I regret that every day. I wasn't the man you deserved back then, but I've changed. I've learned to face my shit instead of running from it. Therapy helped me see that. I've learned to be honest with myself, with what I feel. And I know I can be that man for you now—emotionally, mentally, all of it. I'm not that same Zay from before."

I let the words settle between us, the truth of them lingering in the air like a promise. "I know it'll take time for you to believe that, and I get it. But I want you to know, I'm here. Not just for now. For good. I'm willing to do whatever it takes to show you I'm different. I want to be the man who can stand by your side, not just when things are good, but when they're bad, too."

Her lips parted, but she didn't speak. I could see the doubt warring in her eyes. I pulled her by her waist, pulling her against me, one hand firm against her waist, the other cradling her chin. "I'm not going anywhere, Nessa. I've spent too long being closed off, and I won't make that mistake again. If you ever decide to give me a chance, you'll see. I'm all in this time."

For the first time, her gaze softened. She didn't say anything, but there was a shift, something that told me she was starting to see it—starting to believe I wasn't the same man who had let her down.

"Okay."

"Okay?" I cupped her face in my hands, waiting for a little sign of reassurance.

"Yes, okay."

Chapter 17

Xavier

After the conversation with Vanessa, the absence that followed hit harder than I expected. Sure, she responded to my texts—short replies, keeping the conversation alive but barely. It wasn't the same as having her near, feeling her warmth in the same room. I knew she felt the pull too, the magnetic thing between us, but something held her back. Hell, maybe it was me. I didn't make it easy back then, shutting her out when I needed her most. She was the one who walked away, said she couldn't handle dealing with me anymore.

But was that warranting never speaking to me again? Acting like the connection we had wasn't stronger than that?

Maybe she needed time now, space to process what it might mean for us to be in each other's lives again. The way we kept circling back to each other like this—it had to mean something, right?

Coming home to the dimly lit confines of the living room in my house in New Orleans, memories replayed like a reel in my mind—Vanessa's laughter, the way her eyes crinkled when I teased her, the soft brush of her fingers against mine, accidental but deliberate all the same. A reality show about ex-wives and girlfriends of football players played in the background—our show. The one we used to laugh at together, side by side, trading jokes as if everything in the world made sense.

Funny isn't it?

A part of me, the part still tethered to this city, found itself missing things I used to take for granted. Houston had its drawbacks for sure. No city could ever replace the foundation New Orleans gave me, but time spent in Houston shifted something in me. It had the potential to fill the cracks and grooves left behind by my shaky upbringing. I couldn't even look around this house, the one I'd dreamed of renovating, without feeling the hollowness of it now.

My gaze landed on the painting above the fireplace, a piece I'd picked up in the French Quarter years ago. It reminded me of her—the colors, the boldness, the layers hiding beneath. It was like looking at the piece of my soul I'd let drift away.

That was on me.

I built that wall first, back when I pushed her away, drowning in my own shit and shutting her out. I destroyed the trust she had in me, and I could see the cracks now, even when we were trying to rebuild. But damn, I wanted to show her I was different now. I wanted her to trust me again, to feel safe with me like she used to. I exhaled deeply, the blunt in my hand a poor substitute for the peace I was chasing.

THE MORNING SKY STRETCHED heavy and low, a thick quilt of gray smothering the light. I stood in front of my grandfather's grave, my breath mingling with the cool air that seeped into my bones. The stone was weathered now, but his name, carved deep in granite, still stood firm. My fingertips traced the letters, each one a small reminder of his presence—solid, unwavering. I needed him now more than ever. The quiet strength he gave me slipped further away with each passing year.

"Hey, Pops," I whispered, my voice carried away with the wind. "I miss you. There's so much happening, and I really need your advice right now."

The silence of the cemetery held my words, cradling them in the cool, still air. I closed my eyes, imagining his voice, his steady hand on my shoulder like he'd done when I was a boy. But all that came was a soft crunch of footsteps behind me. I turned, and there was Mr. Ted, his presence as comforting as it was expected in this somber place. His salt-and-pepper beard and calm, thoughtful expression gave him a dignified air, much like a wise sage. He reminded me of a younger Laurence Fishburne. He'd been there for Ma for the past few years, filling a space that my father, and even Pops, left behind. Something like an old tree growing in the shadow of giants.

"Morning, Zay," Mr. Ted greeted, his voice warm but soft, like he knew exactly where I'd been and why. "You didn't stop by the house yesterday. Your mom said you might be out here."

I managed a weak smile, my eyes flicking back to the grave. "Yeah...I just needed some time with him." Today marked another year since Pops had passed. It took me two years after graduating to finally come to his grave alone, to face the stone and all it meant.

Mr. Ted placed a firm hand on my shoulder, grounding me in the moment. "From what your mom says, he was a good man. He'd be proud of you, you know."

I looked back at the grave, the weight of everything I carried pressing down on me like that thick sky above. "I hope so. I'm just trying to figure it all out, Mr. Ted. This life shit...it's stressful."

He guided me to a nearby bench, and we sat in the quiet. "Talk to me, son."

The levees broke open, and I didn't hold back. "Nessa told me she lost our baby. Back in college. When I was fucking around, being stupid. It's like every time I think I can catch my breath, something else comes along to knock it out of me."

Mr. Ted let out a stream of air. "Oh man. How'd you feel hearing that?"

"Mad as hell." I leaned forward, resting my head in the fist of my hands. My chest heaved, struggling to suppress the build up of emotions within me. I sniffled, forcing the tears back inside.

Mr. Ted draped an arm around me shoulders. "Zay, if you're hurting, it's okay to let that out. Losing a child isn't something easy."

"Fuck," my voice cracked out. "I thought us running into each other was a sign. That this was our time." I pinched the bridge of my nose. "How am I supposed to come back from that? Leaving her to deal with that shit all by herself? How is she supposed to trust me with making her feel safe, if I wasn't there when she needed me most?"

"You start by apologizing. Build the trust from there. Be as vulnerable with her as you are right now."

I blinked, the question catching me off guard. "What do you mean? I'm a man. I'm supposed to protect those around me."

"Yeah," he said, his voice steady. "But who takes care of you? In the few years I've known you, I've watched you pour into other people. Be a shoulder for them to lean on. But when your storm drains overflow, who's the one pumping that stress out of your heart?"

His words cut through me, simple but sharp. I hadn't realized how long I'd been holding everything together, or how I'd forgotten to look after myself in the process. "How do I let that go? How do I stop feeling like I have to be everything for everyone?"

"By understanding that it's okay to not have all the answers," he said, his voice gentle. "It's okay to not be okay sometimes. And by letting those who love you help carry the load." He paused, letting the words settle. "You're not your father, Xavier. You're the man who's always stood back up, no matter how hard life hits. But sometimes, standing tall means leaning on others for support. It's not weakness—it's strength in connection."

His words reshaped something inside me, turning over the way I saw strength. It wasn't about building walls to keep the world out, but bridges to let the people who loved me in. "If I do all that, you think she might be willing to give us another shot?"

Mr. Ted smiled, that warm approval in his eyes. "If that's what you both want, start with honesty, and the rest may follow. But if she doesn't, that's not a sign to go back to your old ways."

We stood up, and as we walked back through the quiet rows of headstones, I felt the weight I carried here begin to lift, piece by piece. It was time to break down the walls, let her see the real me—scars, flaws, and all.

Chapter 18

Vanessa

The hum of soft music filled the bathroom as I stood in front of the mirror, fingers gently working a shea butter and coconut hair cream through my damp coils. The air smelled sweet—the hair products mixing together with the lavender vanilla candle I had burning on the counter. I let out a deep, content sigh, feeling the warmth of the air caress my skin. It was one of those nights where everything felt...right. Calm. Almost peaceful.

I loved this time—the ritual of washing, sectioning, twisting my hair, letting it breathe and coil naturally. There was something about the process that soothed me, like I was re-centering myself. My fingers moved methodically through each section, twisting with care, as if each strand was a whispered reminder that I had time—time to be with myself, to nurture, to reflect.

As I reached for the next section, my phone buzzed on the counter. I ignored it at first, not ready to break the rhythm of my evening. But when it buzzed against, the temptation to glance down became too much. *Zay*. The name popped up on the screen, and just like that, the peaceful moment turned into something else entirely.

My heart did a little skip, and I rolled my eyes at myself.

But I couldn't help it. My fingers slowed, my breath hitched slightly. That butterflies crept up on me, the way it used to back in the day when I'd get those random texts or calls from him. It was silly. I knew that. But a girl could still smile, couldn't she? I wiped my hands on a towel and picked up the phone, pulling my lips into a smirk as I answered.

"Hey, what's up?' I said, hoping my voice sounded more nonchalant than the flutters in my stomach felt.

Pulling the phone away from my ear, I saw the video call icon blink on my screen, his attempt to catch me off guard. I tapped the decline button with a quickness. I wasn't about to let him see me like this, halfway through a twist-out, hair sticking up in every direction.

"Zay, I'm in the middle of doing my hair," I said, shaking my head. "You can't just FaceTime people without letting them know first." I could already picture his grin on the other end, knowing he was imagining me rolling my eyes.

"My bad," he laughed softly, the smooth tone in his voice making me smile despite myself. "I'm just checking on you. I wanted to see if you'd wanna see the construction site. I feel like I've seen you in your element. I want you to see me in mine."

"That could work. I'll let you know... How are you doing? We never really talked about how you felt about the baby."

"It fucked with me a lot, not gonna lie. But I've been leaning into the present and what's in front of me now. How are you?"

"I'm fine." My fingers stopped working on my hair. I shook my head, getting back to work. "This project with Wright Horizons aside, you've done some really great things."

"Oh yeah? How you figure?"

"I may have looked up a few of your projects back in New Orleans."

"Well, then you need to come see the renovations in person."

"Yeah, we'll see."

Xavier laughed into the phone. "I'm gonna let you finish your hair. Thank you for checking. I appreciate it."

"Anytime," I smiled.

"Aight. I'll see you this weekend," he added, his voice lowering. "Be listening for your doorbell,"

My hands froze mid-twist. "What for?"

"Don't worry about that," he said, with that playful edge in his tone, leaving me curious. Always leaving me curious.

Shaking my head, I couldn't help the grin that tugged at the corners of my lips. I leaned back into the mirror, staring at my reflection. The girl staring back at me looked amused, maybe even a little...happy.

"Zay, don't pop your ass over here."

"Now why would I do that," he smirked. "Make sure you eat before you go to sleep."

I smacked my lips, laughing softly before hanging up, but that feeling lingered. The one that had started to take root in my chest.

Damn him.

I continued twisting my hair, but my mind wasn't on the curls anymore. It was on him. On what this meant. On the way my heart felt lighter, and the way the corners of my soul started softening again. I wasn't sure where we were headed or what all of this would lead to, but for the first time in a long time, I didn't mind thinking about the possibilities.

My doorbell chimed, breaking my focus. When I opened the door, a brown take-out bag sat at my doorstep.

Vanessa

Are you on a mission to fatten me up before you go home?

Zay

Never that.

I just know how you get when you're focused.

You can't tame all that hair on an empty stomach.
Vanessa
You're ridiculous...
But thank you
Zay
Anytime, love.

I STOOD BEFORE THE full-length mirror, staring down at the third outfit I'd changed into after my shower. *Still not right.* The dissatisfaction tugged at me as I yanked the shirt over my head, tossing it into the growing heap of discarded clothes piling up on my closet floor. I turned back to the racks of sweaters, their colors arranged like a rainbow of indecision. My fingers stopped on a thin, olive-green cropped cardigan. It slid up my arms smoothly, the soft fabric brushing against the lace of the black bra underneath. The buttons closed with a snap that felt final, decisive.

Back at the mirror, I surveyed the pairing with my light-wash, high-waisted jeans. A good match, finally. But my hands—shaky, restless—had a mind of their own, tugging and twisting at my hair. First a high bun, then low for a braid, then loose again, combing through the waves I'd spent too long manipulating. I caught myself, my fingers pausing mid-tangle. Times like this I wish I had my natural hair out, instead of hidden beneath the hair of others. Let my coils be free.

I glanced at my face. My lash refill from my birthday was still in good shape, framing eyes that told too many stories of sleepless nights and quiet worries. The skincare routine I clung to religiously kept my skin smooth, though the faint shadows under my eyes betrayed my restless mind. I dabbed on a bit of concealer over the dark circles and tapped a pinkish-orange blush on my cheeks.

After lining my lips with a brown pencil, topping it with a sheer gloss, a sigh escaped me, long and deep, unraveling in the empty room. Xavier was the only man who could do this to me, fluster me. *No*, I corrected myself. Not flustered, *giddy*. A laugh bubbled up, echoing through the stillness. Yes, I was giddy—the kind of giddy that made me feel eighteen again. The thought of having lunch with my ex-boyfriend, the man who once held my heart so completely, sent a thrill through me. *The former love of my life*, I reminded myself, though it felt like a lie.

This is insane.

A knock at the door interrupted my spiraling thoughts. My heart thudded in time with my footsteps as I made my way down the hallway, each beat a reminder of the history I couldn't escape. I sucked in a breath before opening the door, my lungs deflating the moment I laid eyes on him.

There he stood, the man who still knew how to steal the air from a room. Xavier leaned against the frame, effortlessly casual in a black graphic tee that hugged his chest and arms in all the right places. His black pants sat just so on his hips, loose and easy, like he had all the time in the world. And, of course, the pristine white sneakers—always impossibly spotless, as if they never touched the ground at all. I marveled at this for years, how he treated his shoes with the kind of reverence usually reserved for art or love. Back in college, I swore he had more shoes than clothes, and it seemed nothing had changed.

But what really hadn't changed was the way seeing him still knocked the breath clean out of me.

"Nessa." Xavier's voice wrapped around my name like velvet, his lips pulling into that smile that always left me off-balance. Those perfectly straight, perfectly white teeth gleamed under that hallway light, making me feel exposed, like he could see right through me. "You look beautiful...I can still say that, even though we're friends, right?"

His eyes roamed over me, slow and deliberate, the way you savor water after wandering the desert. It was as though he was quenching a thirst that had been parched for years.

"It's fine I guess," I said, throwing him a smirk with just enough sass to keep my own heart from racing too fast. I cast him a side-eye, a warning. *Don't play with me, Zay*. "You ready?"

"Ready when you are." His voice, low and rich, slipped over me like warm honey, his New Orleans drawl lingering on every word. It made something deep inside me stir, an ache I hadn't felt in years, one I wasn't sure I wanted to feel again.

I shook my head, retreating into my apartment for my phone, keys, and crossbody bag. *Get it together, Vanessa*, I reminded myself, but the steady rhythm of his presence tugged at my composure. When I stepped back into the hallway, there he was, leaning casually beside the door, close enough to unsettle my thoughts. My hands fumbled with the lock, the damn key refusing to cooperate. I finally managed to hear the click, only to find Xavier standing right behind me, his frame slightly towering over mine. I had to draw in a deep breath to steady myself as he loomed, close enough to feel the heat radiating off his body.

"So, do you actually want a tour of the city, or are you just trying to find a good food spot?" I asked the teasing in my voice meant to cover the flutter of nerves he stirred within me.

His smile grew, slow and knowing, like he understood the effect he had on me. "How about both?"

That smile melted something in me, the way it always had. I rolled my eyes, moving past him toward the elevator. "You are asking for a lot. I'm busy later, so you have time for food. That's it." My tone was sharp, but it was the only defense I had. "And I'm driving."

"You? Miss 'I Hate Driving?'" He chuckled, falling into step behind me.

"Yeah. I don't want you getting any ideas. This is not a date." I said over my shoulder, entering the elevator car.

"Of course not. We're friends, remember?" His voice dropped, and our eyes locked as the elevator doors slid shut, trapping us in the tight space. Words unsaid bounced off the metal walls. I focused on the elevator buttons, my heart pounding in the confined silence.

In the parking garage, I darted ahead, eager to break the tension, and slid into the driver's seat before he had the chance. Xavier eased into the passenger seat next to me, his arm resting comfortably on the center console, brushing against mine. The warmth of his skin seeped through the soft knit of my sweater, a distraction I wasn't prepared for.

I started the ignition, the car humming to life as *Thee Sacred Souls* filtered through the speakers, their soulful sound wrapping around us. Xavier's low hum joined the music, his voice blending in so perfectly that for a moment, I forgot about the road ahead and focused solely on him.

"What do you know about Thee Sacred Souls?"

He grinned, those dark eyes twinkling. "Aww, this my shit. You know I stay on that old school type shit." I continued the drive to Mikki's Soul Food Cafe, as the album played on. His voice laced through the song, and I couldn't help but steal glances, watching the way the music seemed to settle him. Each note carried us deeper into a rhythm we hadn't shared in so long, and for a fleeting moment, it felt like no time had passed at all.

As "Lady Love" began to play, I noticed the shift in him—his thumb tapping his leg in time with the music, his teeth catching the inside of his cheek. It was a small habit, but one I knew well. He was anxious.

Why is he anxious? My hand twitched on the steering wheel, wanting to reach over and stroke the back of his neck, to calm whatever stirred inside of him. But I held back. My car's lane assist beeped, snapping me out of my reverie as I realized I was drifting between lanes.

"Damn, so you trying to kill me?" Xavier laughed, breaking the tension. "I knew something was up when you offered to drive."

"Shut up, Zay," I shot back, heat rushing to my face, joined by a soft smile. "If I wanted to kill you, I would've done it a long time ago."

He chuckled softly, his voice curling around me. "I'm just messing with you, Nessa baby." His arm nudged mine, and the simple touch felt like a current running through me. I tightened my grip on the steering wheel. "So what you been up to since you left college?'

I hesitated. "I, uh, took a gap year before I went to work at my dad's company for a few months and started grad school, then left. Wasn't really feeling the corporate world."

"Well, yeah. That's why you switched your major to Art History."

"Right," I laughed, again. Why was I laughing so much? Nothing in this conversation was funny.

"Then what?" he asked, his voice soft, patient, as if he really wanted to know.

"I took a position with my parent's foundation. Been there ever since," I replied, pulling into the restaurant parking lot. I cut the engine and waited for his response.

"That's surprising."

"What's surprising?" I asked, turning to face him.

"Nothing," he said, brushing it off. "Where are we? This doesn't look like one of those bougie places you talked about growing up."

"That's because it's not."

"Are you sure you not trying to kill me?" he teased again, leaning closer.

"Boy, come see for yourself."

Chapter 19

XAVIER

WE MOVED IN SYNC, as we slid out of the car, the harmony between us so natural it felt like we'd never missed a beat. Vanessa rounded the front of her car, and every now and then our hands brushed, sending tiny shocks up my arm with each accidental touch. It was like I could feel the pulse of the past between us, beating faintly, urging us closer. The tension simmered in the air as we walked into the small, hole-in-the-wall restaurant she'd chosen for us. A waft of slow-cooked meats, savory greens, and sweets greeted us at the door, welcoming us into a world where time seemed to move slower, like the food was cooked with patience and love.

"This reminds me of Lil Dizzy's back home," I said, taking in the place. It had that same down-home, no-frills feel, the kind of spot where you knew you'd leave with a satisfied stomach. Pictures of the owners with various Black celebrities wrapped around the small restaurant, adding to the vibe. But I kept my reaction cool, didn't need Vanessa knowing she might be onto something.

"Yeah, something like that," she said with a smirk she tried to hide, those dark eyes of hers dancing with mischief as she looked up at me. She glanced toward the steam trays filled with food, then back at me. "I'm 1,000% sure, you'll find something here that'll make you forget about the food at home."

I laughed, shaking my head. "You sure about that? Nobody do food like New Orleans."

Her eyes sparkled with challenge. "I bet you take those words back." She glanced around the crowded room, searching for an empty table. The place was packed, but her confidence never wavered.

"And if I don't? What happens then?" I asked, a teasing edge in my voice.

She stopped mid-step, turning to face me, her gaze locked onto mine with playful irritation. "When I lose? I'm not going to lose." She laughed, light and carefree, but there was a fire in her words, like she was daring me to try her.

"Then shake on it." I held out my hand, and she paused, her eyes tracing the motion of my lips as I licked them, heat flashing across her face. *Damn*, Vanessa had always been fine, but now...now she was even more. There was a depth to her beauty, a confidence that radiated through her, making it hard to look away.

"What do I get when I win?" she asked, her voice dropping as she bit her lip, eyes rounding with a hint of hesitation, like she wasn't sure she wanted to answer.

"What do you want?" I asked, keeping my tone light, though something heavy hung in the air with us.

"You." She blinked, her mouth quirking into a grin. "I want you to stop popping up everywhere I am."

So that's how you want to play it.

"Fine. It's a bet."

With a small laugh, she nudged me forward, her hand grazing my waist as we moved toward the lunch counter. The contact sent a rush of heat through me, and I had to will myself not to close the space between us. The scent of her perfume—peonies and cashmere—filled the air around us, mixing with the food, and every part of me craved more than just the meal that was about to hit my plate.

As we stood in line, I couldn't help but tease her again. "You're trying to lose on purpose, aren't you? You just want me around."

"I told you, I'm not losing," she said, flipping her hair playfully into my face. The line shuffled forward, and we stood side by side at the counter. When it was my turn to order, Vanessa placed her hand on my chest, stopping me. "Let me order," she said, and turned to the cashier, her voice smooth and confident. "We'll take a plate with oxtails and rice, mac n' cheese, greens, and yams. And another plate with fried fish, yams, and greens. And two waters."

Before she could pull out her wallet, I was already swiping my card. There was no way I was letting her pay for anything.

"I was going to pay," she protested, her eyes narrowing playfully.

"I asked you to show me around, remember? I got it." I replied, flashing her a grin that silenced her, but left a smile on her lips.

We found a table tucked in the back, the hum of the restaurant fading as Vanessa and I settled into a comfortable conversation. She caught me up on the work she'd been doing at her parents' non-profit, her passion spilling into every word. Listening to her, it was clear she hadn't changed at her core—still that same woman who gave her heart to everyone around her. Back in college, I thought I was just another one of her projects, but I was wrong. She didn't do charity; she did love. And I had been too blind to see that then.

"Are you going to keep staring at me, or are you going to try it?" she teased, pushing the plate of oxtails toward me, her eyebrow raised.

I smirked. "Now, I know you are trying to lose on purpose. You know my mama oxtails the best around."

"Just try it," she insisted, taking a bite of her fried fish, her lips closing around her fingers in a way that made me swallow hard.

I forked a piece of meat, eyeing her with skepticism before taking a bite. Instantly, the rich flavors hit my tongue—the slow-cooked beef melting into garlic, onion, and peppers. My eyes closed as I chewed, the taste bringing me right back to my mother's kitchen. It was damn near perfect.

Vanessa smiled knowingly, stealing a piece of meat from my plate, her moan of satisfaction filling the space between us. "I told you."

I opened my eyes to find her watching me, confident and radiant. "It's aight," I admitted with a smirk.

"Aight?" she laughed, shaking her head. "Your face says more than that. You lit up like you just ate at your mom's house."

I shook my head. "Fine. It's cool," I chuckled.

"You're full of shit. You know that right?" Vanessa's soft voice jingled in my ears, so light and feathery amidst the energetic conversations around us in the restaurant.

Now and then, our eyes would lock, and it felt like the rest of the world blurred away. The rhythm of the past was still there, lingering in the spaces between us, waiting to be rekindled.

"Deja vu," I laughed, leaning back in my chair, still watching her.

Vanessa cocked her head, scrunching her nose in that cute way she did when she was curious. "What's funny?"

"This. Us. It feels like deja vu. Like the day I met you at Essence Cafe."

She bit her lip, trying to hide her smile. "I remember. Y'all had us all over New Orleans that day."

"Yeah," I grinned, the memory warming me. "And you still look the same. A little more buttoned up, but the same nonetheless."

Her eyes narrowed, playful but challenging. "Buttoned up? What's that supposed to mean?"

"Your vibe. It's different. I don't know if it's because of me being around or what," I shrugged, taking another sip of my drink. "I don't want you to be uncomfortable around me."

Vanessa shrugged her shoulders, biting her cheek before saying, "I'm not uncomfortable. We're just... in a different space now. I've already told you, I'm not going down that road again."

I leaned forward, resting my elbows on the table. "You keep saying that. Are you trying to convince me, or yourself?"

Her eyes darted away, but I reached for her hand, gently lacing my fingers through hers. She hesitated, her gaze meeting mine as if deciding whether to pull away, but she didn't.

"Zay."

"Nessa," I said softly, my thumb brushing the back of her hand. "I'm just trying to be here, in the present."

"Same," she whispered, though there was a trace of uncertainty in her voice. "So, are you ready to tell me I won?" Our fingers toyed with each other as we finished our meal.

"Naw. It was aight."

"Stop lying."

"I'm not." A devilish grin took over my face. "Where are we off to next?"

"There is no next. I have plans later." I picked up and threw away our trash as we walked out of the building, heading toward her parked car.

"Nessa, come on," I teased, a playful grin curling at the corner of my lips. "You really gonna leave me hanging? We were having a good time."

She shot a look at me, folding her arms but clearly amused. "I am leaving you hanging. I've got to check out this exhibit before it leaves."

"What exhibit is it?"

"*Souls of Black Folks* at the Contemporary Arts Museum," she replied, then quickly added, "but it's not your thing."

My eyebrows raised, pretending to be offended. "You think art about Black life isn't my thing? I'm hurt."

She rolled her eyes and smirked, trying to keep up her front. "I just figured you'd be busy, that's all. You know with meetings and networking."

"Please," I chuckled, stepping closer into her space. "The only thing on my calendar for today is hanging with with you. And you are making it the best day I've had since I've been in Houston, friend."

"Fine," she sighed, then laughed. "You can tag along. But only because I don't trust you to actually pay attention anyway."

Vanessa walked beside me, her movements fluid and easy, like she was a part of the air itself, always grounding me but just out of reach. She entered the car, as I did on the passenger side, backed out of the parking spot and drove toward the street. We sat in silence for a while, as she maneuvered through the rush of traffic.

"You putting anything on to listen to?" I asked, leaning back, feeling the tension that always bubbled when I was near, now her settle into something softer.

"Yeah. See if you can guess who this is." Within moments, the bass-heavy beat of classic Houston rap filled the car, a chopped and screwed melody that was unmistakable. I listened closely, trying to place the voice that drifted through the speakers, but the slow drawl didn't belong to anyone I recognized.

"Is he rapping in cursive?" I teased, cocking my head. "I know it's not Kevin Gates, but whoever it is, sound like him a little."

"Definitely not Gates," she laughed, a sound that rippled through the stillness of the car like a memory. "It's Mexican OT. And the other guy is Sauce Walka. Some of the kids at the center put me on. I had the same reaction as you."

"That's crazy," I said, nodding my head to the beat. "They don't listen to the OG's?"

"They do," she shrugged, keeping her eyes on the road. "But there's always room for new stuff."

"Yeah," I replied, bobbing my head to the music. "How's your Mom and Dad doing?"

"Good," she shrugged. "My dad's retired now, but you know how he is. Always working on something. My mom and I...She can just be so...ugh, sometimes."

"You biting your cheeks again," I said, reaching over without thinking, brushing my fingers lightly against her chin. She stiffened slightly but didn't pull away. "You can't let her get to you like that."

Vanessa's lips pressed into a thin line, her fingers tightening on the steering wheel. "We're working on it, though." Vanessa's fingers flexed on the steering wheel. "I think we're headed in the right direction this time."

"Is that why you've been stressing?"

She glanced at me, her eyes flashing with a vulnerability she rarely let show, then turned back to the road. "What makes you think I'm stressed?"

I smiled, watching the way her hands gripped the wheel. "Biting your cheeks. Your eyebrows are all bunched up, shoulders tense. Classic signs of my Nessa baby in distressed."

"One, I'm not you're baby. Two, maybe you're right," she admitted softly, her voice barely audible above the music. Then, she turned the conversation back to me, a hint of concern in her eyes. "How are the renovations really going?"

I shifted in my seat, rolling my shoulders as my irritation with the project settled over me. Without a word, Vanessa's hand moved from the wheel to my neck, her fingers kneading gently into the tight muscles. A soft moan slipped from my lips before I could catch it, the tension melting under her touch.

"That bad, huh?" she teased, her voice softer now, the intimacy of the moment wrapping around us.

"Yeah, just ready for it to be over," I muttered, the warmth of her hand soothing me in a way only she could. "Let's not talk about it right now."

She nodded, her fingers still working into my neck, and I let out a sigh, sinking deeper into the seat. The music continued, but it was the sound of her voice that I wanted to hear most.

"So, what's been going on with you?" she asked, her fingers finally leaving my skin as she returned her hand to the wheel.

"Now who's giving the third degree?" I teased back, the tension in my chest easing further as I smiled at her.

She laughed softly. "Hey, you've been picking me apart this whole time. It's only right I return the favor."

"Well," I started, thinking back over the past few years, "mostly good, I guess. Ma's been better. But I was lost for a while, especially after you left."

Her face twisted, a mixture of confusion and regret. "I didn't leave you, Zay. You left me."

I raised an eyebrow, a smirk tugging at my lips. "That's not how I remember it."

"Well, that's my story and I'm sticking to it," she shot back, her voice soft but firm.

I let it go, shaking my head as I leaned back again. "When I found out you left New Orleans for good, that's when I knew I had to get my shit together. Ma suggested a grief counselor when things got bad with her cancer, and after that, I kept going. Helped me work through a lot."

"Like what," she asked, her voice gentler now, almost hesitant. I noticed the way she bit her cheeks again, the same nervous habit she'd had as long as I'd known her.

I chuckled softly. "Damn, you want to know everything huh?"

"I'm just giving you the same treatment you gave me."

"Fair enough," I said, nodding. "Well, you for one. Losing my pops. My dad leaving us. Katrina. Life. When you're young, you think you got it all figured out, but then life starts and you realize you don't know shit."

Vanessa's eyes stayed fixed on the road, her face softening as she listened. "Yeah, I get that."

"Therapy helped me be a better man. I needed that clarity, especially after losing you. But I kept going even when I thought we were done for good. Had to do it for myself."

Her eyes flickered with something I couldn't quite place. "So, how are you now?"

"Better. For the most part."

"Do you still go to therapy?"

"Here and there. When I think I need a tune up," I joked, the heaviness lifting slightly.

"A tune-up?" She repeated, glancing at me with a raised brow.

"Yeah. Like when I knew there was a chance I'd run into you again. Figured I needed all the help I could get," I added with a laugh, the weight of old memories slipping away.

Vanessa smiled, her eyes soft as she pulled into the parking garage. Well, I'm happy for you. Genuinely."

As I moved to get out of the car, her hand rested on my arm, her touch lingering.

"I appreciate you being honest with me," she said softly, her eyes locking onto mine. "Letting me in. It's all I ever wanted."

I placed my hands over hers, squeezing gently. "Just doing what I should've done before. And whenever you need somebody to tell what's on your mind, I'm here. Always."

Our eyes held for a moment longer, something passing between us that felt bigger than either of us could name.

Chapter 20

Vanessa

The cool air of the museum was a welcome respite from the afternoon sun as we stepped inside, a hush settling over us that felt almost sacred. Art museums and galleries were my kind of place—quiet, filled with stories told in brushstrokes and colors, each one unraveling something deeply human. And today, with Xavier here, I was lowkey excited to share the moment. Even more, as I watched genuine interest take over his face as his eyes roamed over the exhibit title: *Souls of Black Folks*.

"I feel special knowing I have my own personal tour guide," Xavier spoke, bumping my shoulder with his arm. "Lead the way."

Suppressing the smile that fought to bloom across my face, I nodded, relishing the warmth of his gaze. We wandered through the rooms, stopping at each piece, my heart swelling every time he asked a question about the artwork or commented on the emotions he saw in each piece. Back in college, he would halfway pay attention through my breakdown of different exhibits shown in the New Orleans Museum of Art. But here he was, nodding and taking it all in with careful attentiveness.

We finally came to a large painting, a beautiful mess of color and longing. Two figures, lovers reaching toward each other, painted in shades of blue, gold, and red, their hands almost touching but just out of reach. I felt Xavier come up beside me, close enough for the heat of his chest to spread across my back.

"It's beautiful," I murmured, my eyes tracing the outlines, the softness in their expressions that mingled with their distance. My head couldn't decide if I was thinking about the painting or the feeling creeping over as Xavier stood so close, yet not close enough.

"Yeah," he said softly, something layering his voice—a quiet depth I wasn't expecting. "The way they're reaching...it's like they're so close, but something's holding them back." His gaze shifted to me, warm and intense eyes drinking me in, from head to toe. "Makes me think of us."

A shiver traced down my spine, but I forced myself to look at the painting, hoping he would miss the impact his words had on my expression. "That's one way to look at it."

He let out a soft chuckle, his tone lowering as he wrapped an arm around my shoulders. "Come on, you know what I mean."

I turned to him, finally letting myself look up, searching his face for any hint of the old Xavier—the one who'd had all these walls up, shutting me out when it was most important to let me in. But this version of him felt different. Older, wiser, finer.

"Zay, I still have love for you, but it's complicated," I started. "We've both changed."

He nodded slowly, his gaze steady on me. "Yeah, we have. But that doesn't mean it has to be complicated. I know things ended worse than either of us could've imagined, but we're here now. I want to try."

I swallowed, the weight of his words settling in my stomach. We'd laid out everything from the past and wiped the slate clean. However, there were parts of me that still felt raw, guarded. But the way Xavier looked at me, his gaze so sincere, broke down some of the walls I'd built up.

"Do you ever wonder what it would've been like if we hadn't split up?"

A slow breath left his lips, as we turned to walk through the remainder of the exhibit, hand in hand. "Every damn day. But maybe we needed time to grow, to find our way back. What if we're ready now?"

"Maybe," I said, looking at the ground.

"Look, I'm not trying to pressure you or anything. I just want a chance. Slowly, carefully—whatever you need."

Something about his tone, the patience with which he spoke, his strong stance like he was ready to stay however long it took, softened me. The tension eased throughout my body, and I couldn't help the faint smile tugging at me lips. "Alright, maybe we can take it slow. Test the waters."

His grin was immediate, and soon warmth filled my chest, reminding me why I'd fallen for him in the first place. "So, you wanna keep this "friend outing' going? Show me a few more places?" he asked, wrapping his arms around my waist.

"You think you're slick," I laughed, raising an eyebrow. "Sure, why not."

We wandered through Houston as if discovering it for the first time, eventually making our way to Project Row Houses in Third Ward, marveling at the artwork and installations celebrating the sacredness of Black resilience and creativity. Finally, the day ended with us at a car show, a parking lot full of slabs in every color imaginable—deep purple, electric blue, candy apple red—all polished and gleaming in the late afternoon sun. The cars sat low, some bumping old-school Z-Ro, Lil Keke, and UGK tracks, others shining with intricate murals on the hoods, every vehicle an ode to the city's distinct style and pride.

Xavier checked out a classic Cadillac, his eyes lighting up as he took in the scene. "You know," he murmured, nudging me, "I've always wanted one of these. Can't think of a better ride to show off around town."

I laughed, shaking my head. "You'd have too much fun with one of these."

He grinned, catching my gaze and holding it for a moment that stretched, making everything around us blur. And in that instant, surrounded by candy-painted cars and the hum of Houston's heartbeat, I realized that this day, these moments, were the memories I'd been yearning for. The ones I'd tried to hold back from, fearing they'd only hurt me again. But with him looking at me, so open, so present, all I wanted was to dive back in and see where this could lead.

"Today was perfect," he said, walking us back to my car. "You should let me plan the next date."

"This wasn't a date," I laughed off.

"Exactly, which is why I need to plan it," he replied, with and easy smile that made my knees weak. "Come on, just one night." His eyes sparkled with his signature confidence that told me he'd already won me over.

"Zay." I shook my head, feigning exasperation.

"Stop overthinking it," he said, his hand cupping my cheek. I rolled my eyes, trying not to smile. "What's complicated about dinner and some good music? Give us a real shot to see what this could be."

I opened my mouth, ready with another excuse, but the words caught in my throat as he reached for my hand, holding it lightly, as if he were afraid I'd pull away.

"I promise, no pressure," he said, his voice softer, more serious. "Just a night out. If you're not feeling it, we'll call it what it is—a dinner between friends. But if you are feeling it..." His eyes flicked down to our joined hands before meeting mine again, and I felt a shiver run down my spine. "I'm not coming up off you."

I let out a slow breath, unable to hide the warmth creeping into my cheeks. "You're really not going to let this go, are you?"

He shook his head, grinning. "Not a chance," he said, placing a soft kiss to the back of my hand.

I bit my lip, weighing my options—or pretending to, because deep down, I already knew my answer. "Alright, Zay," I said, trying to sound reluctant, but I couldn't help the smile that tugged at my lips. "One night."

Maybe this time, it'd be better to dip my toe in first.

Part III

"You're My Latest, My Greatest Inspiration" - Teddy Pendergrass

Chapter 21

❖

Vanessa

Xavier University - November 2014

"Mom! Dad! You're here!" I tightly hugged both of my parents. "Come in, come in." We walked into the renovated duplex they'd rented for me for my junior year. My mother's heels clacked against the polished hardwood floors as she raised a judging eye around the entryway.

When Xavier came over after class, it took everything in him to get me to sit still and relax. And yet, my stomach remained in knots. In the two years since Xavier and I were a couple, he'd never met my parents in person. I preferred it that way. I mentioned him in conversation here and there and he popped up in a call home every once in a while, but this weekend would be the first time he'd officially meet Mr. And Mrs. Taylor. So why did I feel like I was walking *The Green Mile*?

"Vanessa, it smells absolutely delightful here. Are you cooking?" My father asked, taking my face gently in his hands like he did when I was little, kissing me on the cheek.

"Now, Douglass, you know Vanessa would burn toast," my mother chuckled. "Come here sweetheart. Your mother deserves a hug, too." My mother's arms squeezed me for dear life. Her strong perfume stole my breath as she left a wet kiss on my cheek. "Now, what's this special reason you begged us to visit?"

"Well, there's someone I want you to meet...officially."

My father gave my mother a knowing glance.

"Zay!" Within seconds, my love turned the corner and swaggered into the foyer. His charming smile brought more lightness to the entryway than the sun outside. *How the hell was he so calm?* "Mom. Dad. This is Xavier Morris. Xavier, these are my parents, Douglass and Vivian Taylor."

"Nice to meet you, Xavier Morris," my dad responded, stretching out his hand to shake Xavier's.

"Nice to meet you too, Mr. Taylor. Mrs. Taylor. Nessa talk about y'all all the time." Xavier extended his hand to my mother, who left it hanging in the space between them. I quickly took his hand in mine, caressing his arm with the other, trying to lessen the sting of her blatant rejection.

"Likewise," my mother said, frost in her voice. "And...Xavier, is it?... Are you a friend of Vanessa's?"

Mom, be for fucking real.

"No, Mom. Don't you remember?" I said between nervous laughs. I looked at Xavier, the vein in his neck beginning to bulge. "Xavier is my boyfriend. I've mentioned him before."

"Obviously things are serious, Vivi, or else we wouldn't be standing here meeting on this special occasion. How about we sit?" My father moved to enter the living room to the left, my mother following close behind him.

I turned to Xavier, wrapping my arms around his waist and pressing my forehead to his chest. The smell of his cologne comforted my anxious soul. "I'm so sorry about that."

He lifted my face with his free hand. "It's all good, love. At least I know you weren't lying about your Momma. Pops seem cool, though." He kissed my lips gently. "Come on."

Xavier laced his fingers with mine and we walked to meet my parents in the cozy living room. They sat on the loveseat facing the window, while Xavier and I took a seat on the couch facing them.

"So, Xavier, you attend Xavier University, correct?" my father asked.

"Yes, sir. It's my last year. Graduating in May, God say the same."

"What are you majoring in?"

"Business," Xavier cleared his throat. "With a focus on entrepreneurship."

My father's eyebrows shot to the sky the same way they did whenever he heard of a new business venture he could be interested in. "Oh really? Are you interested in starting your own company one day?"

"May—," Xavier started.

"Dad," I interrupted. "He has this really great idea to mix eco-friendly real estate development projects to boost affordable housing. Zay, tell him about your concept."

I looked to my mother, hoping to see some sign of acceptance. Instead, she watched me carefully. My father, on the other hand, looked at Xavier with intrigue as he gave my father details on his hypothetical company.

"Well, it's just a concept, really. Something me and my brother Khalil thought about one night in the dorm room."

"Really? I'm intrigued." My father leaned forward and his eyes lit up at the prospect of finding a new company to invest in before anyone else had the chance. "Do tell."

"Oh, Dad. It's incredible, really. There's loads of abandoned buildings around the city and—"

"Vanessa," my mother interjected. "I do believe Xavier can speak for himself."

I sank into the couch and Xavier, always sensing my emotional state, grabbed my hand and massaged the inside of my palm with his thumb. Then, he continued telling my Dad about what he and Khalil were working on.

"Well, yeah, like Nessa said. Beaucoup project buildings been sitting empty for years after Katrina. I read an article about eco-friendly affordable housing and the idea just came from that."

"Tell them the name." I looked at Xavier, smiling brightly. "It's a really good name."

Xavier laughed. "Of course you think it is."

"Well, let's hear it. Every strong business needs a strong name." My father urged Xavier on.

I locked eyes with Xavier, nudging him gently before he started speaking.

"EcoVision Urban Solutions."

Xavier gave my father the breakdown of the name as I looked on with adoration. It was the same breakdown I'd given him that day by the lake. It warmed my heart to see Xavier go back and forth with each of my dad's questions. This friendly spar between two of my favorite people in the world made me smile. Xavier shared concepts about the business I didn't know existed. Clearly, he and Khalil were giving this much more thought than Xavier let on, or even shared with me. Watching my man enthusiastically share about his company made me fall even more in love with him. This moment would've been perfect, if my mother wasn't enveloping us in her icy aura. Her eyes fixated on me, the arch of her brow becoming a permanent fixture on her wrinkle free forehead.

"Well, Xavier. It sounds like you and your friend have something pretty viable on your hands." My father advised. "I'd really like to get in on it. How much capital do you and Khalil have on hand?" Xavier's hands subtly started to shake in mine. I moved to still it with my other hand.

"Well, hardly any right now. It's been hard with both of us finishing school. We're hoping to start saving after graduation and getting full time jobs."

"So, you're broke?" My mother's question felt more like a statement.

"Depends on what you mean by broke. If you're talking about whether I'm happy with the direction my life is going, and who's coming with me, I'd say I'm pretty rich." Xavier retorted.

"I think that's a great way to live life, Xavier." My dad added, leaning back to sweep his arm over and pat my mother's shoulders. "I'd like to talk more about your business idea later. It's been a while since I've heard of an idea as novel as yours."

"Thank you, sir. That's pretty reassuring coming from you. Vanessa told me how you run your private equity firm."

"Oh really? I didn't think she paid much attention to it." I felt my father's nurturing eyes on me. "Just remember, anything is possible, as long as it feels like a sure thing."

My father turned his head toward the dining room. "Now, I have an even more pressing question. I have been wanting to know what that delicious smell is ever since we stepped foot in the door."

I popped up from the couch. "Yes! Dinner. Everyone follow me." The knot in my stomach eased into a loose bow as I ushered my parents and Xavier to the dining room table. Conversation and merriment flowed amongst us—well, most of us. My mother remained mostly unresponsive, only offering one or two word answers to any questions Xavier asked her. Before long, our plates were empty.

"Oh my goodness. I have never had a plate of red beans that good. Xavier, these were delightful." My father praised me.

"Oh, I didn't make these." Xavier corrected, before smiling in my direction.

"Well, what restaurant did you order from Vanessa?" My mother asked, finally adding something to the conversation.

I smiled at Xavier before turning to my parents sitting across the table from us. "I didn't order from a restaurant. I made them." I watched as my parents turned to each other, gobsmacked.

"Vanessa, you've got to be joking."

"Xavier, this is the same girl that set the house on fire trying to make toast." My father added, laughing.

"Hey, now. I worked really hard on these." I felt Xavier's hand rest on my neck and massage just beneath my ear with his thumb.

"She really did, Mr. And Mrs. Taylor. Every time I tried to do something, she pushed me out of the way." He looked down at me. "It was real cute to watch."

"Well, I'm glad everyone got their jokes in today," I pouted. "Xavier, can you help me bring the dishes into the kitchen?"

"Sure, love." We stood to collect the plates before my mother raised from her chair.

"No, let me help. I haven't gotten any alone time with my own daughter."

I followed my mother into the kitchen as Xavier sat to continue talking with my dad.

"Dinner was delicious, sweetheart."

Was that a compliment?

"Thanks mom. I wanted it to be special." I loaded the empty plates into the dishwasher. "So, what do you think?"

"About what?"

I rolled my eyes. "You know what. What do you think about Zay?"

My mother pressed her lips together before sighing. "You know, he's not what I would have picked for you."

"No, Mom," I sighed. "He's not, but he's a great person. And he's so intelligent. You heard him and Dad talking about his company. You of all people know how hard it is to get Dad excited about a company."

"Vanessa, sweetheart, you shouldn't be getting serious with him. Think about your future."

"And what if I am?" I turned to see my mother standing stoic with her hands on her hips. "We've been together for almost two years, Mom."

"Vanessa, listen to yourself. We did not send you down here to chase some boy around. If you wanted to do that, you could've done that at home. We have a plan."

"Plans can change, mom." I fixed myself a glass of water as the fire brewing between my mother and I made the moisture in my body evaporate. The hair on my arms and neck stood at attention. "And I'm not chasing Zay around."

"Oh please, Vanessa. We've been here for four hours, and not once have we heard anything about what you've been doing or how school is going. It's been Xavier this, Xavier that."

"Yes, because he's amazing. I've been trying to get you to see that. You've been too judgmental to see or hear any of it."

"Look, Vanessa. This was cute, but you can't expect me to be onboard with this relationship. What's going to happen when he graduates next semester? When you graduate next year? You'll be back in Houston and Xavier will be here. Long distance relationships don't work, Vanessa. Especially with someone who won't have two nickels to rub together and visit every time either of you gets lonely. And if you think you're going to be flying your narrow ass down every weekend, you're mistaken." My mother's poised demeanor slipped. She never cursed or let her country twang out unless she was truly upset. *Upset for what?* This was my life and she couldn't control my decisions any longer.

"I'm not coming back to Houston," I said under my breath, taking in the details of the beige tile floor of my kitchen.

"Excuse me?" My mother walked over to stand directly in front of me by the sink. "What the hell did you just say?"

Looking up, I couldn't escape the disappointment filling my mother's eyes. It made me hesitate before repeating it. "I'm not coming back to Houston. I'm staying here."

"Like hell you are!" Fire raged in my mother's eyes. "Thirteen years of private schools, tutors, internships...and you're throwing that all away! Do you know how hard your father and I worked to give you the life you had? Do you know how many sacrifices my mother made so you could stand here and make selfish decisions?"

"Mom, I appreciate everything, really. It's just...I want something different."

"Like what, Vanessa? Playing Susie Homemaker to someone who can't afford you the lifestyle we've given you?" My mother responded curtly. "We have a plan. We let you come here so you could fill whatever void you think you've missed out on. The next step is graduating with your business degree, then grad school, then working in your father's company."

I bit my lip, nervous for my mother's reaction to my next words. "I also changed my major."

"What the hell do you mean, you changed your major?! I filled out those forms out myself, Vanessa!" Her eyes glared at me with the sadness and fury of all the ancestors that came before us. But if she wanted a screaming match, that's what I would give her.

"I changed it this past summer! I'm majoring in Art History now!"

"For fuck's sake, Vanessa! Why do you insist on throwing your life away?!" The carefully coiffed waves of my mother's hair shook frenzied around her face. "You're not a child anymore. Grow the hell up and start acting like an adult!"

"I'm not throwing my life away, Mom!" Our raised voices caused my father and Xavier to make their way to the kitchen. "And maybe you'd see I am being an adult, if you'd stop treating me like a child!"

"Whoa, what's all the racket? The neighbors are going to call the police." My father questioned, looking with worry between my mother and I.

"Mom thinks I'm childish because I don't want to go back to Houston and I changed my major."

"Everything I worked for and fought so hard for, she's throwing it down the drain, Douglass." My father moved to rub my mother's shoulders. Xavier came to stand beside me. I rolled my eyes at my mother's attempt to play victim.

"Sweet pea, what's your mother talking about?"

"Dad, I don't want to work at your company. I hate business. I'm staying here. I found this really amazing non-profit where I get to paint and teach kids about art. I love the work I've been able to do with the kids. I can't leave."

"Are you sure about that, Vanessa?" My father asked me, still consoling my mother. "You know we do have the foundation at home."

"I know, Dad, but it won't feel the same."

"Enough with the damn feelings! Vanessa, you're being ridiculous! You're moving back home and that's final. Douglass, tell her she's coming home, even if I have to drag her ass back myself."

"Slow down, Vivi."

"Mr. And Mrs. Taylor, the kids really love her. She's been exposing them to local artists and everything. A few of her students got some of their pieces on display in a gallery in the French Quarter."

I watched my mother shoot an accusatory look in Xavier's direction. "You know what, Xavier? I think I've heard enough from you this evening. It's best if you leave. This is a family conversation."

"Vivian. That's enough." My father's grasp tightened around my mother's shoulders, trying to temper her anger.

"No, it's not. Somebody needs to say it."

Zay moved me behind him, his hand on my waist, as he addressed my mother. "Look, Mrs. Taylor. I mean no disrespect but—"

"Then don't say anything I may take as disrespect." The air in the room was charged. A line had been drawn separating Xavier and myself from my parents. The already too small space and division of the counter felt stifling.

"Mom! Don't talk to him like that!" I felt hot, wet tears falling from my face. Xavier's strong arms held me tightly. He whispered something but I couldn't make it out from the ringing in my ears.

"So now you're sticking up for him?" My mother's voice sounded different. Weak. Pained.

"She ain't gotta stick up for me, but you should listen to what your daughter wants." Xavier cut in. The tight way in which he spoke let me know he was trying hard to keep his cool and stay respectful.

Vivian laughed hysterically. "And what is that supposed to be? To be stuck here with you? Oh, I forgot. You're rich. In case you didn't know, love don't pay bills, Xavier."

"Vivian, stop." My father took my mother by the arms, turning her to face him.

"No, I will not stop!" Vivian broke free from Douglass' grip and started her march toward me. "Don't you come crying to me when you start missing what we've provided for you! If you think we're going to foot the bill while you throw your life away, you're mistaken!"

"I don't give a fuck about what you've done for me!" I screamed back, getting into my mother's face. Xavier's efforts to hold me back were in vain.

"How dare you say that?! Do you know what I gave up to raise you?!"

"Clearly it was pointless, because I can't wait to be away from you!"

"I can't believe you've let some Tom, Dick, and Harpo get your mind all fucked up, you spoiled—!"

"Vivi! Nessa! Enough!" My father yelled, slamming his hand on the counter. His voice boomed through the room silencing us all. There were only a few times I'd heard my dad yell at my mom or myself that way. The most recent being when I begged them to attend Xavier with Kelly. My mother was hellbent on keeping me under the microscope of her thumb.

My father turned toward Xavier and I, offering a small but useless smile. The vein in his forehead throbbed with its own pulse. "Look, it's late. Tempers are hot. Vivi, let's go."

He walked over to get my mother, the two of us still in a stand-off with each other. Her eyes turned glassy as he pulled her away. Before turning to leave, my father looked Xavier deep in the eyes. "It was nice meeting you, Xavier. I still meant what I said earlier."

"Yes, sir," Xavier replied through gritted teeth.

"I'll call tomorrow to talk. You both get some rest. Love you, sweet pea."

"Bye, Dad," I managed to choke out. I watched as my mother and father walked down the hall to the door. I listened closely for the latch of the door to click before slumping on the floor and letting all the hurt my mother caused me to flow freely from every pore of my body. I don't know when it happened, but Xavier cradled me. One of his arms kept my head resting over his heart as I sat between his legs. The fingers from his free hand moved along my spine, up and down, trying to soothe my heavy sobs and anguish. The soft hum of the dishwasher filled the silence between us. We must have sat there for an eternity before I was able to form coherent sentences again.

"Zay, I'm so sorry. I didn't expect that to happen." I sniffled.

"Nah, you good, love. As long as you said whatever you needed to say."

"It's always like this. Every time I stand up to her things just blow up."

"It's going to be okay. I'm still here. I'm not going anywhere. Besides, you know I like to prove people wrong," he said, softly laughing.

"Yeah."

I craned my head up to face his. Xavier's head rested against the cabinet next to the dishwasher. His gaze focused on the hallway and I could see his jaw clenched tight. I nuzzled my face further into his chest and felt the thunderous beat of his heart. His body was hot against mine. He shifted against me, burying his face into the top of my head.

"I love you." He muffled into my hair.

I looked up at him and saw the same mixture of pain and anger clouding his eyes that filled my own.

"I love you, too," I said as I sealed my words with a soft kiss on his lips. I didn't know what it was but that night something changed inside of Xavier. I was used to my mother making me feel inadequate. It hurt my heart to think that Xavier may be feeling the same way. I wrapped my arms around his waist to match the intensity in which he held me. Quiet tears pricked my eyes again then fell in heavy drops down my cheeks. I fell asleep with Xavier and I still in the same position. When I woke the next morning in bed, I was just thankful he was still there.

Chapter 22

Vanessa

As I sat on the couch in Dr. Smith's cozy office, my teeth worked diligently on the inside of my cheek—a nervous habit I couldn't seem to shake. The soft smell of sandalwood and lavender filled the air, a calming contrast to the tension swirling inside me. My mother sat next to me, poised and regal as ever. She looked like she was attending a board meeting, not a therapy session. Her curls were meticulously styled, her black wool sheath dress hugging her frame like it was made for her. Well, it was custom made for her, as was the rest of her wardrobe.

Dr. Smith, ever the peaceful anchor, sat across from us, her twisted locs framing her serene face. Her presence was calm yet powerful, like a quiet storm brewing just beneath the surface. I'd been seeing her for almost two years now, and today, she was guiding me into new territory—this long-overdue conversation with my mother.

"Vanessa," Dr. Smith began, her tone gentle but probing, "why don't we start with you? You've mentioned feeling like your dreams weren't accepted by your mother. Can you share more about that?"

I took a breath, steadying myself. I'd prepared for this, but the words still felt like sandpaper on my tongue. "It's just... every time I pursued something I was passionate about, it felt like my mother dismissed it. Like she was always there with a critique as to why it wasn't practical." My voice trembled slightly, but I pushed on. "I never felt like she truly believed in me."

Dr. Smith nodded, her warm gaze encouraging me to continue. "And how did that make you feel, Vanessa?"

Tears pricked at the corners of my eyes as I stared down at my hands. "Small. Like nothing I did would ever be enough."

From the corner of my eye, I saw my mother shift in her seat. Her perfectly composed face tightened, just for a moment, before she responded, her voice laced with restraint. "That's not true, Vanessa. I always wanted what was best for you. I pushed you because I knew you could do more, be more. I strived to give you the world, but it never seemed like it was enough."

Dr. Smith let the silence stretch, allowing us both to feel the weight of those words before she spoke. "Vivian, it sounds like you were coming from a place of love, but it's important to acknowledge how Vanessa perceived your actions. There's a difference between intention and impact."

My mother crossed her legs, her manicured fingers clasped tightly in her lap. "I never stood in her way. Vanessa wanted dance lessons, so we found the best academy. Horseback riding? We hired a private trainer. I never stopped her from doing anything. But when she made her own decisions after high school—ones that weren't good for her future—I had to step in. I've always been there, cleaning up her messes."

That last sentence hit me like a punch to the gut. *My messes.* I bit back the anger rising in my chest, but it still slipped out. "It wasn't about the things, Mom. It was about feeling seen. Feeling like you actually believed in me, in who I am—not just who you wanted me to be."

Her eyes flashed, her body angling away from mine defensively. "This is what I mean! You're so focused on what you think I didn't give you that you can't see everything I did! Who do you think was there when you got pregnant in college? Who was cleaning up your mess then?"

Click. Boom.

I stood up, my heart pounding in my ears. "I never asked you to clean up my messes! I just needed you to be there! To tell me it was okay that I fucked up."

"Vanessa, wait—" Dr. Smith tried to interject, but it was too late. My mother was already on the defensive.

"You think I didn't sit with you? I wiped your tears, your blood! I prayed over you when you lost that baby, Vanessa. But no matter what I did, it was never enough for you!" Her voice cracked, and suddenly, the woman I always saw as unshakable was trembling.

The air in the room grew thick, suffocating, as we stared at each other—two women caught up in the same hurt and misunderstanding. Dr. Smith stood, her energy still calm but now carrying more weight.

"Let's pause for a moment," she said softly, guiding me back to my seat with a hand on my shoulder. "You both care so deeply for each other. That much is clear. But what I'm seeing here is a cycle—one that's rooted in unspoken pain and expectations neither of you asked for. This... this is what we call a mother wound, passed down from generation to generation, sometimes without even knowing."

My mother's face twitched, her composure cracking just slightly. "Are you implying I hurt my daughter, and my mother hurt me?" she asked, her voice barely above a whisper. "That's preposterous."

"I'm saying that often, as Black women, we are taught to be strong, to carry the world on our shoulders. But no one teaches us how to just be vulnerable. To let our daughters see us as human.

What I'm hearing, Vivian, is that you've spent your whole life trying to give Vanessa what you didn't have. But perhaps there were things you needed, too. Things your own mother couldn't give you."

For the first time in my life, I saw my mother falter. Her hands, once so steady, twisted in her lap. She turned to face me, her almond eyes softening. "Vanessa," she said, her voice wavering, "I never wanted to hurt you. I just... I wanted to make sure you were prepared for this world, the same way my mother did for me. It's so hard out there. I wanted you to be ready."

"And I appreciate that, Mom," I whispered, my own voice catching in my throat. "But I needed more than preparation. I needed you to believe in me. To be there with me, not just fixing everything for me."

We sat in that silence, then, almost hesitantly, my mother reached for my hand. Her fingers were warm, trembling slightly as they curled around mine.

"I'm sorry," she whispered, a tear slipping down her cheek. "I didn't know how to be the mother you needed. I was doing the best I knew how."

I squeezed her hand, the knot in my chest loosening just a little. "I know, Mom. And I don't hate you. I just want us to...understand each other better."

Dr. Smith watched us quietly, her presence grounding the moment. "This, is where healing begins," she said softly. "Not by erasing the past, but by acknowledging it. By choosing to move forward with a new understanding of each other."

My mother looked at me, her eyes glistening. "I'd like that," she said, her voice thick with emotion. "I'm tired of us being at odds. I want to be the mother you need."

I leaned into her, resting my head on her shoulder, breathing in the familiar scent of sweet magnolia and amber that always seemed to surround her. "And I want to learn how to let you in."

Dr. Smith smiled warmly, her eyes twinkling as she watched the two of us. "This is just the beginning, ladies. You've both taken the first step toward breaking that cycle. Remember, healing doesn't happen overnight. But as long as you're both committed to the process, you'll find your way."

As we left the session, hand in hand, I realized something I hadn't fully understood before. My mother and I were more alike than I ever wanted to admit—two women navigating the world with the tools we'd been given, doing the best we could. And maybe, just maybe, that was enough. For now, at least.

Chapter 23

Xavier

I PARKED BY THE valet of Vanessa's apartments, sitting on the hood of my car as I waited for her to come out. This was our first official date—a real one, no "friends outing" label, no hedging. Just me, showing up for her the way I should have from the start. When I saw her step out, I felt the breath catch in my chest. Vanessa looked stunning, more beautiful than I'd let myself remember.

Gone were the wavy bundles from her birthday. Instead, she rocked her natural hair, the top half pulled into a bun on top of her head while the rest curled and coiled around her shoulders. Her smooth, chocolate skin glistened in the streetlights. The little black dress she wore showed off all my favorite parts of her, from the low cut neckline to the hem that stopped just under her ass. The dress allowed her mile long legs to take center stage in the strappy heels gracing her feet, complemented by the white polish on her toes. The matching diamond tennis necklace and bracelet were the perfect additions to an already perfect masterpiece.

She walked toward me, and I couldn't help but smile, getting out to meet her on the sidewalk. "You look stunning," I murmured, my voice dropping a bit as I took her in, unable to stop myself from spinning her in a small circle. Her laughter warmed me from the inside out, as I bit my bottom lip.

"Thanks," she replied, smoothing the front of my jacket like it was second nature. "And you clean up well too."

I opened the door for her, slipping into the driver's seat as she settled in. We didn't say much at first, just let the soft R & B hum around us. There was something about this night—being with her, taking her out like this—that felt bigger than anything I'd done in a while. Like I was finally where I was supposed to be.

We pulled up to *Lombardi's*, an Italian spot I'd scouted ahead of time. I wanted the night to be perfect, somewhere intimate enough to talk, where I could remind her that this time, I was all in. Inside, the hostess led us to a table by the window, the dim light casting a glow over Vanessa's face. She looked relaxed, more open than she had in months. I ordered a bottle of red wine, something rich and bold, hoping she'd like it.

"To second chances," I said, raising my glass, and locking my eyes with hers.

She met my gaze, her expression soft. "To second chances."

We clinked glasses, and the warmth of the wine settled into my chest, spreading with every look she gave me. We talked, the conversation flowing easily between us. I listened as she told me about her work, her plans, and I felt this overwhelming sense of pride for the woman she'd become. This was the Vanessa I'd always loved, but stronger, more resilient.

When our food arrived, I couldn't resist watching her pop hearty bites of rigatoni covered in spicy vodka sauce into her mouth and the little dances of satisfaction after. I also didn't miss the side glances she'd make at my plate. "Here, try some," I said, holding out a bite to her.

She leaned in, tasting the piece I offered, her eyes lighting up. "Mmm, I should've gotten that," she admitted, laughing. "Yours is definitely better."

As we ate, the music shifted, the restaurant's playlist moving into smooth R&B. I leaned across the table, reaching for her hand. I could feel the nervousness leave me as her fingers slipped easily into mine. It was like coming home.

"Nessa," I said quietly, my voice low, "I want you to know that I don't take this for granted. Being here with you... it's everything. And I'm not going to let anything get in the way of that."

I watched as she looked down, her expression vulnerable in a way that made me ache to reach across the table and hold her. Instead, I kept my hand in hers, letting her know I'd be patient. I was here for the long haul.

After dinner, I took her to the car, opened the door, and glanced back toward her with a grin. "I have one more place in mind," I said, trying to keep it a surprise.

"Where?" she asked, her curiosity lighting up her face.

"You'll see," I replied, giving her a wink.

We drove through the city streets, pulling up to *Bald Kitty*, a cozy lounge with live music that filled the room with soul as soon as we walked in. I could feel her energy shift, could see her shoulders relax as the smooth sound of R&B washed over us.

I found us seating ducked off in a corner, just past the stage, ordered drinks, and took in the scene. Vanessa looked around, a smile playing at her lips, and I knew this was exactly the kind of night she needed.

The singer took the stage, her voice rich and full, pouring into the crowd. I reached for Vanessa's hand again, leaning in close. "You know, back then... I don't think I ever took the time to just sit back and be in the moment with you. But tonight? I don't want to miss a single second."

She looked at me, her gaze tender, something unspoken passing between us. "We've both had a lot of growing up to do," she said quietly, almost to herself. "Being open looks good on you."

I nodded, tightening my grip on her hand. "You deserve someone who's fully present, Nessa. Someone who sees you and appreciates every single part of you. And I'm that person."

She looked down, and I could see a hint of emotion in her eyes. "And who said you're the right man for the job?" she teased, though her tone was soft.

I chuckled, shaking my head. "You not making this easy on me, huh?"

"Where's the fun in that?" She trailed a finger along my collar, stopping to caress the back of my neck.

The song changed, picking up into a smooth jazz riff, and I stood, reaching out my hand. "Dance with me?"

She hesitated, glancing around, but after a moment, her hand slipped into mine. I led her to the where other couples were dancing, keeping us on the outskirts, resting my hand on the small of her back as we moved to the rhythm, my other hand holding hers.

I leaned in, murmuring, "I'm glad I get to do this with you again."

"So am I," she breathed into my neck.

Her head leaned against my chest, her breathing steady, and I could feel the connection between us, pulsing and alive. It wasn't the same as it had been before; this was stronger, something I wasn't going to let slip through my fingers again.

When the song ended, we stayed close, not wanting to break the spell. Back at our seats, we talked in quiet voices, laughter and soft smiles filling the moments in between. I brushed my thumb over her knuckles, watching her as she leaned back, the candlelight casting soft shadows across her face.

She looked at me then, something vulnerable in her eyes. "Do you really think we could make it work this time?"

I held her gaze, feeling my chest tighten with the weight of her question. "I don't just think so, baby. I know so. If that's what you want, I'll be here, every step of the way."

Her eyes softened, and for a second, I could see a future I hadn't dared to picture in years. We stayed at the lounge long after the crowd faded, our hands intertwined, sharing stories and laughter like we'd never been apart.

Driving her home later, the night felt like a perfect memory already, one I'd hold onto forever. Standing in her entryway, I couldn't resist leaning in, tucking a strand of hair behind her ear, letting my fingers linger just a moment too long.

"Tonight was... everything," I whispered, my voice a low murmur.

"It was," she smiled. "I'm not ready for it to end. Do you want to stay for a bit?"

I followed her to the living room of her apartment. As I looked around, every inch the space was distinctively Vanessa. Vibrant paintings made up a gallery wall, leading to floor to ceiling windows, the Houston skyline a picturesque view just past her balcony. How I missed that large beige couch in the center of her living room was lost on me. The thick cushions reminded me of oversized marshmallows.

"Do you want a drink?" she asked, walking over to her wine fridge. She took out a bottle of red wine, grabbed two glasses from the cabinet, and placed them on the counter. I walked over to meet her, taking the wine opener form her hands, popping the cork and pouring our glasses.

She moved to the fridge, taking out a pan of brownies, cutting two pieces, handing me one. "Don't worry. I used my mom's recipe. I just added a little something extra."

I didn't need to ask what the something extra was, as the smell of weed met my nose before the chocolate of the brownie. "How much of something extra did you put?"

"It's just an edible Zay," she said, a mouth full of brownie. "Don't act like you don't smoke."

"Yeah, but I still need to drive home. I'm not fucking with the cops out here."

"Or, you could stay over?"

I surveyed her face, noticing the hint of uncertainty passing between her eyes. "Are you ready for me to stay over?"

"Maybe."

"Maybe's not good enough." I leaned down, pressing my lips to hers in a kiss that felt like a promise. "When we cross that line again, I want you to be so sure, it's not a question of if, but when." Our lips locked again, Vanessa's soft whimpers making it harder for me to convince myself to leave. "I can tell your body is ready," I started, kneading the flesh of her ass, pressing her close against me.

"But I can wait for your head to be in sync," I continued, running my hands through her scalp, massaging there as well. Leaning down again, I covered her lips with mine, savoring the sweetness of her mouth, our tongues twisting around each other, trying to mesh into one. Her eyes closed as moans sounded from deep within her. I trailed a finger down to her chest, just over her heart, running my thumb under her breast.

"But this is what I want most of all. And for that, I'll wait an eternity. Cause Nessa baby, when you give me all three, you'll have me addicted. And ain't no amount of rehab gonna make me give that up."

We spent the next few hours catching up, reminiscing about our past and the time we lost. Slowly, I watched the effects of the edible mixed with the wine loosen Vanessa. We went from sitting far from each other, on her couch, to Vanessa sitting on my lap, her arms draped around my neck. She shifted, straddling my legs, leaning down to kiss a trail down my neck. My dick strained against my pants, willing me to go against my words from earlier.

"I think it's time for me to go," I said half-heartedly. I brought Vanessa's face to meet mine. It took all my resolve to stick to my words, the pout on her face threatening me to give her whatever she asked for.

"Fine. Can I at least a kiss? I need something to help me get off after you leave," she whined.

Fuck it.

I lifted her into my arms, carrying her to her bedroom. Her face was torn between confusion and anticipation as she laid back on her elbows. I kneeled down in front of her, pushing the hem of her dress above her hips.

"Zay, what are you doing?"

"You said you needed a kiss. I'm about to make it worth it." I pulled her panties off, praying to God to give me strength to stop before I got too far gone. I brushed my nose against the soft velvet of her inner thighs, breathing in her essence. I looked, seeing the "X" tattoo in the valley between her thigh and pubic bone.

"Damn shame."

"What?"

"You gave them other niggas a map to what's mine, and I bet they still couldn't find your spot."

My lips touched the smooth skin above her wet slit, making her grind herself into my mouth. Soft gasps escaped her lips. My tongue slid between her lips, tasting her, lapping up every bit of arousal that leaked from deep within her, my tongue sending her body into convulsions.

"Shit, Zay," she cried above me, her hands finding their way to my head.

Her voice, the way it called out to me, yearning for me, the way she rolled her hips to meet my licks and sucks, drove me wild. Her body began to tense, so I grabbed her hips, keeping them in place, massaging the soft skin of her inner thighs.

"Let that shit go, Nessa baby." I stuck two fingers inside of her as my tongue circled and suckled at her clit. She exploded into my mouth, guttural cries leading to soft pants as she rode the waves of my fingers and mouth. I pulled her back up, bringing her face to meet mine, the dazed, dreamy look of her eyes, made the hardness of my dick ache with desire.

Grabbing her face with both my hands, pulling her close, I kissed her madly, deeply, tenderly, our tongues frantically searching for one another. She moaned into my mouth, making me grow harder in my pants. I moved my hands down to her hips, pulling her closer to me as her arms wrapped around my neck. I brushed soft kisses on her chin, her cheeks, her eyes, before pressing my forehead to her temples. "Whenever you ready, it's more where that came from."

Chapter 24

Xavier

Unspoken frustration filled our office as Khalil and I bantered back and forth about the upcoming NFL game. Beneath our casual jabs, there was a tension neither of us wanted to fully acknowledge. That tension came crashing in when a firm knock sounded against the door.

"Hey, mind if I interrupt for a moment?" Wesley stood at the doorway, his figure framed by the fading light of the late afternoon. The look on his face gave away that whatever he had to say wouldn't be easy.

I waved him in, gesturing to the seat across from us. "Come on in, man. What's going on?"

Wesley hesitated, his usual easy demeanor replaced by something heavier, more conflicted. He closed the door softly behind him before taking a seat, leaning forward with his elbows on his knees. "I had a meeting with my father today."

That one sentence hung in the air like a thick fog. Khalil shot me a look, and I felt the irritation rise. Wright Horizons had become a constant source of compromise.

"What did he say?" I asked, already dreading the answer.

Wesley took a deep breath. "He's putting a hold on the affordable housing project, indefinitely. Says it's not 'financially viable' right now. He wants to shift focus to more upscale, luxury developments. High-end eco-friendly housing for wealthier buyers."

Khalil's face tightened, my own jaw clenching as I processed his words. *Luxury housing?* That was the exact opposite of what we had set out to do. The blueprints and sketches tacked on the walls around us felt like ghosts of the vision we had when we first started EcoVision.

"So... more luxury," I repeated, bitterness lacing my words. "What happened to giving back to the community? That was the whole point, Wesley. To build something sustainable for people who actually need it."

Wesley's face fell further, the tension rolling off him in waves. "Look, I wanted this just as much as you two, maybe even more. But my father's convinced that the high-end market will secure better revenue. And the board agreed."

Khalil rubbed his temples, a deep sigh escaping him. "We didn't come here to sell out. We had a purpose, man. A vision."

"I know," Wesley murmured. "Trust me, I know. But my hands are tied. I don't run Wright Horizons... not yet. Until I do, I have to play the game my father laid out." He leaned back, his eyes betraying the turmoil he felt. "I didn't want this. But it's the reality I'm in. Not all of us can pick and choose. Sometimes the road is already paved."

The room fell silent as we all sat in the thick stew of compromise, frustration, and helplessness. Wesley's words rang with a truth neither Khalil nor I wanted to face, but there it was. We had built our company from nothing, and now we were at a crossroads.

I finally broke the silence, my voice quiet but firm. "We can't abandon our values, Wesley. Not for the sake of money. There has to be a way to make this partnership work without selling our soul."

Wesley looked down, running a hand over his head. "If there was another way, I'd take it. But this is where we're at right now. If we want to stay in this game, we need to adapt."

Khalil, ever the mediator, leaned in. "Maybe there's a middle ground. Maybe we can use the revenue from this luxury crap to fund the affordable housing we're trying to build ourselves. Look, I don't like it any more than you, but this might be how we keep both afloat."

I shook my head, frustration bubbling up again. "You really willing to compromise everything we stand for, just for a check? We didn't start this company to be part of the problem."

Khalil's voice rose, his frustration matching mine. "You think I like this? Hell no. But we can't make anything happen without money. You're acting like we can just snap our fingers and change the system overnight."

"This is the same cycle of gentrification we said we were fighting against!" I snapped, slamming my fist down on the desk. "We're just feeding into it now."

Khalil stood up, meeting my intensity head-on. "I know that, man. But what are we supposed to do? Walk away and let everything we've built crumble? Or are we going to be smart about this, get what we need, and then use that to make real change?"

Wesley, who had been quiet, watching our back-and-forth, finally spoke up. "Look, I know I haven't always been on the same page as you two. But I'm here now, and I'm trying. We all want the same thing, even if the road there looks different. Let's not let this split us."

I looked between the two of them—Khalil, my brother in all but blood, and Wesley, who was slowly finding his way into our fold. Despite the tension, there was a bond here, one that couldn't be broken easily. I sighed, rubbing my hands over my face. "I need time to think."

"Take the time you need," Khalil said, his voice steady now. "But remember what we came here for. We can still make this work."

"Besides, maybe this is all part of a bigger plan," Wesley added. "Speaking of which. What's up between you and Van?" I raised an irritated eyebrow at Wesley. "I'm sorry. Nessa."

Khalil stuffed his face into the crook of his elbow. "You mean his old lady."

"I should be asking you the same thing," I tossed back to Wesley.

"Oh, us?" He laughed. "We've grown up together our whole lives. She's like a sister to me."

"See, Zay. I told you Nessa didn't get down that way," Khalil chimed in.

"What's that supposed to mean?"

"No offense, Wesley, but Nessa don't seem like the type to date somebody as..." Khalil looked to the ceiling, struggling to find his words.

"Stuck up," I inserted.

"Stuck up?" Wesley seemed shocked.

"I was going to say rigid," Khalil started, "But stuck up is more accurate."

"Y'all think I'm stuck up?"

"I mean, at first. But getting to know you a little more now, not so much." I stood to pack my belongings, ready to meet up with Vanessa at the construction site. I turned to face Wesley. "So, nothing ever happened between you and Nessa?"

"Seriously. Closest we've gotten to dating was when I escorted her for her debut. Nothing more. Besides, I've been trying to get in with one of her friends since high school."

"What friend?" Khalil raised to his seat.

"Lynn," Wesley replied with a shrug of his shoulders, shaking his head.

"Uh-huh. It don't feel so good when it's happening to you."

"Man," Khalil started, settling back into his chair, "I don't know what you talking about."

"Well, I'm about to head over to the site. I'll see y'all later." Bag in my hand, I headed for the door.

"Yeah, that sound like a good idea. Wesley you coming?" Khalil said, standing. "We can start looking into some alternative funding. Figure this out."

Wesley stood up, stretching his shoulders. "I'll tag along. I could use the distraction."

"Nah, I'm good. Y'all stay here," I said, trying to keep my expression cool. "I need to show somebody around."

"Somebody like who?"

Chapter 25

VANESSA

PARKING MY CAR, I pulled up to the address Xavier sent me about an hour and a half later. My pulse quickened as I turned off the engine. The evening air kissed my skin as I stepped out, smoothing the silky fabric of my skirt. My mind drifted back to the date night with Xavier— the ease of it all, stirring up a creative storm in me for the next few days, all of the energy manifesting into its final form hours before Xavier requested my presence here. There was no way I wanted to show up in paint splattered leggings and an oversized hoodie. So, I used the extra time to get cute so that I'd be ready for the girls' night Kelly, Lynn, and I had planned later tonight. Knowing Xavier would see me all dolled up was just an added bonus.

Sure, Jan.

I adjusted the fuchsia silk skirt that hugged my hips, cascading down to my mid-calves, swaying slightly with each step. The cream sweater I wore, cropped just enough to tease a sliver of skin, draped off my shoulders, its bell sleeves fluttering in the breeze. My thick curls were tamed into a low, sleek bun, my freshly arched brows framing my face with precision. I could still smell the lingering vanilla scent of my lipgloss, the brown liner making my lips pop. Even in heels on gravel, I glided up to the building, anticipation settling deep in my belly.

Maybe I *was* overdressed for an active construction site, but something about tonight felt like a turning point, a moment I needed to meet with all of me at my best.

As I neared the building, I spotted Wesley standing on the curb, leaning casually as if waiting for something—or someone.

"Van? Let me guess. Here to see your boyfriend?" His voice had that teasing edge I remembered from growing up, the one that never missed an opportunity to meddle into my business.

I smirked, rolling my eyes playfully. "Ha ha, Wesley. What's that I heard, though?" I cocked my head, the faintest hint of challenge in my tone. "Still in your feelings about a certain friend of mine? I know Lynn's finally moved on from your complicated ass."

Wesley's face faltered, just for a second. He sighed, hand pressed dramatically to his chest. "Low blow, Van. You know it's not that simple."

"Maybe it could be," I said softly, my voice dropping with a tinge of empathy. "We're adults now, Wes. It's time to start making decisions that feel right for us, not for our parents or anyone else. You keep waiting, she's going to be gone before you realize it."

Wesley's eyes flickered with something—regret, maybe? But he didn't respond. Instead, he motioned for me to follow him toward the building. I stepped carefully, my heels clicking against the loose gravel as we moved inside.

The air inside the building smelled of fresh paint, wood, and dust—the undeniable aroma of transformation. The exposed beams and modern fixtures clashed against the weathered charm of the old structure, and I could see how Xavier fought to preserve its soul.

Wesley led me down a narrow hallway, past an open office, and with a tilt of his head, gestured for me to enter.

I stepped inside, my breath hitching the moment I saw Xavier. Tailored slacks hugged his hips, emphasizing the strength in his legs. His shirt—black, crisp, and buttoned up to just the right place—clung to his broad shoulders and muscled arms, like it was made to be worn by him. I swallowed hard, memories flooding my mind, uninvited. The way those arms had felt wrapped around me, how safe, how right it felt.

As if sensing my thoughts, Xavier looked up, a slow smile spreading across his face. His eyes traced the curve of my body, lingering in places that made heat bloom low in my belly. He bit his lip, trying—and failing—to hide the spark of desire in his gaze.

"Nessa, I'm glad you made it," he said, his voice low and warm, like honey dripping from a spoon.

The way my name fell from his lips had me momentarily breathless. I fought the urge to fan myself, keeping my cool. "Well, it was on my way to girls' night, so I figured why not," I teased, though my voice came out softer than I intended.

The corner of his jaw twitched, just enough to tell me he wasn't buying it. "Girls' night, huh?" His eyes sparkled with amusement, but there was a heat there too, simmering just beneath the surface.

I tilted my head, unable to suppress the grin tugging at my lips. "Maybe you can tell me why Wesley thinks you're my boyfriend."

Xavier chuckled, the sound low and velvety. "Boyfriend? Shoot, let me know something."

I laughed, feeling the tension between us twist and pull. "Stop, Zay. That's just his way of stirring the pot. You mugged him so hard at our meeting, he thought you were ready to swing."

"I mean, both things can be true." He leaned against the desk, crossing his arms, watching me in that way only Xavier could. Like I was the only person in the room. Hell, like I was the only person in the world.

Our laughter faded, leaving behind a moment that stretched between us. The weight of unspoken words hung thick in the air, making the small office feel even smaller.

"So, what do you think so far?" Xavier's voice pulled me back, and I realized he was waiting for me to say something—anything—that wasn't dripping with tension.

I glanced around, grateful for the excuse to look anywhere but directly at him. "I like it," I said honestly. "You kept the charm of the original building."

Xavier's gaze softened, as if my approval meant something more. "Yeah, that was important to me."

He spoke with such conviction, the passion clear in his voice as he detailed every inch of the project. I always knew he had it in him—that drive, that ability to create something remarkable. Seeing him in his element, I couldn't help but admire him, proud of the man he became.

Inhaling deeply, I focused on the photographs again, trying to calm the stirring in my chest. But even from across the room, Xavier's presence was overwhelming. His scent—sandalwood, fresh and masculine—filled the space, curling around me with tangible force.

I couldn't deny it anymore. This wasn't just a nostalgic pull. This was something deeper. Something I wasn't sure I could walk away from this time. Every second with Xavier in such close proximity had me teetering on the edge of self-control. I wasn't sure how much longer I could hold it together before my resolve broke.

Girl, calm down. You are not about to let Xavier lay you across this table. Not here. Not now. Not with Wesley and Khalil two feet away.

"We don't have to take a tour," Xavier's deep voice rumbled softly, pulling my gaze to his. His eyes dropped to my feet. "Those heels don't exactly look like they're made for walking around a construction site anyway." His laugh was low, teasing, and yet it held a warmth that made my chest tighten.

I smiled back, feeling the edges of my nerves unraveling. "Thank you. I'm not trying to break an ankle. I'm already regretting these shoes," I admitted, shifting on my feet.

Xavier stepped closer, his presence pulling me in like gravity. He grabbed a set of plans and some papers from the table next to me. "Here, sit down," he said, rolling a chair over for me and holding it steady as I sank into it, grateful to relieve the pressure on my feet. His touch lingered for a moment longer than necessary, and I felt the heat of his hand even after he pulled away.

Is he looking at me? I feel like he's looking at me.

I shifted slightly in the chair, pretending to adjust my skirt. When I peeked at him from the corner of my eye, I caught him quickly looking away, his expression matching my thoughts. My heart fluttered in my chest, a slow burn rising to my cheeks.

Trying to distract myself, I reached for the papers on the desk but knocked them over in my haste. "Oh, I'm sorry," I mumbled, bending down to help gather them.

Xavier was quicker, crouching down beside me, his hands brushing against mine as he picked up the fallen documents, sending a soft wave of electricity up my arm. I froze for a split second, my breath catching in my throat. The heat of his skin against mine was intoxicating.

"Still clumsy, I see," he teased, his voice warm and close as he looked up at me from where he crouched. The hint of a smirk played at the corner of his mouth, and my heart skipped a beat. He stood, taking the papers from my hand, settling into the chair next to me.

His scent wrapped around me like a heady fog. I inhaled deeply, feeling light-headed from the proximity, the smell stirring something primal inside me. I glanced at his neck, the slight bulge of a vein pulsing just beneath his skin. The urge to reach out and touch it, to soothe it with my fingers, feel the pulse beats with my tongue, was overwhelming.

"So, what's all this?" I asked, my voice slightly breathless, motioning toward the plans in his hands, trying to focus on something—*anything*—other than the fire building inside me.

Xavier's jaw tightened again, the tension in his body palpable. He clenched and unclenched his fist before finally answering. "Just some of the plans for the building." His voice was gruff, but the vulnerability in his eyes gave him away. I could see the frustration simmering just beneath the surface.

I smiled, my thumb gently brushing the nape of his neck. "Interesting. So, what's the plan for this place?"

He started explaining the details, pulling out the building layouts and walking me through the modifications. His voice grew stronger as he described how each feature would make the building more eco-friendly, more sustainable. The excitement in his tone infectious, and soon I found myself leaning closer, hanging on every word.

Our chairs moved closer together without me even realizing it, and at some point, his arm slipped around my waist, his thumb brushing lightly against my side. The touch was barely there, but it sent a slow, burning flood through my body, making it hard to think clearly.

"Zay, this is brilliant," I whispered, staring at him with wide eyes. "Wright Horizons and Wesley are lucky to be working with you and Khalil."

He smiled, the profile of his face softening, and my heart clenched. God, I wanted to reach out and trace my fingers along the sharp planes of his jaw, to brush my lips against his. I wanted to get lost in the feel of him, the taste of him.

But the moment passed too quickly, and his smile faltered as he turned to face me fully. "I wish they saw it that way."

I reached for his hand, threading my fingers through his. His grip was firm, grounding, but there was a vulnerability in the way he held me, like he was afraid to let go.

"What do you really think about the building?"

"Umm...It's definitely one that needs to be renovated. The kids in my art class talk about the homeless people they usually see hanging around all the time. I'm confident you'll do what it takes to bring some life to the community." I tried to find anything to pull my attention from the man sitting mere inches away from me. The man who, still after all these years, made my knees weak and my body yearn for something more. "Now, the finished product does seem a touch out of place compared to what's here already. Even with some of the original features. Like, it's too big for the small neighborhood charm around here."

"I thought you liked big things?" *This nigga*. My eyes shot up, meeting his gaze, wide with shock and something else I couldn't quite name. "That's not what I meant," he said, but the drawl in his voice wrapped around me, sending a slow burn through my veins.

Oh, he knew exactly what he meant. And, he wasn't wrong.

The room seemed to darken, as if the fluorescent lights dimmed just for us, casting us in a cocoon of quiet intimacy. Time stretched, suspended in that moment, where only the two of us existed. The outside world fell away, and I could feel the pull of him, like a magnet drawing me closer. My body hummed in response, every nerve awake and alive, as if my skin was remembering the feel of his touch, the heat of his kiss.

Without thinking, I moved closer, feeling the space between us evaporate. Xavier's hand reached out, firm and warm, circling my waist, as if it had never forgotten its place there, pulling us up from our chairs. The spark between us ignited into something more, something I had been fighting against for far too long. I felt like I might melt right there in his arms.

God, I could never be just friends with this man.

"You still running from me?" His voice was low, soft, the words brushing against my lips like a feather. His thumb grazed my bottom lip, sending a shiver down my spine. My breath caught in my throat, my pulse racing as his eyes bore into mine, searching for the answer I couldn't give him. Not here. Not yet. But my heart knew. My body knew.

"Why do you think I'm running?" I whispered, my voice betraying the calm I tried so hard to keep.

"I know you. Your brain probably creating reasons for you not to be with me. Why?" His grip tightened on my waist, pulling me flush against him, his words sinking into my skin, branding me. The hard press of his body against mine left no room for pretense. The way I leaned into him, craving the connection I'd been denying, left no room for lies.

I couldn't speak. Couldn't think. His lips were so close to mine, I could feel his breath, warm and tantalizing. The thickening bulge of his arousal pressed into my lower belly, and I knew he could feel the way my body responded to him, the way my nipples peaked through the soft fabric of my sweater, betraying every wall I'd tried to build between us.

"Tell me I'm lying," he murmured, his voice thick with longing. The reality of his words danced in the air, challenging me, daring me to deny the truth that pulsed between us like a live wire.

Speechless, I let the silence answer for me. My heart beat so loud I was sure he could hear it, and the world outside this moment ceased to exist. He saw me—truly saw me, with all my flaws, my fears, my desires—and still, he wanted me. His hand slid up, cradling my jaw as his thumb traced a line along my lips, his eyes never leaving mine.

"Let me make you happy again," he whispered, his voice raw with vulnerability, with a desperation that mirrored my own.

Yes. The word echoed in my heart, reverberated in my soul.

"Stop denying yourself happiness," he continued, his forehead leaning against mine, his voice wrapping around me like a promise. "Let me be the man you need, the man I should've been before. I know it'll take time for you to trust me again, but give me the chance to show you that you can. You're it for me, Vanessa. There's no one else. When you left, you took a piece of me with you. You took you. I should've run after you... Fuck, you shouldn't have even made it out the door."

His words, filled with regret and yearning, tore through me, unraveling the carefully constructed walls I had built around my heart. We were so young, so foolish, thinking we had all the time in the world. But life had a way of teaching us the hard lessons, of making us confront our mistakes.

"Start over with me now," he whispered, his lips grazing mine, just barely. "If you feel even an ounce of what I feel, I'll never let you go again. I just want to love you. For life. Please, give me that."

Yes.

I couldn't form the words, couldn't say what my heart screamed. But Xavier knew. He felt it, the way I leaned into him, the way my body molded to his. One hand wrapped around the base of my neck, pulling me closer, the other gripped my ass, melding my body with his. My eyes fluttered shut as our lips finally touched. It was soft, tender, but filled with so much promise, so much emotion. I clung to his body, fully ready to give myself over to him. My mind, my heart, my body.

Then, the heavy footsteps of reality approached, and I quickly remembered this was not the time or place to get my back broken. The door swung open, bursting our bubble. I turned, my back against Xavier's chest, wrapping my arms around my chest, trying to collect myself, slow the frantic beat of my heart.

Xavier's arms wrapped around my waist, holding me to him, his chest rising and falling with the same ragged breaths I struggled to control. And in that moment, despite the interruption, I knew—there was no going back. Not for us.

Our moment evaporated into slight awkwardness as Khalil sauntered in with that trademark grin of his, all casual like he didn't just barge in on something. "Oh shit, my bad," he said, grinning, clearly entertained by the vibe he picked up on. "Didn't mean to interrupt whatever y'all had goin' on."

Xavier straightened up, the annoyance on his face was too real, and it was almost comical watching him try to keep it together. I couldn't help but smile at how irritated he looked, caught like a kid sneaking around.

"Khalil, knock before walking into a room," Xavier muttered, shaking his head.

Khalil just laughed, leaning against the doorframe, unbothered. "Chill, Zay. The fuck I need to knock for? It's a construction site."

I rolled my eyes, even though my cheeks were still warm. "You and Kelly have the worst timing, Khalil. Honestly."

He winked at me. "Timing is everything, Nessa. And look at it this way—at least I saved y'all from a OSHA violation."

Before Xavier could say anything back, Wesley walked in, glancing between the three of us. "What's going on in here? Y'all look like y'all just got caught sneaking out after curfew."

Xavier shot both of them a look, but his lips curled into a reluctant smile. "Y'all are ridiculous, for real."

Wesley held his hands up in defense. "Don't blame me. I'm just here to check on the upper floors."

Khalil leaned on the desk, shooting me a look. "So, Nessa, Zay said y'all having a lil' girls' night."

I gave him a side-eye, already knowing where this was headed. "Oh no. Y'all are not crashing girls' night."

Khalil held his hands up, all innocent-like. "Come on now, just tell me where it's at. Ain't nobody tryin' to crash—just thinking about sliding through, see what y'all got going on."

"That's literally crashing it though," I sighed, knowing there was no stopping Khalil once he got an idea in his head. "It's at FRNDS. Just a small spot. Only me, Kelly, and Lynn. Nyah's off doing married people things."

At the mention of Lynn, I noticed Wesley's whole demeanor shift for just a second. Quickly, he masked it, but I caught that little spark in his eyes. *I see you, Wesley.*

"Well, now I definitely have to come," Wesley said, trying to play it off like he was just joking. "It's been a minute since I've had a good drink."

Angling my face, I squinted in Wesley's direction. "You sure? This place is a little different from the cigar lounges you prefer."

Xavier folded his arms, looking thoughtful, but the twinkle in his eye gave him away. "I don't know, Nessa. Sounds like it could be fun. You should go ahead and invite us."

I laughed, shaking my head at them all. "Y'all are too much." I held up a hand. "Let me call Kelly. If she's good with it, y'all can come. But don't expect much."

I pulled out my phone, dialing Kelly while the guys stayed quiet, but clearly trying to listen in. She picked up quickly, her voice light and teasing.

"What's up, girl?"

I smiled, already knowing how this was gonna go. "Hey, so how would you feel about Xavier, Khalil, and Wesley crashing girls' night?"

She paused, then burst out laughing. "Oh lord, Khalil's been bugging me all day about linking up. They can come, but they're footing the bill. And Wesley too? What is the world coming to?"

"Girl, you know why," I grinned. "See you soon."

I turned back to the guys, shaking my head. "I guess y'all can come, but y'all are paying."

Khalil raised a brow, trying to act all cool. "Say less."

Xavier glanced at me, his smile softening, that lingering tension still between us. "This should be fun."

I nodded, feeling the flutter in my chest return. "Yeah, it's definitely gonna be a night."

Chapter 26

Xavier

The vibe at FRNDS was cool, and the night had that kind of buzz that made relish in the moment. Vanessa was quiet for most of it, laughing along with Kelly and Lynn, but I could tell her mind was elsewhere. I caught her stealing glances at me, and every time she did, my teeth just had to let her know they missed her.

As the evening wound down, our group continued to throw jokes across the table, Khalil and Wesley caught up in their now usual back-and-forth, trying to one-up each other. But my mind was already somewhere else, focused on Vanessa. We hadn't really talked since earlier at the site, and I was still thinking about the moment we almost had before Khalil interrupted.

I leaned back in my chair, watching her out of the corner of my eye. She was pretending to listen to whatever Kelly was saying, but I could tell by the way she absentmindedly twirled a piece of her hair and leaned into me, that she wasn't really there.

As soon as I caught her eye, her smile softened and she stood, sliding her purse over her forearm. She muttered something about needing to head out early, saying goodbyes to the girls and throwing a quick wave at Wesley and Khalil. Her gaze caught mine, lingering just long enough to say what words hadn't.

I waited a beat before standing up myself. "I'll catch y'all later," I said, already heading for the door before anyone could reply. I barely registered the playful barks and whistles coming from Khalil behind me.

When I stepped outside, she was already a few feet ahead, walking down the quiet street toward her car. The glow from the streetlights cast a soft hue over her, catching in her hair, highlighting the way her silk skirt hugged her hips just right. My steps quickened to catch up, and when I reached her, I called out softly.

"Nessa."

She turned, slow, a small smile on her lips like she'd been expecting me all along. "What took you so long?"

I chuckled, sliding my hands into my pockets. "I had to pay, remember."

"Walk me to my car?" she asked, though I already knew she was going to say it.

We fell into step together, the sound of our footsteps the only thing cutting through the stillness. I kept sneaking glances at her out of the corner of my eye, the energy between us growing heavier with every step.

When we reached her car, she leaned against the door and tilted her head up at me. "I guess this is goodbye," she said softly, her voice quieter now that we were alone.

I didn't say anything at first, just stood there, feeling that same pull I'd been feeling all night, all day. Hell, maybe for years.

"I don't wanna say goodbye yet," I admitted finally, taking a step closer.

Her lips parted, eyes flickering with that thing we'd both been holding back. She hesitated for only a second before speaking. "So don't."

That was all I needed to hear.

"Come over," I said, my voice steady, even though my heart was racing. "We can just...talk. Nothing else. I promise."

Vanessa smiled, the kind of smile that said she didn't believe me but wasn't going to call me out on it. She unlocked her car and slid inside, but not before looking up at me one more time. "Text me your address."

I nodded, already pulling out my phone, my pulse quickening as I watched her drive away.

Unlocking the door, I stepped in with Vanessa right beside me, the soft click of her heels echoing through the quiet apartment. As soon as we crossed the threshold, the familiar scent of sandalwood mixed with the lingering smell of fresh laundry filled the air. I'd set the mood from my phone—Al Green playing low in the background, the warm glow of lamps casting soft shadows across the room. This rental was simple, but I'd made it feel like home, and tonight, I hoped it'd be a place she'd feel comfortable.

I glanced over at her, taking in the way her cream sweater hugged her body, that pink silk skirt gliding just right over her hips. Everything about her looked soft—delicate. I swallowed, trying to keep my cool.

"Make yourself at home," I said, my voice a little rougher than I intended. "I'm gonna change real quick."

She nodded, her eyes tracking me for a second before turning to look around the space. I couldn't help but notice how she moved—how she seemed to take up space in a way that made my heart thud against my chest.

I walked down the hall toward my room, breathing out a heavy sigh as soon as I was out of her sight. I couldn't be around her in these work clothes any longer, feeling like I needed to shed all the weight from the day. Pulling off my shirt and slacks, I threw on a black T-shirt with our company's logo and a pair of gray sweatpants, something chill. Nothing too much, just...me. I glanced at myself in the mirror, brushing over my waves. I wasn't trying to impress, but I couldn't lie to myself—I wanted her to like what she saw.

My nerves hit again as I stepped back into the living room. She was sitting on the couch now, her legs tucked under her, heels discarded to the floor, hands resting in her lap as she looked around. The lamps were dim, casting a soft light over her, and she looked...perfect. The way she sat there, so at ease and so damn beautiful, made my chest tighten. A real life Venus de Milo carved from the smoothest mahogany sitting right in my living room, owning every part of my being.

"You good?" I asked, my voice coming out lower than I intended.

She nodded, but I caught the slight shift in her posture, like she was trying to play it cool. "Yeah, I'm good."

I sat down on the opposite end of the couch, not too close but not far either. The music hummed around us, Al Green crooning about love and loss, filling the room with something I couldn't put into words myself.

"You didn't have to change," she teased, a small smile tugging at her lips.

I chuckled, leaning back into the cushions, trying to get comfortable even though every fiber in me was wound tight. "I figured you've seen enough of me in work clothes. Thought I'd switch it up."

She laughed softly, and damn, that sound made me feel things. "You look good."

My eyes dropped to her lips for a split second before I met her gaze again. "You too, Nessa baby." The way her name rolled off my tongue nowadays—familiar, intimate—made something stir inside me.

"I'm glad you came tonight."

She nodded. "I'm glad I came too. I'm not sure what to expect."

"No expectations," I repeated, leaning back into the couch, trying to keep things steady, even though her presence had me off balance. I ran my hand over my waves like that might smooth over my nervousness creeping into the room. "So, what do you want to talk about?"

Vanessa shifted, inching her legs closer to me on the couch. Her fingers played absently with the hem of her skirt, but when she looked up at me, her eyes were direct—too direct. "Did you get with anyone else? After us?"

Her question hit me like a curveball out of nowhere, and I almost laughed at how blunt she was with it. We'd been dancing around the deeper stuff since she walked through the door, and now here she was, diving right into it. "You don't want an answer to that," I said, shaking my head.

She raised an eyebrow, her lips curving into a half-smile. "What, ashamed of your hoe-tivities?"

I rolled my eyes, leaning forward and resting my elbows on my knees, trying to deflect her teasing with a grin. "You think I want to know about the clowns you been with?" I couldn't stop the grimace that twisted my face.

"That's different," she shot back, smoothing her hair behind her ear. "It's not my fault you left the door open for others to get a better shot."

I glanced at her, my voice low, but the edge in it was undeniable. "What you mean a better shot?"

"You know what I mean, Zay." She rolled her eyes at me. "There were other guys I could've made do."

I leaned back against the couch, crossing my arms, my voice dipping lower. "That makes it worse."

Her brows furrowed, her lips pressed into a thin line. "How so?" she asked, her voice tight.

"'Cause it meant you were willing to settle," I said, staring at her. "You should never settle."

Her lips parted slightly, like she didn't know what to say to that. I could see her biting her lip, her leg bouncing a little—a telltale sign she was feeling some type of way. The room went quiet between us, like we were both waiting for the other to break the silence.

"Answer my question," she said, softer now but still pushing. "I want to know."

I sighed, feeling the weight of her gaze on me. "Are you gonna drop it after I answer?"

She nodded, her eyes never leaving mine. "Yeah."

I exhaled slowly, knowing this wasn't going to be the answer she wanted to hear, but we were already here now. "I did," I admitted, watching her reaction, lips tightening, eyes flickering with emotions she was trying hard to keep under control—hurt, maybe even jealousy. I hated seeing that look on her face.

We sat there for a moment in silence, the space between us thick with tension. I reached out and gently tilted her chin up so she'd look at me. "Talk to me, Nessa."

Her voice was soft, barely above a whisper. "You're right. I didn't want to hear that," she said, biting her lip, twisting her fingers in the pillow on her lap. She looked away, her eyes avoiding mine.

"Don't feel like that," I said quietly, letting my hand drop from her chin. "Nobody ever replaced you, baby. Trust me on that."

She let out a small sigh, leaning back against the cushions. Her voice softened as she looked down at her lap, her fingers still twisted. "Nothing serious though, right?"

"Nah. Hell nah," I replied, the tone in my voice matching the truth of what I was saying. "Once I got my mind straight, Khalil and I went all in on the company. Definitely wasn't trying to get into anything heavy after that." I glanced over at her, trying to read her face. "What about you?"

She smirked, her laughter breaking up some of the tension in the room. "Nothing serious," she mimicked, shaking her head. "I needed a break, so to speak."

I raised an eyebrow. "A break? From what?"

Her laughter bubbled out of her, full and warm, the kind that could ease every tight knot in my chest. "From you, nigga! My heart was broken. I needed time to heal."

I couldn't help but smile at that, even though it stung a little to know I'd hurt her like that. "I feel you," I murmured, watching her closely.

She shifted beside me, her voice turning more thoughtful. "You don't have to keep apologizing, Zay. I *guess* I added to it by walking away, but...we were young. You were stupid. I was naive. We both made mistakes."

"Wait," I laughed. "Run that back. You trying to throw shade?"

"If you caught it, you caught it," she said, raising her hands in the air. We laughed again before our eyes met and locked tight. Longing and regret made its rounds in the space between us.

"Are you still painting? Aside from the murals and classes?" I took Vanessa's feet into my hands, kneading into the her arches and lower calves.

"Yeah...Something like that." She placed her free hand at the nape of my neck, stroking the back of my head with her nails grazing through my waves.

"Oh, really? Show me what you've done."

"One day." Vanessa looked at me as she bit her lip. "Five years later, and we still can't keep our hands off each other."

"Six, almost seven years. And is that a problem?" I asked, leaning my head further into her hand as I stared into her eyes. They held a conversation with each other as she hesitated to answer me. "Get out of your head and come here." I opened my arms, gesturing for her to come closer.

Slowly, she moved to sit on my lap, nestling herself into my chest, as I laid us back, my head resting on the armrest. One hand toyed with the collar of my shirt while the other rested on my abs. Wrapping my arms around her waist, I let myself relax into the moment. So many nights, I prayed to be in this position again.

"My head is pounding," Vanessa spoke softly into my chest.

I freed her tightly pulled hair from its cage of a bun, running my fingers through her scalp to loosen the compacted strands, allowing its volume to reach its maximum capacity. Wafts of coconut, mango, and shea butter filled my senses, as I massaged her scalp. The warmth of her breath matched the fever pitch of desire growing within me. Not just for her body—for her mind, her heart, and her soul. Soft exhales escaped her lips as I continuing massaging her scalp with one hand, kneading gentle circles on her back with the other.

"Mmm. That feels so good," she whispered, snuggling closer against my frame. Her soft hand found its way underneath my shirt, stroking my lower abs and hovering just above the waistband of my sweats. "I've missed you so much, Xavier."

The crack in her voice caused me to lift her chin, tilting her face to mine. "I'm right here, Nessa baby. You don't have to miss me anymore." Pulling her body up, so that our faces paralleled each other, I guided her lips to mine and kissed her deeply. Her lips parted, allowing me to explore the sweet warmth of her mouth. Our tongues tangoed in a dance of longing and hungry desire. As our kisses grew ravenous, she straddled my hips, her skirt rising up her thighs, and moved her body rhythmically against my dick trying desperately to seek orgasmic relief.

"Why do you do this to me?" she moaned, pulling back and staring down at me. Her breaths came out in little ragged puffs.

"Shit, I'm struggling, too." I grabbed her neck to lower her to me again. My thumb grazed her chin as I took in her beautiful form. "You are my weakness and strength all in one."

I kissed her with all the intensity of my love that grew for her in her absence. My hands moved to cup her ass, pressing her closer to me. One hand moved under her sweater, and smoothed across her taut stomach. The soft, supple skin felt like butter in my hands. I found my way under her bra, cupping her left breast in my hand. The urgent moans coming from deep within her made my dick jump against her warm center. Meeting her hungry kisses with moans of my own, my thumb ran circles around her pebbled nipple. Her intoxicating scent of arousal wrapped itself around my being, taking ownership of my senses.

"I need you, Zay," she rasped against my lips.

"You sure?"

"Stop asking me that stupid shit," she fired back at me. "Yes, I'm sure."

I wasted no time grabbing my phone, then taking her into my arms and carrying her to my bedroom. I laid her on the soft comforter, her eyes locking with mine. I transferred the music to the speaker in my room. The smooth, sultry tones of Lauryn Hill and D'Angelo floated through the air, wrapping me and Vanessa in its soulful embrace in our serene intimate atmosphere. Lauryn's voice, tender yet powerful, seemed to caress each note as D'Angelo's deep, velvety tones wove around hers. As the song played, it felt like time slowed down. The lyrics spoke directly to our hearts, reinforcing the sense that, in this moment, nothing else truly mattered.

Dropping the phone on the dresser across from the bed, I joined Vanessa on the bed. Kneeling over her, her soft warm hands tugging at my shirt, pulling it over my head and throwing it across the room. Slowly, I peeled her clothes off of her body revealing a matching black lace bra and thong. I bit my lip to contain my excitement, a guttural groan breaking free from deep within me. Vanessa's body writhed beneath me. Her thighs pressed close together, struggling to bring some relief to the bundle of nerves between her slit. Her hands roamed over her brown skin glowing irresistibly in the warm light of the room.

Grabbing one of her legs, my hands kneaded the balls of her feet before my lips left trails of kisses from her ankles, to her calves. My tongue circled the space behind her knee before savoring the sweet velvet of her inner thigh. Vanessa's essence led me straight to the source. When I made it to her center, my nose brushed against the chantilly lace, my lips gently kissing those precious lips. Vanessa's hips bucked against my face. My eyes lifted to hers, lustful fire shooting from them. As she moaned, my thumb slid underneath the mesh of her thong. I stroked her wet folds and hardened bud, sending her arching to me again, her cries more beautiful than the music in the background.

Pulling back on my knees, I took in the sight before me. My dick protested in the confines of my boxers. I needed to be within Vanessa's walls and take up residence in the house custom built for me.

"Fuck me, Zay," Vanessa whimpered.

Shaking my head side to side, I denied her request. "Nessa, we've been apart too long for me to just fuck you. You don't need to be fucked. You deserved to be savored," I said, kissing the inside of her other thigh. "Treasured. Adored." I continued, leaving a trail of kisses up to her belly button. "Let me do that for you. Let me love on you. Let me love you. Can I do that for you?"

"Yes."

"So you'll stop running? From me? From us?" My lips met hers again, my nose brushing her nose.

"Yes."

"You sure? Cause ain't no going back."

"Yes." She grabbed the nape of my neck, lowering my head to meet her mouth. We kissed hungrily, just two people trying to satiate an appetite too long starved. I gripped the lace of her underwear and snatched the thin fabric off her body.

"Fuck, Zay. Those cost over $200."

"You acting like I can't replace them ten times over."

Tossing the ripped threads to the side, I ran my fingers up and down her hot, slick folds. Massaging her throbbing pearl with my thumb, I slipped a finger inside her to make circles around her spot that brought forth waterfalls. I lowered my head to lick the shelf of her breasts, still caged in her bra, breathing in the heavenly scent nestled between them before using my teeth to free them from the cups of the lace fabric. My mouth feasted, longing for sustenance only Vanessa could give me. Her chest arched into my mouth as I suckled her right nipple in my mouth, snaking my tongue around the pebbled left nipple in time with my fingers. Her walls quaked as she grew closer to the release she craved.

Releasing her nipple with a juicy plop, I huskily whispered into her ear. "Come for me, love."

"Not yet. I can wait. I want you inside of me," she rasped.

"You've done enough waiting," I said before littering her face with soft pecks. "I'll fill you up soon enough, but I need you to come for me right now." My fingers moved quicker as my thumb applied pressure to her clit as she unraveled around me. Her head pressed against the pillow, eyes shut tight, and teeth biting her pillowy lips as wave after wave of pleasure coursed through her body.

Seeing that sent every ounce of blood left flowing in my veins straight to my dick. I reached into my wallet on the nightstand to pull out a gold foil packet. After slipping on the condom, I aligned myself to her opening, her wetness making it too easy for me to slip inside, with an all too comfortable snug.

Fuck.

As I circled my hips, moving in and out of Vanessa in rhythmic strokes, electricity sparked in my veins. The growls escaping my mouth made her thrust back onto my dick with fervor, her breast bouncing from the recoil of each smack of our bodies coming together. The walls we'd built to protect ourselves from each other crumbled in ruin around us. I dared myself to look deep into her eyes as she cried out in ecstasy. Dark vulnerable eyes met my gaze and stared into the depths of my soul. Tonight, I lit a match that started a fire within me. I only hoped I would have the strength to control it before it threatened to engulf everything around us in flames again.

Chapter 27

Vanessa

After our routine Pilates class, Kelly and I settled into our favorite smoothie shop across from the studio. The place had this kind of peaceful vibe, all-natural light filtering through the large windows, casting a warm glow over the wooden tables. The soft hum of people chatting and the gentle clinking of glasses created the perfect backdrop for one of our deep conversations.

"One of these days," Kelly groaned, stretching her legs out in front of her, "I'm gonna strangle Kathy. I swear, she's trying to set some secret record for breaking us in half. That last series of moves? Cruel and unusual punishment."

I chuckled, running a hand through the damp coils of my hair, which were still tightly bound in my post-workout bun. "Maybe, but if she keeps my waist snatched, I'll take the pain."

Kelly shot me a look, her eyebrow arching in disbelief. "Girl, that's because you're a glutton for punishment."

I grinned, taking a long sip from my smoothie. "No, I'm just committed to the glow-up."

"Is getting good dick a part of that glow-up plan?" She snorted. "What? You thought I didn't notice you walking in here all bow-legged?"

"Kelly, shut up. You're too much in my business." I leaned back in my chair, letting the calm wash over me, but there was something bubbling beneath the surface—something that had been gnawing at me for weeks. I pushed my half-empty smoothie away and drummed my fingers lightly on the table. "But here's something you can know. I'm going to save the community center. Does that sound crazy?"

Kelly's eyes softened immediately. She reached across the table and took my hands in hers. "Not crazy at all. It actually sounds perfect for you. What's on your mind?"

I glanced out the window for a second, collecting my thoughts before speaking. "The closing of the community center's been bothering me more than I thought it would. I can't stand the idea of those kids having nowhere to go, no place to dream or create. I want to give them that space back—somewhere they feel safe, seen, and loved."

Kelly's expression shifted from surprise to admiration. "Nessa, that's beautiful. You've always had such a big heart. These kids need someone like you fighting for them. And let me tell you, working in the ER, I see too many kids who get pulled into the wrong things because they don't have a safe place to go. Gangs, drugs, violence... It's a cycle. You stepping in could change everything for them."

Her words filled me with a warmth I hadn't felt in a long time. The kind that comes when you know you're being seen for who you truly are. "Right. It's still formulating in my brain. When we get to Lynn's place, I'll ask her for advice about the legal stuff. I want to be prepared before I go to my parents. If I come correct, they'll have no choice but to support me."

Kelly smiled, her hands finally letting go of mine. "That's my girl. And remember, this is your journey. Take your time. Listen to your heart—whether it's your career, love life, or anything else. Just be honest with yourself, and don't rush into decisions."

I smiled, grateful for her wisdom. "Thanks, Kelly girl. I needed that."

THE NEXT DAY UNFOLDED slowly, like frozen syrup dripping from a spoon, what with fall finally transitioning to something like winter. Morning slipped into afternoon as I worked on the details for the Foundation's Gala in March. But the weight of it all—my ideas, my goals, the community center's fate—kept pressing on my mind. I left early, grabbing a quick bite before heading to teach my art class at the community center. Mrs. Collins and I had a long conversation about what it takes to run a place like Heritage. She shared insights, her soft yet determined voice guiding me through the possibilities—foundations, grants, partnerships. She even suggested talking to my parents. The Taylor Foundation, she reminded me, was the biggest in Houston. And the truth is, that'd been hovering in the back of my mind, too. Going to them for help, for backing, for approval.

Leaving the center that evening, I felt a bit lighter. A plan was forming in my head, and I had enough information to present to my parents. It was time.

As soon as I parked in the wide circle drive of their home, the familiar weight of everything hit me. The sprawling mansion loomed ahead, its columns catching the last rays of daylight, glowing softly like it always had. My parents' home was like that—constant, unwavering, a place where expectations lived and thrived.

I headed straight to my father's study. The faint smell of cigar smoke hit me before I even reached the door, and as I entered, I saw him—standing by the large bookshelf that took up the entire wall at the back of the room. The golden light from the setting sun filtered through the tall windows, casting long shadows over the dark, rich wood.

My father looked up and smiled, already pouring two glasses of amber liquid. Whiskey, as always. He crossed the room and handed me one without a word.

"Thanks, Dad," I murmured, taking the glass and sinking into one of the deep leather chairs by the window.

He sat across from me, his posture relaxed but his eyes sharp. "I was surprised when you called," he said, his voice calm, but with that undercurrent of curiosity. "It's been a minute since you've come by for dinner, too."

I leaned back, draping my arm over the edge of the chair. "I was just here a few weekends ago, remember?"

He raised an eyebrow, swirling the whiskey in his glass. "So, things are going good with your mother?"

I nodded, taking a sip of the whiskey—strong, smooth, with just the right amount of burn. "Yeah, actually. She's letting me oversee the PR for the gala."

My father's eyes twinkled as he chuckled. "Well, that's something. Your mother letting go of the reins, even a little, is a miracle in itself." He leaned forward slightly, a serious expression creeping into his face. "But something tells me there's more on your mind than the gala."

I met his gaze, feeling that familiar tug of vulnerability. He could always tell when something was weighing on me. I sighed, lifting the glass to my lips again. "Well, I wanted to talk to you about something."

My father didn't flinch, but his eyes sharpened. "Is it about Xavier Morris being in town?" His voice was steady, measured.

I nodded, setting the glass down on the small side table. "Wesley's dad told you about his project near the community center, didn't he?"

A knowing smile played on my father's lips. "He did. Richard wasn't happy about the partnership ending. Said something about Xavier and Khalil pulling out after the construction's done."

"Good for them," I muttered, trying to keep my tone neutral.

My father raised an eyebrow. "You sound like you knew all about it."

"I did. Mom even suggested I do a mural for the project, but I passed. Xavier and Khalil should've never gotten involved with Wright Horizons in the first place."

My father sighed, leaning back in his chair, cigar smoke swirling around him. "You know, I offered to invest in their company once."

I blinked, caught off guard. "Speaking of which. Why did you do that?"

He chuckled softly, his eyes glazing over as he recalled the memory. "You of all people should know I can't turn down a good investment. That's where Richard went wrong. He tries to force things into his vision, instead of letting them flow naturally."

My heart tightened in my chest. "Daddy, he didn't want a handout. He and Khalil built their company from the ground up. They didn't need your help."

My father nodded, his eyes narrowing slightly as he took another puff of his cigar. "I wasn't offering charity. I saw potential in them. But I respected his decision. Whatever happened between you two?"

"Xavier and I...we're good now," I said, feeling the conversation shift. "We've talked about the past, and we've agreed to move forward."

My father's gaze sharpened, his voice lowering slightly. "Move forward, huh? What does that mean, exactly?"

I downed the rest of my whiskey, the burn trailing down my throat. "It means we're figuring things out. Seeing where it goes."

He studied me for a long moment, his eyes softening as he leaned forward, resting his elbows on his knees. "Vanessa, do you know when you're meant to be with someone?"

"How did you know with Mom?" I asked, my voice barely above a whisper.

My father's smile returned, soft and nostalgic. "She made me work for it. And we made each other better. We almost didn't make it a few times, but love...love is work, Vanessa. It's commitment."

I nodded, letting his words sink in. "I don't know if I'm ready to dive back in like that. It's complicated."

He chuckled again, standing and offering me his hand. "Life's always complicated, sweet pea. But you don't have to have all the answers right now. Just take it one day at a time."

I stood and let him pull me into a tight embrace, the familiar scent of his cologne mixing with the lingering smell of whiskey and cigars. "Thanks, Dad."

"You're welcome. And remember, no one else's expectations should shape your happiness. Not mine, not your mother's. Not anyone's."

I smiled, the tension in my chest easing just a little. "I'll keep that in mind."

"Is that what you came over here to talk about?" My father asked as we left the study, his arm around my shoulders.

"No actually, something else entirely."

"My two favorite ladies," my father called out as we walked into the kitchen together, pulling my mother into his arms and pressing a kiss to her forehead. His gaze shifted to me, and before I could say a word, he wrapped me into their orbit, pulling me close with an arm around my shoulder.

"Vanessa, sweetheart. How's your day going? Are you staying for dinner?"

"No," I smiled, leaning into the warmth of the moment. "I came over to run something by both of you," I began, my voice hesitant but growing steadier. "The community center is closing. I can't stop thinking about it. I don't want those kids to lose their space. It's become important to me."

My mother raised an eyebrow as she adjusted her gold bracelets, listening intently. "What exactly do you want to do, Vanessa?" she asked, her tone soft but curious.

Taking a deep breath, I stood a little taller, the weight of the idea solidifying in my mind. "I want to save it. I'm thinking of starting my own nonprofit, something that provides safe spaces for kids and teenagers. Somewhere they can grow, learn, and not feel like the world is against them."

The words spilled out, flowing faster than I expected. I wasn't just talking about saving the community center anymore; I was talking about building something, leaving a legacy.

My mother exchanged a glance with my father. I braced myself, ready for the questions, the doubts, the lecture on logistics and feasibility.

But instead, she surprised me.

"That sounds... wonderful," she said, her voice coated with something deeper. *Pride.* "You've been thinking about this for a while, haven't you?"

I nodded, biting my lip. "Yeah. I just didn't know how to start."

My father chuckled softly, walking over to cut himself a piece of the brownies my mother pulled out of the oven when we'd first entered the kitchen. He handed me a piece without asking, knowing my weakness for her baked goods. "Well, you're on the right path, sweet pea. And you know your mother and I will help however we can."

I blinked, a little overwhelmed by her enthusiasm. "Are you sure?" I asked, still half-expecting her to tell me I wasn't ready, or that I needed to think it through some more.

"Absolutely," she said, stepping forward to place a hand on my arm. "You're my daughter. I've watched you struggle with decisions before, but this... this feels different. You're not just chasing an idea, Vanessa. You're following your heart."

A smile tugged at my lips, and I let out a breath I didn't even realize I'd been holding. "Thank you. I'll make you proud," I whispered, my voice steady now, my resolve growing stronger.

"You already have," my mother said softly, pulling me into a hug.

As I stepped back, my phone buzzed in my pocket. A message from Xavier. I couldn't help but smile. "I'll stay for dinner another time," I said, starting my departure.

"Vanessa, let me walk you to the door. I'll be right back, Dougie." Following my mother to the exit, I prepared myself for the barrage of questions she would assault me with, before letting me walk out of the house. "Where are you off to? I thought we could spend more time together tonight?"

"We will another night. I need to see a man about a horse." *And ride it into the morning light.*

"Vanessa Ann Taylor," my mother scoffed, looking around to see if anyone overheard me. "I know we're working on communicating, but I'm still your mother. We have to have some boundaries."

"Okay, okay. I have plans, Momma. I gotta go."

My mother nodded as she settled into her understanding. "Do these plans concern a certain ex-boyfriend who's in town?"

"Maybe..." I hesitated. "Yes, they do." And there it was. I braced myself for the bullets of disapproval that had my name etched on them. I was prepared though, my kevlar in place, as I waited for my mother to speak. Sure she was receptive to me starting my own nonprofit, but how far would that grace go when it came to my choice of a partner.

"Well, as much as I want to tell you what to do about that situation, I'm not. Whatever you think you need to do concerning Xavier, whatever comes of it, I'll be here to support you."

Shock entered my body. I was fully prepared for my mother to tell me I shouldn't be seeing Zay. Hearing that she would support my decisions would be something I'd have to get used to, so long as it lasted.

"Thanks, mom. I appreciate that."

"I told you, I'm trying. You have no idea how hard it is at this moment, but I'm trying. Can you at least let me know how things go? I'm sure you'll discuss it with Dr. Smith, but I'd like the opportunity to be there for you as well."

"Sure, once I make it make sense to me, we can talk about it."

"Okay. Well, let me not hold up your plans. Call me if you need anything, no matter what."

"Yes, momma. I will." Leaning forward, I placed a kiss on her cheek, giving her arm a squeeze. "Love you. Have fun with Daddy...but not too much fun."

My mother's face brightened. "Don't worry about me and your Daddy. You're the one who doesn't need to have any fun, you understand?"

Narrowed soft eyes looked me over as a chuckle escaped my lips. "Bye," I exclaimed, walking from the bar to my car park around the corner.

Chapter 28

Xavier

"So what you think about that other company?" Khalil asked after we reviewed the slide deck we'd been given by a potential investor. Since we decided to part ways with Wright Horizons, we've been on the hunt for a new company to help us reach our expansion goals.

"They seem straight. But so did Wright Horizons, and you see how that turned out."

"I feel you, bruh...Where my beer at?"

"Negro, you got two legs. Go get you one." I laughed.

Khalil moved to grab him a beer from the fridge, continuing with his previous statement. "Like I was saying, Evergreen Capital Ventures is legit. I know I messed up with Wright Horizons, but remember, my initial conversations were with Wesley, before his dad took over." Khalil plopped down in the armchair next to the couch. "We have some time in the New Year to set up a meeting, so think about it."

"I will. What's the alternative? Besides, I have some shit brewing in my mind that I need to figure out how to make happen."

"Shit, let me know something. Until then, I keep searching for investors."

I knew of one person who might be able to help, but I didn't know if he'd have any hard feelings about Vanessa and I breaking up. Mr. Taylor didn't seem like the type of man to hold grudges, but any man is capable of anything when it comes to their children, especially their daughters.

"Say, you think Vanessa's dad might know somebody we can use?" Khalil asked, as if reading my mind.

I leaned my head on the back of the couch. "He might. Nessa said he don't fuck with Wright Horizons like that."

"So let's hit him up, see what he say. Especially if things don't work with Evergreen." Khalil looked hopeful. I appreciated that most about him. He had a natural ability to see the best of every outcome. It's most likely what caused him to miss the red flags with Wright Horizons. *Shit, I missed them, too.*

"I don't know, man. What if he's feeling some type of way because of what happened between Nessa and I? I would."

"Shit, man." Khalil was uncharacteristically quiet, deep in thought.

"What if we're biting off more than we can chew?" I looked at the emails on my phone. One of our assistants back at home sent an update on a project. We were trying to get permits approved by City Hall to start construction on the historic Clabon Theatre located in the Treme neighborhood, but it was like pulling teeth. City politics was making it hard for us to save the historic building that was once a center of Black entertainment and symbol of the neighborhood's artistic roots. "Johnny just forwarded the response from city hall about the permits. They denied them again."

"Man, this is just a small obstacle. We overcame bigger roadblocks starting out. I'll see who I can talk to when we get back to New Orleans." Khalil took a swig of his beer then looked at me earnestly.

"Push come to shove, we just keep doing what we've been doing. What's meant for us will come when it's time."

"Yeah, true." I swigged the remainder of the beer in my bottle. "But right now, it's time for you to get on up out of here. I got places to be." We stood in sync, grabbing our belongings to leave my apartment.

"Man, where the fuck you going?" Khalil judged, rushing to grab some chips from my pantry.

"See my love, of course." I cheesed, my smile taking over my face, as I picked up the empty bottles and threw them away in the kitchen. With us nearing the end of our project with Wright Horizons, I didn't want to waste time spent with Vanessa on things outside of my control. My focus was on her right now.

"Damn, again," Khalil joked. "Nah, but for real, happiness looks good on you my boy."

"Man, what. Happiness not even the word. I feel like my world is complete." I picked up my keys and wallet, stuffing them into my pockets, before pulling on the camel colored overcoat over my black hoodie and jogger combo. "Which is why I might need something to come together here in Houston. I just got my baby back. I don't want to give her any reason to believe it won't work out this time."

"You taking her on a date like that?" Khalil joked, looking me up and down.

"Chill man. It's not a date. I'm keeping her company while she works on her nonprofit plan."

"Man, what kind of date is that?"

I pushed Khalil out of my apartment, locking the door behind me. "Like I said, it's not a date. She said she was tired and didn't want to do anything too major." We walked down the steps, heading in the direction of our cars.

"I might have to give that lovey dovey shit a try one day," Khalil grinned, as he stopped in front of his car. "Not any time soon though."

"Aww, it ain't all bad. You just gotta be patient" I dapped up Khalil before entering my car. "Ain't that what you told me?"

"Ahh. Get on to your date before she change her mind."

I revved my engine before pulling off. As I cruised through the streets of Houston, the weight of our partnership with Wright Horizons dissipated, making room for the excitement I had at spending the evening with Vanessa. The moment I stepped out of the car, the cool night air hit me, washing away the lingering stress. From outside her door, I could hear a faint melody, the kind of music that made you want to settle into a quiet night.

When she opened the door, it felt like time slowed down. Vanessa stood there, her hair loose and free, framing her face just so. That oversized sweater hung off her shoulder over one of my company t-shirts barely concealing a pair of boyshorts, casual yet so got damn tempting. I couldn't help but take it all in—the way she looked at me, tired but still radiant. She had that magic, the kind of beauty that isn't even about how she looks. It's how she carried the weight of everything without letting it crush her.

"Hey, Zay," she said softly, her voice low, like she hadn't spoken to anyone all day.

"Hey my baby," I replied, stepping inside and closing the door behind me, pulling her into my arms, littering her face and neck with kisses. Her place felt warm, lived-in, like it belonged to someone who poured love into every corner. Candles flickered on the tables, the smell of something comforting lingered in the air, papers scattered across the coffee table, laptop still open, glowing like it had seen too many hours of work.

"You've been busy, huh?" I asked, watching her as she sank into the couch, her hands rubbing her temples. She looked worn out, like she'd been fighting a battle only she could see.

She sighed and leaned back, looking like she was ready to collapse into the cushions. "Yeah, I've been at it all day. Trying to perfect this proposal for the nonprofit. The board meeting is right after the holidays, so I need to finish it now before I get consumed. It has to be flawless, but every time I think I've got it right, something else feels off, and I'm back at square one."

That same expectation she carried—perfection. Always trying to make sure everything lined up exactly how it should. It was something I knew well, but it seemed like it was swallowing her whole tonight.

"Nessa," I said, lowering myself beside her, close enough to feel her energy. "You don't have to do this alone. You're trying to carry it all by yourself, but I'm here. Let me help."

"No, Zay. I need to figure this out by myself. For myself. To prove to myself I can do it."

I stared at her for a moment, waiting for her to see the irony in the words she'd just used. Those same words I'd used that led to our breakdown before.

"Nessa baby, look at me." She stared at me, the most adorable pout on her face, eyes bleary from staring at her laptop all day. "I learned the hard way about trying to do stuff by yourself. Let me help you. I won't tell you what to do. I'll be your assistant."

For a second, I wasn't sure if she'd let me in, but then she nodded, her eyes softening in that way they did when she let her guard down.

"Okay," she whispered. "I could use a hand."

We got to work, bouncing ideas back and forth. It felt natural—like we'd always done this, building on each other's energy. She had this way of making ideas come to life, turning them into something real and meaningful. I was just glad to be part of it, to give her some relief. I could see the stress slipping off her as we talked, replaced by that spark I loved so much.

But right when we were making progress, my phone buzzed in my pocket. Khalil's name popped up on the screen.

"One second," I said, stepping away. "What's up?"

"That greedy muthafucka," Khalil's voice was tight, laced with frustration.

"Who?" I asked, already knowing it wasn't good.

"Wesley's dad is playing dirty. He's trying to block us from getting new investors. Mad that we pulled out of the deal."

"For real? After everything we did for him?" I felt my chest tighten, anger bubbling up. "How did you find that out?"

"Yeah, man. Wesley tried talking sense into him, but you know how that goes. He called to give me the heads up. I just got off the phone with him and called you."

I looked out the window, my mind racing. "Alright, we'll figure something out. Right?"

"I'll keep trying, but we need a hail mary. Hopefully he ain't gotten in contact with Evergreen yet." Khalil's frustration mirrored mine. "Look, I didn't wanna mess up your night. Hit me up when you can."

After the call ended, I just stood there, staring out into the Houston night. We had put our hearts into our company, building it from nothing. Now it felt like all of it was being ripped away over someone else's pride. Right when I was getting used to the idea of expanding. Right when all parts of my world were aligning.

"Zay?" Vanessa's voice was soft behind me. She stood there, concern written all over her face.

I shook my head, trying to process it all. "Khalil called. Wesley's dad is trying to block us from getting new investors. He's mad about the deal we ended, and now he's blackballing us."

She moved closer, her gaze locking onto mine. "I'm so sorry, Zay. That's not fair." Her arms wrapped around me from behind, her face resting against my back.

"It's just...we've worked so hard for this. And now it feels like it's slipping away because of someone else's bullshit ass ego."

She didn't say anything at first. Instead, she took my hand, pulling me back to the couch where we'd been sitting. Her grip was firm, steady, like she was anchoring me.

"You're not going to let it fall apart," she said, her voice sure. "I know you. You always find a way. Look what all you've accomplished with just you and Khalil."

I looked at her, taking in the sincerity in her words. "What if I can't fix this one?"

"What was it you told me earlier? We'll figure it out together," she said, her hand still holding mine. "You've got Khalil. And you've got me. We'll get through this."

"Even if it means going long distance?"

A realization neither one of us anticipated bubbled between us. The partnership with Wright Horizons was supposed to give us access. Access I now realized would make an expansion to Houston possible. Access that would allow whatever was blossoming between Vanessa and I to flourish until everything was in its right place.

Vanessa took my hand in hers, placing two of my fingers over her heart, doing the same to me. No words needed to follow the act. For the first time that night, I felt the tension in my chest ease, even if just a little. She made it seem like, no matter what happened, I wasn't in this alone.

She stood up, pulling me with her. "Come with me. I want to show you something."

We headed down the hall, into a room I hadn't been in before. Her guest room—half-bedroom, half-studio. Canvases leaned against the walls, some covered, some in progress. But one stood in the middle, draped in a large sheet.

Vanessa pulled the sheet off, revealing a painting of me. I stared, speechless. She'd captured me—everything. The strength, sure, but also the weight I carried, the vulnerability I tried so hard to hide. Deep brushstrokes filled in the space around my profile, deep grays imitated the storms I've faced in my life. It contrasted with the richness of the colors she'd used for my skin, rich browns and blacks, gold foil replicating the cuban link chains and cross around my neck.

"How long did it take you to do this?" I chuckled as I examined the painting further. "You even got my waves."

"You wouldn't believe me if I told you," she said chuckled. "Do you like it?"

"I love it." I ran my hands over the painting, the different textures amplifying what she was trying to convey. "Tell me about it. I know you have a story."

"This is how I see you," she whispered, stepping beside me, grabbing hold of my arm, resting her head against my shoulder. "I know now that chaos that consumes your mind, thoughts running rampant as you try to solve everything. Be everything. I get it. Unless we're looking in a mirror, we don't get to see what the world sees. And when you step into the world, this is what people get to see. Silent strength," she said, running her fingers along my shoulders. They smoothed across my chest, up my neck, stopping at the temples of my forehead. "Brilliance beyond measure." She took my chin in her palm and turned my face to meet hers. "Someone who faces everything head-on, no matter what. A person who changes the world."

I swallowed hard, not knowing what to say. She saw me in a way no one else did. For once, I didn't feel like I had to keep it together. Not with her.

I turned to her, my voice low. "Thank you, baby," I said, pressing my forehead to hers, brushing my nose with her own.

"No thanks needed. Sometimes we need someone to remind us of who we are," she smiled, and just like that, I felt like I could breathe again. "Come on," she said, pulling me out of the room. "Let's get out of here for a bit. I know a place where we can clear our heads."

I laughed softly, grabbing my keys. "You always know what I need."

She winked. "That's my job."

Chapter 29

Xavier

Walking into Post HTX, a dining, shopping, coworking space in Downtown Houston, with Vanessa was like stepping into an alternate universe where time stood still but every detail thrummed with life. I held the door open for her, and she glided past me. We were here for food, but my mind was already racing with excitement about the building she told me used to be the historic Barbara Jordan Post Office.

"Damn, this is crazy," I marveled, sweeping my arm to high ceilings and open space. When entering the doors, you could still make out the original mailroom counters, albeit with a facelift to fit the modern aesthetic of the building. "It's like they took the bones of the old post office and gave it a soul."

Vanessa chuckled beside me, her eyes sparkling. "You sound like you're about to propose to the building."

I smirked, nudging her playfully. "Maybe I am. I mean, look how they integrated the industrial elements with the original mid-century modern design. It's genius. This is something Khalil and I thought about doing at a shopping center in New Orleans East, but the building sold before we could get our hands on it."

She shook her head, a smile playing on her lips. "Okay, Mr. Architect. Let's get something to eat before you start drafting blueprints. I can see the wheels turning in your head."

We wandered further into the building, toward the food hall, a sprawling marketplace of culinary delights from around the world. My stomach rumbled as we passed various food stalls. Ramen, Tacos, Burgers, Cajun, Sweets. There was something here for everyone.

"Follow me." Vanessa pulled me toward a West African stall called CHÒPNBLỌK. She ordered something called the Golden Bowl and an Oga Palmer. After a short wait, we were seated, at one of the tables in the heart of the food hall. She pushed the tray in my direction, beckoning me to take the first bite. I placed a little of everything on my spoon. The smoky jollof rice mixed with the African spiced chicken beautifully. I took another bite, dipping the spoon into the curry. This was a dish I could get used to eating.

Soon enough, Vanessa joined me in eating. I couldn't help but watch her. The way she savored each bite, the little sounds of satisfaction she made, she was a sight to behold, even with a dollop of curry sauce on her chin.

"Hold still," I said, reaching over to wipe the sauce off with my thumb. She caught my hand before I could pull away, holding it for a beat longer than necessary.

Her lips wrapped around the current luckiest member of my body, sucking the curry clean. "Thanks," she murmured, her eyes locking onto mine.

My heart did that weird thing it always did when she looked at me like that, like she could see right through the false confidence I plastered on my face, to the guy who still was in disbelief that she was sitting here with me. I sipped the Hibiscus Lemonade drink to quench my thirst. Finishing the cup, I realized my thirst for Vanessa would never be satisfied until we were in each other's lives forever.

After we demolished our meal, we stopped to get ice cream at Flower & Cream, Chocolate Brownie for me, Biscoff Cookie Butter for her, sharing tastes as we took in the various art installations and quirky shops in the building. I felt like a kid in a candy store, pointing out every unique architectural feature, reclaimed wood, exposed ductwork, even the minimalist lighting fixtures. Vanessa listened patiently, occasionally teasing me about my "building crush."

We eventually found ourselves back in the center of the food hall, taking the stairs that led to the rooftop. I pushed the doors open to reveal a lush rooftop garden with sweeping views of the downtown Houston skyline. We stepped further out, and I could see the awe in her eyes, the silvery gleam, from the skylights, highlighting her cocoa skin.

"Beautiful, isn't it," she asked, looking back at me.

"You have no idea," I replied, slipping my arm around her waist. "Who would've thought an old post office could turn into something this beautiful?"

She leaned into me, her head resting against my shoulder. "You would. You have a way of seeing the potential in things, when no one else does."

We walked closer to the edge of the garden, getting a closer view of Aquarium's Diving Ferris wheel and I-45. The city stretched out before us in glittering lights and shadows. The air was markedly cooler than when we'd left Vanessa's apartment. The wind whipped around us, carrying a faint scent of the herbs and flowers planted around us.

I turned to face Vanessa, lifting her chin gently so our eyes met. "Nessa," I said softly, so the other guests walking around the rooftop couldn't hear me. "There's a feeling I get each time I'm looking at blueprints, where I can see how everything's going to come together. How the chaos of lines and mess will transform into something amazing."

She nodded, her gaze unwavering.

"That's how I feel about us," I continued, my voice whispered into her ears. "Even when things were messy and we were apart, I always knew we had the potential to be something incredible."

Her eyes glistened, and for a moment, I thought she might cry. But then, she smiled, that radiant, heart-stopping smile that always knocked me off balance.

"I feel the same way," she said, her voice breaking slightly.

I leaned in, capturing her lips in a kiss that was both tender and fierce, a promise and a plea all at once. The world around us seemed to blur, the city lights fading as we lost ourselves in each other.

When we finally pulled apart, breathless and slightly dazed, I couldn't help but laugh. "You are unforgettable."

"You too," she laughed, resting her forehead against my lips. We stayed like that for a while, just holding each other and soaking in the moment. Eventually she pulled back and kissed me gingerly on the lips. "Zay?"

"Yes, baby love?"

"Take me home."

And with that, we left the city behind, ready to create something even more beautiful together.

Chapter 30

Xavier

As I walked through the door, I took in the scene of Vanessa's art class, tables covered with art supplies, kids already engrossed in their own worlds of creativity. Vanessa hadn't told me exactly why she needed me here today, just that it would be fun.

I shrugged off my confusion, thinking back to her cryptic text, and took my place at the front of the classroom next to Vanessa. Her eyes sparkled with a playful glint that set my heart racing. She had that effect on me, ever since we reconnected. As the kids started filtering in, a few of them surrounded me, peppering me with questions.

"Mr. Morris, have you ever done any modeling before?"

"What's it like running your own company?"

"Do you have any tips for staying motivated?"

"How do you manage stress with everything you've got going on?"

I chuckled, answering as best I could. "I wouldn't call it modeling," I said, glancing at Vanessa, who was trying not to laugh. "Running a company is a lot of work, but it's worth it when you're passionate about what you do. And staying motivated? It helps to have a good support system—and take breaks when you need them."

Vanessa's eyes met mine with a reassuring look. Those flutters in my chest? They were back in full force.

"Alright, everyone!" Vanessa's voice cut through the noise, pulling everyone's attention to the front. "Today, we're diving into the world of portraits!" She paused, letting the excitement build. "And guess who our special guest model is?"

The kids exchanged curious looks, buzzing with anticipation. I shot Vanessa a questioning glance, and she just grinned, mouthing, "You."

"Y'all remember Mr. Morris, right?" she announced, stepping aside and pointing at me like I was some sort of celebrity.

"Oh, so this is why I'm here," I muttered, shaking my head with a bemused smile. I walked over to the stool next to Vanessa, playing along. "Looks like I'm the chosen one today. Don't make me look too crazy, alright?" The kids laughed, throwing out playful jokes at my expense, which only made me laugh harder.

Vanessa's eyes softened as she looked at me. "Now, before we start, let's talk about the importance of observation in drawing. We'll focus on capturing the essence of our model, Mr. Morris, on paper." Her gaze held a hint of admiration, making me stand a little taller despite the nerves bubbling up.

"Observe the details—the curve of his smile, the shape of his eyes," she continued, turning her attention back to the kids. "It's not just about copying; it's about understanding and interpreting what you see."

The kids nodded, faces set in serious concentration, sketch pads poised and ready. As they started sketching, Vanessa moved around the room, offering gentle guidance. I tried to stay still, which wasn't easy when you're the center of attention and your old lady was sneaking glances at you that make you feel like you've won the lottery.

"You've got a really good profile," one of the kids remarked, their pencil already moving quickly over the paper. "Miss Nessa, do you use Mr. Morris as a model a lot?"

"Focus on your drawing," Vanessa replied, grinning across the room.

"Can you do a serious pose?" another kid asked. Never one to disappoint, I struck a more composed pose, trying to keep a straight face.

"Remember," Vanessa said, trying to get the class back on track, "it's not just about capturing physical features. Think about the emotions you see, the stories behind the eyes. Let your drawings reflect the personality of our model." She threw me a playful wink, and I had to stifle a laugh as the kids giggled.

Vanessa walked over to a table where Payton was hard at work. "Miss Vanessa, are you and Mr. Morris a thing?" she asked, a mischievous glint in her eye.

I watched Vanessa chuckle, a little caught off guard. *Payton sure is direct*, I thought, hiding a grin. She was talented, but man, could she dig for gossip.

"That's not what we're focused on today," Vanessa replied, her voice warm but firm. "We're all artists focused on creating beautiful portraits, okay?"

"So that's a yes?" another student teased.

Vanessa glanced at me, and I couldn't resist winking at her. "Yeah, maybe a little," she relented, and I had to bite my lip to keep from laughing out loud.

As the kids poured their creativity into their sketches, I found myself engaging with them more, complimenting their efforts and offering tips. "Great job on the eyes," I told one kid, then to another, "You really captured the shape of my jaw. That's impressive."

"Okay, everyone, let's take a moment to share our drawings!" Vanessa called out. Hands shot up, eager to present their masterpieces. The room filled with applause, admiration, and good-natured jokes as each kid showed off their work. It was humbling to see myself through their eyes—each drawing unique, each perspective fresh and honest.

"You're all incredible artists!" I told them, genuinely touched by their efforts. "I might need to hire you as my personal portraitist." Their faces lit up, their pride contagious.

"Mr. Morris is correct," Vanessa added. "Today was about more than drawing. It was about capturing the essence of a person, expressing emotions on paper, and having fun with it. I'm so proud of each and every one of you."

As the class wrapped up, the kids swarmed us with their sketches, eager to show off their work one last time before heading out. I turned to Vanessa, my gratitude spilling over. "I loved watching you in your element. And hey, being a model is not a bad gig." I wrapped my arms around her waist, pulling her closer.

"You alright. Don't go getting a big head on me."

"I already got that, love." I nuzzled her neck, pressing a light kiss to her lips. Lost in the moment, I didn't hear the heels clacking into the room until it was too late.

I glanced over Vanessa's shoulder, and my stomach clenched. *Vivian Taylor.* She entered the room, a striking figure with her tall, statuesque frame, flawless caramel complexion, and meticulously styled hair framing her face. Her sharp, almond-shaped eyes were assessing, as if she could see straight through any pretense. She carried herself with an air of effortless authority, her posture perfectly poised, exuding a refined confidence that always left me feeling exposed. Her elegant, tailored clothes hinted at her sophistication and the high standards she set for everyone around her.

The moment her gaze landed on me, my stomach tightened, pulling me back to the first time I'd met her during my college years. Back then, her mere presence put me into defense mode, as if she were all too aware of my shortcomings. The way her eyebrows arched, just slightly, as she took in the sight of Vanessa in my arms now, brought back that familiar sensation of inadequacy.

Vanessa quickly stepped back, smoothing her clothes with a slightly guilty smile. "Mom," she said, a hint of nervousness in her voice. "I thought you were going to drop by next week?"

Mrs. Taylor's eyes moved between us, her expression unreadable but not entirely unkind. "I was nearby and thought I'd check on your class." Her gaze landed on me, assessing. "Xavier Morris. It's been a long time."

I swallowed, trying to read her reaction. "Mrs. Taylor. Good to see you." My palms were suddenly clammy. *Would she ever truly approve of me?*

Mrs. Taylor nodded, her lips curling into a small, enigmatic smile. "Am I interrupting?"

"Not at all," Vanessa said, a little too quickly. "We just finished. The kids were working on portraits."

"Portraits, huh?" Mrs. Taylor's eyes scanned the room, taking in the scattered sketches. "That sounds wonderful. Vanessa, you've always had a gift for uplifting others."

Vanessa's face lit up, and a rush of pride for her swelled in my chest. She was incredible with these kids, helping them see their own potential. "Thanks, Mom. We were about to discuss the proposal for the nonprofit community center."

Mrs. Taylor's expression turned business-like. "I'd love to hear more. Can I join?"

As if on cue, Mrs. Collins, Vanessa's mentor and a force in the community, breezed in with her usual energy. "Vanessa! Mr. Morris! Oh, and Mrs. Taylor, too?," she added warmly, her eyes twinkling as she saw me. "Good to see you all."

Vanessa outlined her proposal: a community center offering art programs, career workshops, and resources for underprivileged youth. I couldn't help but admire her passion and vision as she spoke, Mrs. Collins adding a few remarks here and there. "We're still finalizing some details, but it's coming together well," she said, her excitement contagious.

Mrs. Taylor listened carefully, nodding. "It's ambitious, Vanessa. I'm proud of you for taking this on."

"Thank you," Vanessa beamed.

"I know she keeps telling me not to get my hopes up, but I can't help it," Mrs. Collins added. "Whatever happens, I'll be eternally grateful for your help, Vanessa. Can I pull you away for a moment? I want to show you some other things you might want to consider adding."

"Um, yeah." Vanessa looked between her mother and me, cautiously. "I'll be right back." As Vanessa and Mrs. Collins moved to exit the classroom, I felt Mrs. Taylor's eyes on me. I shifted uncomfortably, uncertain of what was coming next.

Deciding to break the ice, I started by apologizing. "Mrs. Taylor, I want you to know, that I never meant for all that happened between Vanessa and me to go down that way. Especially..." The words strangled themselves in my throat. "Especially the umm..."

"The baby, Xavier. Your child." Vivian took a deep breath, her gaze steady. "I don't fault you for that... I know we haven't always seen eye to eye. I want you to know my concerns were never about you personally. They were about ensuring Vanessa had the freedom to discover herself before committing to anyone else."

I nodded, the knot in my stomach loosening. "I get it, Mrs. Taylor. I think I was so focused on trying to be what I thought Vanessa needed that I forgot to just let her... be herself."

Her eyes softened, a rare warmth there. "We both wanted to protect her, but maybe we didn't give her enough space to decide what she wanted."

A small smile crept onto my face. "Mrs. Taylor," I started.

"Call me Vivian, please?"

"Vivian. Since Nessa and I have been apart, I've learned a lot about supporting someone without trying to control the outcome. Vanessa deserved that back then. It's my mission to give it to her now."

Vivian's expression brightened. "I completely agree." She hesitated for a moment. "I've enjoyed seeing the light come back in my daughter's eyes. I like to think you've had a little something to do with that."

Emotion welled up in my chest, unexpected and overwhelming. "Thank you Mrs. Vivian. I could say the same for you."

"Xavier, can you do me a favor?" I nodded my head up and down, anticipating what Mrs. Taylor would say. "Vanessa told me you'll be moving back home after the holidays. My daughter is stepping into the exceptional woman I've always known she could be. But, I'm learning that growth isn't linear. And old habits are hard to shake.

"I never doubted the love you have for my daughter. And as much as she won't allow herself to admit it, I know deep down, she feels the same. If the two of you plan to continue whatever it is you have going on, and it becomes too stressful, promise me you'll catch her.

"If you love my daughter, even half of what I think you do, I need you to be there for her where I can't. Some wounds can't be fixed with a mother's hands. I don't want to be on the verge of losing my daughter again. Do you understand what I'm trying to say, Xavier?"

"Yes, ma'am. I understand." The knot that lodged itself in my throat struggled to force its way down, as I swallowed Mrs. Taylor's words.

Vanessa returned, her discussion with Mrs. Collins seemingly wrapped up. Her eyes sparkled with a mix of surprise and pleasure as she looked between us. "Everything okay here?"

"Perfect," Vivian replied, a genuine smile touching her lips. "Xavier and I were just catching up."

Vanessa's face lit up. "Oh, really?"

I nodded, catching Vanessa's eye, feeling a renewed sense of hope. "Yep. Turns out we have a lot more in common than we thought."

Vanessa squinted her eyes at both her mother and me. "Okay."

"Well, I'm heading out to meet your father for dinner. Xavier, I do hope to see more of you in the future." Vivian hugged her daughter before exiting the classroom.

"What was that about?" Vanessa turned to face me, her eyebrows raised.

"I think your mom and I just had a truce," I replied, pulling her close and kissing her nose.

"Interesting...You ready to grab some tacos?"

"Yeah, hungry ass."

We gathered our things and headed out into the evening, a playful anticipation in our steps. The promise of dinner at Pistoleros added a lightness to the air, and for the first time in a long while, the future seemed brighter.

Chapter 31

VANESSA

Setting my phone on the holder next to the pepper grinder, I rummaged through my pantry, pulling out jar after jar of foreign to me seasonings. Kelly, Lynn, and Nyah's faces were on the screen, all watching me with expressions that could only be described as part concern, part entertainment.

"So, what exactly are you trying to make again?" Kelly asked, arching an eyebrow with a skeptical smile.

"Spicy bolognese," I replied, holding a random box of noodles. "With parmesan-crusted chicken."

Lynn squinted at the screen, then burst out laughing. "Girl, that's spaghetti and fried chicken." Kelly joined in her laughter, Nyah smiling and shaking her head.

"Nessa, do you even know what you're doing?" Nyah asked, looking between the screen and behind her.

Heat rushed to my cheeks as I shoved the box of noodles onto the already crowded counter. "Yeah. How hard could it be?"

"True," Kelly snickered, "but you're more a bring the drinks type of cook."

"Come on, now, y'all. You got it, Nessa," Nyah cheered me on. "Just keep it simple, tomato sauce, garlic, a little Italian seasoning, if you have it."

"See, simple." I nodded, glancing around as if "simple" ingredients would magically appear. "I do have a question. When do I add this red wine? Oh, and can I substitute shallots for garlic? I grabbed the wrong thing."

My friends' witch-like cackles came through on the speaker of my phone. Glancing at the phone, I swear Kelly and Lynn had tears in their eyes. "Girl," Lynn started. "Y'all, she's going to burn down her kitchen."

"No, I'm not. Ye have little faith," I huffed, finding a bottle of garlic powder hiding behind something called paprika in my cabinet. I held it up triumphantly, ignoring their giggles. "I found garlic powder. That counts, right?"

Kelly shook her head, smiling. "It's not as good as fresh garlic, but desperate times, girl."

I popped open the lid and gave it a good sprinkle into the saucepan, trying to channel my inner Tabitha Brown. I stirred it around with a wooden spoon, my heart hammering as the sauce began to hiss and pop.

"Nessa, you're stirring like it's a science experiment. Be gentle!" Nyah advised, wiping tears from her eyes. "And did you drain your ground beef?"

Fuck. My neck almost broke with how fast I looked at my friends staring back at me. "I forgot to get the ground beef. You can have bolognese without ground beef, right?" I paused, letting the question hang in the air, my friends' expressions of bewilderment making me nervous.

"Wrap it up, Nessa," Lynn said, breaking the silence. "I can't even laugh at this point. This is just sad."

"At least she's trying," Kelly added. "But for real though. Why are you doing the most? You could've just gotten takeout, and Zay wouldn't know the difference."

A small, genuine small spread across my face as I kept stirring. "I don't know. It felt like something nice to do for him."

"Wooowww," Kelly said looking into the camera. "A bitch start getting dick on a regular basis and turn into Betty Crocker."

"Uh-huh," Nyah drawled, her tone teasing. "Look at you being all domestic."

"Y'all can shut up," I said, sitting the spoon off to the side. Deep down, their teasing only made my heart race faster. It felt strange, wanting to impress him, but also wanting to just be in the same space with him. My phone buzzed, as my friends continued with their own conversation. "Oh, he's pulling into the parking garage. How do I look?"

I spun around, letting my girls see the cute loungewear I wore for Xavier's arrival. The short, long-sleeve, soft-knit cotton lounge dress felt cozy against my skin. The knitted, thigh-high socks and slippers on my feet added an extra layer of warmth from the outside chilliness I tried combatting with my electric fireplace.

"I give it ten, fifteen minutes tops before all that shit is on the floor," Lynn joked.

"Let's make this a bet. Nessa's dropping the panties in five minutes. I can guarantee it," Kelly said.

"Nah, I'd say thirty, forty minutes max," Nyah added. "Y'all know she's stubborn. She'll wait it out just to prove us wrong."

"Nyah, they're just jealous we're getting New Year's dick and they're not." I looked at my married friend, her smile not fully reaching her eyes as she nodded her head.

"Nessa, shut the hell up," Lynn said, laughing.

"I know one thing. Next year, we need to be on somebody's yacht, a bar, something." Kelly said.

Knocks sounded on my door and I froze, my heart skipping a beat. I wiped my hands on a towel, taking a deep breath so I wouldn't seem to excited. I headed for the door, fluffing my twist out. Opening it slowly, a wave of warmth spilled over me as soon as I saw Xavier standing there. He held a large bouquet of white roses, a soft grin spreading across his face as he looked at me.

"Are these for me?" I asked, taking the flowers into my arms, blushing as I stared into his eyes.

"A dozen roses for everyday we've been apart." He walked into my entryway, kicking the door closed and locking it, then pulling me into his arms. He captured my lips in a kiss so deep, so sweet, I became lost in the taste of us. He dropped his keys on the table next to the door, swooping me into his arms, securing my legs around his waist, and led us toward my kitchen. Not once did he let up on the willful assault he had on my mouth. Securing my free hand at the base of his neck, I fought for dominance, my moans and his growls a lustful battle cry in the short hallway of my apartment.

The way he palmed my ass, pressing my hot center against his dick, had me ready to wave a white flag. My girls would have to just say "I told you so" and move on with their petty lives.

Entering into the kitchen, he sat me on the island counter, trailing kisses down my neck to my breasts, my nipples peeking through the thin fabric of my dress. "Come up out this shit, Nessa baby. I been feening for this pussy since I left after Christmas." He tugged at my clothes, peppering kisses along my shoulders and back up to my jaw

"Damn, Zay. Not you over here pussy-whipped," Kelly yelled from the phone. I dropped the flowers on the counter, hopping off to end the call. "We should've bet money. I told y'all asses five minutes and the panties were coming off."

"It was good talking to y'all, but I gotta go," I rushed, grabbing my phone.

"Bye, Zay," they said in unison, as I ended the call. I walked back over to Zay, wrapping my arms around his waist, a sheepish grin on his face. "I'm sorry about that. I thought they would've hung up by now." I tilted my head up, pursing my lips as I waited for a kiss.

"Nah. I think you wanted to give them a little show." He nipped at my lower lip, sucking it gently as he slid his hands under my dress, kneading my ass. Melting into his embrace, I explored his mouth, tugging at the waistband of his joggers, searching for the trapped steel I desperately needed. He squeezed my ass harder, moaning into my mouth, pressing me closer to him, letting me feel the power I had over him. Each twirl of my wrist, heavy length filling my hand as I stroked him up and down, was met with thrusts of his hips.

"Didn't I tell you take this shit off. Now if I rip it, you gonna want to curse me out." His voice was dark, alluring, hypnotizing. My eyes were locked on his, my chest heaving, breaths short and quick, waiting for the next command. He spun us around, my back to the counter. He walked backward, drinking me in, biting his lip as he stroked himself. "Strip."

My hands were quick to peel the dress over my head, my eyes losing sight of his for the brief moment it took to work it's way over my hair. My breasts felt heavy, my nipples pebbling with aching desire, longing for his mouth to cover them. My fingers slid my thong to the floor. His gaze had me stuck, transfixed, relenting prey ready to be devoured. When I went to slide the socks down my legs, Xavier shook his head.

"Nah, love. Leave them on," he crooned, the deep rasp of his voice making my center purr. "Mmph. Beautiful perfection."

He kicked off his shoes, discarding them to the side. When he shrugged his hoodie and shirt off, my eyes loitered across his chest and abs. Every inch of his skin covered with tattoos I'd sketched myself. He walked toward me, eyes narrowing, biting his lip. Each step he took toward me built anticipation within my core, my body going into overdrive, desire and want coursing through my veins.

We came face to face, shallow breaths escaping my lips as my body arched into his. "Turn."

Slowly, I turned, until my back was to his front, the only contact being the warmth radiating from his torso, the slight taps of his dick as it knocked for entrance into my slick center. My body trembled as he stepped even closer, his dick nestling into the gap between my thighs, the warm caress of his breath snaking down my shoulder and across my chest. His lips brushed against my neck, his arms circling my waist, depleting what remaining space we had between us. He bit into my neck, following it with soothing licks and kisses, one hand moving upward to grab my breast, squeezing it gently, rolling my painfully erect nipples between his fingers.

I cried out, happy for some relief, begging for him to claim other parts of me. His free hand moved lower, covering my mound. I grinded into his hand, desperately seeking a release. The air was scorching, magnified by the toying Xavier did to me.

"Yeah, my pussy missed me, huh?" He slapped my ass, the smack reverberating around the room.

"Fuck, Zay," I cried behind me.

"Mmph," he groaned, rubbing the sting away. His footsteps shuffled behind me, followed by the soft scrape of one of my dining chairs.

"Come here." I turned around, taking in the leisurely way he sat in the chair, my own personal staute of David, except way more supreme. My steps were light as I walked to the rhythm he set stroking his length, the tip glistening. When I made it to him, standing between his spread legs, he gripped my thighs, easing me down, covering him. "Ride."

My eyes rolled to the back of my head as our bodies joined as one. His hands guided us in a rhythmic dance of passion and ecstasy, the melody soft sucking sounds of kisses across my chest, heavy pants and moans, lyrical cries and growls, as we rode to the crescendo of our own love song. Up and down he moved us in harmony, my thighs in the crook of his arms, his biceps firm and strong as he lifted me over and over, his thrusts into my center unrelenting. I gripped his shoulders tight, my nails burrowing into them, my chest arching into his, as my peak washed over me, again and again, his release coming with the final chorus.

"Fuck," he growled. "Shit sweeter than sugar." He pulled my face down, swallowing my mouth into his. My body was spent, leaning into Xavier for support, my arms draped around his neck, my legs dangling over his. He stood, walking us to my bathroom, holding me in his arms, my legs wrapped around his waist.

There, he sat me on the counter, turning on the water, waiting for it to get just warm enough to wet a towel and clean us up. I watched everything, still stuck in my lustful daze. He came to stand between my legs, sprinkling kisses over my face, saving my lips for last.

"You know I love you, right?" I nodded my head, still in a dreamy state. "And you know I accept all of you, flaws and all."

"Yes, Zay," I smiled, giving a little giggle. "And I accept you too." I puckered my lips, closing my eyes.

He laughed to himself, indulging my silent request. "Nessa baby, answer me this."

"What?"

"What is you in there burning?"

My eyes shot open as I hopped off the counter. "No, no, no," I screamed, running into the kitchen. I grabbed Xavier's shirt from the floor, slipping it over my head just as I made it to the stove. I searched the counter for the spoon I'd used earlier, finding it amidst a splatter of caked on red sauce spread across the stove and countertop. "Fuck, fuck, fuck.

I tried stirring the sauce, the once red concoction now reddish-brown cementing the pan. I tried salvaging a drop but failed. Xavier walked up behind me, pulling his joggers up.

"Baby, what happened?" He asked, placing a hand on the small of my back, taking in the chaos of my cooking shenanigans.

Who did I think I was? Ina Garten?

"I tried to cook dinner for you, but that was a disaster," I fretted, bringing my hand over my eyes.

"I see that," he laughed. "But what?"

"Spicy bolognese and parmesan-crusted chicken," I pouted, crossing my arms over my chest.

"Baby, it's a lot of things I love about you. Cooking is not one of them."

Picking up the nearest knife, I glared in his direction. "Keep laughing and I'll make you eat it." I sighed, watching Xavier move the pan from the stove, cutting the burner off.

"I'm just playing," he said, kissing me on the nose as he placed the pan in the sink. "Next time, let it simmer on low, instead of keeping it so high."

"What are we going to eat now? I worked up an appetite."

"Was the sauce the only thing you cooked?" He asked, making sense of the mess on the counters.

"Yeah, the chicken is still in the fridge."

"You sit here," he said, guiding me to the barstools at my kitchen island. "Drink this red wine and let your man take care of you." He placed a soft kiss on my lips, then gathered the things he'd need for our replacement meal.

"Mmmm, my man. I like the sound of that."

Xavier moved around the kitchen with a surprising ease that drew me in. I watched, leaning against the counter, fighting the exhaustion seeping into my bones. As I poured myself another glass of wine, he methodically seasoned and breaded each chicken cutlet, his focus intense as if Gordon Ramsey himself peered over his shoulder. The warm, savory smell of cheese and garlic filled the kitchen overpowering the burnt tomato sauce, the last few traces wafting out the open balcony door. I couldn't help but lick my lips, my stomach grumbling with anticipation.

He glanced up, catching me watching him. "I know you not over there judging?"

"I'm just trying to make sure you're not going to give me food poisoning," I deadpanned.

"Nessa, drink your wine." He turned back to the stove, the steady sizzle of the chicken in the pan making my mouth water. My eyes lingered on the way his muscles rippled as he moved with care.

Eventually, he plated the pasta and layered the crispy chicken on top. After placing a plate in front of me, he drizzled a generous amount of pesto over top. "Open," he commanded, holding a forkful of food to my mouth.

I took the bite, savoring the crunch of the chicken against the soft noodles and fresh pesto, closing my eyes in exaggerated delight. "Mmph. Much better than what I was going to make."

"Thank you. Now eat up." He tossed the kitchen towel over his shoulder, smiling as he walked back with a plate of his own.

After dinner, we settled onto the couch with the warmth of the fireplace crackling in front of us. Fireworks lit up the night sky in the distance, illuminating the Houston skyline view from the windows of my living room. The countdown to midnight played softly on the TV in the background, a playlist of soothing R&B playing overtop.

He wrapped his arm around me, pulling me close as we watched the lights of the city twinkle outside. "You know, I'm gonna miss this," he said quietly, his voice thoughtful. "I know New Orleans is home, but this feels like home too, in a different way."

I looked up at him, a bittersweet ache settling in my chest. "I'm not looking forward to you being back at home. I feel like we were finally getting into a groove. Like, we're exactly where we're supposed to be."

He nodded, squeezing my hand gently, and placing a kiss on the back. "Then let's make a promise. No matter how hard it gets, we'll figure it out. You lean on me. I lean on you. Can you promise me that?"

I leaned forward to kiss his chest, right over his heart. "Yeah, I can."

As the ball dropped, he kissed me softly, his warmth blending with the crackling fire as the world outside faded away. In this moment, the future felt limitless, as long as we faced it together.

Part IV

"Simply Beautiful" - Al Green

Chapter 32

XAVIER

XAVIER UNIVERSITY - MARCH 2014

THE BREEZE COMING OFF the lake sent chills across my arms. I watched as the wind moved through Vanessa's hair. Her warm, floral, sweet scent circled me. She was going on and on about the students she was working with at the Boy's and Girl's Club, and how much fun she was having with them. She could have been talking about anything, but Vanessa would always have my full attention. A smile crawled to my lips as the twinkle in her eyes warmed my heart.

"Zay, are you listening to me," she asked, swatting my shoulder.

"Of course, I am." I kissed her hand. "I'm always listening to you."

"Then what did I just say?"

I stared at the space just beneath her ear, exposing itself as Vanessa tilted her head. I'd grown too comfortable kissing and tasting that spot over the last few months. Licking my lips, I repeated her words back to her. "Some of the kids have potential and you wanted to take them to an art gallery, to show them where their art can take them." Vanessa peered at me through her thick, dark lashes, squinting ever so slightly, before pursing her lips.

Fuck, I love this girl.

"What, you shocked?" Her silence made me laugh. "Not I got you speechless."

"Anyways," she said, rolling her eyes, "do you have homework?"

"Yeah, I'm almost done though. You?"

"Ugh, yes. I have to write a business proposal. I haven't started and it's due tonight."

I studied my girl, *my love*. "Let me ask you something."

"What?"

"Why ain't you changed your major?" I held her palm in my hand, pulling her close to me.

"What's wrong with me majoring in business? Aren't you majoring in business?" She asked, looking up at me.

"Yeah, but I like it. You don't." I kissed her lips gently. "You talked about it with your mom, huh?"

"Maybe." I never understood Vanessa's need to get her mother's approval on everything. Every time they had a difference of opinions, it dimmed Vanessa's light. I had to work double time to bring her back, even though I didn't mind.

"What'd she say about you switching?"

"That it would be a horrible decision," she said, sighing. "Art History isn't part of the plan."

"Whose plan? Yours or hers?"

"Both." She responded, but sounded more like a question.

I kissed her again. "If you could do anything you wanted, what would that be?" She gazed out to the water. The fading sun cast a honey-gold light across her face, highlighting the golden flecks within her round brown eyes.

"Maybe something like what I'm doing right now. Teaching something. Working with kids. Painting all day."

"See, now that I believe."

She laughed into my chest, resting her head there. "So tell me, why'd you pick business?"

"Easy, That's how you operate out here. You wanna make any kind of change around here, you gotta do it from the inside." My fingers brushed her cheek. Her skin was so soft beneath my fingertips.

"And what exactly is it that you want to change?"

"The world, love," I said with a laugh.

"I'm serious." Vanessa looked at me again, smiling. "What's the first thing you'd change?"

"First thing?"

"Yeah, first thing."

"The projects. It's beaucoup buildings just sitting since Katrina. Something could be done to them, instead of them being left abandoned."

"Really? Like what?" She stared up at me with those round eyes that made me want to give her whatever she wanted.

I smiled sheepishly. "Don't laugh." Vanessa tapped two fingers over her heart. "I read an article about how people been using different types of materials and technology for affordable living solutions. Like eco-friendly, sustainable stuff. It sent me down a rabbit hole. I think a lot of what they were saying could help the people in the projects." I looked down at Vanessa, my heart beating faster, anxious at how she might respond.

"Zay, that's ingenious." She reached up to kiss me. "So how do you start that exactly?"

"Business," I said, flicking her nose and laughing.

She joined my laugh, making my heart melt. "So what would be the name of your company?"

"Company? Nah, I'm not going to have a company."

"Zay, you can't change the world without your own company. At least that's what my dad says."

"I never thought about having my own company," I replied, looking at our intertwined hands.

"Well, we are now. So, what's the name?"

"Uhhh. I don't know, Morris Urban Development."

"Cute, but you want something that speaks to the purpose of the company. Try again."

I began to seriously think, pushed on by Vanessa's excitement. "Check this. EcoCity Innovations."

She raised her eyebrow. "Does that feel right in your gut? My dad says your gut is never wrong."

I tossed the pretend company name over in my mind. Vanessa was right, it didn't feel solid. "Nah, not really." She drummed her fingers on the ground.

"What about, EcoVision Urban Solutions? Eco, for the environment. Vision, because it's your vision. Urban, for affordable inner-city housing. And Solutions cause your solutions are going to change the world." She looked at me hopeful.

Do you even see how brilliant you are?

"EcoVision Urban Solutions," I said aloud. I let the company name roll over my tongue a few more times. Eventually, my thoughts turned to the girl sitting before me. I didn't think I'd fall for someone as hard as I had while in college. I was just here for a good time while I got my degree so I could level up in life. She looked at me, smiling, awaiting my answer.

Yep, she's the one.

"Sounds good right?" Vanessa exclaimed, sitting up.

"I don't know. We're going to see." I kissed her deeply this time. "How do you do it?

"Do what?"

"Stay so optimistic. You think of something you want to do and do it."

"I don't know. I usually don't. At least not growing up."

"I don't believe that."

"No, I'm serious. People in my world, we're like soldiers. From the moment you're born, your whole life is planned out for you."

"Really? Must be nice not having to think about what you're going to do with your life."

"Maybe. But you don't get to know who you are."

"What about Kelly? Didn't she grow up with you?"

"Yeah, but Kelly's different. She fits there, anywhere really. She knows what she wants, and how to move and navigate. She doesn't care about the status quo."

"You think I'd fit in."

She studied my face. "Yeah, I think you could...No. I know you can."

She had me blushing, again. *This girl was doing numbers in my heart.* "Yeah, we gon see about that." I looked deep into her eyes, the setting sun making them twinkle.

"I'm serious. You can be anything you want to be Xavier Morris." Her gentle pat against my chest sent butterflies going through my stomach, which intensified as she grazed her fingers along my abs.

"Says the girl who won't change her major." Vanessa was so good at encouraging the people around her, and supporting their dreams, it frustrated me that she thought about herself last. I would be certain to change that.

"What happened to you always keeping it real with me?"

"I am keeping it real. Your stuff looks good. Better than them stuck-up people in the actual art program."

"Yeah, good. But not great."

"It's better than great." She became silent, as she looked to the ground. I picked up her chin and kissed her lips. They were so sweet and supple. I felt her tongue searching for mine, making me grow inside my boxers. I pulled back, catching my breath. "You can do anything you want, don't forget that."

"Thank you." She smiled at me. "You either."

"I love you." I didn't give her a chance to respond before I kissed her passionately again. I was undeniably, irrevocably in love with her. Vanessa captivated every fiber of my being. With every heartbeat, a rush of emotions took over me, a river of longing a simple 'I love you' could never capture. When she smiled, it lit the deepest, darkest corners of my soul. She was the missing piece I never knew I needed, the glue that kept me whole. I didn't know if I would ever find the words to express how deeply I felt about her, all Vanessa needed to know was that I did, and I would tell her every chance I got. "Let me get you back to your room."

I'm going to marry this girl.

Chapter 33

VANESSA

THE EARLY SUNLIGHT STREAMED through the expansive windows of my office, bathing the room in a golden, inviting light. I glanced around, taking in the familiar sights: the stack of reports on my desk, the framed photos on the wall, and my parents sitting across from me, their expressions a mix of pride and concern.

"Tell me again why you two won't be in the presentation?" I fretted about the slide deck on display on my computer.

"Vanessa, we've discussed this." My mother got up from her seat and moved to stand beside me at my desk. She fluffed a few hair strands of the twist-out I rocked, before smoothing circles on my back. "It's important for you to present yourself as capable of directing this project. If your father and I are there, it'll be a huge conflict of interest, one that may deter donors."

"Sweet Pea, don't look so nervous, you've got this," my father said, his voice steady and reassuring. His bald head and distinguished features lent him an air of authority that had always comforted me.

I nodded, trying to absorb his confidence. "I know, Daddy. It's just... I want this so much. It's not just a project; it's a part of me."

My mother turned my face to meet hers, her eyes, a mirror of my own, brimming with support. Her elegance was effortless, her dark hair pulled back into a neat bun, her makeup understated but flawless. "We know how important this is to you, honey," she said, her tone gentle. "But remember, you've done everything you can. You're ready for this."

Her words settled over me like a blanket of calm. "Thanks, Mom. I just... hope they see it the way I do."

"They will," she assured me. "Your passion shines through in everything you do. Just be yourself."

I took a deep breath, feeling the weight of their support lift my spirits. "Okay. It's time."

THE CLOUD NINE I'D floated out of the boardroom on earlier deflated once I made it back to my apartment. I tried finding my parents to give them a rundown, but they insisted on waiting to hear what the board said, as they would for any other project. Xavier and I played phone tag for the rest of our workday. I messaged my girls' to see if they wanted to grab drinks during happy hour to celebrate, but then the crazy Texas weather decided to pour down the rest of the afternoon. Needless to say, my high from earlier was very much grounded.

I switched to my food delivery app, quickly closing it after finding it hard to pick a restaurant. I decided to soothe my sorrows by watching a few episodes of reality housewives. Kelly and I enjoyed the show, casting our version for Houston, picking women from our mother's friend groups. I laughed as the two older women shouted and screamed at each other in the middle of the made for tv event. "Oh, that would definitely be Mrs. Devonschild and Ms. Rockforth." My phone buzzed in my lap. *Xavier.* I took a deep breath to calm my excitement.

"I love you," he answered, his face filling the screen. "What you doing?"

"Watching *Real Housewives* reruns."

"Lawd, still?"

"Yes, still." I laughed, remembering how I'd gotten Xavier hooked on the show during college. We'd watch the newest episode every Sunday, while he held me in my bed.

"You know it ain't been the same since what's her name left."

"Because she was that girl!" I laughed into the phone. Lighting bugs swam through my body at the realization that he'd been keeping up with one of my favorite shows. "I didn't know you still watched."

"Yeah, let's just say somebody got me addicted." He laughed, the low vibrations sending the lighting bugs into a flurry. "It might be my comfort show now." We fell into a light dialogue, discussing previous seasons and rotating cast members. I felt at ease, talking to my person again. I grew silent as he recapped his day and the issues he was having securing the permits for a building he and Khalil wanted to renovate.

"Hey, why you over there looking all sad? You said your presentation went well, earlier."

"It did...I just thought I'd be more excited right now."

"You should be," he encouraged.

"I know. I'm just thinking, what if it wasn't enough." I turned over, burying myself deeper into my sofa, snuggling the soft, thick blanket under my chin. The heavy drops of rain beat against my floor-to-ceiling windows, the already black skies competing with the darkness of my dimly lit living room. "They can still say no."

"If they say no, find someone else. Stay optimistic." I focused on the screen of my phone. Xavier looked so relaxed, sitting in his car. The white glare of his phone screen magnified the brightness of his teeth. The hidden ambient lighting bathed the silhouette of his body in a warm glow, making him look every bit the calm, reassuring presence he was. His laughter, warm and unguarded, resonated like a cherished melody, each note a reminder of the depth of our connection and the void his absence left in my heart.

And there it was. The reason for the emptiness I'd been feeling since leaving the offices of the Taylor Foundation. At that moment, the vivid clarity of his face on my screen seemed to whisper of a life more complete, a love that I yearned to feel wrapped around me once more. I'd prioritized so many facets of my world, since he'd moved back home, the community center, the progress with my mother, spending time with my friends, and putting my name to recent artworks.

But here, in the emptiness of my apartment, I felt a profound ache, a delicate yearning for the other half of my soul. Despite the joy and successes showering down over my life, there lingered a void, a subtle hum of incompleteness that only the melody of his laughter and the warmth of his embrace could fill. I realized then that even in the fullest bloom of my dreams, the tender presence of his love was the light that made my soul truly shine. Tears pricked my eyes as I bit my lip to quell its subtle tremble.

The smile faded from Xavier's face as tears poured from my eyes. His brows knitted together, and his eyes filled with immediate concern. "Nessa baby, what's wrong?" He leaned closer to his phone as if trying to reach through to console me directly.

"I just...I didn't expect to miss you this much," I admitted, my voice barely above a whisper. "Even though everything else is going well, great even, my heart aches because you're not here."

His expression softened instantly, and he leaned closer to the screen, his eyes searching mine with a tenderness that melted my defenses. "I miss you too, baby. Every damn day," he replied, his voice rich with sincerity. "I've been having a hard time too."

I tried to muster a smile, but my heart was heavy, my eyes still wet from slowed-down tears.

Xavier's eyes flickered with a hopeful light as he spoke, his voice a soothing balm. "How about I come see you this weekend?"

"You can't. You have that community event, remember?" I used the thickness of my blanket to wipe my eyes.

"You right," he laughed. "Why don't you come visit me? Spend a weekend here. I'll have a lot of time off with Mardi Gras around the corner."

I looked up at him, my heart lifting slightly at his words. "You think that could help?"

He nodded, his smile warm and reassuring. "I know it will. We've been apart too long, Nessa baby. I want to see you, hold you, make sure my baby alright."

A deep breath steadied my nerves, and a tentative smile tugged at my lips. "Okay. I'll come. I want to be with you, Zay."

His grin spread broadly across his face, and the relief in his eyes mirrored the joy that started to bloom in my chest. "You have no idea how much I needed to hear that. We'll be together again in no time, okay?"

A soft laugh escaped me, the tension easing from my shoulders. "Okay."

Chapter 34

Xavier

I stood outside Vanessa's door, my heart thudding against my chest like a steady drum, anticipation twisting and curling inside me. She'd sounded so raw the past few days, her voice carrying the weight of the distance between us, and I couldn't bear to hear it without doing something, without being *here*. Each time we hung up with each other, the second I hung up the phone, something in me couldn't stay put, couldn't wait. The drive from New Orleans to Houston was too long and I tried to keep my visit a surprise. It hurt me to dodge her calls, but all I knew was that I had to hold her. I had to make sure she knew I was right there, no matter what.

I knocked three times and waited for her to come to the door. Finally, it swung open, and there she was. Her eyes, usually so bright, were damp and red from crying, her cheeks blotched with the emotions she'd been keeping locked up inside. She looked like she was struggling to smile, but it was there—a faint flicker in the sea of her sadness.

"Zay?" she whimpered, her voice barely holding on.

I didn't say anything at first. There was no need. I just stepped forward, closing the distance between us in one swift movement, pulling her into my arms like I'd been craving to do since we were together for New Year's. She melted into me, her soft body fitting against mine like she belonged there. Like she always had.

"I couldn't wait," I murmured into her hair, breathing her in. That familiar scent, that warm, soft, comforting essence of *her* filled my lungs, and for the first time in days, I felt like I could finally breathe.

Her arms wrapped tighter around me, but there was still a weight hanging between us, something she hadn't let go of yet. I leaned back, just enough to cup her face, tipping her chin so I could see those beautiful eyes of hers. Even through the tears, they were the most stunning thing I'd ever seen.

"What's going on, Nessa baby?" I asked softly, my thumb brushing her cheek. "Talk to me."

Her sigh was heavy like the weight of the world was sitting square on her shoulders. I could see it—the battle she was fighting inside, trying to keep it together when all she wanted to do was break. She always tried to carry more than she should. She pulled away from me, leading us into her living room. I sat down first, letting her crawl into my lap.

"I don't know, Zay," she said, her voice trembling. "I should be happy, right? The Taylor Foundation approved everything with the community centers. I worked so hard for that, and now it's happening. But I still feel like... like it's not enough. Like I'm chasing something, but I don't even know what it is."

"You've done so much already," I said, keeping my voice low and steady. "But maybe it's because you've been working for everyone else. For the community, for your family. What about you, Nessa? What do *you* want?"

Her lips parted as the question caught her off guard like maybe it hadn't even crossed her mind until now. "I think," she hesitated, her fingers nervously fidgeting with the edge of my company shirt she'd stolen from the last time she stayed over at my place. "I want to open a studio. A place where I can create and teach kids—somewhere they can come and express themselves. I want to give them access to the things I took for granted when I was younger."

"Nessa baby," I whispered, pulling her close again, my lips brushing her hair. "That's it. That's exactly what you're meant to do. You're so talented, baby. And the world needs to see what you can create."

Her eyes shimmered with something close to hope, but there was still a flicker of doubt in them. "You sound like my therapist."

I kissed the top of her head. "'Cause it's the truth."

She leaned into me, nuzzling her face into my neck, her body softening as the weight of her uncertainty seemed to lighten. I pulled her close again, my lips pressing against her forehead. "Thank you," she whispered, her voice cracking. "I don't know what I'd do without you."

I smiled into her hair, as her fingers traced lazy patterns on my chest. "You'll never have to find out."

We stayed like that, just holding each other in the quiet, letting the world and all its problems fade into the background. For the first time in what felt like forever, I felt like maybe everything was going to be okay.

"You know what?" I said after a moment, pulling back just enough to see her face. "We need a break. Let's take the night off, forget about work, and just have fun."

She leaned over, eyes locked on mine, her lips just inches away. "That depends. Do you consider losing to be fun?"

My pulse quickened. Her confidence, the way she leaned into this challenge like she knew she had the upper hand—it was maddening. "How can somebody with the face and voice of an angel be so competitive?" I murmured, my eyes lingering on her lips, imagining all the ways I could silence that smart mouth of hers.

"How can I be competitive when there's no competition?" she fired back, her words a smooth purr, as if daring me to cross that line between us. The tension hung heavy in the air, thick with the promise of what was to come.

I let out a chuckle, but my heart was racing. "Let's say we make a bet, then," I said, my hand drifting lower on her thigh, testing the waters.

Her eyes flickered with amusement and something darker—desire. "What's the wager?"

"You win, I owe you whatever you want. I win, you owe me whatever I want."

She grinned, and I knew I was in trouble. She was playing me, but I didn't care. I was all in. "Alright, bet. I know the perfect place."

As I drove toward our next destination, my mind was a million miles away from the road in front of me. Vanessa's energy filled the car, warm and intoxicating. The way she leaned back in the passenger seat, her body relaxed but humming with that quiet intensity I knew all too well, had me feeling some type of way. She had this glow about her like she was ready to set the world on fire, and the way she talked about her plans for the gallery made it clear she was about to do just that. It was the Vanessa I'd always known—ambitious, determined, and full of passion. It's what drew me to her then and what kept me locked in now.

"That sounds like a bomb ass idea," I said, patting her thigh gently. I left my hand there, fingers slowly tracing lazy circles over the fabric of her leggings, letting her feel the warmth of my touch. Her material was soft beneath my fingertips, and every pass of my thumb had my mind wandering into dangerous territory.

Vanessa shifted in her seat, crossing her legs and trapping my hand between her thighs. The move was intentional, teasing, and I knew it. I swallowed hard, trying to keep my focus on the road, but the heat between us was undeniable, palpable. She wasn't making it easy for me to keep things cool, but then again, when had she ever?

Two can play that game, I thought, glancing her way as I pulled into the parking lot of The Puttshack. The way she looked at me, with that glint in her eye, let me know exactly what was on her mind too. I parked the car, letting out a slow breath as I turned to her with a raised brow.

"Golf? Really?" I asked, my voice lower than before, my hand inching back up her leg.

"Yes, really." Her smile was all mischief, and I knew right then that she had plans beyond just the game.

"Not fair," I groaned as I got out of the car. I rounded the front, opening her door, and I couldn't help but admire the way her body moved as she slid out of the seat, that confident sway in her hips meant just for me. "How many years did you take private lessons again?"

She laughed, flipping her hair as we walked toward the entrance. "Chill. It's just a mini-golf, Zay. Not the Master's."

I grabbed her waist, lifting her slightly off the ground just to remind her that I wasn't about to let her win so easily. "I wouldn't be so cocky, love," I whispered into her ear, my lips brushing the soft skin of her neck. I could feel the shiver that ran through her, and damn if it didn't light a fire inside me.

She let out a soft laugh, but I could tell I'd gotten to her. That's the thing with us—no matter how much we pushed each other, we both knew where it was headed. The tension between us wasn't something you could ignore. It was real, electric.

As we played through the course, the black lights cast a neon glow on everything around us, but I couldn't focus on anything other than her. Every time she bent over to take a shot, my eyes were glued to her body. It wasn't just the way she looked—though, God knows that was enough to drive me crazy—it was the way she carried herself. The confidence. The fire.

I couldn't resist anymore. When she bent over to swing, I slipped my hand onto her ass, giving it a firm squeeze, and watched as she missed the ball completely.

"Stop, Zay. You're cheating," she scolded, turning to me, but the smile tugging at her lips told me she didn't mind. Not one bit.

I shrugged, feigning innocence. "My bad. Didn't know you were ready to hit yet."

"If you see me bent over like this, clearly I'm ready to hit."

I swallowed hard, trying to keep my cool, but the heat in her words was enough to set me on fire. "Back up so I can concentrate," she ordered, and I did as she asked, watching her with a hunger I couldn't deny.

She hit the ball, sinking it into the hole, and turned to me with that victorious grin. "Now I'm only down by two."

"Yeah, I guess so," I laughed, stepping up for my turn. I swung the club, but my eyes never left hers. I wasn't playing the game anymore—I was playing her. The ball missed the hole, and I moved closer, closing the distance between us. I swung again, missing on purpose, but I didn't care. All I cared about was the way her body responded to mine, the way her breath quickened as I leaned in.

"That's two," she teased, her voice barely above a whisper.

I swung one last time, my eyes locked on hers, and let the ball roll toward the hole, sinking it easily. "Damn, guess you won."

"You let me win."

"Only because I want to give you whatever you want."

We stood there for a moment, the game forgotten, the tension between us building to a breaking point. I grabbed her hand, pulled her close, and led her toward the exit.

"You hungry," I asked, my voice rough with the desire I couldn't hide any longer.

She blinked, pulling herself out of whatever trance I had her in. "What did you say?"

"I said, do you want to grab something to eat, or you ready to get home?"

The corner of her mouth lifted into a slow smile, one that sent a jolt straight to my core. "Let's grab something to eat. But after that..." She leaned in close, her lips brushing my ear, her voice a sultry whisper. "Take me home."

I smiled, pulling her even closer. "You got it, love."

Chapter 35

Vanessa

As soon as we pulled into the parking garage of my apartment, my heart began to race. The anticipation, the energy between us, it felt electric. The petty way he teased me on the drive back, thumbing just over my clit, building up the pressure but not letting it go off. I would've fought him if he weren't driving. Before I could even reach for the door handle, Xavier was already there, pulling it open for me like he always did, with that quiet strength of his. His hand found mine as he led me inside, the warmth of his touch grounding me, sending tiny sparks up my arm.

The door closed behind us, and the air between us shifted, the tension simmering just beneath the surface. I barely had time to register the keys he tossed to the couch, hearing them plink to the floor before his hands were on me—steady, firm, yet infinitely gentle.

Xavier slipped my hoodie off, letting it fall forgotten to the floor, his hands finding my waist and pulling me close. I felt the heat of him, the way his body pressed into mine, making it impossible to ignore how much I wanted him. His hands cupped my face, and before I could even think, his lips were on mine. The kiss was deep, and needy, every part of me responding to the fire he stoked within.

My hands reached for the hem of my shirt, but his were already there, sliding it up and over my head, his fingers grazing my skin, igniting something raw inside me. His thumb brushed against my nipple, sending a shiver through me that made my breath catch. I moaned softly into his mouth, my body arching toward him, every nerve alive and humming with desire.

I could feel him, his readiness pressing against me, and it was all I could do not to lose myself completely. When he began to slide my leggings and underwear down my hips, his lips moved from my mouth to my neck, trailing hot kisses that left me trembling. Everything slid to the floor, and before I knew it, he lifted me effortlessly, carrying me to the counter like I weighed nothing at all.

The cool surface met my skin as he set me down, and his lips found mine again, but this time, the kiss was deeper, hungrier. His hands roamed over my body, one sliding down my back while the other drifted lower, his touch making my body pulse with need. When his fingers slipped between my thighs, finding my center, a gasp escaped me, my body instinctively leaning into his hand.

God, the way he touched me—like he knew every inch of me, every soft spot, every place that made me come undone. He circled my clit with his lips, soft sucks followed by teasing licks, his fingers moving inside me, and I could barely keep still. My breaths came out in ragged gasps, and I could feel myself teetering on the edge, his touch sending me spiraling higher.

I tugged at his shirt, desperate to feel him, to have him closer. My fingers brushed against the hard muscles of his chest, but before I could get his shirt off, he pulled his hand away, leaving me aching for more. My body clenched at the sudden absence of his touch, but the way he looked at me, with those deep, smoldering eyes, left me speechless.

Xavier kissed me again, slower this time, like he wanted to savor the moment like he wanted to savor me. And God, I wanted to give him everything. I needed him, and I wasn't ashamed to ask for it.

"Do you have a condom?" I asked, my voice barely above a whisper, my body still trembling from his touch.

He nodded, reaching for his pants, but as I watched him, something inside me shifted. The hunger, the longing—it overwhelmed every other thought. "Shit. I left my wallet in the car. I'll be right back."

"No," I whispered, pulling him back toward me, my fingers threading through his shirt. "Just you. I need you, Zay."

He paused, uncertainty flickering in his eyes as he searched my face. "I can't do that," he said softly, but there was a war in his voice like he was holding back for reasons he couldn't quite explain.

I held his face between my hands, pressing my lips to his, my voice trembling with desire. "Please, Xavier. I need you."

He hesitated for only a moment before he nodded, his hands gripping my hips as he lifted me off the counter. He turned me gently, facing me toward the counter, his fingers trailing down my spine, making me shiver in anticipation.

And then, with one smooth motion, he slid into me, and the world disappeared.

It wasn't just about sex. It was about everything—the love, the grief, the longing, the years we'd spent apart, the distance that kept us away now. His hands gripped my hips as he moved inside me, slow and steady at first, his body fitting mine perfectly. Every thrust sent a shockwave through me, pulling me deeper into the moment, deeper into him.

I could hear my moans, soft at first but growing louder with each movement. Xavier's breath was ragged in my ear, and I could feel his heart pounding against my back as he pushed into me, deeper and deeper, his touch setting me on fire.

I braced my hands on the counter, my body arching into his as he filled me. "This is mine," he growled into my ear, his voice low and rough with possession. "Tell me it's mine."

"It's yours," I cried out.

"That's it, Nessa baby. You were made for me and me for you," he growled between thrusts. "Don't ever forget that."

His words sent me over the edge, and my body trembled as I came, the waves of pleasure washing over me, taking me somewhere else entirely. And yet, even in the midst of it, I could feel Xavier there with me, holding me steady, keeping me grounded.

He didn't let go. Not even when I felt him tense behind me, his breaths coming faster as he reached his release. His hands gripped me tighter, and for a moment, it was just us, tangled in each other, lost in the feeling of finally being whole.

When it was over, he pulled me close, his arms wrapping around me as we both tried to catch our breath. He kissed my shoulder softly, the tenderness of the gesture making my heart swell.

"I love you," I whispered, turning to meet his gaze, my hand resting against his chest.

He pressed his forehead to mine, his voice low and filled with emotion. "I love you, forever."

After showering together, then going another round, and then showering again, we lay in my bed. Xavier held me close, his breath warm against my skin. The weight of his body against mine was comforting, soothing me in the moment as our breathing slowly steadied. I could have stayed like that all night, wrapped in his arms, safe and content.

But after a few hours, he shifted slightly, I felt it—the quiet tension in the air, the unspoken words sitting heavy between us.

He kissed the top of my head, his lips lingering there as if he was reluctant to say what I knew was coming. I closed my eyes, savoring the warmth of his embrace, trying to hold on to the moment just a little longer.

"Nessa baby," he whispered, his voice low and almost apologetic.

I knew what was coming before he said it. I didn't want to hear it. Not yet.

"I have to go, baby."

My heart sank at his words, even though I knew he couldn't stay forever. I swallowed the lump forming in my throat, refusing to let it show how much it hurt. "I know," I whispered back, trying to keep my voice steady. But it wasn't enough to hide the sadness creeping in.

He lifted his head to look at me, his eyes soft and filled with the same reluctance I felt. The weight of the moment hung between us like a thick fog. I hated how habitual this had become—saying goodbye, again and again.

"It's just…" he began, running his hand over his haircut, "I have to drive back to New Orleans. I still need to be at the community event. It's the anniversary of when we opened it for residents. I have to be there." He sighed, his thumb brushing against my cheek, his touch gentle. "I don't want to leave, Nessa baby. You know that."

I nodded, biting the inside of my cheek to keep from crying. I didn't want to make this harder for him. For us. "I know," I murmured. "I get it. You've got responsibilities, and I'm proud of you. But…"

"But it's hard," he finished for me, his eyes never leaving mine. "I know. I hate this part, too."

I turned away from him slightly, my chest tightening with the familiar ache of watching him leave, again. The hours we'd spent together were filled with so much love, so much passion, but now they felt fleeting, slipping through my fingers as the night turned into the early morning.

"I just miss you," I admitted quietly, the vulnerability in my voice surprising even me. "Even when everything else is going great—my art, the students, the proposal—I still miss you, Zay."

He tilted my chin up, forcing me to meet his eyes. "Hey, look at me," he said softly. "I'm always with you, even when I'm not here. You know that, right?"

I tried to nod, but the sadness still weighed heavily on my heart. He leaned down, brushing his lips against mine in the softest of kisses, his thumb tracing slow circles on the back of my hand.

"I promise, this is temporary," he continued, his voice low and reassuring. "We're building something here, together. You, me... This distance won't last forever. We'll make this work."

Tears stung my eyes, but I blinked them away, trying to focus on his words. He was right. We were building something—something strong, something real—but the distance still gnawed at me in moments like these, when all I wanted was more time with him.

"You believe me, don't you?" he asked, his gaze intense, searching my face for reassurance.

I nodded slowly, wrapping my arms around his neck and pulling him closer. "Yeah, I believe you."

"Good," he whispered against my lips, kissing me deeply as if he could seal the promise in that kiss. "Because I'm not going anywhere, Nessa. You and me? We're it."

I held onto him tightly, savoring the warmth of his body against mine for as long as I could before he finally pulled away, his forehead resting against mine for a brief moment.

"I'll call you when I make it, okay?"

"Okay," I whispered, my voice barely audible.

He grabbed his shirt from the floor and slipped it on, the sight of him getting dressed sending another pang of sadness through me. The room felt colder without him.

As he gathered his things, I stood there, watching him in silence. My heart ached with the weight of the goodbye we were about to say, but I knew it wasn't forever. Just another part of our story—one where we had to endure the distance to reach the future we both wanted.

He walked back over to me, his eyes soft, and full of love, and cupped my face gently. "I'll see you soon, Nessa. I promise."

I nodded, leaning into his touch, memorizing the warmth of his hand on my cheek, and the way his eyes softened when he looked at me. "I love you."

"I love you more. Get some sleep. I'll lock the door behind me," he whispered, brushing one last kiss against my lips before heading for the door.

And then he was gone.

As the door clicked shut behind him, the silence of the apartment felt deafening. I laid there for a moment, letting the sadness settle in, before burrowing myself deep in the covers. His scent lingered in the air—sandalwood and sage—and I breathed it in deeply, wrapping my arms around myself for comfort.

I knew he had to leave, but it didn't make it any easier.

Sighing, my fingers tracing the fabric absentmindedly as I tried to shake the loneliness creeping in. The excitement of seeing him, of having him here, was quickly overshadowed by the emptiness of his absence.

But his words echoed in my mind, grounding me.

"We're it."

I clung to that promise as I curled up, waiting for the morning light to remind me that our time apart was temporary, and soon, we'd be building our life together—one where there'd be no more goodbyes.

Chapter 36

XAVIER

KHALIL AND I STOOD under the white tents set up in the parking lot behind Dooky Chase's on Orleans Ave. Because of the notoriety of our company, we were able to rent out the lot for our employees' families and friends to enjoy the Zulu Parade, a parade that symbolized the cultural experience of African Americans in New Orleans. Marching bands and auxiliary groups from various high schools and colleges around the city and country performed numbers every so often on the parade route, in between cartoon-painted, jungle-themed floats. The black and white painted faces, some with large black afros and grass skirts, others with glittering feathered headdresses and women in fur coats, drove the pack-line streets wild with their array of throws; Mardi Gras beaded necklaces, hula hoops, and other trinkets being displayed on the floats. Even with the slight cold and cloudy weather, hundreds of people still lined the street, waiting for a chance to cop one of the coveted decorated coconuts.

It felt good seeing the number of people that came out. Local businesses from all over the city had different stalls set up on the street, retailers, other non-profits, food trucks, and vendors, just as Khalil and I did. We'd even set up a refreshment spot for the residents of a housing community we'd renovated a few years ago. The current residents were able to grab drinks and food, and have places to sit while waiting for the floats to pass. This was part of the dream Khalil and I manifested in our dorm room. It was truly grounding to see it all come to fruition, and so fast. Elation and pride took over me knowing that Vanessa would see what we'd built out here.

Because of her.

"It feel good to be home, huh? I almost forgot." Khalil said, breaking my concentration.

"Yeah, man. Ain't nothing like the city." I looked down at my phone, checking Vanessa's location. She, and her friends, should have made it to our spot by now. The invitation was initially for her, but then Kelly and Lynn decided to tag along since Kelly's birthday was around the corner. The trio arrived yesterday morning and spent the day celebrating together. After Khalil and I ensured we had everything ready for today, we met up with them Uptown for Orpheus, another Super Krewe parade.

"I don't know how I'm functioning right now. I ain't get no sleep," Khalil said, taking a sip from his styrofoam cup. "How about you?"

"Nah. Soon as Nessa and I hit the pillows, I was out like a light." I looked back over the streets again, hoping to see my girl. "If it wasn't for Ma calling me, I'd still be asleep."

"Man, what? When we went back to their rental house, I thought I was about to make a move to one of my lil' yeah's houses. That damn Kelly had me bringing her and Lynn all over the place until I said they were going to need to call an Uber."

"Yeah, the three of them are a menace. I see why Nyah stay out the way." I checked my phone to see if Vanessa responded to my messages trying to see where they were.

"Where they at, anyway? You told them where to find us?" Khalil laughed, then nodded to the crowd. "Oh, look."

Oh my god.

Vanessa walked toward our set-up, Kelly and Lynn in tow. She hadn't yet seen me, as familiar faces from college stopped the friends as they maneuvered the crowded streets leading to my company's spot.

Her hair was a cascade of braids, the tips reaching just above her butt. I could make out her glossed lips from where I stood, her long, thick lashes, making her eyes stand out. She wore a white, long-sleeve polo, with yellow, green, and purple stripes going across the chest. The shirt was halfway tucked into the top of high-waisted, distressed jeans that fit snugly across her hips, before tapering down her long legs to meet her black Doc Martens. My heart raced as she and her friends made their way to us, finally noticing the company tents we had set up. The gentle sway of her hips as she strutted toward me sent me into a trance, the parade around me disappearing. I only saw her, her beauty, her exuberance for life.

That's gonna be my wife.

"There's my pretty baby," I said, pulling Vanessa into a tight embrace. She felt so good in my arms. I pulled her chin up, leaning in to kiss her soft, shiny lips.

"Here I am." she squealed.

"You look beautiful." I couldn't stop smiling.

"You don't look so bad yourself." She laughed, then looked behind me, taking in our set-up. "This is quite the set-up. What happened to this being a little thing?"

"Compared to last year it is," I replied, shrugging my shoulders. It was smaller than the previous two years. Since Khalil and I were focused on the project in Houston, the rest of our immediate executive team stepped in to focus on the development projects we had going on in the city. Otherwise, we'd have time to get the restaurant rented out too.

"Y'all look bright-eyed for people who had me out all night, and this morning," Khalil said over the noise of the crowd around us. Kelly glared, while Lynn laughed, as Vanessa snuggled closer into my chest.

"Oh, trust. We're running on fumes right now," Lynn added. The shorter friend looked like walking Mardi Gras beads with the sequin purple, green, and gold top and matching boots.

"Yeah," Kelly said, dropping her head on Khalil's shoulders. "We stopped for beignets and coffee on the way here, but I'm almost positive we walked that off already."

"We have Morrow's catering toward the back of the lot. Grab a plate and come back. The parade still has a while before it's over." Khalil said. "We need to finish showing our faces a little bit." Vanessa and her friends walked away, disappearing into the crowd behind us.

Khalil flicked my nose. "Wide open. I told you that shit was going to happen."

"I don't even care."

"So, what? Y'all doing this long-distance thing?"

"Yeah. Hopefully not for long, if all goes well with Evergreen Capital Investments." Khalil and I shook the hands of some businessmen who passed us. "If we end up taking their investment, what do you think about opening a new office in Houston?"

Khalil let air stream out of his mouth, before taking another sip of his drink. "I'm bout it. Besides, the team here more than proved they can handle things without us being around full-time."

"That's what I was thinking too…I don't know. We'll cross that bridge when we get there."

Amid the sea of revelers, I spotted my mother making her way toward us. Even in a crowd, she was impossible to miss. Her presence was magnetic, commanding attention without effort. She wore her rich, deep mahogany skin with pride, the sun casting a warm glow that accentuated her maternal instincts. Her short, curly hair, cropped close to her head, framed her face with an elegance that spoke to both her strength and grace. Her eyes, sharp and knowing, seemed to catch every detail around her, always seeing more than she let on. Each step she took radiated the quiet confidence of a woman who had seen life in all its facets and faced it head-on.

Trailing beside her was Mr. Ted, a tall, solid figure whose presence was as reassuring as Ma Josie's was commanding. Together, they moved through the crowd with a natural ease, their hands linked in a subtle but endearing show of unity.

"Ma Josie!" Khalil's voice rang out as he waved her over, his grin reflecting my excitement.

Her eyes lit up at the sight of us, and I could see that familiar mix of pride and amusement dancing in her gaze. "Look at you two," she teased, her voice rich and full of warmth. "Y'all not out here cutting up without us, huh?"

As she enveloped Khalil, then me in a hug, I felt that comforting wave wash over me—like coming home after a long journey. "I'm good, Ma," I said, returning her embrace. "Just here to soak in the Zulu floats. You know I wouldn't miss this for anything."

She released me, her smile broadening, crinkling the corners of her eyes. Ted nodded, placing a gentle hand on her shoulder. His gaze was steady, grounding. "Always good to see you, Zay and Khalil. I tell people all the time, if I had sons, I'd want them to turn out just like you two."

I looked around, the sounds of brass bands and the laughter of the crowd filling the air, but at that moment, everything seemed to pause. There was something profoundly grounding about having the most important people in my life here with me—Ma Josie with her unwavering support, Mr. Ted with his silent strength, Khalil with his neverending support, and Vanessa with her forgiving love.

Their presence reminded me of the roots that ran deep, anchoring me to who I was and from where I came. Roots from which I could grow beyond my wildest dreams.

"We made a pit stop at the housing development a couple blocks down. Everybody look so happy with how y'all got them set for the parades. You and Khalil are doing good things. I'm proud of both of you."

"Aww, thank you Ma Josie," Khalil beamed. I looked back over the crowd of our event, seeing Vanessa, Lynn, and Kelly making their way back to our table.

"Ma, guess who's in town?"

"Who?" I nodded my head behind me, where she instantly spotted Vanessa, trailing behind Kelly and Lynn. "That's not who I think it is, is it?"

"Ms. Josie!" Vanessa exclaimed, pushing past her friends to head for my mother's outstretched arms. "I'm so happy to see you!"

"Nessa, girl, come here. I ain't seen you in a month of Sundays. Give me a hug sweetie." I couldn't contain the happiness inside me, watching my mother and Vanessa embrace, genuinely happy to see each other after all these years.

"How have you been, Ms. Josie?"

"Good. I'm still here. I got my health, my family, my man."

"I see," she giggled to my mother, as she introduced her boyfriend. All these years the two women in my life still had their indescribable connection.

"How are you? My son taking good care of you, I hope. You know I beat his ass, before. I'll do it again."

"Ma!" The group laughed. "Mr. Ted, get your ol' lady. Please."

"Nah. When she right, she right." the older man shrugged, giving me no sympathy.

"Ms. Josie, you remember my best friends, Kelly and Lynn." Each girl hugged my mother as Vanessa introduced them.

"Yes, I do. Kelly, how ya mama 'nem doing?"

"She's fine," Kelly said with a twinge of sadness.

"What y'all got planned for the rest of the day," Mr. Ted asked.

"Whatever it is, I hope sleep is involved," Kelly blurted.

"Nah, not Miss 'I'll sleep on the plane,'" Khalil joked.

"Some things never change, huh? Vanessa, come talk with me right quick. Give me a second Teddy." My mother grabbed Vanessa by the elbows, and the two stepped off to the side of the group, just out of everyone's earshot. I tried to listen closely to what they were talking about, but between the music and shouting from the crowds, all I could make out were the laughs and motherly touches Ma gave Vanessa, especially the stealthy swipe of a tear coming from Vanessa's eye. Shortly after, they were on their way back to Khalil, Ted, and I, Kelly and Lynn disappearing into the crowds closer to the passing floats and bands.

"What were y'all talking about?" I asked, wrapping my arms around Vanessa's waist.

"Nothing," my mother said, answering for both of them. "We're about to head up out of here. Y'all stop by the house and get something to eat when y'all done running these streets. I got a pot of gumbo with y'all name on it."

"Oh," Vanessa started, her face lighting up. "You don't have to tell me twice."

"Alright, then." My mother and Mr. Ted said their goodbyes, before disappearing into the crowd.

"I'm happy you came," I told Vanessa, tightening my arms around her waist, and nuzzling my face in her neck.

"I'm happy I came too," she said, snuggling herself under my coat. "Much better than the last time I came out for Mardi Gras." She leaned forward to kiss me. "Let's go join the others."

I watched happily as Vanessa and her friends swayed and sang along to every song the DJs blasted as they passed along the street. Vanessa turned to me, wrapping her arms around my neck, singing along with a bounce remix of an Anita Baker classic, serenading my ears. I bent down to kiss her lips before she turned around to continue dancing and singing along with the crowd.

The Zulu parade had wound its way through the streets, leaving behind a trail of excitement and debauchery. Beads hung from tree branches and power lines, shimmering in the late afternoon sun. The rhythmic beats of the marching bands still echoed in my mind as we walked through the vibrant aftermath, the energy of the crowd slowly dissipating into the hum of the city.

As we made our way toward their car, I couldn't help but notice the number of people who stopped to greet us. It seemed like every other block, someone recognized Khalil or me from our work with EcoVision Urban Solutions.

"Xavier, Khalil!" A middle-aged man, his face creased with a hard-earned smile, waved us over. "Y'all doing the Lord's work with them apartments, man. My cousin's got a place in Plaza Towers—best thing that's happened to him in years."

"Thanks, Mr. Douglas," Khalil replied, clasping the man's hand with a firm grip. "Glad to hear it's making a difference."

Mr. Douglas nodded, his eyes shining with genuine appreciation. "Y'all keep it up. We need more folks like you in this city."

We exchanged a few more pleasantries before continuing down the street, the weight of his words sitting heavy and hopeful on my shoulders. It was moments like these that made all the late nights and uphill battles worth it.

As we approached a street corner, a group of teenagers hanging out by the corner store called out, "Yo, Mr. Xavier, Mr. Khalil! What's happenin'?"

"What's up with it, lil' brudda'!" I responded, giving them a wave. One of the kids jogged over, his eyes wide with excitement.

"Y'all really own that big building on Canal Street? My uncle said it's gonna have a community garden and everything."

"That's the plan," I said, a grin spreading across my face. "A place for everyone to grow and thrive."

"Cool! Maybe I can help out this summer?"

"Absolutely," Khalil chimed in, handing the kid a business card. "Reach out when school's out. We always need more hands."

As we walked away, Vanessa slipped her hand into mine. I felt her fingers tighten slightly, and I glanced over to see a shadow of uncertainty clouding her expression.

"You okay?" I asked softly.

She gave me a small smile that didn't quite reach her eyes. "Yeah, just... thinking about how far you've come. It's impressive, Zay."

I squeezed her hand, trying to convey the reassurance I felt in my bones. "We've come a long way, Nessa."

She nodded but didn't say anything more, her gaze drifting over the bustling streets as if searching for something she couldn't quite name. Her silence wrapped around my heart, leaving me with a nagging sense of unease. I couldn't shake the feeling that something was troubling her, something she wasn't ready to share just yet.

Chapter 37

Vanessa

The familiar, welcoming scent of gumbo filled Ms. Josie's kitchen, wrapping me in its comforting embrace. The living room was a patchwork of memories and warmth, every corner reflecting a life well-lived. Childhood photos of Xavier with his mom and grandpa adorned the walls, their frames catching the light from the overhead chandelier and ceiling lights. I giggled inside as my fingers traced his kindergarten graduation picture, sans his two front teeth. He must've been about six years old here. *They would've been about six years old now.* I shook my head, clearing the thought, and joining the rest of the group in the dining room.

The old dining table in the center bore the marks of countless meals shared during college. Tonight, it was laden with fleur de lis centerpieces and Mardi Gras beads. The gumbo, a rich, velvety concoction, bubbled softly on the stove, its aroma mingling with the laughter and conversation that filled the adjoining living room, as Kelly, Lynn, and Khalil made themselves at home.

Xavier, standing by the stove, seemed so at ease, stirring the pot with practiced hands. His tall frame moved with a familiar rhythm, his broad shoulders relaxed as he teased his mother. Ms. Josie matched his banter effortlessly. She'd pulled her short natural hair back with a silk scarf, revealing her high cheekbones and the soft lines of her face that deepened when she laughed. Mr. Ted maneuvered between the fridge and living room, making sure everyone had a good-spirited drink in hand.

"Watch it, Zay. You're stirring too fast," Ms. Josie admonished playfully, adjusting the heat on the stove.

"Ma, I done stirred a pot of gumbo plenty of times over. I got it," he replied, his lips curving into a grin that was impossible not to love.

Love.

The four-letter word that made life's decisions so much more difficult. It had the power to break you and lift you the same. I took a seat at the table, observing their easy rapport with a bittersweet pang. This house, this family, was once a second home to me.

The laughter around me felt like a balm, but beneath it lurked a gnawing uncertainty about our future. How could we sustain our connection when our lives seemed to be pulling us in different directions? Xavier was having an immense impact on his city. Who was I to pull him away from that?

Kelly, Khalil, and Lynn breezed into the kitchen to fix themselves a bowl, their lively chatter adding to the room's infectious energy. Khalil, ever the charmer, began setting up the table for a spades game, while Lynn filled us in on the crazy things she saw at the parade. Her laughter, bright and clear, contrasted sharply with the turmoil swirling in my mind.

"Hey, Nessa, you remember how to play spades?" Khalil called out, winking as he shuffled the deck.

I forced a smile, pushing my doubts aside. "I practice here and there."

"Is that what you call 'watching YouTube tutorials'?" Kelly teased, sitting at the table, a bowl of gumbo in hand.

"Let's see if those tutorials help you win, Vanessa," came a deep, resonant voice from behind me. Mr. Ted stepped into the dining room with laid-back charm. He greeted everyone with a nod and a warm smile, setting a bottle of cognac on the table. "This should complement the gumbo nicely."

"Teddy, you play around with these kids, your ass is gonna be on the floor before 9:00." Mr. Ted's eyes twinkled with amusement as he took a seat across from me. "Nessa, I know it's been years since you been here, but you know your way around the kitchen."

"I know, Ms. Josie," I laughed. "I'm not hungry just yet."

"Too late," Xavier cut in, placing a bowl in front of me. "I already made you a bowl. Picked out all the bones and everything. Mr. Ted, you trying to start some trouble with that bottle of Crown."

"Thank you, Zay." The first taste of the gumbo was like a hug in a bowl—rich, complex, and deeply satisfying. I glanced at Xavier, who was now deeply engaged in a playful argument with Khalil about the game rules, his eyes alight with the enthusiasm I had fallen in love with. Could we still have this, even as we walked our separate paths?

"Alright, let's get this show on the road," Khalil announced, dealing the cards with his signature flick, while Kelly sorted her hand with an easy grace. Lynn looked on with excitement as she continued to eat. Her spades skills were worse than mine.

Xavier leaned back in his chair, a confident smirk on his face. "Better watch out."

I gave him a playful side-eye. "Don't start Zay."

He chuckled, glancing at his cards. "We'll see about that. I got two and a possible. How about you, baby?"

I surveyed my hand, biting my lip in thought. "I think I can go three. So, six books for us."

Khalil and Kelly exchanged a glance, a silent conversation passing between them. "Alright, we're going seven," Khalil declared, a mischievous gleam in his eye. "Let's see if y'all can back up all that talk."

The game kicked off, and the familiar rhythm of spades took over. The clatter of cards, the strategic silences, the bursts of laughter or groans of frustration—it was all part of the dance. As the game wore on, I found it harder to keep my focus. I was playing my cards, but my mind was elsewhere. The doubts, the uncertainties—they were all creeping in, despite the warmth and familiarity around me.

"You okay?" Xavier's voice cut through my thoughts as he laid down a club.

I glanced up, trying to muster a reassuring smile. "Just thinking. Trying to focus."

We were nearing the end of the game when Khalil laid down his ace of spades, claiming the last book. "That's game! Four for us, y'all got nine. Y'all cheated anyway."

I forced a smile, though the weight in my chest hadn't lifted. "I'm going to get something to drink. Anybody want something while I'm up," I said, standing from the table. "Mr. Ted, you take my spot."

"Remember, Mr. Ted, Khalil talk a lot of shit," Xavier said, his competitive edge showing. "Him and Kelly together are twice as bad."

"Only because I taught him everything he knows," Kelly shot back, making everyone laugh.

I busied myself hiding in the kitchen, when I heard the taps on the tiled floor, as someone approached.

Ms. Josie made her way to the stove and pulled out the bread pudding she'd baked "You okay? You seem a bit off tonight."

I nodded, forcing a smile. "Yeah, just a lot on my mind."

"Like what?"

"I knew Xavier and Khalil were doing great things with their company. He's shown me the different projects. I googled them and read all the articles," I laughed. "But to see everything in person..."

"It's something, huh," Ms. Josie said, drizzling her homemade rum sauce over the bread pudding. "I'm proud of them. They came a long way from where they started. Plenty of people around the city think so too."

"It's everything he's ever dreamed of. I'm so happy for him." I looked to the floor as Ms Josie studied me carefully.

"And what about you?"

"Things are good," I smiled, trying to ensure my face showed the excitement I felt about that and not the sadness I felt creeping around the edges. "I found out my parent's foundation accepted my nonprofit proposal."

"Umm huh." Call it mother's intuition, but Ms. Josie kissed her teeth before going to the cabinet to grab plates. "Then why was your face all twisted up when I walked in here?" She handed me the plates as she began cutting slices of the bread pudding for everyone.

I struggled to find something to say, as she would read through my excuses with a quickness. "Ms. Josie," I began, my voice barely above a whisper, "can I talk to you about something?"

She turned to me, her eyes warm and understanding. "Of course, baby."

I took a deep breath, feeling the familiar sting of old wounds. "I don't know if I'm okay."

Ms. Josie's hand stilled on the knife. She set it aside and turned to face me fully, her expression gentle. "What makes you say that?"

I nodded, tears welling up despite my efforts to hold them back. "Zay and I lost so much time. But now, even with the time we've spent together, I keep thinking what if we're not meant to be. As if this is our time to end things the right way. He has a whole life here, and I'm building mine elsewhere."

She reached out, taking my hand in hers. "Sometimes, we need a do-over, Vanessa. Life gives us second chances, but we have to be ready to take them. You need to decide if Xavier is part of your happiness."

I looked down, the tears threatening to spill over. "But what if the long distance and our busy careers make it impossible? What if we just hurt each other more? I can't go through that again. You saw what it did to me. We both have too much at stake now."

Ms. Josie squeezed my hand. "The truth is, you need to look deeper, sweetheart. It's not just about the distance or your careers, is it?" Wise eyes peered into my soul as she patted my shoulder, finding understanding. "You're still holding onto that guilt of losing the baby, aren't you?"

Her words struck a chord, and I felt the dam inside me break. "I haven't," I admitted, my voice breaking. "He doesn't deserve me bringing this negative energy into something that's supposed to be so positive."

Ms. Josie pulled me into a hug, her embrace warm and comforting. "And why do you think you deserve it? You need to forgive yourself, Vanessa. What happened was not your fault."

I nodded against her shoulder, the tears holding steady to my lashes.

"Vanessa, you can't move forward until you let go of that guilt. And you need to be honest with Xavier. If you want to be him, you have to be all in. If not, you need to let him go, so you both can find your paths. The same way you were broken, so was he. And I refuse to watch him go back to that sunken place."

Her words lingered in my mind as I wiped my tears and gave her a shaky smile. It was the bitterest of pills I've had to swallow in a long time. "I understand. Thank you for hearing me out."

She smiled back, her eyes twinkling with affection. "Anytime, Vanessa. Now, let's get this bread pudding in there. That big piece is for Teddy. It's my grandmama's recipe and his favorite."

As the game continued, the laughter and camaraderie around me provided a temporary respite. We cleared the table, the evening's joy still resonating in the room, and moved to the living room. Hours later, the evening wound down, Xavier and I stood in the doorway, watching Khalil, Kelly, and Lynn help Ms. Josie tidy up. True to her words, Mr. Ted went to bed early after trying to keep up with the shots of cognac Khalil poured. Xavier's hand found mine again, and I squeezed it, hoping he could feel everything I couldn't put into words.

"Ready to go?" he asked, his voice a soothing balm to my frayed nerves.

"Yeah."

As we left his mother's house, a sense of unease settled over me. Xavier seemed excited, too excited to say he was bringing me to his house. The joy oozed from his pores like the rum sauce from the bread pudding we ate. We drove through the familiar streets of New Orleans toward Gentilly and Lakeview, the vibrant life of the city, still thrumming with Mardi Gras celebrations, a stark contrast to my inner turmoil.

When we pulled up to a beautiful one-story house, my breath caught in my throat. It was the house we had dreamed of back in college, the one we'd sketched out plans for on lazy Sunday afternoons, imagining a future that seemed so certain back then.

Xavier looked at me, his eyes shining with pride. "Look familiar?" He got out of the car, grabbed my suitcase, and opened my door.

I stepped out of the car, my legs feeling unsteady. The raised cottage, with its elevated foundation and wide staircase, was painted in a palette of soft neutrals—creamy whites, pale grays, and muted taupes—accentuated by wrought iron railings and shutters. The white stucco stood out from the lush green lawns and mature oak trees lining the streets. The wide front porch, supported by sturdy columns, was the perfect spot for leisurely afternoons watching children play. But as I took it all in, a pang of sadness hit me. This was everything we had talked about, everything we had wanted, but now it stood as a painful reminder of all that had been lost.

Xavier took my hand, sensing my hesitation. "Come on, let me show you around."

We walked through the front door, and I was immediately struck by the warmth and beauty of the interior. Hardwood floors gleamed under the soft lighting, and the open floor plan made the space feel expansive yet intimate. He led me from room to room, each one a tribute to the plans we had made together. The kitchen, with its large island and state-of-the-art appliances, the cozy nook by the window in the living room, perfect for morning painting sessions, and the spacious master bedroom with its high ceilings and elegant furnishings—all of it was exactly as we had envisioned, back in my dorm room.

As we entered the living room, my eyes were drawn to the fireplace. Above the mantle hung one of my paintings, a piece I created just before moving back home. The canvas was large and imposing, capturing the raw anguish and confusion I felt after ending my relationship with Xavier, losing our child, and spiraling into depression. Seeing it there, in the heart of the home we had dreamed of, brought tears to my eyes.

The background was a chaotic swirl of dark, stormy colors—midnight blues, deep purples, and intense blacks—that churned and clashed like a turbulent sea, representing my sorrow and the overwhelming sense of being lost in a storm of my own making. In the foreground, a central figure emerged—a woman who bore my likeness but appeared ethereal, almost ghostly. She stood with her back partially turned, her posture hunched and defeated as if burdened by an invisible weight. Her face, partially obscured by shadows, revealed a mix of despair and longing, her eyes vacant and her mouth slightly open in a silent cry.

Surrounding the central figure, fragmented images floated like haunting memories. A delicate, almost translucent infant was cradled in her arms, our lost child and the fragile hope that had been shattered. Intertwined with these images were broken chains and shattered glass, the chains representing the ties that once bound me to Xavier, now severed and scattered, while the shattered glass reflected my fragmented sense of self and the dreams that lay in pieces.

To the side, almost blending into the dark background, a pair of hands reached out, as if trying to grasp the central figure. These hands, though faint, were unmistakably Xavier's, representing his lingering presence in my mind and the unresolved feelings that still clung to me. Above the entire scene, a heavy, oppressive sky pressed down, filled with dark, swirling clouds. However, in one small corner, a sliver of light broke through, hinting at the possibility of hope and healing, even in such profound pain.

Xavier noticed my reaction and pulled me into a gentle embrace. "I wanted this place to be a reflection of both of us. I know things haven't been easy, but I believe in us, Nessa baby. I believe in what we had and what we can still have."

"H-h-how did you get this," I stuttered. "I thought I'd thrown it out when I moved back home."

"I was looking around for pieces to put in a few of our projects. I came across it in a gallery in the French Quarters. The owner said it didn't have a tag, but it reminded me so much of your work, I had to get it."

His words stirred something deep within me, a mix of longing and fear. The emotions swirled inside me, overwhelming and confusing. I looked up at him, my eyes searching for answers. "Xavier, this house... it's everything we dreamed of, but it also feels like you're holding onto something that's already slipped away."

He cupped my face in his hands, his gaze steady and reassuring. "I understand, Nessa. But this house isn't just about the past. It's about the future we can still build together. I want us to have a chance to make new memories, to create something beautiful despite everything we've been through. Give us that chance, baby."

My eyes flitted around, taking everything in.

"Vanessa," he murmured, his fingers tracing patterns on my back, "we can take this one step at a time. We don't have to have all the answers right now. But I want you to know that I'm here, and I'm willing to fight for us. I love you, and I always will."

Tears slipped from my eyes, but this time, they were tears of a complex mix of sadness and hope. "I love you too, Zay. I'm just... This is a lot for me to process."

Anguish swept across his face as he took in my words. "Then give me tonight," he said softly. "Give me this moment where this house is our home. If only for one night. Please." His voice cracked on his last word.

Before I could think, I found myself leaning in, capturing his lips in a desperate kiss. It was as if all the pent-up emotions, the pain, the love, the longing, all came rushing to the surface. The kiss deepened, and soon we were a tangle of limbs and heated breaths, losing ourselves in the intensity of the moment.

Xavier lifted me effortlessly, carrying me to the master bedroom. We barely made it to the bed, our clothes discarded in a flurry of urgency. Desperate hands clung to my skin, as his lips trailed soft kisses from my shoulder up my neck. Xavier moved a hand to the base of my neck, pulling at the coils of my head, turning my face where he wanted. He devoured my mouth, his kisses urgent as he sucked my tongue into his mouth. Light traces of cinnamon and cognac lingered on his tongue and breath, dizzying me into his enchantment. I pressed my heated mound against his thigh, seeking relief from the flood of arousal cresting within me. The coolness of his sheets tempered my heated flesh. For one night, I could pretend everything was right in the world.

"Nessa baby," Xavier spoke into the skin between my breasts. "You are the light of my life." His lips grazed down the center of my stomach, making little pit stops along the way to savor my flesh. The tender touches sent flutters along each spot he kissed. I gasped each time the warmth of his mouth gave way to the chill in the air.

Xavier pulled back on his knees, pure adoration dripping from his lowered eyes. "I've been so grateful for every moment I've spent by your side," he started his voice a gentle murmur in the quiet of the room. His hands caressed the sides of my thighs before swooping me up in his arms and resting me on his lap. "Your presence makes my world brighter and my heart fuller."

He wrapped my arms around the broadness of his shoulders, then pressed his forehead to mine. "I am thankful for your love and the way you see me." One hand tilted my lips to meet his whisper-soft kiss. "You understand me in a way no one else ever has," he continued, as the hand on my chin smoothed its way down to my burning core. "I cherish that deeply."

The feel of his hand covering my mound sent my hips gyrating against his palm. He pulled me closer to his chest, as two fingers circled my begging hole. "You bring me so much joy," he said, pushing the fingers inside of me, rocking me to the rhythm of the words being whispered into my ear. "You bring meaning into my life. Your laughter is my favorite sound, your smile my favorite sight." In and out, round and round his fingers moved within me, pushing me to the brink of euphoria.

The action, in addition to the declarations he affirmed, cast a spell over me. My replies were neverending moans and short catches of breath. I kept myself afloat by the life raft that was his shoulders. Time stood still. There was no present, no past. Just here and now.

"Nessa baby, I am grateful for your strength and resilience. You inspire me to be better, to do better, just by being you."

The tidal waves brewing within my walls grew larger and larger, ready to crash against the shores of his palm. Xavier used his thumb to apply pressure to the swollen bundle of nerves at the top of my folds. The single movement sent me over the edge, my essence releasing into his hand. His lips crashed into mine, as he massaged the orgasm out of me, bit by bit. Wave by wave. Before letting the feeling fully subside, he lifted me to cover his hardened length, filling me up again. One hand trailed its way to the base of my neck, turning my head to stare deep into his eyes.

"Thank you for your patience and your kindness." The exaltations Xavier bestowed upon me wrapped around me like a favorite hoodie. Our bodies moved in tune with one another. Each thrust he made was met with a circling of my hips. "You are my rock," he continued, "my anchor, my haven. I am so lucky to have you, to hold you, to love you.

"I am eternally grateful for you, Vanessa. You complete me in ways I never thought possible, and I will always be thankful for the gift of your love."

Our bodies created an opera all its own. Xavier made expert work at worshiping my body through his sensual touches, while his adorations made love to my mind. It was all too much. Were it not for the frigid, wet chill hitting my cheeks, I would not have known I was crying. Here, I had a man praising every fiber of my being. Ready to give me everything and more. Yet, I struggled to stand ten toes down with him. Struggled to muster up the courage to take that risk again.

I'm going to ruin us.

"Nessa baby, get out of your head. Come back to me. Come back to us." Xavier kissed the remainder of the silent tears that ran down my cheeks, before making his way to my neck. "Whatever you're thinking about, release it. Give me all that pain," he pleaded against the space beneath my ear. "Let me carry it."

Xavier moved deeper inside me, desperately trying to give me the release I so desperately needed. I clung to his neck as my body bounced up and down along his length. The devotion he gave me captivated me. He continued to sing affirmations into my ear as he brought us closer and closer to our peak.

"You are my heart, my soul, my forever." As we came together, it was more than just a physical act—it was a moment of connection, of finding solace in each other's arms amidst the chaos of our emotions.

Afterward, we lay intertwined, the room filled with the soft glow of the moonlight filtering through the windows. I rested my head on his chest, listening to the steady beat of his heart, my own turmoil slowly settling.

Chapter 38

Vanessa

THE MORNING SUN, FILTERING through the sheer curtains, made my eyes blink. A dull throb pulsed through my temples, a relentless reminder of all the alcohol I'd had from the day before. The room spun around me as I shifted, a dry, parched sensation clinging to my mouth. A groan escaped me as I tried sitting up, gingerly, the weight of my hangover settling in, and memories of the previous evening slowly piecing themselves together in my hazy mind.

Heavy limbs connected to joints that seemed to protest my movements with a dull ache. I dropped my head back on the pillow, relinquishing the fight against my sore body. I inhaled, satisfaction spreading across my lips. The sheets smelled like the perfect combination of Xavier and me, sandalwood and patchouli mixed with fresh peonies and warm vanilla. I heard the soft mumbles of his deep, baritone voice down the hallway.

With him out of the room, I had a moment to take in everything around me. Clean, sharp-edged furniture lined the walls of the room. A flat-screen mounted on the wall above an ebony dresser that matched the nightstand between the bed and window. A glass and black metal bookshelf stood guard on the other side of the bed, filled with books, framed photos, and other trinkets. As I took in the space, a large, framed print of Basquiat's "Pez Dispenser" took me by surprise.

The heavy thuds of his feet against the hardwood floors made their way down the hallway. I mustered all the strength I had to pull myself up in the bed, wrapping the covers around my chest. He came into the room carrying two mugs, shirtless, wearing long soft pants. I felt myself tighten and warm watching the ripple of his abs with each step, compounded by the gentle sway of his dick beneath the thin, loose fabric.

"Don't look at me like that, love." He crawled into bed, handing me one of the cups.

I blew gently before taking a sip. "Mmmh." I took more sips. "I needed this." I looked at Xavier's face, my eyes swimming in the deep waves of his low haircut, the sides tapering into a fade. The sun's rays flickered across his skin, bringing out the richness of his deep mahogany complexion. Muscles flexed beneath his skin as he adjusted himself on the bed, propping himself up on one elbow.

"Did you enjoy last night?"

"Mmph. I think too much. I can barely move." We shared laughter as Xavier turned to place his cup on the nightstand. He turned back to take me in his arms, pressing my back against his chest.

"I can fix that." His hands moved across my body, instinctively finding the dull aches, massaging away the soreness of my languid limbs.

"Not too much." I let my body relax against his.

He kissed my temples gingerly. "Can I tell you something," he questioned, his voice soft but firm, filled with emotion that seemed to radiate from his very soul.

"Yeah," I replied, drinking more of the warm, caffeinated liquid.

Xavier took a deep breath, his eyes locking onto mine with a mixture of intensity and tenderness. "I've loved you since the moment I first saw you," he began, his gaze unwavering. "And that love has only grown deeper, more profound, with every passing day. Even when we were apart, when life took us down different paths, my heart never stopped beating for you."

He continued, his voice breaking slightly with the weight of his feelings. "You are the most incredible person I've ever known. Your strength, your passion, your kindness—they inspire me every single day. I see the world differently because of you. You've taught me what it means to truly love, to give of yourself without hesitation, to dream without limits."

Tears welled up in my eyes as he spoke, each word a stitch to my bleeding heart. He reached out, gently brushing a tear from my cheek, his touch sending shivers down my spine.

"I know we've faced our share of pain and loss," he said softly. "And I know that the future is uncertain. But what I also know is that my love for you is unwavering. It's a part of me, as integral as the air I breathe. I can't imagine my life without you in it."

His eyes searched mine, full of sincerity and devotion. I couldn't hold back the tears any longer. They flowed freely, a mix of overwhelming love and the lingering fear of the unknown. Xavier's words resonated deep within my soul, breaking down the walls I had built around my heart. He took the coffee mug from my trembling hands and placed it next to his on the nightstand. He pulled me into his arms, holding me close as I cried against his chest.

I took a deep breath, pulling away slightly to meet his gaze. "Xavier, I love you too, more than words can say. But... I'm hurting, and I can't make it stop, no matter how hard I try."

His expression faltered, pain flickering in his eyes. "What you mean?"

"I'm scared," I admitted, my voice trembling. "Being here is triggering me in ways I didn't expect. Seeing what you've built, in person. Everything we dreamed of, it's all here, except... I wasn't. I don't know how to explain it, but it's like I'm grieving a life I never got to live."

I couldn't finish. My throat tightened, words trapped under the crushing weight of the grief I'd buried so deep, I didn't know it was still there until now. My chest felt heavy, and I gasped, trying to suck in air, but it wasn't enough. Nothing felt like enough.

"Baby, we lost a lot," Xavier said softly, his thumb brushing against my cheek as if his touch could ground me. "The plans we had...they didn't go the way we thought, and I hate that too. But we're still here. You're still here."

"I'm not, Zay," I whispered, barely able to get the words out. "I haven't been since... I thought I was okay, I thought I'd healed. Things were on track. I was living again. But being back here, with you...it's like I'm seeing all the pieces of what could've been. And I...I...I can't handle it."

My voice cracked as the tears finally spilled over, hot and unstoppable. All the pain, all the guilt, all the shame that I'd buried, it all came rushing up, hitting me so hard it felt like I was drowning in it. I tried to pull away, to push the feelings back down like I always did, but it was too much. The grief was clawing its way out, and I couldn't stop it.

"Nessa baby, breathe." Xavier held me tighter, his hands firm but gentle as they gripped my waist. "Breathe, baby."

"I can't," I gasped, panic setting in my heart as it pounded against my chest. The room spun around me, dizzying the scrambled mess of my brain. "I can't make it stop."

"Yes, you can. You're safe. Right here with me." His voice was low, and soothing, like he was pulling me back from the edge. He kept his forehead pressed to mine, his breathing slow and steady, and I tried—God, I tried—to match it. But the panic intensified, burning the oxygen left in my lungs, making it impossible to catch air.

"You don't have to fight it alone anymore," he whispered, his voice breaking through the storm in my mind. "I got you. I'm right here. Let yourself go. I'll catch you."

Tears fell harder now, heavy drops burning down my cheeks. "I don't know how to let it go, Zay. I don't know how to stop feeling like...like I failed you." Sobs escaped from deep within my chest. "Like I failed us."

His hand slid to the back of my neck, pulling me closer like he was trying to absorb my pain. "You didn't fail anyone, baby. What happened was out of our control. We couldn't change it, no matter our circumstances. But we're still here. You're still here. And I'm not letting go."

The way he said it, so sure, so steady, it hit something deep inside me. I wanted to believe him, but the grief, the guilt—it had been my constant companion for so long. It felt like I didn't know who I was without it.

"I'm sorry," I whispered, my voice cracking as the sobs shook through me. "I'm so sorry."

"For what?" He lifted my chin, forcing me to look into his eyes. "Vanessa, you don't owe me an apology. Not for this. You didn't do anything wrong."

"I know, but our baby should be here. That's a piece of us we'll never get back," I choked out, my chest tightening with every word. "I don't know how to move on."

His eyes softened, and he kissed my forehead, lingering there like he was pouring all the love he had into that one touch. "You don't have to figure it all out right now. But you're not alone in this. You never were. We'll get through it. Together."

The sincerity in his voice broke something inside me, and I let go. I let the grief take over, let the tears fall without trying to stop them. I crumbled into his chest, shaking as the weight of everything I'd held onto for so long finally came crashing down.

He didn't let go. He didn't move. He just held me, his arms wrapped tight around me like he could shield me from the world, from the grief, from the pain. His hand stroked my hair, his breath steady against my ear as he whispered soft reassurances, grounding me while I spun out of control.

"I got you, baby. You're not alone. Just trust me."

His words seeped into me, slowly calming the chaos inside my chest. I took a deep, shuddering breath, the panic finally starting to loosen its grip on my life.

"Okay," I whispered, barely audible. "I trust you."

Chapter 39

VANESSA

DR. CAMILLE SMITH'S OFFICE smelled like eucalyptus and lavender, with a hint of sandalwood in the air. It felt like walking into one of those herbal shops in the Heights, where energy and calm just wrapped themselves around you. Her large wooden desk was covered in crystals, stacks of books, and a burning sage stick near the window. She always made sure her space felt like more than just a therapy office—it was a sanctuary. I exhaled, feeling the tension in my shoulders relax a bit as I sank into the plush velvet chair, already bracing myself for the deep dive ahead.

"Vanessa," Dr. Smith said, her voice low and earthy, like she carried all the wisdom of our ancestors in her tone, "you've come a long way since the day we met. You feel that, right?"

I nodded, acknowledging the truth in her words. I had come far, but still, the memory of that panic attack in New Orleans, of the grief that had consumed me, hovered in the back of my mind like a dark cloud. "I do. I mean, I know it... logically. But some days, it's like, damn—am I healing? Or just doing a better job at keeping it bandaged?"

She smiled, leaning forward just a bit, her long, silver-streaked locs shifting against her shoulders. "That's a real question. But the truth is, healing doesn't mean you won't have moments where you feel like it's too much. It means when those moments hit, you know how to move through them, instead of being consumed by them. That's growth, baby."

"Then why did I have a panic attack?"

"I want to focus on that moment in New Orleans," Dr. Smith continued, her pen tapping lightly on her notepad. "When you were there with Xavier and you broke down about the miscarriage. Let's talk about that. How are you feeling about it now?"

I took a deep breath, closing my eyes for a moment. It was still hard to articulate—the sharp pain, the gut-wrenching realization of all that had been lost. I looked down, fiddling with the bracelet on my wrist. "I just... I didn't expect to fall apart like that in New Orleans. It was like being hit by a wave I didn't even see coming. One minute I was okay, and then the next—bam—I'm drowning in it. Seeing him, seeing how everything kept moving forward without me... it triggered something deep inside. Like I was standing in the middle of everything we planned, but I didn't belong there anymore."

The memory of that morning—my body trembling as I collapsed into Xavier's arms, all the pain and regret crashing over me—was still so fresh.

Dr. Smith nodded, her eyes soft and understanding, but she wasn't about to let me fall back into self-pity. "It's not surprising, Vanessa. That kind of grief, when it's buried for so long, has a way of catching up with us when we least expect it. And you let yourself feel it. You didn't bottle it up this time. That's the difference between who you were and who you're becoming. You didn't run from the pain—you faced it."

I breathed deeply, trying to take that in. She was right. I didn't run. But it didn't make the weight of it any less crushing at the time.

I nodded, wiping away the tears that escaped. "I just feel like... every time I think I've moved past it, something pulls me right back," I said, my voice shaky. "I feel stuck sometimes, even though I'm trying. But the miscarriage... it's like a shadow that follows me, no matter what I do."

She sat back, letting her fingers graze over the crystals she kept near her. "That shadow is part of your story, Vanessa. But it doesn't have to define your journey. The fact that you even let yourself break down in front of Xavier, in New Orleans of all places? That's proof you're healing. You can grieve without being consumed by the grief."

Her words settled into my chest, like the softest of comforts, wrapping around the raw ache inside me. "I just wanted so much for us. What if we...I... never fully get past what happened?"

Dr. Smith smiled softly like she was letting me sit with that question for a moment before responding. "And what if it's not about getting past it? What if it's about learning to carry it differently? You lost something precious, something that'll always hold a piece of your heart. But you can still move forward. You can build new things with that same heart."

Her words hit me in the gut, pushing me to see beyond my pain. "I don't know how to carry it without falling apart sometimes," I admitted.

"And that's okay," she said, nodding. "You're allowed to fall apart. You're allowed to have moments where the weight of it is too much. But don't let those moments define you. Look at where you are now. You've healed your relationship with your mother, opened up to Xavier, and even let yourself grieve. You've been making moves, sis. You just have to believe in the strength you already have.

"You're trying to hold on to this idea of perfection, like if you don't keep everything together, then you're failing. But that's not real. Growth isn't linear, Vanessa. It's messy, and sometimes, it's ugly as hell. But it's still progress."

"But I still feel like I'm failing sometimes," I admitted, my voice shaky. "Like I'm just piecing myself together, but the cracks are still there. Why?"

Dr. Smith nodded, her expression unwavering. "That's because you're human. The cracks don't mean you're broken—they mean you've lived. You've survived. And you are still *surviving*. You're on the right path, Vanessa. And the fact that you're even sitting here, acknowledging the cracks, shows me how far you've come. Long live the rose that grew from concrete."

I inhaled deeply, allowing myself to absorb that truth. The cracks didn't mean I was broken. They meant I was whole in a way I hadn't understood before.

Her gaze softened, but she didn't baby me. "Baby girl, you've spent years letting other people tell you who you are. Your mother, Xavier, even the nonprofit you want to build—it's all been about proving yourself to others. But now... it's time to pour all that love you give to them back into yourself. You deserve that."

I exhaled, my shoulders slumping in the chair as I wiped a tear away. "I've been trying, though. I'm doing everything I'm supposed to—therapy, starting a nonprofit, trying to balance my life..."

"You've spent your life pouring from a barely full cup. And it's time you stop. You're a grown woman, Vanessa. You've got dreams, and desires—things that are yours alone. You're not that scared little girl anymore, trying to make everyone proud."

The air felt thick, her words sinking deep. I opened my mouth to respond, but she held up a hand, stopping me before I could deflect.

"I'm not talking about going through the motions, Vanessa," she pressed gently. "I'm talking about truly loving yourself. Giving yourself the same grace, patience, and care that you so willingly give to everyone else."

Her words hit me in a way that felt different this time like they finally broke through a wall I didn't even realize I'd built. "I think... I think I'm ready to do that," I whispered.

She smiled, that deep knowing smile, like she'd been waiting for this moment all along. "You're ready, Vanessa. You've been ready. Now, it's just about believing that."

I stood, feeling lighter, more grounded. The heaviness wasn't gone, but it wasn't dragging me down anymore. I could see a way forward, and this time, it was on my terms.

"Thank you, Dr. Smith," I said, my voice steady.

"Don't thank me," she replied, standing as well. "Thank yourself for showing up. Every day. You've got this. Just keep moving."

As I walked out of her office, the sunlight kissed my skin, the breeze felt fresher, and lighter. I could breathe again. This path I was on—it wasn't perfect, and it wouldn't be easy. But for the first time, I was walking it for *me*.

THE RENEWED WARMTH OF my parent's house, beckoned to me as it had during my childhood, before puberty ignited the rift between my mother and me. It was alive tonight with the buzz of laughter and the irresistible aroma of her famous chicken and dumplings, simmering away in the kitchen. I couldn't remember the last time she'd cooked anything in the massive, restaurant-grade kitchen.

Kelly and I sat cross-legged on the plush rug, the flicker of the fireplace casting a golden glow across our faces. Vivian and Charisse, our mothers, reclined on the overstuffed sofa, each holding a glass of wine, their eyes sparkling with the kind of mischief that made me think they had something up their sleeves.

Vivian leaned back in her chair, a mischievous glint in her eyes as she sipped her wine. "You know, Charisse and I weren't always the respectable women you see before you."

Charisse laughed, shaking her head. "Oh no, we certainly were not. Remember the secret party we tried to throw senior year of college?"

Kelly and I exchanged curious glances. "Secret party," I asked, intrigued.

Vivian grinned, her eyes sparkling with the memory, sipping more of her wine. "It was finals week, and the library had become our second home. One night, we decided we needed a break—something to blow off steam. So, we came up with a plan. We'd sneak into the library after hours and set up a surprise party for our study group. "

Charisse took over, her laughter infectious, a mirror image of Kelly. "We dressed in all black like we were on some covert mission. I even had pantyhose over our faces, for dramatic effect. We entered through a door to the basement that stayed unlocked."

"We snuck around, avoiding the security guard on patrol. What was his name, Risse?" Vivian continued, clearly enjoying the trip down memory lane.

"Old Albert," Charisse replied. "He was a cue ball of a man. Potbelly out here and shiny bald head."

"I swear, that man wasn't securing anything on campus," my mother added. "Anyways, we set up floor lamps with red bulbs, dusted off the chairs down there, and even brought a boombox with the best '80s hits. I was obsessed with Teena Marie back then. By the time our friends arrived, it looked like the library had been transformed into a nightclub."

Kelly's eyes widened. "You two threw a party in the library? What happened when you got caught?"

My mother and Charisse looked at each other before turning into fits of laughter. Charisse, still chuckling. "Oh, we didn't get caught," she explained, pointing to herself and my mother.

Kelly and I looked at each other in confusion. "Mom, y'all threw a party, in the campus library, after hours. Surely you got caught."

"Let us finish the story, Nessa."

"See," Charisse chimed in. "That's what's wrong with your generation now. Y'all are too busy moving so fast, you don't take time to sit down and listen." Kelly and I rolled our eyes.

"So, we must've had our group down there for about an hour, before your father and Kenneth walked in with a few of their frat brothers."

"Nessa, your Mama about passed out," Charisse added, topping off everyone's glass of wine. "She'd been playing cat and mouse with Doug for two years. He finally caught her that night."

"Hey, if memory serves me correctly, I wasn't trying to get caught. It was a setup. Kelly, your mother told your father to bring him."

"The apple didn't fall too far from the tree," I said, looking over at Kelly.

"Hmph. That was back when he knew how to listen. Before his head got too big for his ass."

"Come on, Ma. Not too much. That's still my Dad," Kelly pleaded. As strong a front as she put forward, I knew she was troubled by her parent's recent separation.

"Let me get back to the story," Charisse said, giving her daughter a regretful smile. "Picture this. It must've been 2:00 AM. Teena Marie's 'Out On a Limb' was playing on the stereo. Kenneth and I were tucked away in a corner."

"Doug had me swaying out on the makeshift dance floor. Then, all of a sudden, Old Albert came barreling through the door, his mangy mutt and the Dean flanking him on either side," my mother managed to get out between giggles.

"Mom, stop. Are you serious?" Kelly and I looked at each other, eyes wide, ready to pop out of our sockets.

"Yes," Charisse laughed. "He kept asking, 'Who's running this juke joint?' over and over, as people scattered to leave. It's so funny looking back, but at the time, your mother and I were frozen."

"Y'all dads stepped in and took the blame, for us. Said the whole thing was their idea. That they were profusely sorry for the turning of what was supposed to be a study session, into a nightcap."

"Well, what happened to them?" Kelly questioned.

My mother laughed, shaking her head. "Their parents were not amused. Luckily, those two clowns were able to talk themselves into a few weeks worth of unpaid work-study and got a stern lecture about the sanctity of academic spaces."

Kelly and I laughed, the sound mingling with the gentle hum of the room, a brief escape from the weight we each carried. Our mothers, perceptive as always, exchanged glances that spoke volumes, a silent agreement passing between them.

Vivian set her glass down with a soft clink, her eyes sparkling with a mix of determination and mischief. "Vanessa, come with me. I want to show you something."

I followed my mother out of the living room, leaving Kelly and her mother behind. We ended up in the library of my parent's home. My mother shuffled over to her desk, picking up a large brown portfolio, similar to the one I used for my art projects during high school. As I stepped closer to where she stood, the realization hit me that it was indeed my old portfolio.

"Mom, where did you find this?"

"I've kept it in that closet all these years." We flipped through the different sketches and canvas sheets housed in the worn brown sleeve. Staring at the works before me, I stood in awe of the progress I'd made since then. "You've always had impeccable talent. I hated what losing the baby did to you."

"Mom, why have we never talked about what happened in college? About the miscarriage?" My voice wavered, the words heavy as they fell between us. It was a question I had been too afraid to ask for years, and now that it was out, it lingered in the air like something sacred, something fragile.

My mother's hand tightened around mine. I could see the tension in her shoulders, the way her jaw clenched subtly, the restraint she was trying to maintain. She had always been like that—poised, composed, like nothing could touch her. But I knew better. I knew the cracks in her armor, and right now, they were beginning to show.

Her eyes, so often sharp and discerning, filled with unshed tears. "I don't know, Vanessa. Maybe I thought not talking about it would protect you. Maybe... Maybe it was to protect myself too."

I blinked at her, unsure of what she meant. "Protect yourself from what, Mom? It wasn't your mistake. It was mine."

She looked away, her gaze wandering, settling on the window as if she could find the answer somewhere outside. "You were so broken," she whispered, her voice softer than I'd ever heard it. "You weren't... You weren't you. And I couldn't bear to see my baby like that. I thought if we moved past it quickly, if I could push you through it, you'd find your way back. I didn't know what else to do."

I swallowed, trying to steady myself. "But moving on didn't heal me. I've spent years trying to live with this hole inside me. I spent my whole life trying to be this version of myself you'd be proud of, but deep down, I'm just... I'm broken."

Tears blurred my vision, but I saw the way my mother flinched at my words, like they hit a part of her she wasn't ready to confront.

"Oh baby," she said, her voice trembling as she brought her hands to my face, her palms warm against my cheeks. "It wasn't your fault. Losing that baby was never your fault. Don't you remember what the doctor said?"

"No, Mom. I don't remember any of it," I said, choking back the sob in my throat. "I blocked it all out just to survive, just to make it through graduation. I saw the pitying way people looked at me"

She let out a long breath, her own eyes glassy. "Vanessa, no one was pitying you. We were grieving right along with you. I... I didn't know how to show it, but I was devastated. Kelly was too. But when I saw you in that state, I couldn't let myself fall apart. I had to be strong, for you and me. That's what I knew. That's how I've always operated, and maybe I was wrong."

Her voice wavered as she continued, "I remember the day I flew to Louisiana like it was yesterday. Kelly called me. She told me she hadn't heard from you in days, and the moment I picked up the phone, I knew something was wrong. When I got to your apartment, it was like stepping into someone else's life. The light was gone. The Vanessa I knew wasn't there. I found you on the floor, Vanessa curled up like a little girl, and I wanted to scream. I wanted to bring you home right then, to fix it all."

Her voice cracked, and I saw her wipe a tear from the corner of her eye. "But you were bleeding. And when I called 911... I knew. I knew I couldn't fix it. That's when I decided the only way to save you was to push you forward. To force you to keep moving."

The admission broke something inside me, the image of my mother—Vivian Taylor, always so strong, always so immovable—standing in that hospital room with me, powerless. I had never seen her this vulnerable. For the first time, I saw her not just as my mother, but as a woman, a Black woman who had raised me in a world that demanded strength and resilience from us at all times. A woman who had carried the weight of her expectations and mine, trying to protect me from a world that had no mercy for women like us, even if it meant suffocating both of us in the process.

"Mom," I whispered, my voice barely audible. "I didn't know you were hurting too."

Her face crumbled. "Vanessa, you were my baby. You *are* my baby. I didn't know how to let you hurt. I thought I had to hold it all together for both of us. I've been holding everything together for years, for this family, for your father's career, for you. I just... I didn't know how to stop."

A tear slipped down my cheek, and I didn't wipe it away. "You don't have to do that anymore, Mom. You don't have to carry it all."

Her eyes softened, the vulnerability between us palpable. "And neither do you, Vanessa. You don't have to keep proving yourself, not to me, not to the world. I see you. I've always seen you."

"I've been so scared to disappoint you. To not live up to your expectations."

Her lips quivered into a smile, one laced with sorrow and pride. "Baby, my expectations were never about you proving anything to me. I've always wanted you to have the life you deserved, to be happy in whatever path you chose. That's why I pushed so hard. That's why I was so tough on you after college. I didn't want you to be lost."

I shook my head slowly, feeling the years of miscommunication, of unspoken pain, unraveling between us. "I'm not lost, Mom. I'm finding my way."

A smile broke across her face, small but genuine, the kind I hadn't seen from her in a long time. "I know you are. You've been building something beautiful. The community centers, your art. You've taken control of your life, and I'm so proud of you for that."

My chest tightened, but this time, it wasn't from grief. It was from something else. Something lighter, something hopeful. "I've been thinking... After I finish with the centers, I want to open my own gallery. A space where I can show my art, and maybe teach kids who want to be artists too. I think it's time."

Her eyes sparkled with a pride I had always longed to see in her. "That sounds like exactly what you should be doing." She took my hands, squeezing them tight. "I'll be right there, cheering you on. Whatever you need, I'm here."

For so long, I had seen my mother as a force, someone to live up to. But now, sitting here with her, I realized she was a woman like me—flawed, human, trying her best in a world that demanded too much from us. And maybe, just maybe, I could give both of us permission to heal.

"I love you, Mom," I said, my voice thick with emotion.

"I love you too, Vanessa. And whatever comes next... we'll face it together." She pulled me into a tight hug, her embrace fierce and loving.

As we sat there, holding each other in silence, I felt something shift deep within me. I wasn't the same girl who had been shattered by grief and loss. I was a woman now, standing at the edge of something new, ready to claim my future on my terms. And for the first time in a long time, I felt truly free.

Chapter 40

Xavier

Stewing, I sat at a corner table in Felipe's, the hum of conversation around me blending with the upbeat Latin music that filled the air. The scent of freshly made tortillas and grilled meats wafted from the kitchen, but I hardly noticed. My mind was elsewhere, tangled in the emotional aftermath of Vanessa's breakdown. I took a sip of my Corona, the sharp tang doing little to cut through the heaviness in my chest.

Khalil walked in, his usual confident stride somewhat subdued. He spotted me and made his way over, clapping a hand on my shoulder before taking a seat across from me. "You look like hell, man," Khalil said, his voice tinged with concern.

I managed a weak smile. "Yeah, it's been a rough few weeks."

Khalil signaled the waiter for a drink before turning back to me. "So, what's happening with Vanessa?"

"She's fine. I just need to get back to my baby, bruh." I sighed, running a hand over my waves. I needed a cut badly.

"Yeah, Kelly told me about the panic attack." Khalil nodded, his expression sympathetic. "I'm sorry about the baby, again. How you dealing with that?"

"It hurts like hell," I continued, my voice breaking slightly. "Then double that when I saw what it was doing to Nessa. We need time and space to heal together, without this long-distance shit."

"I get it." Khalil took a deep breath, clearly contemplating his troubles. "I've been thinking a lot about Houston lately. I miss it, you know? The energy, the people."

I looked up, surprised. "Really? You sure it's the people or one person in particular?"

"Man hush," Khalil laughed. "But I think it might be time for a change. Maybe it'll help me find some peace, you know?"

We sat in silence for a moment, both lost in our thoughts. The waiter brought Khalil's drink, and he took a long sip before speaking again. "So, what about Evergreen? We have that meeting with the board coming up. We need to figure out a plan if everything checks out."

I nodded, grateful for the distraction. "I was thinking about that too. If the board is truly on board with our mission, we could set up operations in Houston while keeping things running smoothly here in New Orleans. We'll need to strategize, and make sure we have the right people in place to manage both locations."

Khalil leaned back in his chair, considering. "I'm not worried about that. The team held it down while we were gone. And it might be good for both of us, having something new to focus on."

I agreed, feeling a glimmer of hope. I pulled out my phone, glancing at the time. Since Vanessa was back in Houston, the annoying game of phone tag commenced.

Khalil reached across the table, giving my shoulder a reassuring squeeze. We clinked our bottles together, a silent vow to support each other through whatever came next. As we began to discuss our strategy in more detail, I felt a renewed sense of purpose. That being getting back to Houston was necessary, come hell or high water. My baby needed me just as much as I needed her.

KHALIL AND I STOOD at the entrance of our office, a sleek, modern space that reflected our vision for EcoVision Urban Solutions. The minimalist decor, with its clean lines and tasteful art pieces, exuded sophistication and success. Sunlight streamed through floor-to-ceiling windows, casting a warm glow over the polished hardwood floors. We welcomed the men of Evergreen Capital Investments, a group of distinguished gentlemen whose presence commanded respect.

As they entered the meeting room, I felt a sense of ease wash over me. This was a stark contrast to our previous dealings with Wright Horizons, where every interaction was fraught with tension and regret. Here, the atmosphere was different—more welcoming, and more aligned with what we wanted for EcoVision Urban Solutions.

Patrick Hall, a tall man with a powerful build and a commanding presence, stood to greet them. "Gentlemen, thank you for flying in. I'm excited to solidify this partnership with EcoVision Urban Solutions and discuss how our investment can benefit both parties."

Khalil leaned forward, his voice steady and assured. "Thank you, Mr. Hall. EcoVision is all about sustainable urban development. We aim to create green spaces and energy-efficient buildings that not only benefit the environment but also improve the quality of life for the communities we serve. I know we didn't have a set place during our previous conversation, but we hope to expand these efforts to Houston, and with your support, we believe we can make a significant impact."

A board member nodded, a smile playing on his lips. "That aligns well with our values at Evergreen. We have a strong commitment to uplifting our communities and creating opportunities for growth and development. Our board is particularly interested in ventures that offer both financial returns and social impact."

I glanced around the table, making eye contact with each board member. "We're glad to hear that. One of our core missions is to foster economic empowerment within underserved communities. We believe that by providing access to green technology and sustainable living, we can help bridge the gap and create lasting change."

"Excuse the interruption," Patrick chimed in, "but our last two members finally arrived."

"Good afternoon, everyone. Sorry, we're late."

My heart stuttered when I heard the familiar voice. Vanessa's father, Douglass Taylor, entered the conference room, with Kelly's father trailing behind him. He noticed the shock on my face, and gave me a slight head nod, before sitting in one of the empty chairs around the table. Khalil looked between me and Vanessa and Kelly's fathers, his expression mirroring mine.

"Mr. Taylor. Mr. Reid. I didn't know you both were involved with Evergreen," I managed to get out, trying to preserve my professionalism.

"Yes. We're silent partners, like Tim over here. We only make an appearance when Patrick insists."

Another board member, a distinguished gentleman with silver hair, chimed in. "What are your plans for the Houston expansion?"

Khalil took this one. "We've identified several key areas in Houston that would benefit from our green initiatives. Our plan includes developing affordable, eco-friendly housing, as well as revitalizing existing infrastructure to make it more sustainable.

We're also looking at partnerships with local organizations to ensure we're meeting the needs of the community."

The men around the table exchanged nods of approval. The second board member spoke again, "I'm certain we'll be able to make that happen. We have a similar project in mind. Douglass, isn't the Foundation gearing up to overtake a few community centers in Houston?"

"We are. A few of them, like Heritage, are due for much-needed facelifts."

As the conversation continued, I felt a growing sense of optimism. Our goals seemed to align perfectly, and the support of Evergreen Capital Investments would be instrumental in achieving our vision. Just as we were about to conclude, Vanessa's dad, who had been quiet throughout the remainder of the meeting, finally spoke up.

"Xavier, I'd like to request a private conversation after we wrap up."

Quickly, I composed myself. "Of course, Mr. Taylor," I replied, my mind racing with thoughts.

The other board members began to file out of the room, offering their congratulations and firm handshakes. Kenneth clapped Khalil on the back, and one by one, they left until it was just us.

He leaned back in his chair, his gaze steady. "Xavier, I've been following your progress for a while now. You and Khalil have built something remarkable with EcoVision."

I nodded, still processing the revelation. "Thank you, sir. That means more than you know coming from you. Vanessa said you were retired, imagine my surprise you walking in here."

Mr. Taylor smiled a hint of pride in his eyes. "Somewhat. I prefer to keep a low profile these days. But when Patrick mentioned your company as a potential investment, I couldn't refuse to show my face." Mr. Taylor stood from the table and walked over to where I stood. "Our goals are in line with what you're doing. I wanted to see for myself if this partnership would be a good fit."

I took a deep breath, meeting his gaze. "And do you think it is?"

Douglass's expression softened slightly. "I do. But I also wanted to talk to you about Vanessa."

A lump formed in my throat. "What about her?"

"I don't know what happened in the past, but I can tell she means the world to you. I just want to make sure that whatever happens between you two, you both find a way to move forward. Especially since it seems we'll be working together."

I nodded, emotions swirling inside me. "I understand. I love her, Mr. Taylor. I just want to bring her happiness."

Mr. Taylor sighed, a fatherly concern etched into his features. "I know you do, Xavier."

I swallowed hard, the weight of his words sinking in. "Thank you, sir."

He stood up, offering his hand. "Good luck, Xavier. With the business and with Vanessa. I believe in you. I'd love for you and Khalil to come to the gala in a few weeks. Announce the partnership then?"

"Yes sir. That sounds like a plan." I shook his hand firmly, feeling a renewed sense of determination. "Thank you, Mr. Taylor. I won't let her down."

"Oh, I don't doubt that at all," he confirmed, smiling as he exited the room.

Chapter 41

Xavier

The Houston Rodeo was in full swing, the air electric with the scents of fried food, livestock, and the occasional whiff of fresh hay. I tightened my grip on Vanessa's hand as we wove through the crowd. Her laughter rang out above the noise, sweet and full of life. Her curls bounced around her face, and her smile shone brighter than the Ferris wheel lights glimmering in the distance. She seemed so much lighter than when she'd visited me in New Orleans.

"Xavier," Vanessa teased, her eyes sparkling. "Why do you look like you're about to fight someone? We're here to have fun."

I raised an eyebrow, fighting back a grin. "I'm not fighting anyone. Just trying to make sure we don't get trampled."

She leaned into me, pressing her warmth into my side. "You're too much. We're fine."

Khalil came up from behind us, holding a giant turkey leg in one hand and a fried Oreo basket in the other. "Man, y'all taking forever. This food ain't going to eat itself."

Kelly was right next to him, rolling her eyes. "Khalil, how do you even have room for all that? You just ate three corn dogs," she asked stealing an Oreo.

He shrugged, taking a massive bite of the turkey leg. "Because it's always somebody trying to take my shit."

We sat at a nearby table, as Kelly and Khalil started one of their bickering matches, Kelly continuing to take bites of Khalil's food. Vanessa sat on my lap, my arms circled her waist, my face resting in the crook of her neck.

"How you feeling, baby?"

"Good," she said, smiling down at me, and placing a kiss on my forehead. "Really good. Free, you know after... I didn't realize how much I'd been holding in. Thank you for helping me through that."

"That's what I'm here for." I kissed her shoulder, looking back at our friends across the table from us. Now, Kelly completely took over the turkey leg, picking at it with her fingers. "Man, Kelly. Why you taking my man's food like that?"

"Zay, mind the business that pays you." Kelly looked past me, Vanessa doing the same. "Oh look, there's Lynn...And, Wesley?"

"Yeah, he said he was coming kick it with us," Khalil replied, polishing off the rest of the Oreos.

Lynn and Wesley strolled up to the table, caught in some playful argument about bull riding. Wesley leaned in, all charm and persuasion, while Lynn tossed her braids over her shoulder, giving him a look that said she wasn't easily impressed. Yet, the little smile she couldn't quite hide gave her away.

"Hey, y'all. Look who I found by the entrance."

Wesley smirked and side-eyed Lynn, then dapped up Khalil and myself. "Yeah. What have y'all done so far?"

"Not much," Vanessa answered. "Played some games. We just took a break since Kelly was hungry."

"Wesley," Kelly started. "When did you start coming to the rodeo like us common folks?"

Wesley chuckled, glancing at Lynn. "Kelly, I always come to the Rodeo."

"You do, but it's normally the fancy stuff with all the company sponsors and whatnot. When's the last time you came to the rodeo?"

"Hey, hey. Sorry, we're late." Nyah walked up with her and her husband's son, TJ.

"Hey, Nyah boo." Vanessa stood from my lap to hug her friend, then scooped her son into her arms. "TJ, you're getting so big. Where's your daddy?"

"Girl, at home. He's trying to finish a report for work," Nyah added skirting around the table to hug everyone.

"Umm huh," Kelly said, her mouth full of turkey.

"Is this Wesley I see? Before my very eyes?" Wesley hugged Nyah. "If I had known this was a couples thing, I would've told Antonio to take a break."

"Girl, it's only one couple," Lynn smirked. "Those lovebirds." She pointed to Vanessa and me, her face dumbfounded. I looked at Wesley and Khalil, suppressing the laughter that wanted to come out. I knew how each felt about the women who stayed just out of their grasp.

Vanessa sat beside me, holding TJ on her lap, as the group continued to talk, taking jabs at Wesley, Lynn defending him now and again. When everyone finished eating, the girls insisted on taking pictures. They found the photo op and took picture after picture, Kelly and Lynn making sure only the best pictures were saved.

The night air buzzed with excitement as we made our way to the rides. Vanessa tugged me toward the Ferris wheel, her eyes alight with mischief. "Oh, Zay. We have to get on the Ferris wheel. Come on."

I tried to play it off cool, but I could feel the nerves prickling up my spine. Heights and I had never been on good terms. "Nah, I'm good right here on solid ground. Take Nyah. Y'all have fun."

She tilted her head, raising an eyebrow. "Xavier Morris, you can't still be afraid of heights?"

Khalil overheard and burst out laughing. "Hell, yeah. Anything that put him in the air is dead."

"Oh baby," Vanessa cooed, throwing her arm around my waist, and leaning in close. "You've faced tougher things. What's a little Ferris wheel ride?"

The way she looked up at me, full of love and trust, made me weak. She knew my fear, and yet there was no judgment, only gentle encouragement. I sighed, feeling my resolve crumble. "Fine. But if I die, it's on you."

Kelly snorted. "A Ferris wheel, Xavier? Really?"

"Let the man live," Wesley defended me, though he was amused.

Vanessa pulled me toward the Ferris wheel, and soon we were stepping into one of the small, swinging carriages. As we ascended, the city lights spread out below us like a galaxy, and the hum of the rodeo faded into the background. I swallowed hard, my palms sweaty.

Vanessa placed one of my arms around her shoulders, secured her arm across my waist, and tossed her legs over mine. "Breathe with me," she whispered, her voice steady. "We're okay."

I exhaled, focusing on her voice, on the warmth of her body pressed close to mine. Slowly, the panic ebbed away. I turned to look at her, her face soft and radiant in the glow of the lights. "You something else, you know that?"

She grinned, leaning her head on my shoulder. "I know. And so are you."

For a moment, the world melted away, leaving just the two of us. Being with Vanessa felt like coming home, like finding solid ground even in the most uncertain moments. "I'd do anything for you, Nessa," I murmured.

"Anything?" She looked up at me, her eyes shining with emotion. "Even if I asked you to move here?"

I laughed, feeling freer than I had in years. "You want me to move here?"

"Yeah," she said. "I know it'll take some time to figure out logistics. Like what will happen with you and Khalil's company. Finding a place to live."

I ran a thumb up and down her arm, staring into her eyes. "When do you want me to move here?"

"Yesterday," she laughed. "This long distance is for the birds. I just want to wake up next to you."

"Okay," I said, kissing her lips gently.

"Okay?" Her face twisted up, making her look even more adorable.

"Yeah. Okay. I'll move out here."

She sat up quickly, sending our cart rocking back and forth. "Don't you need to think about it?"

"Nessa," I spoke between clenched teeth. My hand gripped the back of the car as we reached the peak of the wheel, the creaks and moans of metal rubbing against each other sending a mini panic to my heart.

"Zay," she started, still moving, still adding momentum to this death trap. "Moving is a big decision. You need to talk it over and make sure it's possible. As much as I want you here now, I can wait until it's the right time."

"Nessa, please," I begged, as the car lurched forward, ready to make its descent. "Come here and stop moving."

"What?" She resumed her earlier position, arm across my waist, legs over mine. I latched on to her, willing my heart to calm down.

"Baby, if you're ready for us to take that step, so am I. It's nothing for me to think about."

She snuggled into me, our heartbeats syncing as we stared out at the skyline slowly morphing into the buzz on the ground. "See? It's beautiful," she whispered, her eyes wide with wonder.

I looked at her instead of the view. "Yeah...It is. I love you," I whispered in her ear, the words coming as easily as breathing.

She turned in my arms, her smile radiant. "I love you too, Zay. Thank you for always being here, even when it's hard."

As our cart stopped at the exit, I was grateful for stepping on solid ground, Vanessa right beside me, I knew I'd follow her anywhere. It didn't matter if it meant facing my fears or finding new dreams. As long as she was there, we were locked in.

Chapter 42

Vanessa

The grandeur of the gala hall shimmered with opulence, a lavish display of wealth and influence. Crystal chandeliers adorned the ceiling, casting a soft glow over the gathering of dignitaries, philanthropists, and socialites. I wore an elegant gown that accentuated my grace and moved through the crowd with poise, attempting to immerse myself in the spectacle. In reality, I wanted to be home, curled up in my bed, watching reality TV with a platter of sushi and fried rice. I looked across the room at my mother, easily charming her guests with her bright smile and warm demeanor. She dangled on my father's arm as he looked at her with pure adoration.

Kelly walked over to me, her sparkling, purple gown trailing behind her, making her look like a goddess dropped down to Earth. "Hey, girl. You look like you need a hug." She pulled me into a tight embrace that made my eyes water.

"Me? You're the one walking around in a funk here lately."

"I'm just over this back and forth with my parents. Like, either stay together or divorce." A waiter passed with a tray of champagne flutes. Kelly grabbed two, handing me one. "I just don't get it. A few weeks ago she was calling him a bastard and now they're back under the same roof."

"I don't know what to say, relationships are complicated," I shrugged. I felt bad for my friend. This back-and-forth was a constant in her life, for as long as I could remember. I had no doubt her parents loved each other. And, most people, outside of my mother and father, believed in the facade they portrayed to the world. Deep down, I knew Kelly just craved some sort of stability. She used to want that stability to be in the form of her parents ending their bickering ways and focusing on her. Now, she just wanted them to pick a struggle and stick with it.

"Can I ask you a question?" Kelly's question interrupted my thoughts.

"Yeah," I said, sipping the champagne, its bubbles tickling my nose.

"How does it feel?"

"How does what feel?"

"Love." Kelly clarified. "Being in love. What does that feel like?" We started to move to our seats as the host announced dinner would be served shortly.

"Umm, I suppose it's different for everyone. But, for me, it's the feeling of being vulnerable and knowing the other person is going to keep you safe. An ease, where nothing feels forced. When they're not around, their absence is magnified so much, you swear your heart is calling for them. When the two of you are together, the world seems to disappear around you. Kind of like that."

"Is that how you feel about Zay?" Kelly implored. I knew my friend. Her analytical brain was trying to find the one solution that would make everything make sense. I couldn't bring myself to tell her the only thing that made sense, was that nothing made sense.

"It's exactly how I feel about Zay. You have no idea how many times I have to stop myself from saying 'My man, my man, my man.'" I laughed, getting a small giggle out of her. "I wish he were here now, but, that's just where we are right now. Hopefully, not for much longer."

"I just hope I find what you have one day."

"You will Kelly. Just, don't run away from it when it hits you. Okay?"

"Yeah, sure."

The gala was in full swing, with shimmering lights and soft music filling the air. I sat next to Kelly, trying to focus on the conversation at our table, but my thoughts kept drifting to Xavier. The room seemed to spin with elegant couples and laughter, but all I could think about was how everything I ever hoped for was manifesting before my eyes, and the one person I wanted to share it with wasn't here.

"Vanessa, are you okay?" Kelly asked, noticing my distant expression.

I blinked, forcing a smile. "Yeah, just... I wanted Zay to be here." Tears built in my eyes, ready to rain down my heated cheeks. "Cover for me. I need to get some air, and calm down before I'm sobbing all over the place."

"Still a crybaby at your big age," Kelly chuckled, handing me one of the linen napkins on the table. "Are you pregnant?" she whispered.

"Shut up," I laughed, sneaking out the door closest to our table. "No, I'm not."

As I walked back toward the balcony opposite the hall, I froze. Standing just a few steps away, looking just as stunned as I felt, was Xavier. Our eyes locked, and the world around us seemed to fade away.

"Xavier," I whispered, my voice barely audible. "What are you doing here?"

"I told you I would be here," he replied, taking a step closer.

"But..but how?" The words stumbled out of my mouth, disbelief covering my face. "You said your meeting ran late. That was four hours ago. I wasn't expecting you until well after I made it home."

"Yeah, and when we got off the phone I asked Khalil what flight he was taking and joined him." He wrapped his arms around my waist, his thumbs strumming my back. "Nessa baby, what's wrong?" He looked toward the empty balcony a few steps away. "Come with me."

As soon as we stepped outside, tears flowed from my eyes again. My whole body felt hot and sticky from the early humidity creeping into the city. I could just make out the music filtering out from the ballroom. I covered my eyes with my hands, willing the tears to stop. "You got on a plane," I sobbed out between breaths. "You hate flying."

"I know that." Xavier's eyes softened, and he closed the distance between us, cupping my face in his hands. "But I had the best incentive in the world. You."

A giggling sob escaped my lips as I leaned into his touch. "I just assumed you'd drive."

Xavier held me tightly. "I told you I got you. From here on, we face everything together, every high and every low. I promise."

The warmth of his embrace and the steady beat of his heart against mine lifted the weight of my fears and doubts, replacing it with the certainty of love.

"I promise too," I whispered, my voice breaking with emotion. "I love you, Xavier."

"I love you more than words can say," he replied, pressing a gentle kiss to my forehead. "And I always will."

"I'm sorry for being a hot mess," I said, pressing a kiss to his lips.

"Nah, you're not a hot mess. You just love and feel freely. It's what I love most about you. My lil' crybaby," he joked.

"Ugh," I whined, joining his laugh, "I probably look a mess." I patted the napkin around my eyes to soak up the remaining tears that lingered.

"Never that, love." Xavier pressed his forehead against mine while caressing the small of my back. "How about we head back in? Can't miss your dad's speech, right?"

I nodded my head, letting him take me by the hand and lead me into the ballroom. When we arrived at my parent's table, Khalil was there, seated amidst the rest of the group. Representatives from each organization Taylor Foundation supported were standing on stage, giving reports of what they were able to do with funds received from my parents' foundation. The hostess did her best to bring laughter to the room, shouting out jokes in between each part of the program, and hyping up the winners from the silent auction and award winners. The laughter was a welcome relief from my mini-meltdown from earlier. Through it all, Xavier never let my hand go. Every so often, I saw my parents smile over at me, beaming with a hint of secrecy.

By the end, the hostess welcomed my parents to the stage. It was time for them to make their obligatory speech to the guests, thanking them for opening their pockets and guilting them into donating to the foundation for another year.

"Ladies and gentlemen, our very esteemed guests," my father started. "We wholeheartedly thank each one of you for being with us tonight. For ten years, we've worked tirelessly to give back to the community around us. Without you, we never would be able to have the impact we've been able to have."

"It is with this love and support we were able to start this foundation. Douglass and I wanted something we could leave behind, as a living memento to the values we share as a family, as a community. We couldn't let this night pass, without acknowledging the tireless efforts of our daughter, Vanessa."

Immediately, I felt the room's eyes on me, the spotlight helping the guests sitting at the back tables. I continued to look at the stage, seeing my mother's eyes turn glassy. "Her unwavering dedication, not only to the inner workings of this foundation but to the greater community of Houston has been nothing short of inspirational. Vanessa, we are so proud of the passion you put into the things that mean the most to you, and the vision you have for elevating our family's legacy. Your father, and I, are so very lucky to call you our daughter." Kelly tapped my arm, handing me a folded napkin, as Xavier smoothed his hand up and down my arm. I dabbed the inner corners of my eyes, emotion spilling out of me in droves, my mother's eyes locked in with mine.

Fuck, am I pregnant?

My father took the microphone from my mother, sensing her vulnerable state. "After ten years of helping various organizations in and around Houston, Vivian and I are thrilled to announce the inception of our non-profit, under the umbrella of our foundation." Claps and cheers circulated in the room around us. My heart beat faster, my ears hungry for the remainder of my father's speech. Instead, he passed the microphone back to my mother.

"As you all know, the Taylor Foundation is in the process of taking over a few community centers around Houston, saving them from the hacking away of safe spaces for the children of our city. To further provide areas for kids to find and pursue their passions, we've partnered with another company to ensure these centers are fully equipped with everything staff and center directors will need to make this a possibility. Please help me welcome to the Taylor Family, the founders of EcoVision Urban Solutions, Xavier Morris and Khalil Grant!"

Rounds of applause went through the room, as Xavier and Khalil stood to accept the applause. Stunned I was at the revelation. So many questions ran through my mind. How did this happen? When did this happen? Where did this happen? I knew just about every piece of business that went on with my parents' foundation, so how did I miss this? Recounting the past few weeks, I realized I'd been so wrapped up meeting with the different community center directors, I'd barely spent any time in the office.

"Nessa, baby, close your mouth before you let a fly in," Xavier grinned, sitting back down.

"When did this happen? Did you know about this when you came for the rodeo?" My brain was about to explode with this news.

"Perhaps. I wanted to wait until everything was confirmed before I said anything," Xavier whispered, as my parents wrapped up their speech. "Khalil and I met with his investment firm shortly after we moved back home. We didn't find out your dad was on the board until a few weeks ago. Your face is exactly how I looked when he walked into the conference room."

I looked at my parents, standing together on stage. Two powerhouses of love and strength. My mother beamed down at me and then gave me a smirk, while my father threw a quick wink my way as they posed for pictures. I shook my head in disbelief.

"Xavier, what about your life in New Orleans? What about your mom? Your company's there. Your home is there." I rattled off every reason he had to stay in New Orleans, reasons for which I would compromise parts of my future.

"Khalil and I were already planning to expand out here. My mom doesn't need me, she has Mr. Ted." Xavier grabbed both of my hands and stared deeply into my eyes. Sincerity swam in his chocolate eyes. "And my home is wherever you are. Regardless of whether we got the investment or not, I was finding my way back to you. I just hoped and prayed you'd open the door. I don't care what successes I achieve. If you're not beside me when I do it, it don't mean shit."

The increasing claps and cheers around us pulled Xavier and me out of the bubble we were in. My parents walked back to the table, as the hostess took the microphone and ended the gala.

Afterward, I stood with my parents, in addition to Xavier and Khalil, as we said goodbye to all of the guests. When most everyone was gone, we all huddled near the front of the building. Khalil walked away to catch up with Kelly, leaving Xavier and me alone with my parents.

"Momma, why didn't you tell me about this deal Daddy made?" I smirked, throwing a hand on my hips. "I thought we were getting closer than that."

"Sweetheart, I have no idea what you're talking about," she replied with a hint of a smile.

"Daddy, aren't you retired?"

"Sweet pea, I sold my former company, but I never retired. I just diversified my portfolio." My father laughed then stuck his hand out to shake Xavier's. "I'm glad you and Mr. Grant could make it."

"Yes sir. And thank you for hooking us up with the private jet. We would've never made it." After shaking my father's hand, he wrapped his arm around my waist, tucking me against his side, her face full of surprise.

"Daddy, you're keeping secrets from me now?"

"Not secrets sweet pea. Just business," he laughed.

"Well, tonight was another successful night for the books. Let me get this old man home." My mother tapped Xavier on the arm before saying, "I'm glad to see you again, Xavier."

Xavier and I departed ways with my parents. We walked hand in hand toward his car. All the unease that filled my body for the past several weeks dissipated into the night air. When we made it to the car, he turned me to face him. His hand cupped my face as his thumb grazed my cheek.

"Vanessa, you are mine forever."

"Forever? Are you sure you can handle me forever?"

"Without a doubt." We stared into each other's eyes for what felt like an eternity. "I'm so grateful to be loved by you." He pulled me close to him, the outline of his perfectly carved chest and abs snug against the thin fabric of my dress. My heart stirred as flutters overtook my tummy. Our mouths met as our tongues searched for each other. One of Xavier's hands drifted down to palm my butt, as his hand pressed firmly into the small of my back. Our mouths danced a tango that revved up the desire between us.

"Xavier," I started, pulling back. "Take us home."

Epilogue

One Year Later

Vanessa

Flutters of sweet kisses brushed against my nose, cheeks, and lips. Zay's scent—sandalwood and fresh sage—mingled with the warmth of our bodies, the remnants of last night's slow, beautiful joining still lingering in the room. My head rested against his chest, the rhythm of his heartbeat a melody I'd grown to crave, even as my mind flickered with thoughts of the last few months. It had been a whirlwind—a beautiful, exhausting, fulfilling whirlwind—of him going back and forth between Houston and New Orleans as he and Khalil expanded their company into my city. And I had been lost in my own storm of community center visits, creative outbursts, and late nights painting, with Zay's presence grounding me whenever he was here.

But this morning... This morning, I was tired.

We'd both been moving at full speed, building our lives, and our futures, but for the first time, I felt a quiet peace, even in the chaos. I stretched beneath the sheets, letting out a deep breath as I gently pulled away from Xavier, his lips still hovering near my ear. The day was calling me—my last day at the Taylor Foundation, the transition of the community centers was finally complete. The past year had been filled with meetings, visits, and negotiations, but I had done it. The centers were now under our foundation's wings, their futures secure. And it was time for me to close this chapter.

I had spent the morning ensuring all the logistics were in place for the programs to run smoothly without me. The weight that used to sit on my shoulders lifted slightly as I walked through the hallways of my last official visit. My parents were supportive, of course—especially my mother, who had surprised me by not only stepping in when I needed her but also offering genuine advice. The woman who had once been a towering figure in my life had softened, and in that softness, I found room to grow.

As I wrapped up the meeting with the staff, I felt a mixture of relief and excitement bubbling beneath the surface. I was ready for what came next.

My gallery show was a week away, and every ounce of creative energy I possessed poured into my art. Each piece told a story—a blend of personal triumph, heartache, and the vibrant world around me. But one piece, the one I had been pouring myself into for the last few days, had become a reflection of my transformation.

Tonight, I added the finishing touches to my last piece. It was a portrait of myself. Bold, yet vulnerable. The strokes of paint captured the deep brown of my skin, highlighted by warm hues of gold and amber as if kissed by the sun. My eyes were wide, full of hope but tinged with the weight of everything I'd overcome. The background swirled with vibrant blues and purples, a storm of color that framed the image like an emotional landscape—chaotic, but beautiful.

I had painted myself standing tall, a figure of strength, but with an openness to the world. The layers of color blended into each other, the same way all the parts of me did—daughter, artist, lover, dreamer, crybaby—finally felt like they were converging into something whole.

I felt Xavier before I saw him, his presence filling the room as he stepped behind me, wrapping his arms around my waist. "It's beautiful," he murmured into my freshly washed and twisted hair, his breath warm against my skin.

"I'm almost done," I replied, my voice soft. "Just need a few more details."

He smiled, kissing my temple. "Take your time. You're not rushing through this, are you?"

"No," I whispered. "I want it to be perfect."

Xavier stayed with me as I worked, his conversation energizing me into the late-night hours. There was something comforting about his presence—his words that made me feel like I could do anything, that whatever doubts I had could be smoothed away in his embrace.

The morning of my show, I woke up alone, Xavier already off bringing the last of my paintings down to my studio, preparing for my gallery opening later in the day. Slowly, I slipped out of bed and padded across the room to the bathroom. The cool tile felt soothing beneath my bare feet as I stood in front of the mirror, my reflection staring back at me. My fingers grazed the edge of the countertop, eyes flicking down to the small white box I had hidden in the back of the drawer. My hands trembled slightly as I removed the small white stick from its wrapper, resting it on the counter. I had been feeling off lately—fatigue settling in my bones in a way running around town and painting late into the night couldn't explain, my body suddenly attuned to every subtle shift. Waves of nausea came and went like an ebbing tide. Maybe it was the stress of preparing for the show tonight or the endless hours poured into the community centers, but something nagged at me. Deep down, I knew there was more to it.

I inhaled sharply, turning my gaze back to the pregnancy test. My heart raced in my chest, my mind swirling with thoughts, possibilities, and what-ifs hanging in the air, thick and unspoken.

Is this even possible?

My hand hovered over the test for a moment before I snatched it up. I couldn't look. Not yet. I placed it face down on the counter and let out a shaky breath. The soft strains of my morning playlist drifted through the apartment, calming me slightly. This wasn't how I expected to start the morning of one of the most important days of my life.

The gallery opening was tonight. My first solo show. The culmination of years of work, dedication, and sacrifice. The nerves that had been building inside me for weeks now seemed almost insignificant compared to the anxiety twisting my stomach into knots. But still, there was hope mixed in, a fragile thing, but growing.

By the time evening arrived, the gallery buzzed with energy. The space was alive, humming with the chatter of guests mingling among my paintings. I stood near the entrance, greeting people as they walked in, each face glowing with excitement or curiosity. The walls were adorned with pieces of me, fragments of my soul laid bare for the world to see.

My heart swelled with a mix of pride and nerves. This was it—my moment. But beneath it all, a quiet hum of something else remained, something I pushed away in favor of soaking in the atmosphere around me.

"Vanessa," my mother's voice called out, breaking through my thoughts. I turned to see her and my father walking toward me, arm in arm. They were beaming, and for the first time in what felt like forever, it was with genuine pride, not obligation.

"You've done it, sweet pea," my father said, pulling me into a hug. His embrace was solid, and warm, grounding me in a way only he could.

"Your work is stunning," my mother added, her eyes soft as she gazed at one of my larger canvases. "I always knew you had this in you. And look at you now. Glowing." She cradled my face before leaving a soft peck on my cheek.

I smiled, warmth blossoming in my chest. "Thank you both. It means everything to have you here."

As they moved off to mingle, I found myself scanning the room, searching for the one person who always brought me a sense of calm in the storm. My heart skipped when I saw Xavier, standing tall in a sharp suit made solely for his body, the waves on his head bringing another wave of nausea to my already unsettled stomach. His eyes stayed locked on mine as he swaggered over to where I stood. He smiled, that slow, knowing smile that sent shivers through me.

"There she is," he said, approaching me, and pulling me into his arms. The scent of him wrapped around me, and for a moment, the rest of the room disappeared. "You look beautiful, Nessa baby. This show is everything."

I melted into him, pressing my cheek against his chest. "Thank you. I still can't believe it's happening. It feels surreal."

"You deserve all of it," he whispered into my hair. "This is just the beginning." He lifted my chin and placed the sweetest of kisses on my lips.

We stood like that for a moment, just holding each other, before I noticed movement out of the corner of my eye. Kelly had arrived, and right behind her was Khalil. She had brought a date—a tall, good-looking guy who had no idea what he was walking into. The banter between her and Khalil was immediate, crackling like electricity.

I couldn't help but smile. "They're going to kill each other one of these days," I muttered, nodding in their direction.

Xavier chuckled. "Or fall in love. One of the two."

"Or finally admit they're in love."

Khalil was leaning in close, whispering something to Kelly, who swatted him away, laughing. Her date looked increasingly uncomfortable, and Khalil, of course, found that hilarious.

"You think she brought him just to mess with Khalil?" I asked, raising an eyebrow.

"Oh, no doubt," Xavier said, grinning. "That's Kelly's style."

I shook my head, amused by the spectacle, before turning my attention back to the gallery. The night was unfolding beautifully, and for the first time in a long time, I felt like I was exactly where I was meant to be. A few of my students from the community center, those with remarkable talent, spoke with confidence and ease about their works on display to several of the guests. As much as this night was about me, it was about them. Giving them the access and tools to live out their wildest dreams.

When it was time for my speech, I stood in front of the crowd, feeling the weight of their eyes on me. My heart pounded in my chest, but it wasn't fear—it was exhilaration. I took a deep breath and began.

"Thank you all for being here tonight," I started, my voice steady but warm. "This show is more than just a collection of paintings. It's a reflection of my journey—one that's been filled with love, loss, growth, and everything in between. Each piece on these walls tells a story, not just of my own life, but of the people, places, and moments that have shaped me."

I paused, my eyes flicking to Xavier, who stood at the back of the room, watching me with that same unwavering support he always offered.

"Art has been my way of navigating through the ups and downs, my way of finding light in the darkest moments," I continued. "And I hope that, through these works, you'll find your own stories reflected at you. Because that's what art is—it's a mirror, showing us who we are, where we've been, and where we're going."

The room was silent, the weight of my words settling over the crowd.

"Tonight isn't just about me—it's about all of us. It's about celebrating life, in all its messiness and beauty. So, thank you. Thank you for being here, for supporting my students, and me, and for being part of this journey."

As the applause washed over me, I felt a quiet certainty settle in my chest. I was exactly where I needed to be. And whatever came next—whether in my career or my life with Xavier—I knew I was ready.

❧

Xavier

THE HUM OF CONSTRUCTION buzzed all around me as I leaned against the large windows of our new office in Houston. Sunlight poured into the space, bouncing off the polished concrete floors, the open layout feeling like a breath of fresh air compared to the rigid walls we started with in New Orleans. This place was a dream realized—a tangible mark of the hard work Khalil and I had poured into EcoVision. But it wasn't just our dream anymore.

This was the beginning of a new chapter. One that tied me closer to Vanessa.

"You thinking 'bout how to renovate this place already?" Khalil's voice broke through my thoughts as he walked in, a grin tugging at his lips.

"Nah, man. Just soaking it all in," I replied, turning to face him.

Khalil looked around, nodding his approval. "We really did it, huh? Houston. A second office. Feels good to say."

"It does." I couldn't help the smile that spread across my face. It had been a long time coming, and now, here we were, standing in the middle of something that used to be nothing more than an idea, scribbled on napkins, and bounced around over late-night beers and blunts.

But even at this moment, with everything we'd accomplished, my mind wandered back to Vanessa. There wasn't a day that went by where I didn't think about her, where I didn't feel the tug of needing to be closer to her, to build more than just a company—but a life. A future.

"You know," Khalil started, his voice dropping into something more serious. "This whole thing wouldn't be what it is if you hadn't kept your head on straight, man. Especially with everything that happened in the past. And I can't even lie...It's been good seeing you and Nessa together. Shit motivating."

"She's everything," I said quietly, but with full conviction. "So when you and Kelly gonna stop playing around?"

Khalil raised an eyebrow, a playful grin forming before brushing off my question with a sweep of his hands in the air. "You ready to put that ring on it?"

Before I could answer, Douglass, Vanessa's father, strolled in. His presence always commanded respect, but there was a familiarity in the way he walked toward us now, a kind of understanding that had developed over the past few months since he started working with us. He and the rest of his company became mentors to Khalil and me, helping us navigate the bigger world of business.

"Gentlemen," Douglass greeted, nodding at Khalil before turning his focus on me. "How are things looking? Almost ready for the big launch?"

"Just about," I answered, shaking his hand firmly. "The team's in place, and we've got a few more details to wrap up, but we're on track."

Douglass nodded, satisfied. "Good, good. You men have done something incredible here. People keep singing your praises with what you've done with the community centers."

There was a moment of silence as we all took in the weight of his words. It wasn't just a compliment—it was validation from a man I deeply respected, a man whose daughter had become my entire world. The weight of his approval settled on me, and for the first time in a long while, I felt like I had truly earned a place at the table—not just as Vanessa's partner, but as part of her family.

Douglass glanced between me and Khalil, then clapped me on the back, his hand lingering there with an unspoken message of trust and respect. "Xavier, I see how hard you've worked. How committed you are to this company, and to my daughter." His voice softened, but it still carried the weight of a man who had seen a lot. "I couldn't ask for a better man to be by her side. I can't wait to call you son."

Those words hit harder than anything I expected. For years, I'd carried the weight of knowing I wasn't just proving myself to Vanessa, but to the people who had raised her. Hearing that from Douglass...it felt like the final piece sliding into place.

"Thank you, sir," I said, my voice low, almost reverent.

"No need for the 'sir,' Xavier," Douglass said, chuckling softly. "We're family now. Keep doing what you're doing, and we'll be good."

After a few more exchanges, Douglass clapped me on the back one last time. "I won't hold you up much longer. I know you've got plans for tonight. Vanessa told me you're taking her out."

I grinned, trying to hide the excitement bubbling up. "Yeah, something like that."

Khalil snorted, clearly enjoying the fact that he knew exactly what I had planned. "Good luck, bruh," he teased, as Douglass chuckled softly, already knowing the stakes.

I gave them both a wave before heading out. Tonight wasn't just another date. Tonight was the night I'd ask Vanessa to spend the rest of her life with me.

As I pulled up to Vanessa's apartment, my heart pounded in a way that no business deal ever could. I gripped the steering wheel, my palms a little sweaty as nerves and excitement battled within me. I'd rehearsed what I was going to say a hundred times, but nothing could prepare me for the moment.

Vanessa stepped outside of her apartment lobby, her face lighting up as soon as she saw me. Even after all this time, she had a way of taking my breath away, making me feel like the luckiest man alive. I held the door open as she slid into the passenger seat, leaning in to kiss her softly.

"You're late," she teased, her eyes twinkling.

"I promise it's worth the wait," I murmured against her lips before pulling back and rounding the car.

We drove through the city, her hand resting on my leg as we moved in comfortable silence. I couldn't help glancing over at her, the way the streetlights danced across her face, highlighting the curves and angles that had become so familiar, yet always left me in awe.

"Where are we going?" she finally asked, her curiosity piqued.

I smiled but kept my eyes on the road. "You'll see."

After a few more turns, we pulled up to a quiet street lined with old oak trees. I parked the car in front of the old, weathered house, its once-bright paint faded to a dull gray, its shutters crooked and paint-chipped, but to me, it was perfect—just like everything else in my life since Vanessa had come back into it. My heart raced as I turned off the engine. This was it. Tonight would change everything.

Vanessa stepped out of the car, glancing around at the quiet street and the towering oak trees that lined the sidewalk. Her brow furrowed in confusion as she took in the sight of the house before us, overgrown with weeds and covered in years of neglect.

"Zay, where are we?" she asked, her voice soft and curious.

I walked around to her side, taking her hand gently in mine. My palm was sweaty and my fingers trembled, but I held onto her as if she was my anchor, the one thing that had grounded me through every storm. I led her toward the porch, each step heavy with anticipation.

"This," I paused, swallowing the lump in my throat as I looked into her eyes. God, she was beautiful, standing there under the streetlights, her eyes searching mine for answers. "This is our future."

Her breath hitched, and she glanced between me and the old house, the confusion still there, but now laced with something else—hope.

I laced my fingers through hers, squeezing gently, and led her toward the front door. "Come on, let me show you around."

Vanessa's eyes flickered with curiosity as I pushed open the door, stepping inside with her right behind me. The air inside smelled faintly of old wood and fresh paint, and as we stepped onto the hardwood floors, they creaked beneath our weight. She glanced around, her lips parting slightly, taking in the spacious open living area.

"I know it doesn't look like much right now," I said, scratching the back of my neck, trying to push past the nerves creeping in. "But I see the potential in it. The way I see the potential in us."

Vanessa turned to me, her eyes wide and soft. "I can see it too," she whispered, her voice full of understanding. "It's beautiful, Zay."

I smiled, relieved she saw what I saw. "Wait till you see the rest."

I led her through the rooms, showing her the kitchen with its old, worn cabinets that I promised to restore, the dining area where I envisioned us hosting family dinners and the cozy living room that I knew could one day be filled with warmth and laughter, pitter-patters of feet running across the hardwood. She took it all in with a quiet, thoughtful expression, occasionally glancing up at me with that spark in her eyes that told me she was already imagining our future here.

But there was one room left. The one that mattered the most.

"Come here," I said, gently tugging her toward the back of the house. I pushed open the door to a large room filled with pinky-orange sunlight streaming in through tall windows. It was empty, bare walls and floors, but it was the perfect blank canvas.

"This," I said, stepping inside and pulling her along with me. "This is for you."

Vanessa blinked, glancing around the room, confusion momentarily flickering across her face. "What do you mean?" she asked, her voice soft.

I grinned, stepping behind her and wrapping my arms around her waist, pulling her close as we stood in the middle of the room. "I know how much you love to paint, and I know how much space you need to do it. I thought... Maybe this could be your at-home studio.

A place for you to create, to put your heart and soul into your art. Just like you've always wanted."

Her breath caught in her throat, and she spun around to face me, her eyes filling with tears. "Zay..."

I took a deep breath, feeling the weight of everything we had been through, everything we had lost and found again. I reached into my pocket, my fingers brushing against the small velvet box that had been burning a hole in my jacket all night.

"I've been thinking about this moment for so long," I said, my voice barely above a whisper, raw and full of emotion. "Ever since you came back into my life, baby, it's like I've been breathing for the first time in years. You're everything—everything I've ever wanted, everything I never knew I needed."

Her eyes filled with tears, glistening as her lips parted, but no words came out. She just stared at me, her heart in her eyes, her soul wide open.

"I know we've been through it," I continued, my voice breaking, the weight of my words hanging heavy between us. "I know I've made mistakes. I've hurt you. I've let you down. And I never forgave myself for letting you go. But you—" I reached out, cupping her face gently, my thumb brushing away the tear that spilled onto her cheek. "You're the love of my life, Nessa. You're my heart. And I don't want to spend another second without you by my side."

Her breath hitched again, her eyes never leaving mine, her tears falling freely now, but she didn't wipe them away. She just let them fall, her lips trembling as she struggled to speak.

"I—" she whispered, but I stopped her, shaking my head softly.

"Let me finish," I said, my voice thick with emotion. "I never thought I'd get a second chance to make things right with you. And every day, I wake up grateful that you're still here with me. That you chose me. But I don't just want you here, for now, Vanessa. I want you here forever."

Her tears fell harder now, her shoulders shaking slightly as she pressed a hand to her mouth, trying to stifle the sob that threatened to break free.

I couldn't hold back any longer. Slowly, I lowered myself to one knee. As I slipped the velvet box from my pocket, my heart hammered in my chest. This moment had played out in my mind a hundred different ways, but nothing prepared me for the reality of standing here, ready to ask Vanessa to be mine forever. Her eyes followed my hands, excitement dancing in her gaze, now knowing what was coming.

I opened the box slowly, revealing the ring I had spent months choosing. It wasn't just any ring—it had to be perfect, something that captured everything I felt for her, something that matched the beauty she carried within and the life we were building together.

The ring gleamed under the soft light, an oval-cut diamond set in a vintage-inspired gold band, the original ring I'd bought before, with a few upgrades. The once plain band now had delicate floral engravings trailing along the sides, roses growing from the concrete of the time we lost with each other. The diamond was radiant, catching the light in a way that mirrored the brilliance Vanessa brought into my life every day. The intricate design of the band felt like her—a touch of artistry, a blend of old soul and new fire. It was a ring that symbolized the journey we'd taken and the life we were about to build.

Her lips parted slightly, her breath catching as she stared at it. I knew, at that moment, I had chosen right. Not just the ring—but the woman.

"Vanessa," I started, my voice thick with emotion, "I want this ring to be a reflection of everything we've been through, everything we've overcome. I want it to represent the love I have for you, the depth of it, and the future we're about to create together. Will you marry me?"

For a second, everything went still. The world faded around us, leaving just the two of us, our hearts connected in a way that went beyond anything words could express. And then, her hand flew to her chest, and the sob she had been holding back broke free.

"Yes," she choked out, her voice shaking with emotion. "Yes, Zay. A thousand times, yes."

I slipped the ring onto her finger, feeling like the luckiest man in the world as she pulled me up, wrapping her arms around my neck and pulling me into a kiss that was full of every emotion we'd shared over the years—love, hope, joy, pain, forgiveness. It was all there, pouring out of us as we held each other in that empty room that was now full of everything we were and everything we would be.

When we finally pulled apart, breathless and laughing through our tears, I cupped her face in my hands, my thumbs brushing away the wetness on her cheeks. "This room—it's where you can paint your masterpieces. But this house, it's where we'll create our masterpiece together. Our life. Our family."

Her eyes softened, and she rested her forehead against mine, her voice a whisper as she said, "Zay, there's something I need to tell you. Something that makes this moment even more perfect."

I held my breath, waiting.

"I'm pregnant."

The world tilted for a second, the word hanging in the air between us. But then, like a rush of wind, joy surged through me, overwhelming and powerful. "You're pregnant?" I repeated, my voice breaking.

She nodded, tears of happiness streaming down her face. "Yes. I'm pregnant," she whispered again, her voice thick with emotion.

A laugh broke free from my chest, and I pulled her into my arms again, holding her so close it was like I could feel her heart beating with mine. My tears mingled with hers as I buried my face in her hair, whispering words of love and joy into her ear.

This was it. This was everything we had ever wanted, everything we had ever dreamed of. Our future. Our home. Our family.

"I love you," I whispered, my voice thick with tears. "You make me the happiest man in the world."

She pulled back just enough to meet my eyes, her hands cupping my face as she smiled through her tears. "I love you too," she whispered, her voice breaking. "I love you more than anything."

We stood there, holding each other, letting the reality of what had just happened sink in. We were going to have a baby. We were going to build a life together, a family. And in that moment, everything felt like it was exactly as it should be.

But we weren't done yet. I had one more surprise for her.

"You ready for one more surprise?" I asked, my voice still thick with emotion.

She blinked at me, her eyes wide with disbelief. "There's more?"

I grinned, wiping the last of her tears away, kissing her knuckles gently, my eyes shining with excitement. "You'll see."

Little did she know, our closest family and friends were already waiting for us, ready to celebrate our love. But this moment? This moment was ours. Our family and friends were waiting—waiting to celebrate our love, our future, our forever. And as we drove off into the night, hand in hand, I couldn't stop the smile that spread across my face.

Our forever had just begun.

Afterword

As you close this book, I want to take a moment to reflect on the social issues that were woven into the fabric of this story. While Vanessa and Xavier's journey was one of love, growth, and reconciliation, it was also a backdrop for issues that deeply affect the Black community—issues like gentrification, mental health, and the wounds caused by fractured family dynamics. These themes were not just fictional challenges; they are a reality for many individuals and families across the country, particularly in historically Black neighborhoods like the ones depicted in this novel.

Gentrification has displaced countless Black communities, stripping away cultural roots and economic stability. Entire generations lose access to homes that once belonged to their families, and with it, a piece of their history. The effects are not just physical but emotional, as people are torn from the spaces they call home.

Mental health in the Black community remains stigmatized, especially among Black men and women who feel they must suppress their emotions or trauma to survive. Too often, people suffer in silence, believing they must carry the weight of their struggles alone. This novel explored the importance of creating safe emotional spaces for Black people to be vulnerable and supported.

Parental wounds—the unresolved pain passed down through generations—affect the relationships we build and the way we see ourselves. These wounds can be deep, and the healing process is often long and complex.

Lastly, and perhaps most importantly, the story focused on healthy Black love—a love that is often overlooked in mainstream media. Black men and women deserve to see themselves loved fully, tenderly, and without reservation.

These are not easy issues to fix. As you step back into your world, I encourage you to reflect on the issues raised in this story and think about how you can contribute to meaningful change. Together, we can create a world where people of all backgrounds—especially those in the Black community—are supported, heard, and loved.

Thank you for taking this journey with me. I hope Vanessa and Xavier's story touched your heart and left you with a deeper understanding of the complexities that shape love and life in the Black community.

ACKNOWLEDGEMENTS

To my readers,

Thank you for going with me on a journey woven through the heartstrings of passion, the trials of deep personal growth, and the enduring power of love. In these pages lay a story born from the moments that challenge us and the relationships that define us. This was more than just a love story between two people; it was a narrative about the kind of love that can inspire, devastate, and ultimately transform us.

This book was inspired by the human capacity for resilience—the incredible ability to rise from the ashes of despair and to forge paths where none seem to exist. It explores the dynamics of love lost and found, the deep scars left by abandonment, and the healing that only time and tenderness can bring. The characters you met, though forged from fiction, embody the spirit of real-life struggles and victories, some of my own, some from others. They are each a composite of bravery and frailty, mirroring the complex beauty of human imperfection.

Thank you to every person who played a part in helping me bring this vision to fruition. To my students, past, present, and future, thank you for inspiring me with all the many conversations we've had about the dream you have for your future. It was my job to teach you, but I learned the most valuable lesson of doing what's important for you. To all my beta readers, I don't know if you'll ever read this, but your comments and advice helped push me to make this book what it is today. A version filled with so much depth and meaning. When I wrote my first draft, I set out to do something easy and light-hearted. You helped me see how much further I could push myself.

To everyone who encouraged me as I stole moments between meetings, buried my nose in my keyboard nights and weekends, and shared my enthusiasm in bringing something like this to life. Without you, I would have lost steam months ago. To my closest family members, who marched along with me every step of the way. My sister helped me get the therapy bits just right and gave me the suggestion of Puttshack for a last-minute date addition. To my son for giving Mommy the space to pour her heart out into these pages, even though Paw Patrol is so much more exciting. To my husband for so many things, I can't list them all.

This story was for anyone who has ever faced a crossroad of heartache and promise, and for those who believe in the redemptive power of love. May you find both an escape and a reflection in these pages—a mirror of your challenges and triumphs in love and life.

Thank you for picking up this book, for walking this path with me, and for finding in it the echoes of your own experiences. May you turn each page not just as a reader, but as a fellow traveler in the journey of life.

With all my heart,
Alexandrea LeChelle

About the Author

Born and raised in Houston, Texas, with roots stretching across Louisiana, Alexandrea has always felt a deep connection to the stories of the South. Having lived in both Texas and Louisiana all their life, she noticed a gap in literature representing the real, complex issues faced by people in these regions—particularly within the Black community. This gap sparked their journey as a writer.

Inspired by a desire to bring untold stories to life, Alexandrea writes to shed light on critical topics like gentrification, mental health in the Black community, parental wounds, and the importance of creating safe spaces for Black women and men to express their emotions. But above all, her work emphasizes the beauty of healthy Black love and the power of Black women being cherished and celebrated.

An avid reader, bullet journaler, crafter, and cook, Alexandrea finds creative fuel in everyday activities and the work of influential authors like Toni Morrison, Zora Neale Hurston, Kennedy Ryan, and Sadeqa Johnson. Many of the themes explored in her debut and future novels are drawn from personal experiences or those of close friends and family, making each story a deeply personal and authentic reflection of life.

What began as a hobby during a winter break from teaching quickly evolved into a passion that brought her newfound purpose.

Through their writing, Alexandrea hopes to offer readers not only an escape but also a deeper understanding of the challenges and triumphs within the Black community. For anyone aspiring to write, her advice is simple: "Just start. There is someone out there who needs to hear your story."

DOUBLE BACK IN 2025

Thank You for Reading!

I'M SO GRATEFUL YOU'VE joined me on this journey with *Loved by You*—it means the world to me! If you want to stay connected and follow along with my author adventures, be sure to follow me on TikTok and Instagram: @alexandrealechelle! Your support keeps me writing, and I can't wait to share even more stories with you. Speaking of... keep reading for a special sneak peek of what's coming next!

Kelly

Playlist: "B.A.S (feat. Kyle Rich)" - Megan Thee Stallion

People say nothing is invincible—not against the seductions of power, the lure of wealth, or the pitfalls of love. Obsessions that have unraveled better souls than mine. But me? I am invincible. Power? It pulses through my veins effortlessly. Money? I was born with a silver spoon, cradled in comfort and privilege. And love? That's for the naïve and the needy. I am Kelly Reid, MD, the prodigious pediatrician whose charm wins over every child at my father's family medical practice. I sailed through residency, aced my boards, and clinched my medical license without breaking a sweat. Life couldn't be better.

Tonight, I'm on top of the world, ready to celebrate one of the four people who mean the world to me—my sister Vanessa, my ride-or-die, my confidante. It was her surprise engagement party, and nothing could dampen my spirits. Not even my parent's incessant bickering.

Adjusting the strap of my dress, my date—Marcus Blackwood, a strikingly handsome financial analyst with a smile that could sway a jury—offered his arm. We stepped into the grand ballroom where Vanessa's engagement party was in full swing. Despite Marcus being the epitome of a dream date, I kept our conversation light, but my mind and heart were guarded. This evening was about Vanessa, and I had no intention of weaving tangled heartstrings into the night's festivities.

The room buzzed with chatter and laughter of old friends and new faces. I scanned the crowd, my gaze lingering on familiar faces: Lynn with Wesley, each sneaking intimate touches, their smiles soft and telling. They may be trying to keep their attraction a secret, but anyone with two eyes could see what lingered between them. In another corner, Nyah and her husband, Antonio, posed for pictures, the picture-perfect couple to any onlooker. Yet, I knew of the storms that brewed beneath their calm seas; whispers of discontent that not even the flashiest smiles could dispel.

And then, there was Khalil. He stood by the bar, his dark eyes catching mine across the room. The air between us crackled with an unspoken history, a chemistry we both denied yet couldn't ignore. I felt Marcus's hand on my back, a polite reminder of his presence, but my attention remained anchored across the room.

The night unfolded with celebratory toasts and dances. As the party neared its end, Marcus excused himself to get his car from the valet as I made my rounds, saying goodbye to friends and acquaintances. When I finally reached Khalil, the air shifted. His gaze was intense, almost accusatory.

"You really brought a date?" he said, his voice a low rumble mixed with amusement and a hint of something darker.

"Just keeping things interesting," I replied my voice light, belying the rapid beat of my heart. His proximity was a reminder of everything we could never be.

"Stop playing games, Lily-girl." Khalil stepped closer, his command a whispered bark against my lips.

"It's not a game if no one's playing, Khalil." My reply was a challenge, an invitation.

He chuckled, the sound sending shivers down my spine. "Then why do I feel like you're the prize I keep losing?"

"Careful, Khalil. Someone might accuse you of being jealous."

"And if I am?" His hand brushed a stray lock of hair from my face. "Ditch his ass. I'm pulling through tonight."

Before I could respond, Marcus reappeared, his timing almost too perfect. "Ready to go?" he asked, oblivious to the tension he had walked into.

I nodded, turning away from Khalil with a sense of relief mixed with regret. "Yes, let's go."

As we walked towards the exit, I could feel Khalil's gaze on my back, burning into me with questions and promises left hanging in the air. I glanced over my shoulder, sending him a quick wink.

The drive home was quiet, filled with the soft hum of the car and the occasional flicker of street lights casting shadows inside the vehicle. Marcus had played the perfect gentleman all night, charming and attentive, but as we pulled into my driveway, a palpable tension crept into the air.

We walked up to the front door, and as I fished for my keys, Marcus leaned against the doorway. "How about a nightcap?" he asked, his voice low, a hopeful undertone threading through his words.

I paused, keying in the lock, turning to face him with a polite smile. "I think I'm going to call it a night, Marcus. It's been a long day, and I need some rest."

"Sure, I understand," he replied, though his disappointment was evident. "Maybe another time then."

"Another time," I echoed, not entirely sure there would be one.

He nodded, stepping back as I opened the door. "Goodnight, Kelly."

"Goodnight, Marcus." I watched him walk to his car and drive away before closing the door behind me.

Thirty minutes later, just as I was considering the solitude of the night in the comfort of my bed and current romance read, a knock sounded at my door. Puzzled, I peered through the peephole and saw Khalil standing there, his hands in his pockets, his posture relaxed yet somehow charged with an unreadable intention.

Opening the door, I raised an eyebrow. "What are you doing here, Khalil?"

"Why you acting shocked? I told you I was coming," he said, stepping inside without waiting for an invitation. The air around us vibrated with the tension of unspoken words and pent-up emotions. "We got some shit to resolve."

I closed the door and faced him, my arms crossed. "And what is that exactly?"

Khalil moved closer, his proximity a magnetic pull I found hard to resist. "The one where you think you can just walk away from what's between us."

"There's nothing between us," Khalil, I said, closing the gap between us. "There's your ego thinking every woman wants more than they say."

He chuckled, a sound that echoed in the close space of the foyer. "And here I thought it was your pride pretending you don't want exactly what I do."

I looked up into his eyes, dark and intent, and for a moment, I lost my train of thought. "You're assuming a lot based on very little."

"Am I?" His voice was softer now, and when he reached out, his fingers brushed against the dainty floral necklace around my neck, sending a wave of heat through me. "Then tell me to leave, Lily-girl."

I swallowed, my voice barely a whisper. "Khalil, you're being ridiculous."

"And yet, I still don't hear a no." In an instant, his lips were on mine, demanding, insistent. Our kiss was reckless, fueled by the night's earlier restraint and the raw need that simmered just below the surface.

Khalil's hands framed my face, and I pulled him closer by his waist, lost in the feel of him, the undeniable connection that refused to be ignored. We broke apart, breathless, our foreheads resting against each other.

"When are you getting your hair done again?" he murmured, his breath warm against my lips.

"Next week, why?" I asked, my voice breathy, chest heaving, my body conceding to the tension that had always danced around us, now burning brightly in the dimly lit foyer of my home.

"Make sure I leave you my card," his voice growled, lust and desire dripping from his lips. "I'm fucking this shit up tonight."